W9-CIR-458

EBC
510X3
3.67

THE

BEST

AMERICAN SHORT STORIES

1963

THE
BEST
AMERICAN SHORT STORIES
1963

and the Yearbook of the American Short Story

EDITED BY
MARTHA FOLEY and DAVID BURNETT

HOUGHTON MIFFLIN COMPANY BOSTON
The Riverside Press Cambridge
1963

TO
Dr. Anthony J. Ruggiero

Acknowledgments

GRATEFUL ACKNOWLEDGMENT for permission to reprint the stories in this volume is made to the following:

To the Editors of *The Atlantic Monthly, Esquire, The Hudson Review, The Kenyon Review, The Literary Review, McCall's, New World Writing, The New Yorker, Perspective, Phoenix, Playboy, Prism, Redbook, The Saturday Evening Post, The Sewanee Review, Southwest Review, The Tamarack Review;* to the University of Chicago; and to U. S. Andersen, H. W. Blattner, John Stewart Carter, John Cheever, Cecil Dawkins, George Dickerson, May Dikeman, Stanley Elkin, Dave Godfrey, William J. J. Gordon, John Hermann, Katinka Loeser, St. Clair McKelway, Ursule Molinaro, J. C. Oates, R. C. Phelan, Mordecai Richler, William Saroyan, Babette Sassoon, Irwin Shaw, Peter Taylor, Niccolò Tucci, and Jessamyn West.

Foreword

WRITING a foreword to a book such as this would be so easy if one could paraphrase Gertrude Stein and say, "A short story is a short story." But it would imply that all short stories are alike, and not even the laziest of editors would dare to indulge in such a lie. Thousands of short stories were published in America during the past year and, except for the bad ones featured in the "slick" magazines which do, unfortunately, show a uniformity of contrivance and falseness, they are as varied as the lives of Americans themselves.

Here we would like to quote from the editors of *The Literary Review,* because they have worded so aptly what we believe:

Few great short stories fit into neat academic formulas. Must a story, for example, always be perfectly clear? Frequently, the vaguer it is the better it is as belles lettres. *An Edna Ferber tale is immediately clear and immediately forgettable, but Tolstoy's "The Death of Ivan Ilyitch," Joseph Conrad's "The Secret Sharer," Katherine Mansfield's "The Doll's House," and Willa Cather's "A Wagner Matinee" haunt the memory more deeply with the passage of time.*

Are there "rules of composition"? Yes — one: be interesting. Does some zealous academician say "that every short story must deal with a brief period of time?" Then tell him to read Chekhov's "Darling" which covers half a dozen lifetimes. Does he say that "every short story must have a beginning, a middle and an end"? Then tell him to read Frank Stockton's "The Lady or the Tiger?", which has no ending. Does he say that "every short story must make sense"?

Then tell him to read William Saroyan's "Aspirin Is a Member of the NRA" or his "Ah-Hah, Ah-Hah," both of which are all mood. Emotional impact, moral involvement, mind discernment — these are the drives that matter: every good story-teller creates his own "rules," his own compulsive form.

None of the stories the editors mention is in the present volume, of course, since this book is limited to stories by American authors published during the past year. Most of the stories mentioned by the *Review* were written many years ago. They are excellent examples of short stories that have long been remembered and which will continue to be read for many years to come. The editors of *The Best American Short Stories,* beginning with Edward J. O'Brien who started the series in 1915, strive to give the reader contemporary stories that are also of permanent value.

If some of the readers of this book are newcomers to the series, and have been acquainted with the short story as it is ordinarily published in the big "slick" magazines that have cheated them of worthwhile literary fare, we shall especially welcome them. Perhaps they will learn that there is a different kind of story, a more interesting story, than the flimsy, insincere bits of writing printed in these magazines.

We are stressing the difference between stories in the so-called "popular" magazines and the stories from the literary magazines which make up most of this book because many persons fail to understand the importance of short stories. An incident in the United States. Senate illuminates this lack of comprehension. In some ways it is amusing. Fundamentally, it is sad.

"These great American short stories, what do they concern? You mean they are just novels?"

"We do some fiction, Senator."

"That is the thing that gets me. I don't know this is going to influence anybody to read a lot of fiction written in America. How is that going to impress anybody? Maybe I don't understand it, but I would like you to tell me."

"Senator, when you are trying to run a commercial-type program, you have to put into the program books which have something of an appeal to the buyer. You cannot concentrate entirely on anti-Communist books or entirely on books relating to American history.

*American literature is certainly one aspect of what we try to show
abroad through our libraries and our book programs."*

*"It is very difficult to evaluate this sort of program and what good
they do. I think some books dealing with the history of this country
and dealing with our progress as a nation and a free enterprise system, a representative form of government and all of that are instruc-
tive. I still don't think that a book of short stories or fiction is going
to be of any great value or produce results."*

"The above," says *The Kenyon Review* which reports it, "is not
from William Faulkner's Saga of the Snopes family, a passage, say, in
which Clarence Eggleston Snopes has finally been elected to the
U.S. Senate; it is, rather a portion of the testimony relating to the
budget requests of the United States Information Agency for 1962,
contained in *Hearings before the Subcommittee of the Commit-
tee on Appropriations: U.S. Senate, 87th Congress. The Kenyon
Review* lists the groups that have been sent abroad to inform
the world about American culture, ranging from haberdashers,
advertising men, and chiropodists, to baseball players, lion tamers
and movie stars. John McCormick's article concludes: "A book of
short stories or fiction, to answer Senator McClellan, is of value and
will produce results. Such results are not spectacular nor subject to
analysis by computer, but they are more important than bombs,
more enduring than governments and more sought after than missiles. They are ourselves."

(One of the editors of *The Best American Short Stories* has had
the honor of having one of her own short stories included in the
collection discussed in the Senate. The mail, even gifts, she has received from Asia show how closely people can be touched by "fiction.")

Dr. Wilfred Stone, of Stanford University, expressed it another
way when he told a conference that the idea that literature is as es-
sential as the latest Canaveral launching "is fantastic to most people.
Great stories perform at least two practical and realistic functions.
Stories are the only way we can learn the emotional, psychological
and spiritual history of a certain time. They are the only way we
get history with a beating pulse."

We are grateful to the editors who have kept us supplied with
their magazines and to their authors for generously granting reprint

rights. The editor of any new magazine is invited to send copies to us.

The editors and staff of Houghton Mifflin Company are also entitled to gratitude for their help. Finally, tribute is paid to the memory of Edward J. O'Brien, who founded this anthology.

Martha Foley
David Burnett

Contents

THE
BEST
AMERICAN SHORT STORIES
1963

U. S. ANDERSEN

Turn Ever So Quickly

(FROM THE SATURDAY EVENING POST)

THEY HAD BEEN DRIVING all day along the bright coastline, heading north along rugged shores, with a whitecapped sea blending its blue into the blue of the sky and a lanced army of fir trees marching eastward into shadowed foothills.

"I love this country," the man said. "Wait until you see Myrtle Falls. And the trout. Wait until you see the trout."

"You make them sound like whales," the boy said.

"That's just what they are, you'll see."

Flashes of painted buildings shone through the trees, then a sign said SHELLROCK, and another sign said SPEED 25. The town unraveled swiftly past the car windows — restaurant, post office, general store, garage and gasoline pump — then was gone, weatherbeaten frame buildings huddled in a hollow, only a memory. "The towns look lonely," the boy said. "Where is everybody?"

"They fish, cut logs. Town's just a place to come home to at night."

"I wouldn't like that. I'd want my life to be more exciting."

The man glanced at him. "You wanted to be a policeman once, Tommy. What do you want to be now?"

"Like you, Dad. A salesman."

The man nodded quickly, pleased and embarrassed.

"There's always a job for a salesman," he said. "What do you want to sell?"

"Do you think I could sell paint?"

"Sure." The man laughed. That's what he sold. Then the laugh caught in his throat, and his mouth tasted bitter. He glimpsed something shadowy. It crossed his mind quickly, and he didn't know what it was exactly, but he heard the sound of running water and smelled the sharp odor of pine needles and had a feeling of isolation and joy. He tried to hug the feeling to him, but it vanished like a ghost.

He wanted to be jolly, but there was a sadness in him. He wanted to say something light, but a gall rose in his throat. "You can make lots of money being a salesman," he said. "You're your own boss too." Then in his silent mind he swore at himself, quickly, so that he hardly realized he'd done it.

"It sounds fine," the boy said.

"Selling's a profession. Just like a doctor or lawyer."

The boy didn't answer. He was watching the trees flash by.

"A salesman's somebody," the man said. "Some of the richest men have been salesmen."

The boy looked at his father curiously. "Did you always want to be a salesman?" he asked.

Now the sound of running water and the smell of pine needles came back very strong, and the man saw another boy, with a fort under a waterfall in a forest glade, and a world to conquer just beyond the trees. His head ached.

"I don't think so," he said.

"How'd you get started?"

The man held the wheel hard to the left because the curve of the road wound around the cliff now, and down below, more than a hundred feet, the sea boiled in a small cove. He'd held his hat in his hand, hadn't he? He was sure he'd held his hat in his hand.

"It was after the war," he said. "A friend of mine was in selling and told me about this job. I went to see about it."

"Did you get it?"

The man nodded. He remembered it clearly now. He'd held his hat in his hand, all right. It had been new, pearl gray, and he had soiled the brim with his sweaty hands.

The boy said, "Not many people get the first job they go after, I bet."

"No," said the man. Joe McCloskey had been his friend, and Joe's dad owned the company, and the bald-headed sales manager had stared at him like a snake. But he had been hired.

"What did you want to be when you were my age?" the boy asked.

"Oh, I guess I thought there might be a hidden cave, and if I found it a secret would be there."

"There really might be, you know."

The man turned to look at him. Against the moving green of the fir trees the boy's face was pale and withdrawn.

"I think about it a lot," the boy said. "I always think it's a place that's been lost, that if you just had the right map you could find it."

The man nodded. "It's lost, all right."

"Sometimes I think it's very close," the boy said. "Sometimes I think it's right behind me, that if I just turned fast enough I could see it. But I never can turn fast enough."

The highway veered from the coastline now and straightened out into a wooded lane, black asphalt hurtling through a gash in the forest.

"Nobody can turn that fast," the man said.

The hum of the motor was steady in the enclosure of the car. Wind hissed at the sealed windows.

"Maybe someday I might," the boy said.

The man looked at him again, and the boy was watching him now, and the man wanted to reach out and touch him, to shield him from the future.

"Lots of people have tried," he said. He had tried himself, hadn't he? Hadn't he stood there with his hat in his sweaty hand because he knew it was impossible? "You forget such things when you're selling paint."

"Why should selling paint make you forget?"

"Selling takes a lot of time."

"It wouldn't take all my time. I'd remember."

The man felt a sudden rush of shame and wanted to defend himself. He glanced at the boy, but the boy was looking out the window. And didn't he have a right to his dream? I wish I had it myself, the man thought.

They passed a sign that said Littleport was ahead, and the man asked if the boy was getting hungry, and the boy said he thought he was, and the man said there used to be a restaurant in Littleport that served good fish, and the boy said he would like that fine.

"The Gaff and Reel," said the man. "That was the name of it."
They drove into Littleport, with the sun low in the western sky
and a redness forming out there, staining the ocean with its reflection, and they drove past weatherbeaten storefronts and across
a bridge, and on the other side of town was the Gaff and Reel, a
frame building with two big windows with beer signs in them,
freshly painted and not looking its age, with a fishing pole crossed
with a gaff over the doorway. They parked in front.

Inside the restaurant were booths and a long bar for serving
beer, and a pinball machine with a man playing it. The smell of
fish was strong, but not unpleasant, and there were two men at the
bar and several others in booths. Advertising signs were on the
walls, and there was a blackboard with the menu lettered in chalk.
CODFISH, $1.75, it said. SALMON, $2.00. They found a booth and sat
down.

"It's changed," the man said. "There used to be a fish bar over
there." He pointed. "You could get shrimp and crab and smoked
salmon and pickled eggs. The place was bigger too."

"I like it," the boy said.

A woman came out of the kitchen and walked up to the table
and waited. Her hair was gray, and there were faint beads of
perspiration on her forehead. She looked clean and strong.

"May I take your order?" she asked.

Now a grin was growing on the man's lips. "Do you remember
me?" he asked.

She looked at him closely, but her eyes remained blank. "I don't
think so. Have you been in here before?"

"Lots of times."

"It must have been way back."

"Twenty years."

Her eyes flicked the pages then, and stopped on one, then focused
again, and now she was remembering.

"There used to be a bunch come over from Valley Junction," she
said. "College kids. They fished at Myrtle Creek."

The man's grin widened.

"There was one always caught the most fish." She snapped her
fingers. "George something."

"Wallace," he said.

"That's right, George Wallace. Well, well." She took a step back
and looked them over. "Is this your boy?"

"Yes. This is Tommy." He wished he could remember the woman's name.

"Mrs. Haroldson," she said.

"Glad to meet you, Mrs. Haroldson," said Tommy.

She turned again to the man. "What brings you to these parts?"

"Just a fishing trip. We live down in California now."

"You figuring to fish Myrtle Creek?"

"That's right."

"It's no good any more. There's been a trailer park at the mouth for five years. Tourists drove all the fish away."

He had a hollow feeling and stared at her.

She said, "The state built parks at the mouth of every creek. There's no more trout at all in this part of the country. You could put all the trout caught last year in one pan."

Now the sound of rushing waters was loud in his ears, and he saw the branches entwined above the falls of the creek, a corridor into mystic woods, and the deep and silent eddy at the corner where lurked the giant trout.

"I'm sorry," said Mrs. Haroldson. She pulled a handkerchief and blew her nose angrily. "You want to order now?"

"It's all right, Dad," the boy said. "We can go salmon fishing instead."

"A trailer park," the man said.

"I'll have the codfish," the boy said.

The man said, "I'll have the codfish too."

Mrs. Haroldson left, and they sat there looking at each other, and the man was trying to understand how it could have happened, how anyone could have knifed away that enchanted wilderness. He wished he'd never heard about it. He wished he'd stayed home and worked.

"We could go down and look," the boy said. "Maybe it isn't so bad."

"I don't want to look," the man said. He'd already looked in his mind.

"I'd like to. You told me so much about it."

"It's not the same now, don't you understand?"

"All right. Will we go salmon fishing then?"

"I guess so."

The man at the pinball machine hit some special number, because the machine began clanging and thumping and flashing

lights. Then the boy said, "I'm sorry about the trailer park, Dad."
And the man answered, "It's all right. I shouldn't have expected
it to be the same."

Pretty soon Mrs. Haroldson brought their food on thick white
plates, and the fish were golden brown, and there were fluffy mounds
of mashed potatoes with butter and kernels of yellow corn.

Mrs. Haroldson said, "Mind if I join you? I remembered something you might like to know."

The man was surprised. "Sure," he said. Mrs. Haroldson sat
down by Tommy.

"You remember those trout you used to catch at Myrtle Falls?"
she asked.

He couldn't remember anything else. His mouth was full of codfish, so he only nodded.

"Did you ever wonder where they came from?"

"I guess they came from the sea."

"I don't think so. I think they came down Myrtle Creek, from
a lake somewhere up in the woods."

"What lake?"

"A lost lake."

The man put his fork down now and looked at Mrs. Haroldson
closely, and he saw that she was sincere, that this was why she sat
with them, to tell him this.

"Where did you hear about it?" he asked.

"Martin Kranz told me before he died. He said he used to fish
in it when he was a boy. He said the fish were big and so eager to
bite you could catch them with a bare hook."

"Did he tell you how to find it?" the man asked. The boy had
stopped eating too. He was watching the woman.

Mrs. Haroldson shook her head. "He said there used to be a
footpath to it, that it was way back in the woods and Myrtle Creek
ran out of it, that beavers built a dam there and made the lake.
But he said that brush grew over the path finally, and heaven knows
how anyone could get back in there now."

"We could find it," the boy said.

"Couldn't you just follow the creek?" the man asked.

Mrs. Haroldson shrugged. "Some of the fellows tried that. They
said that back in there a ways the creek runs through a narrow
gorge with no footing, and you can't walk along the bank because
the brush is so thick."

"Didn't Kranz ever try to find it?"

"He said he had all the fishing he ever wanted, that it was up to someone else to find it. You should hear the stories he told about those fish. Most people thought he was making them up."

"Maybe he was."

She shook her head. "I don't think so. The lake really meant something to him."

"Let's look for it, Dad," the boy said. "We could start early in the morning. We'd have all day."

"It would take all day just to get there," the woman said, "even if you could get through."

"We could take our pup tents," the boy said. "We could find it."

"I don't know," the man said. "It probably isn't even there . . . How far do you suppose it is?" he asked the woman.

"Not over five miles, I'd guess. Kranz said he used to walk it in an hour and a half. It's not the distance, though. It's how tough the going is."

"We've got a machete," the boy said, "and an ax. We could chop our way through."

"Do you think we could find it?" the man asked the woman.

"I don't know," she said.

"Have many tried?"

"Quite a few."

"Sounds pretty hopeless," the man declared.

"It doesn't sound hopeless to me!" the boy cried. "We could find it. And we'd be the first one. Those fish are still there, in a lake nobody has seen for years."

The man said, "We'd have to take food. We might be gone a couple days."

The boy let out a whoop.

"I'll fix it," Mrs. Haroldson said. "I'll pack sandwiches and cold cuts and a Thermos of coffee."

"What do you think, Tommy?" asked the man.

"We have to go, Dad."

"All right, then."

Mrs. Haroldson stood up. "I'll have your breakfast ready in the morning. You come in when you get up."

"You don't have to do that," the man said. "It'll be too early."

"I know what I'm doing. After you find the lake, you'll tell me how to get there." She grinned and headed for the kitchen.

The boy chattered. He'd read about a lost lake once, he said. Only the Indians knew about it. They thought an evil spirit lived in it, so they hid all the trails and let brush grow around it. One day a hunter got lost and stumbled onto it.

"Maybe that's the only way you can find one," the man said, and something touched him lightly on the shoulder. He turned, but nothing was there.

They finished eating and paid the bill, and Mrs. Haroldson said there was a motel just down the street where they could stay, and she told them to be sure to get up early, and she'd see them first thing in the morning.

The motel was called Seaview and had ten stucco cabins, painted green. The man checked in and got the key to No. 5 and parked in front, and he and the boy unloaded the luggage from the car — and the fishing and camping gear, too, so they could inspect it and make it ready for the morning.

The cabin was plain inside, with old-fashioned furniture and a light coat of dust on everything. They put their suitcases in a corner and the fishing and camping gear on the twin beds. They sat there, checking the lines and leaders and hooks and weights and lures, testing the reels. Then they looked over the pup tents and sleeping bags and packsacks. They listened to the radio while they did this, an old radio with a tinny sound.

Finally everything was in order, and they undressed and climbed into bed. The man lay awake for a long time, because he could see a rectangle of luminosity in the darkness, and in it were ever-changing pictures of the past. He watched them as he might have watched a movie screen and saw the ribbon of his life unreeling, not as it had happened exactly, but as it might have been.

It was cold when they got up. They dressed quickly, dancing on their toes and rubbing their arms in the chill, and gathered everything together and took it out to the car. They put the fishing and camping gear on the rear seat, then they drove over to the Gaff and Reel and found Mrs. Haroldson fixing bacon and eggs, the smell of them all through the restaurant.

She talked to them while they ate. She told them Kranz had said the lake was in a little valley, that you came upon it suddenly and never knew it was there until you saw it. She said the people who tried to follow the creek to the lake told her that the left bank was best. When they came to the gorge, they should leave the creekbed and come back to it after the gorge ended. The man listened to her carefully and the boy did too. Excitement was flooding them. The vision of the lake was crystal clear, an emerald in the wilderness. They could hardly wait to be after it.

When they came out to the car again, a light drizzle was falling, and the man saw that the cloud formation was slight and there were breaks in it, and the wind was from the east, so he knew the rain wouldn't last long. By the time they arrived at Myrtle Creek, the rain had stopped, and the gray light of dawn was spreading fast.

Now the man saw the scar upon the land, the carved-out symmetry of the trailer park and the outlines of machines and trailers and tents and picnic tables and waste cans and barbecue pits, and he did not even look in the direction of Myrtle Falls, but instead followed the creek through the trailer park to where brush and forest made a wall to the east. They parked and climbed out and began loading themselves with packs and gear. The tops of the hills were silhouetted against the sky now, and objects were emerging from shadow. They locked the car and made their way to the creekbed, threading their way along rocks at the edge. Into the foothills they walked, against the current, and felt the splashing of spray against their cheeks and saw the waters, dark and inscrutable, rushing past them.

They hiked for half an hour and did not talk much, just words of instruction as the man led the way and passed back information: This rock was loose, that low-hanging branch had to be watched, mud made footing precarious on this log. It was tough going. Then the sun broke through and turned the water of Myrtle Creek light blue, and fir trees doffed their shrouds and turned blue-green, and the man felt lighthearted, released somehow, excited about the uncharted region ahead and the lake lost there. Now and again he turned to look at his son, and they burst out laughing.

They came to a place where the creek made a curve, and the land was flat and clear of brush from the creek running over it, and they dropped off their packs and sat upon them and smelled the sweet and ferny odors of growing things, and the air was clear and crisply damp in this primeval forest.

"We're not far from the hills," the boy said.

The man looked up at them. "We're getting there."

The boy searched the hills with his wide eyes, and the corridor through the trees into which the creek disappeared. "Do you think we'll find it, Dad?" he asked.

"We'll find it."

"Maybe it isn't there."

"It's there all right."

"Do you think Mrs. Haroldson believes it's there?"

"Sure. And Kranz believed it."

"But Kranz saw it. It wasn't really a lost lake to him."

The man wondered why Kranz had always talked about it and always about its being lost. Didn't that show that he wanted it lost? Had he ever been to the lake at all? Or had he just manufactured it from his dreams?

"Funny," the boy said. "If we found it, it wouldn't be a lost lake any more. It would just be a lake."

"Don't you want to find it, Tommy?"

"Yes, but why does it make me feel sad?"

The man turned away. There was such a lump in his throat that he thought he might cry. "I guess it's because when we find the real thing we have to give up the dream," he said.

They began walking again, along the boulders of the creek, and the sun cast their shadows on the eddying waters. The boy began singing a hiking song, and the man joined him, and their voices echoed from the hills. They hiked another half hour before they came to the gorge.

It looked impassable. It was fifty feet deep, with steep sides of slippery clay, and there was no footing in the creekbed, no boulders or logs, no way to get through. The man led the boy up the left bank but, when they reached the top, they were in brush as thick as a jungle. Even the creek couldn't be seen. They rested then, and looked at the tangle of undergrowth and listened to the creek below. The man said it was easy to see how the lake had stayed lost when you ran into something like this.

But the boy was excited. Now that he saw how difficult it was, now that the way really looked impassable, he was finding new energy. He kept walking around, peering into the brush, moving branches aside and peering in and listening, keeping his ear cocked in the direction of the wind.

"Something has to be back there," he said, "otherwise it wouldn't be so hard to get in."

It was a truth that no longer held meaning for the man. He was
getting tired. His shoulders were sore from the pack straps, and
he dreaded putting them on again.

"We'll have to cut a path through that stuff," he said. "We'll
need both the ax and the machete. Which do you want?"

"The machete," said the boy. He withdrew it from the pack
and took a swipe at the branches, severing them cleanly. "It's
easy," he said. "Let's go, Dad."

The man got to his feet and put on his pack and felt the tenderness of his shoulders, and he took the ax and walked along behind
the boy, inching along behind the swishing machete, now and again
stepping forward to cut away a heavy branch. It took them half an
hour to cover a hundred yards, and by then the boy was sweating
and getting winded, and the man knew he would have to relieve
him or give him a chance to rest. They had at least a quarter mile
of this to cover before the gorge flattened out and they could follow
the creek again. Finally the boy stopped thrashing and drew a
deep breath, and the man stepped forward and relieved him of the
machete and began a rhythmic slashing that immediately made him
feel better.

He was surprised at first how easily the machete swung, how the
brush disintegrated before it. But then he began to feel the strain
in his arms and the tenderness of his palms, and the pack straps cut
hard into his shoulders, and he could feel the sweat starting on his
forehead. Ahead he could see just the wall of foliage, and he could
hear the sound of the creek running in its gorge to his right. He
was engulfed in endless wilderness, hacking, eternally hacking.

Before long he had to stop, and the boy took the machete again,
and the man looked behind and saw that they had carved a narrow
path, lumpy and shapeless, but marking their passage, and they
could return on it, could find their way back.

He had another turn with the machete, and the boy had another,
then suddenly, it seemed, it was his turn again, and he was just
about to suggest that they both rest for a while when he noticed
that the sound of the creek was different. Through the trees he
saw that the gorge had flattened out, and he caught a glimpse of
the creek out there, winding along bouldered edges. They would
be able to return to it now; the hacking was nearly over. He cleared
the rest of the way himself, though he wouldn't have been able to
if he hadn't seen the creek, and the boy talked excitedly behind

him, urging him on, exuberant because they had fought their way
through the impassable stretch.

Finally they were sitting on packs at the creek's edge, grinning
at each other like idiots, delighted beyond bounds at their accomplishment, the boy already pointing at the hills, wondering aloud
where the lake was, in that hollow or that one, but the man didn't
want to think about it, not yet.

"The creek should wind around that hill," the boy said, "and
go over to the left, see, where that cup in the hills is, right behind
that patch of brown." He pointed, but the man wasn't looking.
He was listening.

He'd heard a sound somewhere to their left, and it wasn't an
animal and it wasn't the forest. It came again faintly, and now
he realized what it was. He looked at the boy, but the boy hadn't
heard it. He was visualizing the lake.

"I think I'll look around," the man said. "There's a knoll over
there. I might be able to see something from the top."

"I'll go with you," the boy said.

"No, stay here. You need the rest."

"I'm not tired. I didn't work any harder than you did."

"Stay here anyway. I won't be long."

"All right. But I hope you hurry. I'm getting anxious."

The man left then, threading his way through the trees. He
hoped the sound wouldn't come again, but even if it did, the boy
wouldn't recognize it. He went quickly now, with a kind of desperation. When he rounded the knoll he saw below in the hollow
a man bent over a notebook. He wore boots and a checked shirt
and a wool cap, and a hatchet was slung at his waist. The man
was a timber cruiser, all right, checking the log stands here in the
forest. The timber cruiser looked up from his notebook and saw
the man, and they were like two strange animals meeting suddenly.
Then the man started down toward him.

The timber cruiser had a red face and eyes that were lined from
squinting, and he was as big and solid as the trees he checked.
When the man came up to him, he said, "You're on private property."

"I'm looking for a lake," the man said. "There's supposed to be
a lake at the head of Myrtle Creek."

"How'd you get up here?" the timber cruiser asked.

"I followed the creekbed."

The timber cruiser looked at the man's clothes. "I guess maybe you did. That's why you didn't see our sign. There's a No Trespassing sign on the road." He looked at the man strangely. "The road's right over there. You could have taken it if you'd gotten permission."

"I didn't know that," the man said. He was badly frightened. He had a sudden insight into what the world was like to a blind man.

"Do you know about the lake?" he asked. "A lake at the head of the creek?"

"Been gone for years. Used to be on the south fork, three miles up. Only the creekbed there now. You can't even tell where the lake was."

The man was tired. He wanted to sit down. He wanted to sit down and never get up. He wanted to ease his sick feeling by getting drunk or yelling at the top of his lungs. He wanted to forget about this timber cruiser, forget what he had said.

"You can ride back with me if you want to," the timber cruiser said. "I'll be leaving in an hour."

"I'll go back by the creekbed."

"You look pretty tired."

"I don't want a ride, see? I want to walk out by the creekbed."

"All right, but remember you're on private property."

The man walked unsteadily back around the knoll, a hard knot of anguish clutching his stomach. The boy was waiting for him, still sitting on his pack by the creek.

"Did you see anything?" he asked.

"The knoll wasn't high enough."

"I didn't think it was. I could hear you talking to yourself."

The man glanced at him quickly, but the boy was smiling.

"I was talking to myself too," the boy said. "Being alone in the woods makes it all right, don't you think? Are you ready to go now?"

"I am, if you are."

The boy stood up and put on his pack, then faced his father. "Can I lead the way, Dad? It will make it seem more exciting."

"Sure, go ahead," said the man, and the boy led the way along the edge of the creek.

The man watched his son moving ahead of him and knew it was good that he was leading and couldn't see what a terrible effort it was for his father to take each step. They would come to the fork soon and follow the one to the north, taking so long that there wouldn't be time to investigate the other. He'd see to it that the boy always believed the lake was on the south fork. If only I could believe it too, he thought. But it was more important for his son to believe.

H. W. BLATTNER

Sound of a Drunken Drummer

(FROM THE HUDSON REVIEW)

DOING FIFTY UP MISSION she said to Rob, sober and upright beside her, "Don't worry, boy, no cop's going to catch us if I have
to do ninety. They'd have to shoot me in the tires," but there
weren't any around, probably all in their station houses counting
poker chips, and when he gave her a glance she said, "That's right,
I don't like cops. Instinctively I don't like them, verstehst Du?"

He seemed to. He always did. It was one of the beautiful things
about him. He had so many: sweet disposition, handsome intelligent presence, a strong uninhibited capacity for love. Plus good
manners. A sterling type.

"Oh love me love me love me true," she sang low with the radio,
"cause there's no one in the world but yew-hoo-hoo," and gave out
there arbitrarily recollecting the woman back in the drugstore
where she'd gone to get the prescription filled that she'd put the
arm on the nice young doctor for: the naive swimming look that
surprisingly often got to them, the young sweet — helpless —
not too much, careful there, that's right, got it now just the right
pitch — "You see doctor I'm a stranger here, I'll be going back
East soon but I'm under rather a severe strain — " Here something quick about the death of a beloved relative — " "And I
can't sleep so if you could let me have something a bit strong perhaps so I'll be sure to get some rest, I do need it badly."

Hadn't failed her yet any of these young ones that at times
jockeyed for the moment with expectation, unlike most of the
older trouts rendered wily and callous by suffering, other people's

of course — for whom it was all déjà vu like the movie operator who dozes on the job. You could practically read the diagnosis forming up behind the scientific foreheads: "Neurotic. Drinks — " But she was always dead sober at these times and anyway she didn't drink so much most of the time that it was anything like a matter of leaping to the eye, when you considered people like Toni and her clique who went in for it seriously in order not to be, as what's-his-name had said, or had he — I think not, therefore I am not — Men, types. Autumn leaves. Oh, sheets.

But where, what had she started to — no matter, possibly some little thing she was going to say to Rob here who understood one well enough anyway so it wasn't actually necessary to say anything, and slowing for the turn into Ocean Avenue she looked at him and coarsely taken with his companionable air of capable interest flung an arm about his shoulders and said cheek to cheek, "I like you, you know? Men are foul. Dogs are noble." He cut a wet swipe at her chin as she let him go raking away roughly tender, and his profile level with hers faced forward.

Tooling along in the ghost-gray night inside the snug tent of the convertible they wound their way to Junipero Serra and idled on through Portola to where the fine houses slept aristocratic, one couldn't picture people snoring inside. "Richard does, though," she said. "Quite obscenely. I don't know, it simply sounds that way. Look," she pointed, "there's where he is this instant, back in his bedroom there, snoring. Perhaps why Mrs. Wrighthill sleeps separate. *And* à cause de moi, it goes without saying. Marriage one long bore, did someone say. Of *course* she knows, silly. You don't imagine this is the first time, do you? But being a lady she naturally resents not being first fiddle. I suppose she kept her eyes on all that gold paving her way up the aisle, and who am I to scorn her for a natural feminine instinct. No, let's be broad about the thing. He must have been young once, oilily tender. Oi Lily — bei mir bist Du a sister under your skin. No, in truth a formidable woman. A lady. Aren't many of them left, it's said. Stepping all in white with hymen intact and cool authority lo these many years to where attended the gentleman who these days pays for our keep, your horsemeat and my scotch and minks. Not that I asked for any of that barbarity of dead skins but he insisted, Richard's that generous. I'm sure he'd offer to put me through college if I didn't already have my sheepskin. Which I got through the skin of my ass being nice to Professor O'Rourke — you're quite right, it does sound like a fart in a bathtub. Old but still service-able, like an international playboy. The genius of the people comes out in these things. Like dirty jokes. And him poor devil, the professor I mean, scared stiff he'd be found out. Those intel-lectuals, they don't overdo that sort of thing although who knows, with the student body constantly changing. If those ivied walls had tongues, mercy. Richard's house too, such a coincidence. Boy, am I in the Ivy League. However that Elise Lynch, she always did turn a hand or an ass to anything. Way back I was told I'd come to a bad end, and that I have testifies to my powers of application because if you think it's anything but a rocky road to hell you're off the beam, boy." She reached over and rubbed the back of his ear. "Did you know, in a happy home even the animals are happy — the dogs, cats, lions, snakes? When I was a kid we had dogs by the half dozen and not one but was a snarler and biter. Pavlov would have been enchanted — you never saw such conditioning. Still it wasn't that so much made me take to other people's beds. I had my smattering of virtue. More of a built-in inclination, I should say. Got it from Daddy, no question. Who couldn't climb off one playmate than he was casting about for another. Kept poor Mother in a constant state of two-mindedness, like having two heads. And the kids getting the psychic fallout, naturally." She rubbed his ear again. He liked it, leaning to get the full satisfac-tion. "Well, all I can say is I bet you'd be every bit as generous as Richard if you were a man, which thank heaven you're not. This way it's a much more satisfactory relationship. Men and women can't help being dishonest with each other, it's one of the unwritten laws. Listen, if they ever went crazy and told each other the truth there'd be a massacre in the streets."

They were wandering around easy like that, just riding around as they did most nights — Richard left around nine or half-past, not alone because of Mrs. Wrighthill. A man of fifty-three had his sedate routines — she going on talking to him who was such a good listener, as she had got into the habit of doing because if you stayed too long in saloons you got stinking and it was more comfortable as well as seemly to do it inside your own subsidized walls or next door with Toni and her crowd who all they had was

money and carrying their cargo of hooch or H according to preference had jettisoned their souls long ago, when of all things there
was a pair of dogs exuberantly copulating on the sidewalk, the
right time if the wrong place but how naturalistic compared to
humans: in the darkened rooms, the walleyed fumbling. Rob spied
them too and whimpered, looking back through the rear window.
"Don't take it so to heart," she said, "or wherever. You've had
yours, if you'll remember the charming bit you ran across in Sutro
Heights last week. In broad daylight too." One walked on pretending not to notice and after a suitable interval turned and
whistled, on his return slipping the leash on with a mild scold to
make it appear as if he'd done no worse than lift a leg on the
nasturtiums. So proud and set-up he looked, similar to Richard
when he'd put over one of his big deals.

"We'll celebrate," he would say, beaming some — he had the
smooth round pink-tinted kind of face to which it came natural,
at such times he definitely did have the bland chic, a combination
of smoothness and éclat, of a minister in charge of a large and
wealthy congregation. By the same token there was his voice to
play around one in clerical compass, warm, resonant yet urbane,
undoubtedly the instrument that had increased him his fortune,
for he came of one of those elite Western clans whose heads
started out grubbily as prospectors and wound up sleeping on gold-
knobbed beds. When they didn't sail off to chivvy simpleminded
natives on tropic isles, trading beads and Mother Hubbards for
the real estate. Or on that order — how could she be expected
properly to know, an effete New Yorker ignorant of their large
Western ways.

"All right," she would say. "Let's." So then he'd have a champagne supper sent in, and top off the whole with some love play.
Not too much. Richard had his age and health in addition to his
dignity to think of.

But she saw she had come around to his house again, and on a
whim stopped the car in front of the tall red-brick white-trim
house back of the fine meandering date-palmed street and observing it imagined how he'd disapprove, silently of course, if he
knew she was sitting there at her midnight loafing. For being a
wellbred man, in the — what, eight, ten months they'd been in
association — so hard to say, they came and they went and when

they came you wished they'd went — in all this time he had never once said a word about her drinking which naturally he abominated, except to refer in a roundabout manner to the evils of liquor. Himself, a wine man and maybe one two martinis a month. Tout à fait comme il faut. A man of breeding and substance. Gentleman, gentleman friend: mousing around sedate, broad-bottomed, always the cheese and never a nip of the trap.

A patrol car pulled in to the curb. The door slammed and a cop walked back toward her on flat, let's see what we've got here feet.

"Having any trouble, miss?" He peered in as into a cave.

"Since you mention it officer yes, some," she said. "Nothing you could fix, though, thanks all the same."

He measured her out of his ruddy bull-terrier face and said with something of a hard, accustomed sigh, "Well now, let's have a look at your license."

"Sure, if you must."

He held a flashlight on it, peering, and handed it back. "Like to know what you're parked here for, if you don't mind."

"Well, taking one thing with another I should say I do but that's neither here nor there, is it."

"It sure isn't," he said heavily, leaning the elbow of a thigh-sized arm in on her. Rob growled but she casually laid a hand on him and he didn't follow up.

She relaxed, hands idle on the wheel and congratulated herself on having drunk vodka and then not enough to cause a hassle. "It's this way, officer," she said. "I like to ride around dreaming nights. Kind of a therapy, you see, when you can't sleep. Therapy, that means — "

"I know what it means," he said, his dewlaps contracting a bit.

"Well, good. They're doing an excellent job of training, aren't they. So I drove in here and stopped because it's so peaceful I can hear my motor purr."

"Sounds all right to me," he said.

"Oh, it's a superb motor," she said. "None better."

They gazed at each other, eyes glistening in the witching light of the dashboard.

"All right now," he said. "That'll be all. Better run along before I change my mind, however."

"Yes *sir*, officer. That's just what I'll do. But may I say it's good to see the law right in there, protecting property and what's the other — yes, life." She turned on her nicest debutante smile. "A rivederci," she said, backed up and swept off around him.

Well, it had got to him of course. Her smile really could have been her fortune, if she'd bothered to lift her little finger instead of her skirt, so much too soon and too often. But then she got to thinking of Wimberley, for no ready reason except the usual: dead now poor devil, done in despite the specialists, all the crazy care. Hadn't belonged to him long, and him on his last lung then, being eaten by the cancer. A bachelor, it had been all right for her to live in and he gave it out that she was his secretary — clever, that. All the same rather a decent solid type, Wim. A shame, wrenched off at thirty-nine and from out of all that wealth, too. One time money didn't talk loud enough. And so thoughtful of him, seeing to it virtually in extremis that she found a fresh bed-down. Befitting a man who inheriting his fortune was above the vulgarity of treating money lightly, and so left every last penny to a foundation bearing his name.

"I'll never forget the day," she said to Rob. He yawned and slid down, paws drooping over the seat edge and snuggling his chin down on them. " 'I've been thinking of your future,' he says in that awful weak staggered voice, and the shadow of death on the wall, 'and I think I've got the answer — ' "

A slant of sun lay on the bed, that if it had fallen on him would have shown him up transparent, rendered down to nothing as he was. Out the window to one side the Golden Gate bridge draped its harp hang in the clear silver air — a wind drove with fury across the sky, blanching it — Tamalpais rising farther on its remote majestic drag, dark blue and the contours fuzzed in silver. Straight ahead and below the ruins of the Palace of Fine Arts foamed up out of the hags'-hair trees, the Yacht Harbor spread out a rich show of boats and over across the blue-iron white-starched water squatted the serene hump of Belvedere like some huge furry animal taking a foot bath. Another eye-jump and there was Alcatraz, a pedantic impregnable reminder, while a further shift brought in the Contra Costa hills beginning to be smogged in, faintly sulphurous, safely far off. Altogether a glorious view, fit to die in sight of.

The man engaged in it — hardly, gamely fighting every inch of the way — courage for the sheer sake of it, a noble thing — laid his egg-size haunted eyes on her and said, "Never got to — know each other right — did we," the words pulled out of him like nails.

"No," she said.

"But no time — go into that." Then it was he said that about her future. "Richard Wrighthill — you know him — "

"I should," she said. "He's been around often enough." And as it didn't sound quite right, "Seems to think a lot of you, Wim."

"Always been — good friend. Wants to — wants you to — come to him."

She thought it over, her dark blue eyes made lighter, more intense by the breezed light so that the effect was of a cool burning, and held in a fixed observance suggesting some jewel-hard inner amusement totally disconnected from the world contemplated. His stare on them was like that of a man walking to the scaffold taking his last fill of the sky.

"Married, isn't he?" she said.

"Not — very. Never — got along. Take good care of you. Told me he's — very much — in love."

"Well, at least sounds as if I wouldn't want for a good home," she said. "And I do appreciate your thinking of me, Wim. Up to now though I've always landed on my feet."

He shook his head, it rolled slowly back and forth on the pillow like a marble in the hand. As if mustering his strength he stared at her with a gaunt longing, a far light deep in his eyes like the twist at the core of a whirlpool — or maybe it was merely his condition accounted for that spectered air. Then he began to talk, weak, halting from the effort of delicacy as well, reminding her of the time she had taken an overdose of sleeping pills, he didn't want to feel she'd ever do anything so terrible and cruel again, and if she had someone like Richard, a steady kind man to take care of her, he felt sure she never would.

He paused, for breath. And said then suddenly, "I'm — dying," without any theatrics, but it cost him a slight gasp. "Elise, you're so — lovely, young — for God's sake live, if you knew — if you knew what it's like — "

As though some merciless outside force were attacking his face it twisted, wrung by a rising agonized ecstasy that dissolving in sudden improbability reshaped with a kind of gradual successive integration and sank like a spear profound, strengthless into the evacuating eyes.

She was on her feet to run for the nurse but weakly, like a tendril his hand caught hers and she saw he wasn't being worked over any more, just infinitely exhausted, and when feebly imperious he shook his head she said at once, "Okay, I won't. Isn't there anything I can — here, let me fix your pillow," and driven to action, with a subtly frowning face smoothed and settled the pillow, fussed around with the covers, all the while trying to keep her face out of his sight because he hated pity. Even her own crude kind, that could extend only a short lawless way.

He lay with his eyes shut and the look of a ghost on him for a considerable time, while sitting on the edge of the bed she held his hand feeling that that at least fit into the picture. And when at length his eyes came open with an ancient, blurred look she said, "All right, Wim, I'll go with this, what's his name, Wrighthill. So don't worry about it. Goodness, I'm not worth it. You lie there and rest, concentrate on that."

A little knife of a smile twisted in on the pale sensitized lips, the smile of a wounded knight. It faded and he said, "You — promise — promise you'll never try — "

"Wim, it was just an accident. Or supposing it wasn't, all I must have been after was some attention. If we have to get Freudish about it. Do you think if I'd really wanted to — no, it's too silly to waste any more talk on."

A feeble frown drew his brows together Christlike. After a little he said, a whisper, "Whole life — before you." Took a minute for breath, and: "Go to Richard — right away. I'll tell him. No good for you — here. Life — you want life."

So what could she do but agree, especially as the door opened and the nurse glanced in anxious at this long visiting.

A buxom elderly type, she said out in the hall with a brisk matron authority, "You shouldn't, dear. It's hard on people that aren't accustomed to it, and you can't do any good anyway."

Elise shrugged her shoulders. "He asked for me. Still stands, does it? No dice?"

The woman shook her head. "Honestly, dear, you shouldn't go in there any more. You come out looking shaky and after all there's nothing you or anyone can do. It's only a matter of time now."

"Looks like I won't be around much longer, anyhow."

"Good, I'm glad. You're too young—"

"Nuts. At twenty-seven who should be so young."

"You're kidding," the woman said, her face ungainly with amazement. "I would have sworn twenty-one, at the most twenty-two."

"It's true, to look at me you wouldn't take me for a lush, would you? It's my peachy complexion. Holding up real good, nothing seems to touch it. So if I look shaky it's more from hangover than poor Wim. By the way, got anything on you? I'm out of Veronal again."

The nurse starched up at once. "No I haven't," she said with a quick severity. "Excuse me." Brushing past she went in to her patient, and Elise ambled on down to her quarters.

That night the Chinese houseboy came to say there was a gentleman to see her, so she went down and there was Wrighthill in the study, nervous as a tomcat on the scent.

He stammered a greeting, they sat down opposite each other and after a short somewhat soggy silence he pitched in, his gaze filmed-over, heroic, the grim dedication of him conferring the seal of acceptance.

"Miss Lynch — or may I call you Elise, I — I guess I'll come right to the point." He cleared his throat, to eliminate the gravel which whether due to guilt or the nervousness of desire or both choked out the resonance: one got vaguely the impression of a man unjustly suffering an indignity, and in the rear of his mind an eventual revenge forming.

"Wim tells me he's spoken to you about a — a certain, *hrrum*, matter," he said, switching around to something like an intransigent distraction.

"Right. You want to shack up with me, that it?"

His eyelids quivered, rose up to expose his stare — cooling, cooler, stopping just short of cold. But at any rate he was jolted out of most of the jitters. "Isn't that rather an unnecessary way of putting it — "

"I prefer straightforward. Look, we don't have to play footsie, being as we're both with it. Make your pitch, I'll listen and if the terms are right it's a deal."

She slid down a little, relaxed in her chair and lit a cigarette.

Silence, a groping. She smoked her cigarette, relaxed, looking as if she didn't have a thing on her mind. Which being exactly the way it was, after a couple more minutes she glanced over at him and grinned. He must have read something of his own into it, because all at once getting up with a sort of twitched nonchalance, and a short rather sad-sounding laugh he came and lowered himself into a chair beside her, taking her hand in his warm pincushion one.

And said richly warm, quite returned to his old harmony, "You're acting this way because you're scared, poor darling. But dearest, you must believe me, there's nothing to be afraid of. I — the fact is I care for you a great deal, a very great deal. I have from the first time I saw you. You were standing at the top of the stairs, and I had never seen a more beautiful girl. Your lovely golden hair, there was a halo — yes, angelic is the word." He paused a moment. "I'm not the kind of man who loses his head easily, but at that instant something happened to me, something I had never expected to feel again. And each time we spoke a few words you — you attracted me more and more. But I don't have to go on, you can see well enough what you've done to me," he said tying it up with a hint of jovial brusqueness — leaving the door open for a dignified exit, just in case.

She was looking at him with an unswerving bright interest not quite amusement but near it, as if for the moment she found him novel in his brash advocate's substance.

Rousing she said, "I suppose Wim's filled you in on the background."

He nodded. "Born in New York City. Married at sixteen, the marriage annulled. College."

"Right, broadly speaking. But you'll want the gaps filled. Where did you leave off — college, yes. Well, it was there I started to go to the bad, really I mean, not just playing around at it like before I got married. And the less said about that the better. Not because there's any pain in it but because it was plain adolescent and birdbrained. But to go on, about the only thing stuck with me from college was a few tricks of copulation. Oh, and I mustn't omit the interval in Switzerland. Shipped me off in a last desperate attempt at regeneration. Came back reeking of the continental polish: rectitude, and when it won't work discretion. So it's good stock you're getting, if the family did kick me out owing to a little scandal involving gin and gigolo. Never touch the stuff now. The gin that is. In any case I don't come at any bargain rates, it's only fair to tell you."

"I'm prepared to go, um, as high as necessary." And he looked, perhaps because the commercialism distressed him, a shade unnerved. Then she thought it might be That Word that had titillated him, warmed his guilt and thus made him doubly determined to get her: since he was suffering already, why not go whole hog. And later simply through the osmosis of association she found out that was about how it shaped up, his puritanism uneasing him despite the out of his wife's spurning though you could say this for him, it never caused him enough discomfort to rumble any foundations.

"Just thought I'd get the lay of the land," she said. "Because it's always best to get clear on the essentials, then everybody knows where he stands. It worked out pretty good with my former comrades."

His eyes that had begun assiduously to stroke her like a collector with a new choice item backed off infiltrated by alarm, suspicion and a gaining uncertainty.

"Sorry," she said. "Forgot that's a verboten word. Now if I had said comrades in arms, but the obviousness of it. Because lovers is pretentious and old-novelish, like soul. That leaves what, intimates, which rings coy, and lays, too defensive. Well, do we come down to the deal or go on with the preambles."

But he remained mute regarding her with a hung lovesickness, caught with his lust down, and for a moment she had almost a compunction. But what, not such a cinch for her either being at constant beck and call and never calling your body your own except when you sneaked some guy pour le sport, which wasn't cricket. But then who after all was perfect and what was so special about her she should do the noble.

So she allowed him some more time but when he just lumped there with that rather dreamy melancholy as though trying to summon up some approvable manner or expression out of her, and his hand now and again contracting hers in slight nervous spasms she suddenly got bored and vulgarly crossing her arms over her chest said breezy, hoydenish, "Well open the safe door, Richard, and let's see the shine of your gelt."

However it happened to amuse him, after a hesitant low-keyed manner. "You write your own ticket, little girl," he said, his smile moving by fits. "I guess I could say I'll live to regret those words, but I don't think I will." And with an assurance as smooth, confident and full-bodied as it was peremptory, "I'm a pretty fair judge of character. And I believe in you, in your basic sweetness, the good stuff you're made of."

Watching his principles pop out all over him she grinned. "All I can say to that is we'll hope for the best. As for me, I'm totally inconnu to myself. French. Had to show off some."

"Your accent is perfect," he said. "I never can get that 'u.' "

"Easy. Purse the lips. U. U. No extra charge for coaching. Little, you said? Five seven and lithe as a panther. And there's two of everything — eyes, arms, breasts, legs. One mouth, one — you'll find everything in satisfactory working order."

He took her hand back in his, which was moist, and twitched it.

"I'm sure it is," he said, his pink richening. Then in a minute with the care of a superficially restored composure, "There's an apartment four blocks from here. Everything's furnished, all you have to bring is your suitcase."

"Plural. There's three. Plus a trunk. Wim's not stingy. I was on my uppers when he took me in and now look at the wardrobe."

"Nothing to what *I'll* give you, darling," he said, and began stroking her arm.

"Keep talking." Just testing, for the hell of it.

"A car will be waiting for you the day you move in."

"Make it a Cad convertible. No mistress should be without one."

He had the good manners to let it flow on past. "When can you make it, tomorrow?"

"No reason why not. I know Wim wants me out the sooner the better."

He darkened somewhat, right off. "It's such a horrible thing," he said. "At his age, with all he's got to live for."

A pause, his lover's clasp settling with a sort of restraint. "It just came to me," she said. "Some say this here, now is Hell. What if it's Heaven, after all?"

The darkening became a frown, then cleared. "You mustn't trouble your lovely head with such things," he said. His hand put loving pressure on hers. "I'll see you then around five at the Rochester Arms. It's at the corner of — "

"I know where it is."

"The eighth floor. Gorgeous view. I happened to hear of a vacancy, a friend of mine moved out so I went right around and took it. I was sure you'd like it."

"I can see you're a man not given to doubts." Her smile was charming, slanted, with a tangle of lashes and her eyes glinting like water through ferns. A certain perverse quirk at the corners of the lips went ignored — he stared with a sudden jowled barrenness before with a uniform snap-to coming out of it he said, "I had talked to Wim and both of us felt, that is we thought since you'd be at loose ends — "

"Now there, that's what I call an apt turn of phrase. Not everyone could have come out with it so neatly. I must say, I *am* a lucky type. It's not every girl can transfer from bed to bed without having to go out and hustle. I'm *so* grateful, Mr. Wrighthill."

"You called me Richard a while back," he said.

"So I did. I like Richard. I won't call you Dick or Rich."

"Nobody ever has."

"Not even your wife?"

"No." A silence came down, and the fallen-curtain sense didn't lift when he said, "Elise, dear, there's one condition — my wife is never to be mentioned between us."

"Of course. Sorry."

He brought his bulk a little closer and she drew away a fraction before noticing it wasn't a threatening but an amorous move. "You're so lovely," he said in a pressured voice and she could hear his breath coming through the hairs in his nose — a rather large one, the kind described as commanding on the face of a successful man and bazoo on a Skid Row character.

"So lovely," he said, breathing, and his arm going around her he drew her to her feet.

Now this is where I clinch it, she said in herself as with a bull dignity his head loomed. Then the large solid pressure of his body was against hers with the large meaty arms wrapping and the warm-breathed mouth coming down quivering, a rabid diffidence.

When in time their bodies parted it wasn't unlike a stopper leaving a bottle. Dark oxblood suffused his face and his eyes were

stunned, dimly questing. They watered as the red sank down
leaving a fevered pink and his breath strongly sweeping from his
nostrils.

"My darling," he said, "my dearest," with the repressed grunted
pain of pleasure, a muted tone of agonized worry. His arms enclosed her with the manipulating lightness of a relentless grasp,
and when his eyes lurched over to the couch she said, "Okay, but
it'll have to be quick. The houseboy could come in."

He smiled hazed, staggered round in a dream. "That's how it
mustn't ever be," he said, mumbled. "There's tomorrow, and all
the other tomorrows — oh, I'll wait for my darling." He drew her
up close, and into her mind came the time she had wrestled a mattress over. "We're going to be happy, so happy," his breath chuffed
in her ear. "Aren't we. My sweetheart, my lovely girl."

"Sure," she said.

"Darling, sweetest," he nuzzled her ear. "I know you're going to
make me the happiest man in the world, in all the world." And
with a sort of trespassing helplessness his hand began making free
of her breast.

"I don't anticipate any complaints," she said. "It's all those
amateurs screw it up for us pros."

His hand came regretful away, he gazed at her gently chiding,
with the hazed smile. "You mustn't be hard, dearest," he said.
"Love is a beautiful thing; the love of a man and a woman . . .
a beautiful thing."

She took his hand and put it back on her breast. "I'm not
hard." she said. "Feel." And when his eyes started to glaze she
said leaning back on the log of his arm with a roll of warm young
passion, audacious and free, "I'm yours. Go ahead. Have some."

So then of course it happened, over on the couch. With him
first jamming a chair under the doorknob, from a stealthed presence of mind. Although no one disturbed them he was impelled
to hurry and fumble, but she accommodated herself and bringing
all her resources into play caused him to cry out once, a sharp
hoarse reaching that was the sincerest form of homage.

And afterwards, sitting on the edge of the couch following his
set-faced, absorbed zippering and resettling and her casual straight-
ening he gathered her in his arms and told her, in a tone mixing
a shining wonder with the dash of gallantry that foresees a dazzling

future, how wonderful she was, with a profusion of darlings, belovedests and sweetests which after a while she interrupted by saying she didn't like to bring it up at a time like this, but shouldn't
she be going up to take some measures.

He rose immediately, a bulked fluster in the movement. "Yes,
I — I wasn't thinking — but how could I have thought of anything
but you, my most wonderful dearest — "

"My goodness, that was only a coming attraction," she said.
"Save the rave notices for the main feature. Well, I've got to get
cracking. Not that it's really too urgent, I've never got pregnant,
can't probably, but why take chances."

He nodded flushing a bit and then quickly said he'd see her the
next day. "I'll try to make it before five — Oh wait, wait, you
wouldn't go without a kiss, sweetheart — "

She grinned before she could think not to, at his bugeyed en-
treaty like a schoolboy demanding a promised lollipop, a tuft
of hair standing up in front, horn of a dilemma. "Sure," she said.
"We'll lip it up a little." But too taken up with the terse acknowledgment of his need to care, or even listen he gathered her up.

Upon her leaving finally she looked back from the door: the
manner of his standing there was remindful of a tree just before
it starts to fall.

In the morning she said goodbye to Wim, who said it took a
big load off his mind and wished her all the best. "I do want you
— to be — happy, darling," he said, in his great eyes the involuntary longing and disassociation of the terminally ill. She bent to
kiss him quick, with almost an intolerance, and got out of the room.
In the hall she was obscurely astonished to find herself undergoing
a sinking spell, or something of the kind, but it went away quietly.

Over at the Rochester Arms true to the man's word a Cad
awaited, and in the evening there was a sumptuous meal with
champagne, which she didn't much go for and afterwards his
heavy middle-aged embrace, ditto, but it kept her in scotch and
silks and Rob in his two pounds of horsement a day, so there was
no cause to grumble.

"Be there soon, boy," she said to him, watching the minuscule
bayonet tips of the fog fall before the headlights. He pricked up
his ears but didn't lift his head, sleepy from his long walk on the
beach that afternoon. "I should be too but I never felt more wide

awake," she said. Only one o'clock, too. Suddenly all those hours to be lived through before daylight heaved up like the horizon from a pitching ship. Something, a slime like a psychic excretion was released, she sat up, stumbling after memory — hadn't Toni mentioned a party or was it the next night — what difference, always one long party recessed by a day or two. Peculiar how it all balled up so one day ran into the next, and harder and harder to remember things. Right in there, working away drilling all those holes and when the job was finished, that would be the day.

She hummed to "Some Enchanted Evening," coming through the radio. Cheesecloth. Wrap that Dutch one in, with the glowing red skin — Edam. Tiny greasy holes, can't tell one from another. From a hole in the ground. No, the other much more sanitary. How the hair sizzles in the fierce blue flame. Yes, dear, that's Auntie Elise doing a slow burn. Anne, safe and sound with husband and child. Junior League. Suckering the poor. Deeply ashamed of the kid sister and trying not to show it, poor dear. Go in peace, Annie girl. She shall never darken your heart again. Well, one in every barrel.

Motion, a shift, oblique — the woman in the drugstore on Mission, prototype of the embattled respectable poor: virulence like a fling of acid in the look. "Stands to reason," she said. "Us representing the beautiful and damned — nobody ever counts the ugly and damned. And them, the plain and saved, backs to the wall and showing a coyote tooth."

But he just gave a tiny yelp well into his sleep and they rode on carried in the womb of the car past the dark houses and apartments and their own less than two minutes away when in the crashed-monument way of it the entire unit started to give coming deadly alive to the swift scurry of the brittle iced brilliance lashing out the trail of iced fire and then fast, windrush the quaked gathering, stream-up for the giant bursting and up, up — straining to the higher — highest —

No. No. — The shuddered braking.

Under the dead hand the car swerved to the curb.

The break, as into a death. Long, strong temblor drag. Penultimate: erratic, capersome almost the spasms of decline, down waft by sighed levels. And the arrival, touched bottom: organization of drummed calm, gears meshing in cotton wool.

As in a return to consciousness, new-grotesque the street emerged to perception, the gray gauze-bandage fog over a recognizable front of building.

And now the cold. Oh, the cold. Teeth chattering she shook so it woke up Rob who pulled himself up and in calm wakefulness sat by, a mute staff.

She said rattling, tattered, with a lamenting dribble of laughter, "Not this time, not yet," and shaking with the laughter dribbling grabbed hold putting her face to him and he braced strong, grave, planted firm by her side.

Took a spell but then it was over, the worst of it. From time to time she would be hauled tacking on her side but the worst was done: twister receding to distance. Digging with a hand cold and rigid as a spade for cigarettes, "Boy, that one really whirled me," she said. Voice with a timbre like nickelodeon piano. The match kept hitting up beyond the cigarette tip but eventually she got it going, and smoked it down to the tar.

"All right, boy, end of the line." She got out and held the door for him in a prickled dizzy glitter that passed off in a couple of shakes, waited while he took a leak on a small snobbish maple planted in the concrete, then they went through a tall glass door backed by scrolled iron.

Jay the elevator boy said hello with his usual soft look disordering on a devious concern for her stormed whiteness with the bluish corpse tinge she had glimpsed in the lobby mirror: poor kid, kind of a job never went anywhere and his head turned by all the plush living, a wonder more of them didn't fetch up in Alcatraz. Giving him a dollar bill she said, "Put it to bed for me, will you, Jay?"

"Sure will, Miss Lynch. Thanks."

In the corridor she followed the low sounds of revelry to Toni's door and pushing it open the voices and music blew up warm, broken up. A burn of light, active mouths party-loud and suddenly Toni's elegant parrot screech: "Where *have* you been, baby. We've been brawling here for hours." She laid a predatory hand on her, her sleek mouth writhing with her talk under the harassed eyes, a party was a desperate thing to Toni because if they didn't have a good time they wouldn't come back and she'd drown in the silence. "And I want you to come and meet an Indian, honey

— a real one, not one of our scrofulous kind. A superb fawn of a boy, you wouldn't believe the lashes. He's been at the blondes already but wait till he sees *you.*"

Elise obligingly said she'd have at him and asked Rob to lie down. His forelegs slid out sticklike, he laid his chin on his paws and narrowly, with a well-mannered skepticism eyed a woman who leaned over to shriek baby talk at him.

"This way, sweetheart," Toni took her hand. Following the working machinery of the sleek parceled hips she felt her own slapped and said hi to one of the hard core, a specimen who for some time had been trying to get close, whose dank Hitler look and the mouth with the spittled corners made her feel objectively sick so when in a warning voice he called, "Elise, I want you," she kept going, deaf. Then her hand was caught and a face young still but with an old-boy rakishness looked down braced, a tipped desperateness barging in and out of the eyes. "Hello, what's this."

"Not now, Og," Toni pulled on Elise's other hand. "I'm taking her to meet Sri. Later, baby."

He reared, an ineffectual rage and said withering, "Just because he's dark-skinned. And I'll bet only one diaper to his name."

"*Shhh.* If he should hear think what it'll do to Asian-American relations."

He stared with a pointer desperateness at Elise. "Hell with 'em, I say. I've got my rights, a full-blooded American boy. Honey, I'm telling you, they itch under those diapers and when they die their wives go up in smoke. Gee, baby, you and me could have a ball. Ah, come *on* . . ."

"Later I said," and Toni yanked her off.

To set her before a milk-chocolate young man with large ogling mahogany eyes in a beautiful face alive with a gay and sportive charm, the overall look of him, passionate and dashing, outlandish as an antelope among cattle.

"Sri Rhamapandra, darling — he's here to study our primitive migrant workers aren't you sweetheart," Toni said and in a streak was off in pursuit of a couple at the door, leaving. Her screech cut through: "My God you're not *going.*"

Their eyes on a level Elise and the beautiful young man confronted each other. A sparkle and effervescence swiftly came over him, as if he was being shaken up and all his manhood rising to the surface.

"This is a pleasure, well, I must say," he said in a half gabble with a British accent and a joyful shoulder play, his ravished eyes all over her like a frisking. "My word, yes. *Indeed.*"

"How's the name again," Elise said.

"Sri Rhamapandra."

"I had a panda once. Lost it in a blizzard outside a saloon in Nebraska."

"Pandra," he said. "And yours, please? It is all so noisy."

She told him.

"Charming, charming. You are French?"

"My mother was."

"Elise," he said with a small sportive wrench of delight. "I love the sound. It fits you to perfection. My word, you are a beautiful girl."

She glanced casually around. "I'm dry, where's she got the booze this time?"

For a second mystified, then overcome by delight he charmingly laughed, pointing. "There."

"Think she'd keep it in the same place so a person could find it blind," she said. "Well, what're we waiting for."

He started forward with her. "I shall accompany you with pleasure but I drink only fruit juices and what is that, soft drinks."

"Stomach trouble, religion?"

"Religion." And laughing, with a giddy happiness he suddenly performed a little dancing quickstep, screwing up his face at her with an enticing charm. "Forgive me, but I am quite bowled over."

She briefly regarded him with the absence of a jailer watching the futile escape antics of a prisoner and at the bottles helped herself to scotch with a splash of water while he chose a Seven-Up.

Moving off to a side, away from the worst of it she gulped a large swallow and said past a light belch, "Toni says you're studying our peons."

He gazed at her as if just to look excitedly, supremely enchanted him. "Not quite," he said gabbling on a joyous tilt. "I am studying sociology at Stanford University. My word, what a beautiful girl you are. A real smasher."

"The things one learns in those seats of higher whatchamacallit," she said, closed her eyes and leaned back stiff on the wall. Tacking her to windward somewhat, not too rough. Through her closed eyes she could feel him fizzing in front of her.

"An excellent university, yes," he disposed of it. And with a stab of maddened bliss, "But you are without *question* the most beautiful girl I have seen. Please, please may I see your eyes."

They opened, on a stagger. "Precisely," he said confirming with almost a fanged triumph. "In a novel I read it was stated that the heroine's eyes were an angel's blue. I scoffed since rationally they could as well have been brown or green, but now I unreservedly accept the fact of it . . . Oh, but there is an angel's shining about you."

"Then there's my hair," she said. "Spun gold."

"Yes yes — precisely. And your features, in the classic mold — really I do not know why in America the truly beautiful women with one or two exceptions are not to be found in the films. Those are merely pretty. Shallow tinklers. But you . . . you . . . Oh, I am at a confounded loss of words." And standing on one foot he lifted the other behind him wobbling a little as with a delirious drinking expression his face lowered towards her, on the point of losing his balance bringing his leg back down and making her a deep arm-swinging bow in the nature of a passionate wallow. Yet curiously it wasn't altogether freakish: like a shaft of sun falling on a jungle an appreciable area of feeling was lit up.

"Beauty is as beauty does," Elise said and took another large dose of the scotch. She leaned back on the streaming wall. "So what's your opinion of our culture, if it's not too strong a word."

He raised on tiptoe as if to lift himself above the rising swell and boister, cackle of the party. "Good Lord, it is an intelligent angel in the bargain," he said loud, accusing with appreciation. And coming down slowly on his heels marveled, "You are the first person to refer in that fashion — it is singular is it not that they should resent admitting to flaws when all cultures, being human inventions, are of necessity flawed. Thus *your* flaw is excessive materialism, ours excessive mysticism." Winding up with a lively shrug of the shoulders, "Well then, in brief I should say I am appreciative of American culture while not an enthusiast, primarily I think because in this country the word 'intellectual' has acquired an aura of indecency, do you not find?"

"I find for the accused," she said as it seemed involuntary, with a kind of numbness, and with a lankiness blinked around. But then delivering him a remote-control glance, "After all there's something crummy, not the first-class ones but those others, with their domed earnestness. Cheeeese."

He made a grab for her hands, laughing with a startled admiration. "Splendid, I instantly recognize the genus. The attitudinizers, yes. All the same my angel there are those who make forays into the outside to drink whiskies and pinch the world's bottom — no, I *like* intellectuals, truly."

"Just thought I'd bring in the niggling human element," she said and leaned back, yanked for the prick of an instant. "Maybe it's different chez vous, but here we're all sick to death of each other, you know? Life and death and all that jazz, like a mental heave." Then with a sluttish, naïve sway, "But who am I. The hell, poor crapped-up bastards, keeping going on nothing."

He laughed on a tortured burst of love, lust, perplexity. "If you knew how inexpressibly lovely you are, angel of blue and gold, you who are laying waste my poor bloody heart. Oh my heavens . . ." He stilled like the victim of a holdup, sluggish, his head quivered. With a sleeper's fumbled motion he raised her hand, kissed it, laid it by the side of his. "So gloriously white," he said, quivering. "How good that you did not spoil it by sunbathing."

She stood remarking with a careless depression their two skins, until laying on her waist his trembling hands he softly turned her around so they were reflected in the mirror above the fireplace. "See," he said. "The twain who have met." Joyous tears came brightening, distorting into his eyes. "Oh, I — oh — "

"Ohio, yes, I should say," she said, a diffident nearing little smile forming.

Then her elbow dug him in the ribs. She was grinning. "Pull yourself together, man," she said. "The cavalry are on the way."

He tried for a smile to disguise the wretchedness of a forsaken dog. "You do not believe me because I am sincere. No one here believes me when I am sincere." His hand dashed the tears away. "Ah, you are too much, too much for me. I adored you from the first moment," he said with a deep stitched sigh, resigned.

She cast a draggled look around. "Getting gamey in here — better beat it before the management comes pounding. By an odd coincidence I live right next door."

A startled, then adoring gratitude overran his face but she had started off and single file they tracked through the rout, the voices got whooping out of hand, the smash of a glass, on a fringe a pair of drunks trading punches, butting solemn as goats. Sprawled in a chair a woman sobbed with drunken persistence while a man stood over her making pacific gestures with a glass in each hand. Luckily Toni wasn't in evidence. Elise dodged the lunge the sodden Og made at her and Rob becoming visible through the shifting latticework of bodies she said, "He's mine. We'll collect him and run for it."

"A fine breed, German shepherd. Gentle, trustworthy," said Sri, like a manual.

They found a man with a precariously tilted glass leaning over Rob saying with a phlegmed roll, "Deutschland über alles." Rob lying at full stretch had his head lazily raised eyeing the man incurious and was about to drop it back when spying Elise he got to his feet and the three of them slipped out.

Closing the door of her apartment Elise turned the key in the lock and led the way into the living room. "Made it. If Toni should bang don't pay any attention. She's people-hungry. Other-directed, in the current coinage. Christ, labels. All of 'em phony, like where it says sugar and it's arsenic inside."

Sri threw himself full length on the sofa, stretching in luxury. "Peculiarly, rather a child-dominated society," he said. "Really most puzzling for so industrious and efficient a people. Or is it unreasonable to expect maturity from the majority of adults. Then also, pragmatism may tend to retard the growth of intellectual maturity . . ."

"Baby, you don't know," said Elise behind the bar fixing herself a screwdriver and a ginger ale for him. "Take the man pays for this layout. Couldn't ask for a more mature specimen. Dotes on responsibility. A rescuer of waifs and strays. Why, I'd be in the gutter. More daddy than sugar, actually."

She carried the glasses to the sofa. Swinging his legs down he took his and set in frankly, avidly to study her. "A girl so beautiful, and clever also," he said wondering, with a sadness but predominantly fascinated.

"Instead she makes do with the other end," she kicked off her pumps and slid down putting her head back. "That's life for you. And death. What's your thought on death, *toi?*"

"A release, a commencement." His hand clasped hers in a soft desirous grasp. "My dearest Elise, you are terribly lovely," he said, both fantasy and passion muted: around his eyes lurked a faint barbaric rarefaction like an inchoate suffering. "Do you know, my angel, I believe I perceive in you a potential mysticism . . ."

Elise took a long swallow, the shadowy lamplight fuzzing her profile to a lineament of abstraction. "Is there a Suicides Anonymous," she said with a sauntered wag of the head. "I suppose so — not a one of our whims is left unsatisfied. Rushing in to fill one void with another. You need it? We got it."

His head slowly approaching hers hesitated a moment, then continued until the nose of his hazed face came to rest on her cheek. "My eyes are gluttonous of your beauty. Elise, Elise . . . you cannot possibly know your bewitchment." His breath warm and clean was like a child's, but with a man's strained shortness.

"So they could get together and discuss ways and means, easiest roads to the great beyond," she said taking another swallow. "But then of course there's always the chance they'd talk it all out and decide not to. Words are tricky bastards."

"Quite so. Your skin of alabaster, your hands like flowers," and he nibbled on a finger. "What an exquisite ring."

"Sapphire. Compliments of my current owner."

"And does he truly love you, is he kind to you?" he worked his lips across the palm of her hand.

"He's never hit me. Not like one of my types who came in one day and gave me a drubbing, saying it'd teach me but not what."

He held her arm out like opening a folding rule, getting the perspective, and sensuously ran a finger up to the elbow. "Never have I seen a skin to approximate this — it is absolutely an idealization of a skin."

"Evidence of things unseen. That part's even better."

The meaning sifting in immobilized him, then suddenly with the ferocious ardor of a man groveling before a deity: "Do not torment me . . . You could not be cruel, not you. Other girls yes but not you, beloved, never you — "

Raising her head she looked at him down her nose with the fragile scintillance and mystery of a movie queen. "Good gracious, we both knew what was up when we ran out on Toni," she said and kicked him intimately in the ankle. "But I'll just have another drink first. Priming the pump, what it's called."

Feeble he smiled and his eyes hung on her like a train as she went to the bar.

She came back and in a flash he was cozily loving, drawing her close, hugging, patting her all over like a cushion, crooning and gabbling a speech of love as passionate as it was disjointed.

She drank her drink allowing him his play as she would have a puppy, but of a sudden he said in a fainting voice, "Ohh, I love you. Oh my heavens how I love you," and his rounded mouth fell on her neck like a hot petal. But she had lost him somewhere along for some time so she just moved off a little as one does from too importunate a puppy, while like a puppy he clung on.

"Because it's certain to get lousier as it goes along, no getting away from it," she said. "No use fooling around. Either-or, and the devil in between." With a scarcely registering annoyance she found that he had uncovered her shoulder and was working on it pet-tiger fashion. "So in the long run it makes sense. The only sense there is, when you analyze it. It's all very well to say, but what do they know. If ignorance is bliss, knowledge is death. Wonder if this guy. Hey there, you with my gland in your hand."

"Oh heavens," he said, and was all over her.

"All right then," she said. "Your need's greater than mine."

Getting up she walked him off stiff-legged, Rob following. "You don't mind him, do you?" she said. "Because of course they don't know. I suppose. If they do they approve. All for the natural life."

"An utter love," he muttered holding on, sliding his hand up and down her front, not offensive, only to the navel. "Utter precious bewitching love."

In the bedroom she stripped, with a run leaped on the bed and rolled herself up in a ball. "Come along, baby," she said. "Don't be so slow on the drawer." But when he came up a bit diffident in his slender brown nudity his eye met hers peering up at him, a bright blue bloodshot marble, and he paused. "This is how it was in the womb," she said and snuggled her face into her drawn-up knees. "Some ancient races buried like this too. Try it. Feels good."

Crawling in a trifle self-conscious he looked on as if undecided whether or not to smile, becoming then unknowing an observer of a darkened meditating tenderness.

"Feels good, honest," she said muffled, the golden hair shining in the light over the bed with a rioted childish frailness.

"My dearest," he said gently making no move to touch her, and presently she peered up at him with a gleam of cockeyed insight, unwound and brought her upper body down on his. Staring with a kind of jaded curiosity into his love-warm, lazy eyes as into a mirror she said, "Who knows, it might even be a success. If the cycles are right."

With a soft unsteady passion his hand stroked her back. "My most beloved angel. Words cannot express — "

"They never do. Deeds, baby. Incidentally, would you be ambi-sextrous?"

"Eh?" His hand stopped.

"Take on male or female. A new fad, starting to catch on."

"Good Lord no. How could one, when it is so good like this. *Oh* so very good." He groaned with ecstasy, squirming.

"Just checking. Okay, ready?"

"Yes, oh *yes* . . ."

Her mouth lowered in a sweet rough grinding. From the outer dark sounded the thump of Rob's scratching leg followed after a space by the low wrung-off yowl of his yawn, his licking settling chops.

And silence, of a sort.

"Oh my darling," said Sri, on his back and his eyes sliding away and closing in ecstasy. "Oh, oh, oh. . . ."

Propped on an elbow with her cheek in her hand she watched him, smoking. "You're a nice kid," she said. "But you sure go all out. Whyn't you save some for the next round."

His eyes opened and darkly barbaric rolled round to her. "Beloved," he said on a moan, like a sick man. "Beloved beloved beloved," and crawled dragging the weight of his love over to her.

He left towards dawn protesting his love and rapture — he acted like a man hounded by happiness — ("Don't call me," she said. "I'll call you — ") and she slept on and off till nearly nine which was better than average and lay waiting for Nettie to show. Who blew in at a quarter past on a rush of excuses: the bus again, they didn't no way know how to run a transportation route, that was for sure, her brown face wearing its usual hectic anxiousness. She dashed off to put on the coffee water and draw the bath while Elise had a quick one to start off on, which even with the first hot shudder was one of the nicer things of the day. Then breakfast, three cups of coffee, nothing solid with her peckish stomach, at the window with the View to the gaze and after that Toni bursting in indignant because her showpiece had been snatched. "Honey, how lousy — I said *entertain* him not kidnap," and in the next breath said come downtown, want to buy one of those new bucket hats and we'll have lunch and rustle around see who else we can scare up.

Getting back around three she put the leash on Rob and drove out to Sutro Heights. One of those terrific days when the whole city under a free-swinging wind had the translucence of things seen through clear ice, everywhere a flap and toss and glitter, a gloss to the buildings as if they had sprung new-made out of the ground. And currents of energy in the air like a vast electric network — the kind of day that made some people swear because their hats blew off and others want to leap in the streets. A bad day for the incitement of alcoholics and potential suicides, and people in love. Hardly anybody out on the Heights where the wind ripped and stream, shook and flung the trees like a furious spirit released for one day of magnificent destruction. Barking his elation Rob raced up the path now and then turning to see if she was coming, rushing on with a bound of dizzied joy and freedom.

She let him run himself out before going on out to the point where in one great sweeping disclosure ocean and sky came rising up, the sheet-metal water striking away the eyes. Away off to the left boiled the spray-misted beach on which crept a few solitary figures, with nearer at hand the powered heave, curl-over of green glass and foam-toothed onslaught petering out on the sand in overlapping caracoles that sloped up to a bubbled nibble mild and poignant, the exhausted end. Out on their rocks the seals took the sun, about the Cliff House people congregated, fell away, formed fresh groupings like insects carrying out an intricate project. Up the street the Victorian dome of Sutro Baths stood out quaint and somehow dismal, like a building where a crime has been committed. Farther along on the other side Playland wasn't doing much playing: onion-sizzle, spin and lurch and dazzle, rifle-plink and lopsided revolving blare was for the shoddy glamour of the night, neonstain smudged by the mist, lone seawind tumbling candy wrappers — sailors and teenagers, older folk come to gamble, couples snaking off into a hot-oil metal black and coming out shift-faced, having gone the crooked circle. And over it all light or dark the sword of the wind, and the sense of paucity, the starved grasping for what didn't have a name — full stop, and the beginning of nowhere.

Her gaze went back to the scaled sea, the sky whose clear strong blue deepened in the west to a silken burning. The wind punched at her, blew the hair wanton about her face. Her eyes stung with cold, her ears ached, but she stood on braced before the parapet with Rob leaning his shoulder on her knee.

Unannounced as always it came on, then — the thrown darkening, growing tumor of nightmare. Very gently, almost caressingly the ground swelled and dipped, she lost her footing an instant, clumsily regained it. A knotted interval, and like a blow from behind, the silence. Slicing of the cord. Shut in, closed off. Bone in the earth. Shell at the bottom of the sea.

Bludgeoned Christ-dangle —

Now. Now. Scalpel, prying: collapsed loosening like bowels — a hemorrhage of light poured.

Far down in the core of the earth, thunder.

Slow, mammoth the intermeshed movement. Crust, grind down. Gray slime of brain, meat pulped glistening the warm blood, gut twined loving in the shard of bone. Wormed mass, grave-drip — take, stuff in the sodden flesh bottle-green, gorge on the purple-toed meat of the obscene Christ and jazzed cathedral lights flying in crossed trajectory —

"You all right, miss?"

Raw cut of danger: retreating in confusion, the accelerated beginning descent. "What — "

"You seem faint, may I help you to a bench?"

"No." She made speech from marble lips. "It's all right. Thanks."

The cataract, terraced strip-off. Bearing her derelict self gone over irreversible to the crumbling, a vague driveled solace in the knowledge her eyes bungled at a sweep-back of silver hair under a crush hat, black lair-thick eyes and brows, pink and white skin fed by the cream of self-esteem. Black overcoat with velvet collar, cane. Large gestures around a gleaming dinner table — old-time impresario, and/or molester of shopgirls.

"Are you sure you wouldn't like to sit down."

"No, I'm all right. Dizzy spell. Nothing to speak of."

He smiled, the carved wrinkles jumping to attention. "Surely. We all have, at some time or other — that's a nice dog you've got there. Here sir, here. I'm very much of a dog fancier myself."

"I'm afraid he doesn't take to strangers," she said, and began to saunter off. "Well. Time to go." She put a bit of an effort into making a pleasant face.

He tipped his hat. "Good afternoon," turning of course to watch the careful stagger. Drunk. Such a lovely girl. Great pity.

In a small sunny hollow she dropped down on the sand with her back against a bank and gradually the feeling of walking on balloons passed away. Her eyes closed, taking the good warm sun, ignoring the rear-guard skirmish. A moisture seeped out rolling cool and erratic down her cheeks. The wind. Stimulus on the duct — ductless — anyway it was good, the impersonal undertaker handling of it. "You like it too boy don't you," she said not bothering to wipe off the moisture, sun take care of it. Panting already a little from the sun and then he yawned, ran his tongue around his mouth and looked at her: what next.

She laughed and pulled him to her. "Rob," she said, "Rob," and found that she was shaking, shaking him too along with her. His tongue flipped out to her cheek. She hugged him hard. "We'll go in a little while," she said and suddenly there was a stony swell of excitement like heartburn — she grew still, her arm around him jogging to his panting. Then abruptly she rose and they walked off, but glancing at her watch she broke into a run and Rob into a lope alongside.

At a bend under the trees she ran square into a young man, rocking him, almost knocking him down. Steadying his hands grasped her shoulders, and swiftly his stare of annoyance gave way to a softening, a mellowing, and then the mold to a deep-lighted smile. In a moment with a twist she was free and running on up the path.

Panting, a pain in her side, she rested a minute in the car before turning the key, dizzy, but it soon quit and they were off on a jackrabbit start.

At three minutes to five she opened the door, listened — beat him to it, and sprinted in to the bar. Putting the empty shot glass down she heard him at the door. She just had time to fling off her jacket, light a cigarette and sit down with a magazine.

"Hi there," she said and rose to get him the sherry he had lately taken to having on arrival. And that he made last a long while, taking small sips and toying with the stem. You could see he really didn't go for the stuff but it went with the stance and served to loosen him up some besides — he hadn't got over a certain stiffness at first and usually it wasn't till after dinner that he unlimbered. And naturally nothing so obvious as a kiss on entering, after all he was no Frenchman or even anything like the man to flaunt an emotion. For it looked as if that night in Wim's study had proved to be the impetus from which he was still revolving but on a narrower orbit, adjusted to the proper discretion and reserve. Which moreover if you cared to look at it that way tended to put *her* in the proper perspective of things. And why not, part of the job.

"Well, dear," he said as she came up bearing the sherry. "Have a nice day?"

With her bending to set down the glass a frown, a very small one, made its appearance. There, see. Should have stuck to the vodka. However it smoothed off and he regarded her calmly, a wide calm solid man — the benignity still there but not nearly so detectable any more — attendant upon a problem he had lived with for some time and had no doubt he could solve. When he judged the time to be ripe. Which from the look of it could be any time now, and she couldn't say it was unexpected.

"Pretty good," she said. "I had lunch with Toni and furnished moral support while she bought a hat. Then I took Rob over to Sutro. You should have seen the wind. Like to tear you apart."

"We usually get it around this time," he said, and dipped into the sherry.

"Run out of cigars? I can send for some." By this time he'd usually lighted one.

"I've decided to give up smoking. All this lung cancer, and other diseases. It's foolish to take chances."

"Thought cigarettes were supposed to be the culprit," she said, conversational.

His glance lowered to hers. "The evidence certainly seems conclusive that they're very dangerous. It would be wise to cut down,

if you can't or won't quit. Two packs a day is suici — is entirely
too much."

"You can say it, Richard. I don't mind a bit. My one silly little
gesture, goodness. I thought it was long buried and forgotten."

A complimentary urbanity spread over his face. "I like to see
you taking that sensible attitude, dear. I will say this way you
have of not brooding is just about your most attractive trait," he
said with the fine gloss of a man who perfectly trusts his intuitions.

"Well thank you, Richard. But you're an optimist yourself. It's
our great American heritage, think where our pioneers would
have been without it. Pessimism simply isn't in us."

"For which we should be everlastingly grateful," he said going
rather into the mature overseer, or flock-addressing bit. "Defeat-
ism will always be alien to us. This existentialist rottenness, for
instance." Of all things to get around to, gee. "I feel kind of
sorry for a man like that French fellow, Sartre — I started to read
one of his things and had to quit — who's degenerated that far. It
takes a warped brain to go against the grain of its own great tradition and culture."

"Doesn't it. Not so long ago though they were shooting down
Arab women and children, which does seem kind of a funny end
result of a culture. But now if you don't mind Richard I think I'll
have a drink to celebrate our being so well in accord," she said
rising and going to the bar. "Which we are practically all the time,
when you think. What I mean, pretty unheard of in this quarreling
world, wouldn't you say?"

Abruptly, in almost a harsh tone he said, "That's the Com-
munist line," but in a moment moderating his expression to a kind
of upper-class reticence.

Going back to her chair she swallowed a good third of her highball and smacked her lips. "Mm, good. What kind things it does."
And looked over at him sociably, disposed to pass the time in a
civilized manner. "Is it? No, actually any resemblance is purely
coincidental. Just that it does look like a whimsical way to bring
civilization to the untutored masses."

He gazed back congealing in composure, every inch the informed man of affairs dealing with a fowl-brained female. Of
distinction you couldn't quite say, first because of the too too solid
flesh. If he shed about forty pounds. But no, since thick or thin
the parvenu quality would remain, legacy no doubt of the grubbing

ancestor on whom nonetheless his own brand of plucky vulgarity must have looked rather good, aside from being an indispensable in that bearded milieu: a bona fide rawness packed its own picturesque punch. While Richard here, with his sad little crust of nice-nellyism. But hold on there, gal. Come now, be nice to the man, the stranger in our midst.

She said, "So here we are, the two of us with our drinks and the sun setting beyond the Golden Gate just like in the ads," and looked out the window. "Sure is a hell of a view. Whenever I look at this time of day I get that wanton Frisco feeling — worldly, but with verve. Sort of rich-meaty. As if something in the air said get going and do all the good things fast — *live*," she made a devil-may-care squandering gesture, "in a word."

Didn't fetch a thing. Maybe he didn't fancy the Frisco, they were so touchy about it. Or more likely the honeymoon was over. Time was when he'd at least have sent out a mild beam, if only from good manners, but now nothing, except his sausage finger kept sliding sedate up and down the stem of his glass. Then in the dusking light she took note of the subtle frown, of a sort of sublime concentration, way off somewhere: wrong, in effect quite close to home, for just then with a level air he said, "Elise — I feel there's something I should talk to you about."

"Really," she said, interested. "I'm listening."

For a second his level gaze dug in on her like a brand, then it paled back to normal. "It concerns this woman, this — Toni. I have no intention of regulating your choice of friends. But this woman and her crowd aren't the kind of people I'd care to have you associate with. A divorcee — "

"Three times, and a fabulous settlement from each."

"A divorcee," he said plowing on past the irrelevance, "can of course also be a decent person, but from my impression of this woman I don't think she can do you any good. Frankly I consider her a bad moral influence. The manager's received complaints about those parties of hers, and he told me not long ago he'd be glad to get her out of the building. As a matter of fact and strictly between us he's going to try to break her lease. In view of all this don't you think it would be wise to taper off, when she asks you to go out with her you could say you have other plans. And I must ask you not to go to any more of her parties. I understand there was one last night."

"Oh, I didn't stay long. An hour, maybe less."

"I'm sorry you went at all. A bad crowd, very bad. Ever since that woman moved in the place hasn't been the same. I'm surprised they allowed her in in the first place, and if they don't get her out soon I guess I'll have to move my girl to better quarters," he said giving a hitch to his trouser leg, and on his face a look close to a kind of arid archness.

"Well, I'm only a woman," she said. "Do with me what you will."

But he wasn't amused, where back in the beginning her every quip had brought his smile. Definitely a case of the honeymoon being over. "I hardly think that was called for," he said.

She traced the hair-fine sneer of sensitivity, lost almost among the solidity. Funny too how he rarely came out with his sweetests and belovedests anymore. Always dear nowadays. Well, maybe she did cost him more than he'd expected. "By way of a gag, all it was," she said. "To jazz it up some. Been turning all-fired serious lately, hasn't it?"

A stolidly enduring look moved in on him: most of his expressions took time rising, like yeast. "I've always been a serious person," he said. "I should have been obvious from the start."

"Can't say it wasn't. But a mistress's touch, you know. Supposed to bring out the frolic in a man. Or so goes the tradition."

She stood up well, never batting an eye under the long unmoving stare that ten to one caused junior executives to freeze in their flannel suits and women secretaries to run for a bit of quiet hysteria in the washroom. Blowing their nose on the toilet paper and flushing it down the bowl, wishing peevishly murderous *he* were along —

Then she noticed another thing: underlying the stare she caught like a furtive movement in the dark, an attenuated equivalent of what had blazed out of the face of the woman in the drugstore. Universality of hate and contempt. Rich, poor, everybody knew how to hate. While it was the rare ones who knew how to love. So much easier, more instinctive to hate. *Wanting* to love didn't do it, on that you could rely. Had to be learned, step by painful twisted step. Herself, high on the roster of accomplished, or intuitive haters. Or as the poet had it, *trau, schau, wem?* Eh? *Ach, du lieber.*

"Elise." Could as well have said Miss Lynch.

"Yessir."

And as he said no more but continued to look, with a hardening of the eyes: "Sorry, no flippancy intended. I seem to be in an un-handleable mood today, like my psyche took the bit in its teeth — ever feel anything of the sort?"

Silence, the lump of it. No steering around this Scylla. And as for Charybdis, yonder — get to you in due course.

"Well, you're lucky," she said. "Possibly due to my bad genes. Put the blame on heredity, so much easier. But enough of these puerile interruptions. You were saying."

The square bulk of his shoulders rose a fraction, moved back in place like a bull quietly rebelling against a weight. "Elise," he said, in tone and manner on the grim side but restrained of course, gentleman's disagreement, "Elise, you force me to have a serious talk with you. I had hoped it wouldn't be necessary, thinking that if you were given enough rope you'd straighten yourself out. But I'm sorry to say it's been just the opposite."

"Richard, you're quite right. People like me should never be given any rope, they think it's to hang themselves with."

With no change in his voice and looking the same, only more so he said, "I'd appreciate it one hell of a lot if you'd consent to be serious for ten minutes. What I've got to say is for your own good, and if you'll use the sense you've got you'll listen to me. Your refusal to face facts stopped being amusing some time ago, and I think I'm justified in saying that any other man would have lost patience long before this. I've had a lot more experience of life than you have — "

"Of a somewhat dissimilar kind, Richard. But do go on. Merely wanted to keep things straight."

"Which is exactly what you should concentrate on doing from now on. You're — it's not pleasant to say it, but it's got to be said — you're not the same girl you were, the girl I saw standing on those stairs. In a relatively short time there's been a change in you, a very great change. You're young, basically healthy I'm certain, it shouldn't be hard to put yourself back on the right track."

"I know," she said in a tone of polite discovery. "What you're trying to say is I'm rather too fond of the drink."

"You understate it. What I'm trying to say is that you're well on the road to alcoholism."

"Richard, it's nice of you to try and spare my feelings. Truth

is I'm there. Why, if you knew," she said. "I can't face the day
without a stiff shot, half a glass full. Water glass. When you've
come to that, well."

"I thought you had agreed to be serious."

"I am. Dead serious. You don't see any smile, do you? Course
it's getting dark, but — "

"And I can assure you I'm not smiling either. In plain talk, and
I don't know how I can say it any more clearly, you haven't got
much more time to pull yourself together. It's — getting more than
objectionable, I'll go so far as to say I'm seriously disappointed
in you. Yet if you'll show me you're really in earnest about pulling
out I'll do what I can to help. There are treatments, all kinds of
aids. Others have been helped, have gone on to become better men
and women. If they did it so can you. Now listen, Elise. You can't
doubt that I'm — that I think a great deal of you. You've given
me quite a lot of pleasu — happiness. I'll go further and say that
I've come in a way to depend on you. But this degrading drinking business has simply got to stop. Now. Before you completely
wreck your beauty and health." He paused, and when he spoke
again a note of quiet anger nullified the intent of persuasiveness.
"I just can't understand why you insist on throwing everything
away when with some plain ordinary will power you could overcome this weakness. Once you've taken the first step the rest will
be easy. If you really want to, I know you can do it."

Here the tone became more stabilized as he went along on his
faith kick for a spell, but it all flowed on by pretty well after the
pleasu-happiness bit. Because translated it meant she was a damn
good lay, best one he'd had in all probability, otherwise he'd have
shown her the exit long ago. Stinking of drink way she did when
he went to fold her in those mattress arms even though she rinsed
her mouth out beforehand. And showered in perfume. My Sin.
And his, for the record. But he could close his eyes in that sublime-
torture look while she had to peg away at the job, keep the rear
end mobile and play it from all angles so as to keep him happy
and well evacuated — damn near died from the ecstasy of it and
then lay gasping and heaving like a beached whale. Christ she
deserved a drink. All right, so he didn't care for her boozy breath.
Well neither did she, particularly. But as long as she was able to
deliver that was all really counted. Stink or no, once it got to work-

ing and the delicious agony shivers flashing around his belly who gave a crumpet. Assuredly not lover-boy. "So how if we can the sentiment, Richard," she said. "And keep our eye on the balls and the hind end in proper oiled operating condition. Which is my fuckuppation, to get coarse for a moment, and yours is to keep me in Black Label. And one or two other necessaries. Thing is, you're worried if I go on belting the mash I'll lay down on the job. But trust me, man. I been trained by experts. You never heard of a firehorse not rearing at the bell."

She noticed his voice had stopped. "Well, Richard, thanks for the pep talk," she said. "And if you're as fond of me as you say you won't object to my having another before we feed, I'm sure. Small short one, or rather medium would be better. You wouldn't want to stop cold this minute, too drastic. D.t.'s likely to result."

In the gloom he could be felt more or less grimly coping, so to take it out of his hands she went to the bar. Silence, of the more bitter kind. Then he said, "I can't very well stop you, can I. But you've got to promise you'll put yourself under treatment."

She grinned, slopping some token water into the glass. "Well now, you know, I'm pretty strong. Good for some time yet. Really you shouldn't let it fidget you. Man like you, all those investments to worry about, fussing about little old me, goodness." Glass in hand she went and sat on the arm of his chair. "The thing with you is you're getting kind of restless," she said. "In the midst of trust funds we are in death. You ought to get yourself a hobby. Like another girl. Then you'd have two of us to fuss with. Take up the slack, like."

A pause. Could be he'd revolved it and decided against. Question of expense, not improbably. Reason the rich were. Moreover, required a certain amount of daring.

Then he was shaking his head, his arm going loglike about her waist. "You don't know me very well, if you can talk like that. My happiness is with you, dear . . . So you *won't* promise."

"Oh, catch 'em young and they'll train your way. Can I get you another sherry?"

But of course he said one was enough. She tossed off her scotch. "Say, I know what. We'll eat out. Here we are in this city of gourmandism and how often have we joined the public trough — twice is it. New place opened on Hyde very Frenchy is the word where it's doubtful anyone'd catch us. Anyway you can always say I'm your niece. Crude I know, but one's got to think of these things."

His silence while consenting also had a constraint, main reason being a worry that if he flaunted her about the missus might take it into her head to raise a stink: scandal, divorce, depleted coffers. Gloomy inbitten sort of woman, from picture in the society section. Type could take a notion to do anything. Wrote verses, only thing he'd ever said about her. With a touch of complaisance grafted on to the armistice kind of enmity. An artistic wife what with temperament and all excusing many a man's peccadilloes.

"I'll go gussy up, won't take but ten minutes," she said.

"But first," and his finger put nervous-roguish pressure on her waist. She swung her legs over and slid down on his lap: not the kind of gambit meant business, he didn't care to exert himself this early. Sort of an imprimatur rather, mouth warm and rubbery-moist as a hot dog. When with a certain complacence he released her she said, "Ask the man who owns one," and went off whistling Shake That Thing.

On her return exquisite in the mink he rose and gazed with the blur of infatuation at the core of which was something of a checked resistance: moments lately when he positively set himself against her for her beauty and above all, her youth. Christ, she said. This beatup bag a million years old. And to him: "Will I do? Nobody'd take me for a strumpet, would they?"

"You look very nice," he said, and went with dignity to get his hat. They went down and got in the Continental.

At the restaurant she let it be known she wouldn't refuse a cocktail, however it came as no surprise when he said it would spoil her appetite. "I want you to eat a good hearty dinner, dear," he said. "You're getting so thin and pale. With some flesh on you you'll look and feel so much better."

And that much more energy for the bedwork. However, one didn't argue — his privilege.

"I'll order for us both," he said. "You sit there looking pretty," a kind of affability went with it, "and sharpen that appetite."

So she sat watching the trays loaded with cocktails go by. And when the food came tried to wade into the opulent sauced stuff for which she had no stomach, while at a regular untiring pace he fell to working his way through.

There was no talk, this eating rite commanding all his attention. All about the elegant room others were likewise engaged, bent obeisant to the plate or chewing with a misted gaze as though the food's inner steaming clouded their vision. And soon the air rich with food-incense in the templed light, the waiters gliding with their offertory trays, the headwaiter presiding with a sharp sacerdotal eye began to have a somnolent, shrinking effect — suddenly she could hardly push the fork up to her mouth.

She started to feel dizzy, queasy, and then a sudden plunged drop into a fatigue pocket caused the food on the plate to loom like a mountain on which the fork couldn't get so much as a toe-hold. She raised her eyes and the sickeningly ornate room was set in motion as though it had been placed on a merry-go-round, the diners rising and falling in stately distortion. Closer, across the shining white cloth upon which the lamp pooled a rosy light like diluted blood, the silver gleaming like expectant weapons, the faintly levitating man continued to eat ponderous, systematic as a boa gorging its prey.

"Eat," he said, "eat," he murmured flushed, copious, a seed-pearl sweat standing out on his forehead and even around his eyes. Tranced, congested they went to her plate. "Good for you. Eat."

In her hand the fork lay inert at the base of the mountain. Segment by segment the mass of food disappeared into the erratically floating rapacious mouth, with a neat tail-flip at the end and the lips closing down smooth grease-glistening over the crushing jaws.

Nausea rushed together, fumed up. Stumbling to her feet she mumbled an excuse and was off, reaching the bowl without a second to spare.

Drained, shaky she found her way back. "Anything wrong?" he said. He had finished his dessert and lighted a cigar. "To go with the coffee," he said a shade curt. "After such a wonderful meal." His eyes sharpened. "There *is* something wrong."

"I heaved," she said. "If you'll pardon the expression. Guess I'll have to stay away from this rich stuff."

He sized her up through a snarl of smoke, the cigar sticking out of his mouth like a small club: his hand stroked up and removed it.

"I've been expecting it to happen any time. You're going to get sick, seriously sick if you go on. I wish you could see yourself. You look half dead." Master's voice dry, dry and hardened, baked on slow anger. Dragged contempt in the eyes, in the slant of the cigar in the power-fleshed hand.

Considerable outlay. Done everything for her. And all because of stubbornness, stupidity — bad blood after all. Maverick, never take a brand.

"All that and more," she said. "No really Richard I see your point. The right is on your side, no question."

"You won't make the slightest effort to stop. You never will."

Bulked, strapped taut and firm in his integrity he expanded, grown larger with the authority of rank. A big man. Leader in the community. Good works. At death, obituaries this long. Of such is the kingdom.

"Pood Wim," she said. "He may not have made it. Too much the shepherd at heart, when organizers is what's wanted."

"You're still drunk. You went to have a drink, didn't you . . . *Didn't* you."

At any rate he still had his good cigar to enjoy. There was a large crap-colored gravy spot by the side of his coffee cup. "Well," she said. "It's like this."

"Answer me straight for once. *Didn't* you."

"I went straight and had a big slug in the bar. It's around the turn there, convenient to the can. Then I went and heaved it up and went back for a refill."

His eyelids came down, blanking his face in a sort of vicious pondering. Then he turned and signaled the waiter, a motion peremptory and harsh as an obscene gesture.

All the way in the car, not a word. Upstairs along the hall like warden and condemned prisoner. Rob came forward wagging and, it could have been accident, the man's knee bumped him hard in the side. She dropped back as he went on into the living room and squatting took the rough-smooth dogface in her hands. "Don't mind it, boy," she said. "Happened to me too lots of times. Sit tight. We'll go out later."

He gave heed with his customary solid rapport. Dropping a kiss on his ear she proceeded to the living room, where slipping out of the mink she said to the held-up newspaper, "What'll it be, scrabble, gin?"

"I thought your taste ran to scotch," the voice issued dry from behind the print.

"Well, vodka's nice too," she said, and went to the bar.

"By all means, help yourself. Take all you want. When it's gone call up for more. They deliver day and night."

"Like me," she said. And laughed, sound of gay abandon. "Gay abandon," she said pouring the vodka. "Name for a bra. More fun at night though isn't it. In the morning too much like champagne for breakfast."

He was looking at her where she stood drinking, over his paper, and she said, "Richard, it'll all come out in the leak. Believe me." It got through. Throwing off a laugh vulgar with revulsion he said, in a new voice, a level run with no inflection, "Come here. Come on here to daddy."

She went, remembering first to down the vodka. He took hold and pulled her down. "Sweetheart," he said, in the voice. "Baby girl."

There was only one light on, from the side. It fell on her breast and left both their faces in a pink overcast in which his with a commencing faint pullback, as though exposed to a savage wind, a dim peaked frown stared at the pale-gold flesh offering twin hummocks perversely virgin, shatterable. Then the hair-knuckled hand entered the light and lay weighted, twitching, blotting — pressed down, lifted, pressed down.

A quiver, as through a great steamer. "Baby girl. Sweetheart. Come to daddy. Come — Give. Come. Come."

Cigar-rancid, widening cave of vellicating snake tongue. The forcep hand dug, ripped the fabric, shook, spilled. "Baby girl. Baby."

She held fast, rigid against the rising constriction of pain.

"Hurry. *Hurry.*"

The laying on of massive flamed hands.

She screamed.

"Baby. Baby girl." Mutter grinding, grunted. "Baby — Baby — Mine — "

She screamed.

In a white silk dressing gown she sat on the bed with a glass and a cigarette facing the other way from the circumspect large-animal movement going on methodical — comb drop, clink of silver, thud-pattern of the controlled sedate feet.

Coming around, halting. Her eyes hitched up the length of

the mannerly bulk, from the polished black shoes orderly on the
carpet to the perfect exactitude of the tie.

"Sweet. You look about ten in that thing."

The white face stared up, directed, the blue eyes full of light.

A laugh. "Come, I'll tuck you in before I go."

The golden head moved, negative. "Not yet. I'll go soon."

"You won't stay up late, will you. Got to get that beauty sleep."

They kept on looking at each other.

"Sweet. My sweet. Mine."

Deep sag of the bed alongside, and inside the silk the warm
bloated hand stroked. "Say it. Say you belong to me."

"I belong to you."

In spasms, brutal-soft the hand pressed and molded the flesh.
"You're mine. Say it."

She said it.

The hand slowly came away, was joined by the other to draw
and belt the silk over the inflamed and bleeding flesh. Pause, a
concentrate of powerful tranquil repletion.

"I want you to go to bed now. Sleep. Sleep deep and good."

"Yes," she said.

The bed slowly rose, snapped in place frivolous.

"Go to sleep now."

The feet in black distinguished shoes, kindly august side by
side. And then empty space, and the crushed twin imprint.

She stood in the shadowed hallway. Blood trickled down her
somewhere and the darkness billowed. Then Rob was there. She
fell down on her knees and said something, the rough coat under
her hand. His tongue flicked out and a wet coolness touched her
cheek.

Then she was in the bedroom throwing on some clothes and
she said, "Be right there," but shaking so much it was hard to go
fast, then she remembered and ran to get it out of the closet,
holding the heavy coil of it in her hand. Cigarettes — yes there
and the lighter for Christ's sake get going get —

"Come on boy run — "

"Sailing along, on moonlight bay," sang the radio. And it was,
smooth and easy on the maternal purr in the crouch of the late
late night. In time for the late late show.

"What's the thing happens at the same time to many people at
different times."

No answer.

"TV show, darling. Live. You live but a show's live. English is a ridiculous language."

The radio sang low in the glow of the dashboard. "I love you," she said. "For being so strong and silent. Keeps right on, drop by drop. Drip, warm, drip. Trickle, tickle. So I *do* know how to love. Where love is due. In lieu of. Mauve. Lovely color. Muller. Boy wrote me mash notes. Engemmed with acne. Took off the umlaut and there he was, virtually British."

The car just drove itself, rolling up the carpet miles. Oil and rubber. Rubbers. Evil flowers of the night growing by the wayside. Among the empty beer cans and whiskey fifths. J'accuse Mother Nature.

Nobody, nobody in all the. "Save the two of us. Sunken bloody world drowning in its own semen. Poetry. A word for everything. Where science, cosmic — the cosmic, the comic probe. Proboscis. Ora pro nobis. Novice. No, not that one. Expert, and that large Italian knows-what's-what nose to prove it. Maria, Mariucia. Eh, Mariucia. Putta somewhere else da stiletto, it makea da hole in you stocking. Sorry, lady. I am an admirer of the Gracchi. Sure you do. Gracchi Bros., the pasta makers. *Ecco.*"

A truck roared down the stretch, crashed past.

A yell: "Go." He gave a short joyful bark, the speedometer jumped and climbed seventy, eighty, ninety. Ripping the night in two and the tatters streaming haggard, smashing forward and the world left mangled and bloody behind.

Yelling, so damn much alive it kicked around inside like a thousand devils. He barked, pitchforked by excitement — screaming in the curves, swaying and lurching into the straight and the wheel sliding from side to side and the rock and roll, buck and reel, righting the forward plunge once more and suddenly the screeching skid: recollected swerve on to humped dirt.

"Now's the time," she said, "and this is the place."

Bump and sway, towards a gather of tall grave trees.

Here. Good. The motor sighed off. Instantly crickets, frogs took over. Smelled good, of eucalyptus and night earth.

Out, and he bounded off for a run. Overhead the light clack of leaves turning silver bellies to the moon. A spray of stars in their tiny immensity, and the sweet play of the breeze. Except for the fiddling crickets it was still, good: the night breathed deep and easy like God.

He trotted back and she opened the door for him, shut it and went back to the trunk, dragged out the coil and dumped it on the earth, where it lay like a great snake. Squatting she took hold of one end and went to work but it was a job getting it on, her hand was too impatient: "Goddam," she said through a grunt, "toujours le —" But then it held good and tight, she dragged the length of it around to the front and feeding it in through the window said, "See, you *can* pull the hole in after you."

She turned the key and the engine sprang on with a hitch, settled and murmured even.

Supposed to be a fifth in the glove compartment. After the good long lasting pull she dropped it in her lap and took him up close to her.

"Because I love you it's all right," she said. "Thank God you trust me."

He whimpered a little but she held him and he quieted, leaning on her. Long and gentle she kissed him and faced forward past the tree clot to where the moon lapped light. Holes in the ground here and there, black as eye sockets.

She scrounged down resting her head on the back of the seat, and took a deep relaxed breath. "Okay, lady," she said in a grinned rounded-off voice. "But it's me that wins."

JOHN STEWART CARTER

The Keyhole Eye

(FROM THE KENYON REVIEW)

MY UNCLE TOM was the last of my grandfather's ten sons and was fourteen years old the year I was born. He left Princeton halfway through his freshman year to join the A.E.F. and was briefly a flier in France. I remember, or begin remembering, him best around 1920 when I would see him at my grandmother's. He looked like Wallace Reid — if you recall. I don't, but I know I thought so at the time. Later I equated him with one of Scott Fitzgerald's rich boys, and for years I scarcely thought of him at all. What has just happened is why I am writing this.

He was always nice to me in an offhand way and called me "kid," which was racy of him because we were not supposed to use the word and were always being told that a kid was a goat, which of course it was not. I suppose I was a nuisance, but he never acted as if I were, and I used to hang around his bedroom at my grandmother's, much preferring it to my own. I know he was the first adult male I ever saw walking around naked, and the sight fascinated me mightily — whatever the amateur psychiatrists will make of it. Also he muttered to himself and used very bad words like "bastard" and "bitch," and even worse. He never said these things outside of his own room, and it was wonderful for me at six to hear them. He would let me get into his bed and watch him dress to go out, and I would keep very quiet — all eyes, all ears — until finally he'd snap up his silk hat, fit his silver flask into his pocket, and lean over the bed to punch me in the belly.

"You think I'll get it tonight, kid?" I had no idea what "it" was;

I don't think I was even curious; the whole thing was a ritual as set as that in Proust.

My answer was, "Sure thing, Tom," and his, as he closed the door, "Keep your pecker up, kid." This left me limp with delicious, giggly laughter. I knew what a pecker was, but that a grownup should use any other than our nursery word to *me* was almost beyond hope. I never had to ask him or beg or anything; he just always left the light on in his bathroom and the door enough ajar so that I saw it but not so far as to be too light or to catch the bulb in his dresser mirror. I didn't have to ask to stay in his bed either. He just left me there, and, when he got home, he'd carry me in his wonderful dance-stinky shirtsleeve arms across the lounge, down the three steps into the east wing to my own room and my own bed, all shivery cool after so much warmth. Most of the time I wouldn't wake up at all, although I always tried to so I would know about being carried, feeling so bundled and sweaty in his arms and all the whiskey and cigarette smoke deliciously sour on his breathing breath, the enormous dark house around us.

Eleven bedrooms gave off the central upstairs hall at my grandmother's. The hall itself — it was called "Palm Court" on the blueprints — was nearly square and was lighted by a series of skylights. We called it the lounge, and it was furnished as a living room; in fact it was the main living room of the house for the children who were visiting. My grandfather's idea was that each of his ten children should be able to come and stay, and each of the rooms had a name: Tom's room, Fred's room, and so on. All but Tom were married and had families of their own at the time I am writing of, and each of them had a house in town. But in the summer and at Christmas they would come to the big house on the lake where each set of parents occupied the father's old room, and the children, along with nursemaids, the east wing. I don't think all ten were ever there at once, but five or six with their families at a time were not unusual; so the house was run really like a very luxurious men's club. My brother has the household books, and in 1932, when my grandmother died, there were twelve indoor servants. The west wing was more elegant than the east, and that's where houseguests other than the family were put. It had an indoor swimming pool — very Pompeian — in the basement, and there is an entry in the books of $1800.00 for "swimming pool

towels," in case any social historian is looking; and, in case anyone wants a *sic transit gloria mundi* note, the last time I saw one
of them, a sort of Pompeian brown with black pillars across the
border (they must have been specially woven), it was being used
by a great-great-grandson to polish his car.

On each side of the doorway, where three steps led down from
the lounge to the east wing, was a large console with a big pagoda-
shaped mirror over it. If I were just pretending to be asleep
when Tom carried me back, I would try to see us in the mirror.
The lounge itself was light enough because of the skylights, which
in summer were open to the moon and stars. I don't know whether
Tom knew about my habit of peeking or whether he always looked
himself, but one night he stopped before the mirror, and his eyes
came together with mine and we looked full upon ourselves —
upon ourselves, wide-eyed, and each other.

After a minute he said, "You're a faker, kid. Why the hell can't
you walk to your own goddamned room?" I just kept looking at
him and us and he at me. His arms tightened around me and
pushed me to his chest where I could no longer see. He put his
lips into my hair. I could feel its fineness catch on the scratchiness
of his whiskering face.

He put me down then, and we walked, our hands fingered together, down the three steps to my room. We looked at each other
once more, no mirror between, after I had climbed into bed. He
gave my belly its punch and said, "We're the two loneliest goddamned bastards in the whole beautiful world." Even today, when
I see moonlight through an open window in a darkened room,
it is partly the moonlight of that night when weak with love
and happiness I went to sleep.

I don't think he carried me much after that. I was getting bigger. But he didn't stop right away, and, if I were really asleep,
he still carried me for a long time, because in the morning I'd
wake up in my own bed. When I wasn't really asleep, he'd know,
but he'd walk me by hand, and as we'd pass the mirror he'd say
"Hi there, kids" in a conspiratorial whisper and wave, but that's
the only reference either of us ever made to the night. When I
was twelve, Tom married Jay Henry, who was a girl we had always
known; indeed I am married to her cousin now. It was a big society
wedding, and all the cousins read every line in the papers for

weeks beforehand. We were much less sophisticated then. There were dances and dinners, and people came from all over. Lady Moira Burton, the daughter of an earl, was the bridesmaid the papers gave the most linage to even before she arrived, and we were all amazed when she turned out to be nineteen and brought her own lady's maid. We had expected something at least forty. She always said "Thank you, deeply," and so do I and all my cousins to this day.

Of course the family was very much involved with the wedding, which took place in the church we all went to. We didn't really go, but, if we had gone, that's where we would have gone when we were at my grandmother's. The reception was at the Henrys', a mile or so down the road. The night before the wedding, my grandmother gave a big dinner dance with tables on the terraces, marquees in the garden, and my grandmother herself in a completely beaded dress, long gloves, and her diamond tiara. We have moving pictures of the wedding the next day, and we used to look at them on Christmas after dinner. They were very funny with Jay in a dress that cleared her knees, a court train, and yards of Brussels lace, Tom very young and handsome waving at everybody as he got out of his shiny Packard Twin-Six wedding present, and everyone moving in the jerky way movies had then. My Uncle Harry took the pictures, and I suppose they are still around someplace.

But the night before is what I remember without any moving pictures. It was the first grown-up party I was allowed. I was the youngest of the eight older cousins assigned a table on the terrace, and it was the first time — the last time — I saw my grandmother's really *en fête.* My younger brothers and cousins of course never saw it like that, and some of them cannot remember the house; all of them must, I suppose, have some of the furniture, dishes, silver, or pictures. I didn't dance or anything. I just sat and looked. I didn't even talk much to my cousins, who were trying so hard to be old that I was disgusted. I was too young — in knickerbockers I called plus-fours — even to try to be old, to talk about Lady Moira, the dresses, the cars, the two orchestras, the bootleggers who had delivered the booze — that was the word we used — that afternoon in a hearse. Tom himself came in for a good deal of talk.

"I wonder what poor little Miss Payne is thinking tonight." This was my oldest cousin, Edith. A great frump of a girl of whom it was said — in her hearing, I shouldn't wonder, because the family was that way — that it was to be hoped that she would be married for her money because no one would marry her for any other reason. She was, however, a stinker of the first water, and even now I can't feel sorry for her. "Poor-little-Miss-Payne" — at seventeen; you can see the way we were brought up.

"HEARTBROKEN. GNASHing PEARLY TEETH. SIMPLY DEVastated." This was Corinne, who talked like this all the time. John Held, Jr., was her idol, and she had her own subscription to the old *Life*.

"Who's Miss Payne?" Pete, who had told us earlier that he had cut himself shaving. He was always saying, "A man has to," too. "A man has to have at least a dozen bow ties" — that sort of thing.

"Boys never know anything." Slobby Edith again. Tom Charlestoned by us with Jay looking happy, and waved. "She was the blonde Uncle Doctor had one summer for their kids" — that was us — "and they had to get rid of her on account of Tom." I guess we all still looked blank because Corinne said, all in caps, "TOM'S FATAL CHARM."

"Don't you remember, Pete? All that WEEPING and getting SHOVED out of ROOMS, and GRANNY utterly FRANTIC? Some SOPHomore from the University of MassaCHUsetts." Edith began talking like Corinne, but she'd get the accents all wrong. "And her father worked at the BANK, which made it so emBARrassing for poor dear GRANNY and all of us because THAT'S how she got the JOB. A PIECE of imPERTinence is what GRANNY SAID."

"Aw nuts. I'm sure you were just terribly, terribly embarrassed" — my cousin Georgie's voice cracked; nobody could ever stand Edith — "like heck." And then he said the cruelest thing he could have said. I don't think he knew it was cruel, but somehow he always said the cruelest thing without knowing it even though I, who was younger, knew it was cruel and, if it had been anyone but oafy Edith, would have felt sorry.

"Who else ever called Grandmama" — we all used the French accentuation but found our contemporaries' *"grand'mères"* highly affected — "Granny, for Pete's sake. You make me sick." And he pretended to puke into his finger bowl.

Corinne, too, must have seen Edith cower, because she said, "There's no HOPE from THESE SAVAGES, Edie. Let's see what we can find ELSEwhere," and the two of them left, shaking what we called their rumps.

I left, too, and walked down to the lake. Up above me on the bluff the party went on, and the waves lapped the shore at my feet. I sailed some stones out into the water, saying Tom's and my dirty words, and looked at the sky where there were more stars than I had ever seen. I made up a phrase, then and there, which is one of the first phrases I ever made up. I've always remembered it, and I must have used it in almost every story I wrote in school and in college: "The sky was vaporous with stars." To a twelve-year-old, it was a marvelous phrase, and there was the wonder under the wonderful sky of having thought it up. It had nothing to do with the ache in my heart at all or with what was happening. There was no one to use it to in my world; I didn't write poetry yet; I just thought it, and it made up somehow for the sorrow that beat under my thin breastbone.

Edie was probably right. There had been a Miss Payne, but we called her Miss Charlotte. She had taken care of us one summer and had disappeared suddenly in August. She was a wonderful reader and very pretty with naturally curly — she told us — blond hair. She let us play with her curls as she read, slipping them out with our fingers and watching them bounce back into place. I remember one such scene. It must have been raining out and late in the afternoon, because Miss Charlotte is reading to us in the lounge and there is lamplight on her head. She is sitting on the floor and the book is on the needlepoint seat — unicorns, flowers, vines, Persian huntsmen with bows and arrows — of the huge couch. I am lying on the couch, my knees over one of its arms, my head at the very edge of the book from which she is reading. There are children — cousins, brothers, neighbors — all over the couch, some on the floor beside her, but I am looking up at her freckly skin, her golden hair and blue eyes, and she reaches over and pats me. Is it "Rapunzel, Rapunzel" she reads? At any rate, when it is over she puts her head down and spreads her hair as a fan over the unicorns, flowers, vines, and me. The children rush to gather it in their hands, to pull it — "It's all right. She lets you. Pull as hard as you can. You can't hurt her" — but I just lie there still, the hair on my face, and reach out with my tongue to pull a few strands to my mouth to taste. I have just tasted it now as I write.

The purpose of all such girls — there was a new one every summer — was to keep us out of the grownups' way. I don't suppose we really knew this or would have minded if we had. It was just the way we were brought up. We slept in the east wing. We were dressed and taken down to the beach. Now that I remembered it, Tom did play with us a lot that summer, and it might have been that summer that I found a hairpin in his bed, but, if he was tolerant of me, I was tolerant of him.

"What would you have a hairpin in your bed for, Tom?" He didn't start that I could remember, but I do remember his answer even though I didn't think it the least bit strange.

"Well, you're not the only caller I have, kid." I suppose the measure of affection I had for him is that he never underrated me. He knew he didn't have to say "Don't tell on me, kid," or make up an elaborate explanation. That was all he said, and, even though I didn't know the answer, I would never have thought of mentioning it to anyone else.

Couples began to drift down from the party then, and I heard one high-pitched, fashionable voice exclaim, "What wonderful, wonderful stars," as if Grandmama had provided them along with the champagne, and I hugged my "vaporous with stars" even closer to my heart. I heard someone else say, "Oh, it's just one of the kids. There are literally millions; you don't dare imagine," so, when I had a chance, I got up the bluff steps, skirted the party, and went up the billiard-room stairs to my room. I got undressed in the dark and it was very pretty. All the lanterns swaying in the garden, the lighted marquees, and the stars in the sky. The orchestra was playing "I'm Forever Blowing Bubbles" real soft with brushes on the drums, and you could hear the feet shuffling as you sometimes can if you only listen.

I didn't have any definite feeling. There was no sense of loss that I was losing Tom or anything like that. If I had to say, I would have said that I was trembly sad because the night was so beautiful and my vaporous stars so far away. But I didn't have to say. I just had to do what I did, and I did it so naturally that there was no thought behind it at all. Although I hadn't done it in at least a couple of years, although I hadn't missed doing it, or thought about it, I just walked up the three steps, across the lounge to Tom's room, and climbed into his bed. Outside, the party went on, and I could hear the orchestra, the laughter, the glasses tinkling.

I may have been asleep a little time or a long time; I don't remember; but I heard the door open and saw the shaft of light in the dresser mirror. Then I heard a girl say, "I thought you said this was Tom's room."

"It is. Shut up."

"But what's he got there?"

"Will you shut up? How do I know what he's got there? Just somebody's there, that's all." Then the door closed, and I could hear the girl's thin, drunken voice remonstrating, but I didn't know what they were saying and just drifted back to sleep.

It was broad daylight — 10.00 or so — when I woke again, still in Tom's bed. Tom was looking at me, clear as the day, in the reflection which shimmered, hung in the air, somewhere between the dresser mirror in which he was tying his tie and me, whose eyes had been drawn from the sprawl of the bed to meet his looking back.

" 'Bout time you got up kid, huh? Today's the wedding day." My gaze went past the reflection into the mirror, and he looked very happy there. I smiled and stretched, drawing my eyes back into myself. "*You* sure look comfortable."

"I am," I said through my yawn.

I shook my head and found him again in the mirror. "You looked so comfortable, so damned asleep when I came in — rough night, kid, rough night — " (I lost his eyes then when he began to fuss with his cuff links) "that I just went to your bed, and that's where I slept."

Inside of me warm, wet, sudden tears began. I can still feel them flood my heart; so I know and knew what they were. But of course I didn't cry them then and I don't now. They just exist in me and always have. I hope I have them in some poems somewhere. I hope I have them here. Anyway, we never looked at each other, ever again.

Another incident in connection with the wedding I suppose is significant enough for me to tell, although I — and I am the one who is writing this — really don't know, nearing fifty, just how it is important. Jay and Tom were married in the afternoon, so I suppose it was 10.00 or so that night when they got ready to leave the Henrys'. All the cousins had been running around like mad at the reception, although the younger ones had been taken off sometime earlier. I was out on the side lawn with the older ones, but they had given up acting older. The girls had kicked off their high heels, and the boys had thrown their blue flannel blazers in a heap on one of the stone benches. All of us had grass stains on our white trousers because we had played real kid games like stoop tag and even statues, trying to whirl up the girls' skirts, trying to bump into what we called their "boobs." At the end we were all stretched out on the side lawn looking at the stars and trying to catch fireflies without moving anything except our arms and hands. Somehow, without anyone mentioning it, we all knew the rules and would have cried "cheat" had anyone sat up. On the other side of the house, the jazz band was still playing, and beneath us we could hear the lake. We had had a good time all week, but now we were exhausted with excitement the way kids get and just lay there. After a while our grandmother appeared on the side porch and called out, "Edith, Edith, round up those children. Your Uncle Tom and Aunt Jay are going to be leaving soon, and you'll want to be there." She peered over the railing to see how many of us were there, still in her gold lamé mother-of-the-groom's dress, her brown velvet hat still firmly on her head. Only her gloves were gone, and I could see the great diamonds on her fingers — blue fire in the August night. Georgie tried to say, "Last one to the porch is a stink-pot," but it didn't work. The girls had to put on their pumps — that was the word — and the boys had to pick up their coats.

Our grandmother just stood there looking out over the lake, related hands gripping the porch railing. I was the last one to struggle up into the light, and I was the one she caught. "What a mess you are!" This wasn't unkindly. "Come, let me fix your tie. And button your belly button." The big diamonds fiddled with my collar button and pulled my tie up.

"You don't have to choke me."

"I'm not going to have you looking like that. And the grass

stains. But come on." Then she did something that was strange for her; she took my hand and kept it even when I tried to get away to join the others. "I'm not letting you out of my sight, young man."

Now this is what I don't know even though it is my story and I am writing it. It is what I *can't* know unless I pretend I'm Henry James, which I can't do. Did she realize or sense the state of my unconscious excitement and want to protect me from myself, or did she want me for her own protection? All day long people had been saying, "Oh Barbara, your very last baby," and relating things to her, and she'd been smiling and social, and she was as old as I was young. There is so much that you don't know about people. What aches are at work at any given time, what frustrations rage hectic in the blood to ravage so the moment-open heart. She had married my grandfather at eighteen. He was twenty years older than she, the daughter of an Akron judge, and the son of one of the real robber barons. Her wedding present had been the tiara she had worn last night. I sit here now and try to imagine one of my own daughters — and they certainly have had a more sophisticated upbringing than the belle of Akron at eighteen — transported to such a world, giving birth to ten boys, and then standing, nearly sixty, to watch the last leave. It will not work at all. So many truths, facts, operate at the same time that it is impossible to know even your own blood, and, unless the intuition intuits the impossible whole, the separating of it, the ordering, must distort forever the part with which it is dealing.

I say again I do not know why she held me by the hand. Anything I can reconstruct, I can at the same time tumble down. I was annoyed then at being restricted and dragged her around to the scrunchy drive where the ushers were handing out rice and all the guests were standing and waiting for Tom and Jay to appear. When they did come and stopped to kiss Grandmama, I got free so that in their dash to the car I was after them like a skinny dervish — arms and legs flying every whichway, frantically tossing rice more on myself than on them and screaming in my high soprano voice, "Keep your pecker up, Tom."

I don't even know that anyone heard me, but my grandmother got me iron by the shoulder with one hand, there was a cruel flash of diamonds, and I was hit hard across the mouth with those great rings. My inner lip was cut against my teeth. I could taste the salt blood. Thirty-five years later I can put my tongue to the very place my mouth was cut and make physical again what I suppose was a psychic scar. The tyranny, the horror of cruelty, plunged to my heart. But was it cruel? Was I indeed hysterical? The woman had brought up ten boys and diamonds grew from the bones of her fingers. I certainly couldn't be allowed to make a spectacle of myself. At all costs I would want to keep my emotion private, and wasn't she helping me to do just that? All this reasoning comes now. At the time, or if I were to tell the story to a psychiatrist, the diamonds would become symbolic, and she a woman viciously loath to give up her son.

Tom and Jay went to England for two years, Tom to run the London branch, so I didn't see them, and I don't even now know what happened. At any rate Jay went to Reno when they returned, and I saw little of Tom that summer. In the fall he returned to London. When I went away to college, he sent me a check for $2000.00 and one of the three or four notes I have had from him in my life:

Hi Kid,
They tell me your real bright. I am not real bright and never was. But I will tell you something about the family. You can always have any money you want, but somebodies always going to want to know what you do with it. Here is a lot of money just put it into some *other* bank and when you need something use it if you don't want to tell anybody.
                              Keep your pecker up,
                                        Tom

Somebody had always even spelled for Tom, and if the letter had been dictated of course it wouldn't have appeared as it did; but he had written it himself and I kept it and am quite unable, typing it out now, to add the necessary *sic*'s. He was thirty when he wrote it, and I was sixteen.

Two years later he came home for a while when my grandmother died, but we all stayed in town, and he stayed at Fred's. I was only back a few days and returned to Cambridge as soon as I could. The brothers were fantastically busy. It was the bottom of the Depression, and they set about salvaging what they could.

We were still very rich people, but when it was all over the brothers no longer owned the bank lock, stock, and barrel as they had, and none of them could have afforded to keep up the house even had they wanted to. Actually it stood empty until 1942 when, as a tax deduction, it was rented to the Navy for $1.00 a year. My cousins as they married took a few acres here and there and built houses, and finally five years ago the house was torn down and the whole place subdivided into what the ads called (honestly!) "Junior Estates." A kind of Levittown for the rich was the way Corinne described it.

Tom went back to London afterward and was briefly married to an English movie star, whom he himself divorced in a real English divorce case with "m'luds" and corespondents and full coverage in the international press. At the time of the abdication, he was mentioned once or twice, and Edith had a picture of him in the *Tatler* where he was correctly identified and Mrs. Simpson was "and friend." If that's not fame, I don't know what it is. The *sic transit gloria mundi* boys will be happy to know that my daughters didn't even know who Mrs. Simpson was when I mentioned her the other day.

I saw Tom maybe a dozen times in as many years. I had gone through college and got a check, and got a doctor's degree and got a check, and he bought and gave away 100 copies of my first book — I suppose to people who could have had no idea at all what it was about. He came to my wedding and there was some of the old warmth, but I was too excited to pay much attention. Two months later I was in the Navy, and so was Tom, a retread at forty-two. He was in Washington for most of the war, and I was in and out and saw him often. I was the best man when he married Mrs. Paget Armstrong — Nan.

Mrs. Paget Armstrong was not at all what she sounded. She taught French at the University of Maryland and was a quiet, restful, enormously well read, and deeply sophisticated woman. She was five or six years older than Tom — at least she had a married daughter — and two people more utterly unprepared for, although not at all unsuited to, each other, it is hard to imagine. They moved into her apartment in Bethesda amid the department-store furniture that was all that was left of her marriage to a Spokane dentist and which had not been improved by its move across the continent.

Tom was perfectly happy and she was too. I liked going there very much, although the food was lukewarm and ill-prepared and I had to sleep on what she called a "davenport." Even the bath towels were sleazy. She herself simply radiated sympathy, and it was touching to see how proud Tom was of me when the two of us talked books and poetry. Little by little I noticed the furniture being replaced, and the "davenport" became a "sofa," and I thought to myself, "Aha, the little woman is learning."

They had been married a little more than a year when, late in December, I called her up. She told me that Tom wasn't there, but said she really wanted to see me and would I please come. I had a hard time getting all the way out there, so it was later than she thought it would be when I got there and she had already had a couple of drinks. She was wearing a most beautiful navy wool dress — she had had nothing like it that I had ever seen — with a diamond clip at the neck and my grandmother's big ring on her engagement finger.

"What a wonderful dress!" I said as I kissed her cheek. She looked pleased an instant and said, "Molyneux." As I followed her into the living room, she went on, " 'Molly Ner' is what you people say, you know." Never, never act to the rich as if they were richer than you. It floods them with shame. I guess she felt this go through my mind because right away she said, "I'm sorry. But Tom's overdue a week."

"Hush-hush?" My own heart stopped a minute, too.

"Very. I don't know which way to turn or who to talk to."

"Well, talk to me."

"I've been meaning to for a long time, you know."

"The Molly Ner set doesn't go in for talking?"

"Something like that. But even so I don't suppose you generally say to a nephew ——" She stopped and you could see an agony hit her full in the face, and her hand went to her breast as if to ward off a blow. You could tell, too, that it was the sort of thing that recurred, that had been recurring for quite a while. "Why did I marry him? Why did I ever marry him? I could have just slept with him, just slept" — she drew the word out and made it seem simple and beautiful and restful — "with him." She had the trick of repetition even under ordinary circumstances, and now it was exaggerated. "He's an economic primitive. He doesn't read. He can't spell." There were tears in her eyes and you could see that she had just about reached the end of her rope. "He doesn't know anything. Anything at all. Nothing. He's been every goddamned place in the world. He knows every important person in the world. But he's, he's — " she shook her head at the incomprehensibility of it — "innocent." She looked to me for help.

"Is that bad?"

"For me, yes." She twisted the ring in. "When you can't be innocent yourself, yes. I don't even remember when I didn't know. For me there's always a feather of guilt." She looked to see if I understood, and was satisfied, because she went on. "Put me on the witness stand, accuse me of the most monstrous act, and always, always there'd be the moment's hesitation before I could deny it. In that moment I'd remember and I'd think, Yes, I could have done it because I know it has been done by people just as good as me, and I can imagine that I might have done it. I'd feel that it was only accidental — there but for the grace of God go I — that I hadn't done it. The feather of guilt."

"There be much matter in this madness." I tried to laugh her out of it, but you could see that she was hurt at my failure to follow her. I didn't want her to try any harder to make it clear, so I just said, "You mean you could have married him for his money?"

"Oh, you Molly Ners, you Molly Ners. What in Christ's name do you think money is? What's so goddamned special about your money? Of course I could have married him for it and it wouldn't have been any trouble at all. He was married for it twice, wasn't he? That flat-chested Molly Ner bitch. That fantastic bosooooomed Frigidaire. No, no. What haunts me is that I'm really worse than they, I married him for his simple loving kindness." Her eyes drooped closed with a vast weariness, and when she opened them again they were full of love. "You see how that could be worse? Do you know the French word *accueillir?* It means *to receive,* but as a host receives a guest. This is the way Tom loves. He opens himself up completely. He's all there for the taking. But, like a guest, you have to take." Her eyes were so earnest, so pleading, that I took her hand and held it. "You see, he's afraid of embarrassing you by offering you more than you want, more than you are ready for, and yet his own hunger is so deep, his own heart is so transparent, that you can't help wondering — the feather of guilt, and God I love him — if there's enough of you to receive all that he has to give." She took her hand from mine, turned the diamond around and looked at it. "I can't say this sort of thing to him, or at least I haven't yet, so I say it to you. He wouldn't be able to follow. It's not the sort of thing he thinks about; it's not the sort of thing he has to think about. That gorgeous, blooming innocence. But it's sure not a very practical way of loving."

She got up then, smoothed her dress over her hips and said, "I'm glad I said it. To you. To myself. To Bethesda, Maryland. But I don't know if I can stand much more of this kindness, this *gentillesse*, this christawful consideration." I smiled what I suppose was ruefully because she said, "The two with-rue-my-heart-is-laden boys."

"Oh, come off it. It is funny. You're all torn up because you haven't heard from him when you expected, so you complain about his kindness and consideration. Really, now."

She did smile then, but said, "Seriously, you don't know what it is. If he'd just *say*. But no. It's all by the most godawful indirection. How the hell did I know this place was a horror? I didn't know you could pay $350.00 for a wool dress. Yet you come in and your face lights up when you see it in the half dark. As far as I know — really, honestly, truly — it doesn't look any different from $49.95. Why didn't he just buy a house in Georgetown? I — I might feel uncomfortable. Nothing about his being strangled here. D'ya know what he did?" The frantic light came back in her eyes. "I'll tell you. For six months he kept a room at the Shoreham — everybody in Washington is screaming for rooms — to keep his thirty uniforms, his 100 shirts, his forty pairs of shoes in. Because he didn't like to say that there wasn't room for them here. He didn't like to say." She nodded the words out syllable by syllable. "I'm dizzy, just dizzy. I said to him, but they're all alike, aren't they, and he said he supposed so, so he just gave them all away. Just like that. It never occurred to him that I might suppose a room at the Shoreham meant a mistress, you know?"

I was laughing and said, "He isn't acquainted with the subject of French literature."

"It's impossible. Oh, I've seen you in Henry James and Fitzgerald and Proust and all over the place — and you've seen your-

selves, but it doesn't do any good. I'm not prepared for you.
You're not prepared for yourselves."

I've often had occasion to remember that "you're not prepared
for yourselves," and I've wondered just when she said it to him,
for from what happened I am sure she must have. Critics, speaking of Gatsby, always point out his romanticizing the rich; what
they don't know is that the rich themselves romanticize the poor.
It never occurs to Daisy that she is loved because her "voice is
money," and her weeping over Gatsby's shirts — at his thinking
that they can make any difference — is as marvelously revealing
in its way as Nick's last sight of Daisy eating chicken. Take the
ring. Nan wore it as a status symbol — although the phrase had
not then been invented. It was the only way she could wear it.
Twelve-carat diamonds did not grow from her bones. To Tom,
who must have given his movie star an even larger one, it was
his mother's ring. To me — well, I've told you about that.

Tom did get back, did survive the war, and it was Nan who
died cruelly of cancer toward the end of the '40s. She was in the
hospital for nearly a year, and, although he never told her, toward the end Tom had a room on the floor above to be near her.
I saw her two weeks before she died, and, in her own phrase, she
"received me like a guest." She asked me to be good to Tom, to
watch over him as he had watched over her, but then went on,
"But how can you? How can anyone? There always will be the
moment when, like Sartre's man looking through the keyhole
into the empty room, he will see the eye of a stranger looking
back. It happened to me a long, long time ago. I don't think it
has happened to you yet, but it will, and I guess it will be all
right." A spasm of pain came over her then, but she was so intent on finishing that she let it clutch her without closing her
eyes. "What will happen to Tom when he plasters his goddamned,
clear-blue boy's eye to that goddamned keyhole" — you could see
the pain run like a river of fire through her — "I can't even think.
Let Sartre think for me. It's his phrase — 'the burning presence'
of the 'stare of Another.' Never to have known shame. Jesus, I
envy the rich."

I went into the hall to hurry the nurse.

Nan was buried in the family plot. I asked Tom if she had
ever seen it and was sorry that she hadn't. It would have amused

her greatly because it was dedicated to the proposition that even in death we were different. It was in the oldest city cemetery, one of a half-dozen or so national Catholic, Protestant, and Jewish strung along what at one time had been the end of the streetcar line. The street widened out, and when I was little, and went there with my grandmother, there was generally a holiday air about the place. Streetcars clanged; huge Polish, German, and Bohemian families would wander around clutching flags, diaper bags, trowels, and watering cans. You'd see widows in black pricing monuments in the empty lots, shawled women looking at grave plants in the enormous greenhouse, and kids eating popcorn, hot dogs from the whistling wagons. In the summer there was an American Legion carnival with a Ferris wheel. None of these delights was for us. The limousine would have to slow almost to a stop, and we on the jump seats often had to take the thumbed noses — "Pay no attention, children. Act as if you didn't see them" — directed toward us by kids our very own age. Inside the cemetery gates there was none of the egalitarian nonsense of today's "Memorial Parks" where all the markers are the same and everyone has to buy "perpetual care." If you were poor, the stone was poor, the grave sunken, and the grasses grew up around you. If you were rich, you crossed over a little river that our father called the Styx on a rattly bridge, and looking back you could see the welter of domino stones where, crowded more closely even than they had been in life, lay the many dead.

On our side of the river, little hills rose, covered with a chaos of tombs, vaults, angels, columns, Greek porticoes, stone catafalques. The merchant princes, the robber barons sometimes had whole hills to themselves, and one of them had been flattened off for us. There is a picture of ours in the book the family had written about itself, and they used to sell a postcard of it at the cemetery gates — a blue sky, white clouds, and geraniums, aromatic with July, in the flower boxes. Corinne bought a pack of them once and used to send them to us from time to time with "Happy Birthday" scrawled across the back or even, on occasion, "Wish you were here." The robber baron himself lay under an enormous obelisk of polished black marble, his name cut deep in letters as tall as a man. Around him in an ever-widening circle lay the graves of his sons, my grandfather, granduncles, and their sons and sons' sons. Each grave had its heavy slab of matching marble, and, if such a thing can be said to have taste, I suppose the architect's conception can be admired. The obelisk stood as the center of an enormous sundial or clock face, and four flights of three steps each — at 12.00, 3.00, 6.00, and 9.00 — led up to it. The other hours were marked by either black marble benches or flower boxes, and it was because of the filling of these as one set of flowers died that we usually drove out with my grandmother and her gardener.

Well, the streetcar's gone long since; the monument makers have fled; the greenhouses stood empty for a while and were pelted with stones before they were torn down to make room for a shopping plaza, as if the dead could eat, wear shoes, or attend one-cent sales at the drugstore. Very few people are buried there now, mostly people like us who had graves to spare, but even so, when I was there for Fred's funeral, the narrow, winding gravel roads were all marked "One Way." This greatly delighted Corinne, who said, as we rattled over the bridge on our way back, "Remember the Ferris wheel we never could ride?"

Early this year I ran into Tom in the reading room of the public library. I had gone in to look up some things in connection with an article I was trying to do, and there he was, surrounded by encyclopedias, a big blue college notebook in front of him. He was nearly sixty; his older brothers had died, my father among them, and even his grandnieces and nephews were getting married. He only appeared on such occasions, and the members of the family had commented with asperity that, if you wanted to talk to Tom, you had to call him at the bank because he was never home, and half the time your message wasn't delivered. He had even disappeared from the society columns, as indeed had the rest of us, and the only place you were likely to see his name was on the letterheads of charity solicitations.

"Well, look at the elder statesman," was what I said when I saw him, and he really looked caught out.

"I'm sure glad it's you," he laughed, but I felt sorry I had said what I did. A twinge of class consciousness, of course, because we were brought up to act as if there were nothing strange in the behavior, however outrageous, of anyone we knew or were related to. "Come on, I'll buy you lunch." He spoke to the librarian as we left about leaving his stuff out, and she said, "Surely, Mr. Thomas."

He was attending night classes in the downtown branch of the University, and he told me with pride that he was a senior. He hadn't said anything to them about Princeton; indeed, having become committed to education, he was ashamed, much as a Seventh Day Adventist might be ashamed of an Episcopal past. The detail which cost him the greatest effort to confess, however, was his use of the name Richard Thomas, but I quite understood the reservation. He was a trustee of the University; his own name was immediately recognizable. I didn't learn that day, but I did shortly afterward when I began to see a good deal of him, that Tom was living with a girl he had met in one of his classes, and that she had no idea that he was anything other than an older student rather better off than usual. He had taken an apartment for her and her two children — one Negro, one blond as light — in a high-rise insurance company project, and spent two or three nights a week there. Her name was Mrs. Temple — Jo.

She was very beautiful, with long, brown-red dancer's hair, and she moved like a queen. I often had dinner with them, and she went to no end of trouble with paperback French cookbooks and that sort of thing if she felt like it; otherwise we'd just have something sent in. She was witty, well read in a curious sort of way, and never said anything at all about her former life. One of the neighbors sat with her kids while she was in class, and Jo did the same for the girl during the day. It was all very free, casual, messy, highbrow. Tom was not the least self-conscious about it, and I suppose I would never have seen this kind of life if it hadn't been for him. I was fascinated. The idea of Tom's writing a paper on the effect of the restricted vocabulary in Racine and Hemingway was staggering. Yet the paper was very good, and the three of us talked it over, late into the coffee night, for many weeks. We'd argue and walk up and down as if it were the most important literary discovery since the beginning of time. But, if Jo and I were excited about it, it was Tom's idea, Tom's paper, Tom's passion. He really knew what he was doing, and brought to the job the kind of sensitivity that the late or self-educated seldom have, but which no teacher can ever teach.

One night Jo was going to read Cleopatra in a Shakespeare

class they were both taking, and Tom and I picked her up. She was wearing a thin silk dress, cut away to show her magnificent shoulders, and you could tell that she was wearing nothing but a slip underneath — not at all the sort of thing she ordinarily would have worn to class. She must have had quite a reputation around the college, because there wasn't room in the classroom for all the visitors, and the instructor, a Mr. Newberry, laughed and said, "I see that word has got around that Mrs. Temple is to read to-night. I'll have to find us a bigger room." We all moved down the hall then to a chemistry demonstration room.

I suppose those who have never seen one have little notion of what a night course is like at any university, however eminent. On the one hand it is a shabby, heartbroken operation: the university intends to make money out of it; the only big boys who teach are those who want to spend the summer in Europe; the students intend to get credit. Yet if the teacher is any good — and Newberry was good — there is a cohesion, an interest, a completely democratic camaraderie never attainable in day classes where the division into cliques — both intellectual and social — is evident from the very beginning.

I had intended to watch Tom as Jo read, but this was impossible. The students read their parts from behind a long, waist-high sink desk normally used for chemistry demonstrations, the symbols for which still smeared the chalky blackboards. Yet in that bare, dirty room in a reconstructed office building, under fluorescent lights, no one had eyes for anyone or anything but Jo. It was a reading, you understand; they hadn't learned the parts; they didn't act them; there was no business. They would read a scene; Newberry would comment; and they might take up at his cue hundreds of lines later on. Jo didn't even look up very often, and I am perfectly positive that she used only four gestures in the two hours we were there. Her voice was eloquent, varied, and wonderfully colored, but each of the gestures I will remember until the day I die.

When she first stood up — Enobarbus was speaking and she was obviously reading ahead — her hands went to her hair and took out, one at a time, the three or four hairpins that held it loosely up. Each she put to her mouth, never taking her eyes from the text until the hair had spilled, coil by lustrous coil, over

her shoulders, clouding her breast. Her hand went to her lips
then, and I could feel the tiny slick of her tongue collecting the
pins, which she laid between the pages of her book at — oh God
— the spine. There was a little shake of her head and the hair
streamed back as her breasts rose and the marvelously supple voice
began the cadenced lines. If there had been anything conscious
about it, had it for a moment seemed calculated, it would have
been the most naked striptease. But it was pure, unobserved
"Woman Reading" — a woman who knew in her blood that what
she was to read had to be read with her hair down.

I wouldn't be so sure about my recollection, I would distrust
it as over-observed, over-written, except that in the last scene, just
before she got to "Give me my robe, put on my crown," her bare
arm arched, gathered the richness of that brown-red hair with its
shadows, and the flower fingers pinned it again to her queenly
head. Before this, in the scene with the messenger, her voice all
whips and scorns, she had put out her hand, instinctively without
looking up, toward the huge blond oaf who was doubling the
minor parts. As she came to the words, "My bluest veins to kiss,"
she looked him straight in his goggling eyes, and turned her hand
palm upward, baring the underside of her wrist and its bluest
veins. At the tenderness of the coquetry, the boy blushed crimson,
even as Shakespeare must have intended, and the ceiling lifted with
the roar of delight from the class.

The last gesture she used was less overt, but I am just as sure
it was noticed because I could hear the comments as we left the
classroom. When it came to the asp, Jo — at once Jo and Cleopatra, Jo becoming Cleopatra despite the fluorescent lights, the
demonstration sink, Jo with Cleopatra in her bluest veins — put
her hand involuntarily to her breast. Her fingers trembled at the
silk as if exploring the horror of hurt in

> With thy sharp teeth this knot intrinsicate
> Of life at once untie. Poor venomous fool,
> Be angry and dispatch.

Her voice was utterable tears, but when she spoke

> Oh, coulds't thou speak,
> That I might hear thee call great Caesar ass
> Unpolicied,

it whiplashed into such scorn as I have never heard in the human voice, and her hand pressed flesh to its limit.

The power of her reading was such that the others were swept along with her. Antony was Antony and every man there read the lines with him — not only "I am dying, Egypt, dying" and the great bravura passages, but even single lines and phrases. I know because when Antony said "Eros, ho! The shirt of Nessus is upon me," sixty-year-old Tom's hand became a vise on my suit-coat arm.

After it was all over, a bunch of people including Newberry went up to Jo and thanked her, and I suppose *exalted* is the word to express the look in her eyes. I, of course, was irretrievably and forever in love with her.

Tom and I sat back when the others were making over her. He was deep in thought and said nothing. I did say, "That sure was something," but he just grunted and looked very old. We walked out with the rest of the cast and Newberry — Jo had invited them back to the apartment — and they were all laughing excitedly, Jo very flirtatious, triumphant, and young, swinging her hips joyously, tossing her red-brown head. The halls were empty by that time, and a janitor was standing by the elevator, waiting to turn off the lights. Of course it was Tom who said, "Come on. Let's get going. This poor guy wants to get home," but I don't think anyone heard him above the jabber. While we waited for the elevator, the not-at-all pallid Mr. Newberry made a sort of pass at Jo. I don't think he had an idea in the world that Tom was her lover. (I write *lover* now, but when I phrased it to myself then, it was "Tom was the man who paid the rent," and an admonitory shiver went through me that should have warned me of the horror in store.) Jo avoided Newberry with a little dance step — I suppose he was thirty-two or -three — and came toward me, slipping her hands under my coat — cupped palms, moving fingers — across the small of my back.

"Here's the man who's Antony's age, you Dollabellas, you Enobarbuses, you Caesars." It was so outrageous that everyone hooted except Tom and me.

In the elevator going down, I was pressed close to her, and I know she knew my excitement because she murmured to me, "Not every soldier's pole has fallen" in the confusion of getting out.

The party at Jo's was very beery, young, and stupid. Lots of gossip about teachers and classes that greatly intrigued Newberry, who would be sorry the next day, and lots of wandering in and out of the bedrooms, the kitchen, and even into the public corridor. All I did was watch my chance, and it seemed to come when Tom went into their bedroom, saying he was going to make a phone call. I knew that Jo had been watching, too, because she was on her feet right away, pulling me into the front hall. The urgency of our kiss was so complete that when I looked at her there was horror in her eyes, and she could only return my gaze for a moment before she pressed my head to her breast and whispered to herself more than to me, "My bluest veins, my very bluest veins."

I don't think we were gone more than a few minutes; at any rate Tom came back after we had reappeared and were already sitting on the floor.

He stood over us, looking down — paternal, avuncular, what you will — and said, "I just talked to Mary" — Mary is my wife — "on the phone and invited myself out for the long weekend."

"Sure, Tom, fine. The girls will love it." I couldn't find his eyes, and I don't think I would have known what to do with them had I caught them, because I was totally unprepared for what followed.

"They're picking me — us — up in twenty minutes. I told them we'd meet downstairs. They don't know the name on the bell."

To say that my heart sank is less than true. Of course there was that awful, bottomless sinking, but I was flooded with a fire of shame as fierce as my desire had been. A stain, like one of those oxblood birthmarks you sometimes see on faces, spread through me as if to devour my bones. I could look nowhere, least of all toward Jo. Tom mercifully walked away, and in a few minutes Jo got up and went into the children's bedroom. I don't know — I still don't know — if I was meant to follow her, but the fact that she had chosen the children's room stopped me — oh shit on Henry James — for long enough to realize that my knees would never have supported me. I just sat there dazed, and I supposed I would be thought drunk. In a little while Jo came back through the door to their room — there was a bath connecting it to the children's. She had our coats in her hand and said, "The Bobbsey Twins are on their way."

Everyone got up — goddamn them — the way the young do for

the old, and Jo helped us on with our coats. She pecked us both
at the door, but didn't come to the elevator with us. I wondered
if it would be Enobarbus or Newberry. On the way down Tom
said, "When I said *they* were coming for us, I just meant Taylor.
I phoned and told him to bring a car and pack me a bag." His
voice was perfectly normal, but mine broke over the "Sure," which
was all I could get out. I wanted to say with Jo's scorn, "I'd call
great Caesar pretty goddamned policied."

I was on fire with rage at what had been done to me. My
tongue had shot between my lip and teeth as if to ward off the
diamond blow. I was still, as Nan had said, "unprepared for myself."

Taylor came then with the big bank-president limousine, and
it was clear that Tom intended to have him drive us the sixty
toll-road miles to my house in the country. Great Caesar was afraid
to be alone with me, was he? As if he had read my mind, Tom
leaned forward and closed the glass partition, and another wave
of humiliation filled me. "In the morning," I thought, "this is
what I'll wake up to. And every morning it will be there, uneasy
at my heart at first and then known in the blood. The walk to the
bathroom, the very shiver as I pee, polluted." My hands trembled
with *horror carnis* at the thought of touching myself in the shower,
the look in the eyes looking back at me as I shaved. Tom. Tom
had done this to me. Tom. As if I were a little boy who had
disgraced himself at a birthday party. And I had allowed it. Had
been powerless. The Bobbsey Twins. The Bobbsey Twins. Sissy.
Sissy. Shitty sissy.

The paroxysm that seized me was completely real. My teeth
chattered, my feet would not hold still, and I was in the grip of
a wholly involuntary memory: the memory of sitting on a black
marble bench, cold as the death that surrounded me, my six-year-
old thighs, in their thin De Pinna flannel shorts, rigid with ache.
It was the day before my mumps began. I had driven out with
my grandmother in just such a limousine, glassed-in in April, to
see about planting the boxes with hyacinths. It was a weekday,
so we had not had to run the gantlet at the gates. The Ferris
wheel had stopped. There was a poor little funeral — two cars
and the hearse — at one point before we crossed the rattly bridge,
but we scrunched past it. The obelisk was very black against the
dead gray sky, but the branches of the scarcely greening trees

moved, reflected in the elegiac marble. I thought of my grand-father, whom I never knew, dying blind. Of the girl sixteen who had hanged herself. Of the little boy who one hundred years ago had wandered into a Canadian wheat field and died in the August sun, his hair blonder than the wheat which hid him until he was dead. He was a favorite of mine, and the phrases were my grand-mother's as she told the story to impress on us how we must never wander away. She moved now with the gardener, as if the two of them were hands on that enormous clock, from box to box, and I climbed on one of the benches. She called out, "You'd better get in the car, honey; you'll get cold," but I just sat there in terrible sadness watching not the trees or the monument but the move-ment of the trees deep in its blackness.

My grandmother and the gardener had passed to the other side of the obelisk and were out of my sight when suddenly a black cloud of purple martins on their way north hovered above the monument, supposing in its depths a pool. There were literally thousands of them, layered, chirping, their formation abandoned as, purpled black from brown, wheeling, pecking, they swooped down to the marble waters of our graves. I could hear my grand-mother's "Oh! Oh!" and the gardener ran out of the shadows, swinging his rake and waving his trowel. The deceived birds rose with a cry but, in the rising and wheeling round the obelisk, swooped over me on the bench. Their wings beat lice-feathered against my face; their claws caught in my hair; their dirt be-fouled my jacket; they thudded against my hunched breast and back in their wild determination to escape. When they were gone I was frozen with terror that burst within me, and I wet my pants.

My grandmother came running and took me in her arms, but I was far gone in the deep compulsive tremor which had lasted forty years to be relived now with such exactness that I thought it was really urine which trickled through the hairs of my trousered leg and not the memory of a six-year-old shame. I had to put out my hand to know it was not.

After it was over, Tom pressed the button that lowered the window on my side, and I leaned back, limp with quiet exhaus-tion.

"If it's too cold, say so, kid."

"Kid? I'm forty-six years old."

"Kid." I drank in the real air that blew the graveyard air away and felt calmer. My hand lay on the seat between us, and after a while Tom put his hand over it and pressed it.

"Kid, kid, I had to do it."

"Sure."

He withdrew his hand and for a long time said nothing. The revulsions of my original *horror carnis* set up decreasing echoes as we lapped the night in toll-road miles until finally, as we stopped at one of the gates in the blue-green, unreal light and Taylor flung the coins in the basket, I gave a great sigh, and it was as finished as it was ever going to be.

For a while then I thought Tom was going to say, "Please don't see Jo again," or "If I ask you, will you promise not to go by the flat again," or "I'm warning you, don't go back." My mind phrased and rephrased the possible sentences, made up answers in a dizzy succession — evading, consenting, refusing — until the whole jewel-box cab of the limousine seemed ready to explode. I suppose I was never so far away from him as I was in those moments, for, when he did speak, it was to say, "Did Nan ever tell you that about the man looking into an empty room, a room he knew was empty, through a keyhole?"

"And being amazed that an eye was looking back? Yes. A couple of weeks before she died. I've read it since, of course."

"So have I. You don't know who it is looking back. Whether it is the eye of God or your own eye or Shakespeare's eye." He cleared his throat. "You know that's why I went to night school? I never knew any of the things you and she were talking about. She once even told me that from something you said she was pretty sure you were in love with Charlotte Payne. At six? I just laughed. I sure unlaughed it tonight. I guess that's what comes from knowing things."

The old tenderness flooded me, washing clear like sweet water against a bitter clay bank. Poor Tom's a-cold. Did he still think that learning, even understanding, had anything to do with desire or happiness — Nan's *innocence* again?

"She said she didn't know what would happen when you did look through the keyhole and saw the eye looking back. The burning presence."

"Well, now it's happened," he said. "It was your eye looking back."

JOHN CHEEVER

A Vision of the World

(FROM THE NEW YORKER)

THIS IS BEING WRITTEN in another seaside cottage on another coast. Gin and whiskey have bitten rings into the table where I sit. The light is dim. On the wall there is a colored lithograph of a kitten wearing a flowered hat, a silk dress, and white gloves. The air is musty, but I think it is a pleasant smell — heartening and carnal, like bilge water or the land wind. The tide is high, and the sea below the bluff slams its bulkheads, its doors, and shakes its chains with such power that it makes the lamp on my table jump. I am here alone to rest up from a chain of events that began one Saturday afternoon when I was spading up my garden. A foot or two below the surface I found a small round can that might have contained shoe polish. I pried the can open with a knife. Inside I found a piece of oilcloth, and within this a note on lined paper. It read, "I, Nils Jugstrum, promise myself that if I am not a member of the Gory Brook Country Club by the time I am twenty-five years old I will hang myself." I knew that twenty years ago the neighborhood where I live had been farmland, and I guessed that some farmer's boy, gazing off to the green fairways of Gory Brook, had made this vow and buried it in the ground. I was moved, as I always am, by these broken lines of communication in which we express our most acute feelings. The note seemed, like some impulse of romantic love, to let me deeper into the afternoon.

The sky was blue. It seemed like music. I had just cut the grass, and the smell of it was in the air. This reminded me of those overtures and promises of love we know when we are young.

At the end of a foot race you throw yourself onto the grass by the cinder track, gasping for breath, and the ardor with which you embrace the schoolhouse lawn is a promise you will follow all the days of your life. Thinking then of peaceable things, I noticed that the black ants had conquered the red ants and were taking the corpses off the field. A robin flew by, pursued by two jays. The cat was in the currant hedge, scouting a sparrow. A pair of orioles passed, pecking one another, and then I saw, a foot or so from where I stood, a copperhead working itself out of the last length of its dark winter skin. What I experienced was not fright or dread; it was shock at my unpreparedness for this branch of death. Here was lethal venom, as much a part of the earth as the running water in the brook, but I seemed to have no space for it in my considerations. I went back to the house to get the shotgun, but I had the misfortune then to meet up with the oldest of my two dogs, a gun-shy bitch. At the sight of the gun she began to bark and whimper, torn unmercifully by her instincts and anxieties. Her barking brought the second dog, a natural hunter, bounding down the stairs, ready to retrieve a rabbit or a bird, and followed by two dogs, one barking in joy and the other in horror, I returned to the garden in time to see the viper disappear into a stone wall.

After this I drove into the village and bought some grass seed and then went out to the supermarket on Route 27, to get some brioches my wife had ordered. I think you may need a camera these days to record a supermarket on a Saturday afternoon. Our language is traditional, the accrual of centuries of intercourse. Except for the shapes of the pastry, there was nothing traditional to be seen at the bakery counter where I waited. We were six or seven, delayed by an old man with a long list, a scroll of groceries. Looking over his shoulder I read,

6 eggs
hors d'oeuvres

He saw me reading his document and held it against his chest like a prudent card player. Then suddenly the piped-in music changed from a love song to a cha-cha, and the woman beside me began to move her shoulders shyly and to execute a few steps. "Would you like to dance, Madam?" I asked. She was very plain, but when I held out my arms she stepped into them, and we danced for a minute or two. You could see that she loved to dance, but with a face like that she couldn't have had many chances. She then blushed a deep red, stepped out of my arms, and went over to the glass case, where she studied the Boston cream pies. I felt that we had made a step in the right direction, and when I got my brioches and drove home I was elated. A policeman stopped me at the corner of Alewives' Lane, to let a parade go by. First to come was a young girl in boots and shorts that emphasized the fineness of her thighs. She had an enormous nose, wore a busby, and pumped an aluminum baton. She was followed by another girl, with finer and more ample thighs, who marched with her pelvis so far in advance of the rest of her that her spine was strangely curved. She wore bifocals and seemed terribly bored by this forwardness of her plevis. A band of boys, with here and there a gray-haired ringer, brought up the rear, playing "The Caissons Go Rolling Along." They carried no banners, they had no discernible purpose or destination, and it all seemed to me terribly funny. I laughed all the way home.

But my wife was sad.

"What's the matter, darling?" I asked.

"I just have this terrible feeling that I'm a character in a television situation comedy," she said. "I mean I'm nice-looking, I'm well-dressed, I have humorous and attractive children, but I have this terrible feeling that I'm in black-and-white and that I can be turned off by anybody. I just have this terrible feeling that I can be turned *off*." My wife is often sad because her sadness is not a sad sadness, sorry because her sorrow is not a crushing sorrow. She grieves because her grief is not an acute grief, and when I tell her that this sorrow over the inadequacies of her sorrow may be a new hue in the spectrum of human pain, she is not consoled. Oh, I sometimes think of leaving her. I could conceivably make a life without her and the children, I could get along without the companionship of my friends, but I could not bring myself to leave my lawns and gardens, I could not part from the porch screens that I have repaired and painted, I cannot divorce myself from the serpentine brick walk I have laid between the side door and the rose garden; and so, while my chains are forged of turf and house paint, they will still bind me until I die. But I was grateful to my wife then for what she had said, for stating that the externals of her life had the quality of a dream. The un-inhibited energies of the imagination had created the supermarket, the viper, and the note in the shoe-polish can. Compared to these, my wildest reveries had the literalness of double-entry bookkeeping. It pleased me to think that our external life has the quality of a dream and that in our dreams we find the virtues of conservatism. I then went into the house, where I found the cleaning woman smoking a stolen Egyptian cigarette and piecing together the torn letters in the wastebasket.

We went to Gory Brook that night for dinner. I checked the list of members, looking for Nils Jugstrum, but he wasn't there, and I wondered if he had hanged himself. And for what? It was the usual. Gracie Masters, the only daughter of a millionaire funeral director, was dancing with Pinky Townsend. Pinky was out on fifty thousand dollars bail for stock-market manipulation. When bail was set, he took the fifty thousand out of his wallet. I danced a set with Millie Surcliffe. The music was "Rain," "Moonlight on the Ganges," "When the Red Red Robin Comes Bob Bob Bobbin' Along," "Five Foot Two, Eyes of Blue," "Carolina in the Morning," and "The Shiek of Araby." We seemed to be dancing on the grave of social coherence. But while the scene was plainly revolutionary, where was the new day, the world to come? The next set was "Lena from Palesteena," "I'm Forever Blowing Bubbles," "Louisville Lou," "Smiles," and "'The Red Red Robin'" again. That last one really gets us jumping, but when the band blew the spit out of their instruments I saw them shaking their heads in deep moral disapproval of our antics. Millie went back to her table, and I stood by the door, wondering why my heart should heave when I see people leave a dance floor at the end of a set — heave as it heaves when I see a crowd pack up and leave a beach as the shadow of the cliff falls over the water and the sand, heave as if I saw in these gentle departures the energies and the thoughtlessness of life itself.

Time, I thought, strips us rudely of the privileges of the bystander, and in the end that couple chatting loudly in bad French in the lobby of the Grande Bretagne (Athens) turns out to be us. Someone else has got our post behind the potted palms, our quiet corner in the bar, and, exposed, perforce we cast around for other avenues of observation. What I wanted to identify then was not a chain of facts but an essence — something like that indecipherable collision of contingencies that can produce exaltation or despair. What I wanted to do was to grant my dreams, in so incoherent a world, their legitimacy. None of this made me moody, and I danced, drank, and told stories at the bar until about one, when we went home. I turned on the television set to a commercial that, like so much else I had seen that day, seemed terribly funny. A young woman with a boarding-school accent was asking, "Do you offend with wet-fur-coat odor? A fifty-thousand-dollar sable cape caught in a thundershower can smell worse than an old hound dog who's been chasing a fox through a swamp. *Nothing* smells worse than wet mink. Even a light mist can make lamb, opossum, civet, baum marten, and other less costly and serviceable furs as malodorous as a badly ventilated lion house in a zoo. Safeguard yourself from embarrassment and anxiety by light applications of Elixircol before you wear your furs. . . ." She belonged to the dream world, and I told her so before I turned her off. I fell asleep in the moonlight and dreamed of an island.

I was with some other men, and seemed to have reached the place on a sailing boat. I was sunburned, I remember, and, touching my jaw, I felt a three- or four-day stubble. The island was in the Pacific. There was a smell of rancid cooking oil in the air — a sign of the China coast. It was in the middle of the afternoon when we landed, and we seemed to have nothing much to do. We wandered through the streets. The place either had been occupied by the Army or had served as a military way station, because many of the signs in the windows were written in an approximation of English. "Crews Cutz," I read on a sign in an Oriental barber-shop. Many of the stores had displays of imitation American whiskey. Whiskey was spelled "Whikky." Because we had nothing better to do, we went into a local museum. There were bows, primitive fish hooks, masks, and drums. From the museum we went to a restaurant and ordered a meal. I had a struggle with the local language, but what surprised me was that it seemed to be an informed struggle. I seemed to have studied the language before coming ashore. I distinctly remembered putting together a sentence when the waiter came up to the table. "Porpozec ciebie nie prosze dorzanin albo zyolpocz ciwego," I said. The waiter smiled and complimented me, and when I woke from the dream, the fact of the language made the island in the sun, its population, and its museum real, vivid, and enduring. I thought with longing of the quiet and friendly natives and the easy pace of their lives.

That wayward wind that, once or twice a year, carries the sound of church bells out of their native parish, beyond the usual acoustical borders, traffic intersections, rivers, and fields, and scatters the music of chimes over the heads of cows and chickens and lewd and unrepentant sinners, blew that Sunday morning. I heard the bells clearly on the stillness. It had been years since I had been to church, and what appealed to me then was the idea of the changelessness of the liturgy. I washed and dressed, and in my car followed the ringing of bells up a side street to a small brick church. The ringing stopped as I approached the door. I was preceded by three women. They seemed not together, and they were all three past middle age. The first wore a drum-shaped hat, covered with metal discs from which the morning light flashed with the boldness of some advertising lure. Buy Ginger-fluff? Texadrol? Fulpruf Tires? I looked into her face for the text, but there was nothing there but the text of marriage, childbirth, some delight, and some dismay. The other two wore similar hats. I waited until they had entered the church before I went in. I went to a pew way forward, genuflected with a loud creaking of my knee bones, and said my prayers, immersed in the immemorial and Episcopal smell of ancient rains. Then I raised my head to see the place. There was a round window above the chancel, depicting some scene in the Passion, but the brilliance with which the morning light flooded the colored glass made the scene indecipherable and perhaps more beautiful. Then I found myself immersed not only in a smell of ancient rains but in a great violence of odors. The hassocks and pew cushions could account for the smell of straw, the three women could account for the smell of faded flowers, the plaster walls, dusty carpets, and wooden pews all had their exhalations, but the sum of this seemed to be the essence of my specific childhood on a Massachusetts farm; or was this merely the odor of the past, some emission preserved from the turn of the century, some faded distillate of the eighteenth-nineties? The priest came in without his cassock and lighted the order candles. He returned to the altar a moment later, carrying the Host. "Almighty God," he intoned, "unto Whom all hearts are open, all desires known, and from Whom no secrets are hid, cleanse the thoughts of our hearts with the inspiration of Thy holy spirit . . ."

The resonance of the Mass moved into that gloomy place with the sumptuary magnificence of an Elizabethan procession. Perorative clauses spread out the main supplication or confession in breadth and glory, and the muttered responses seemed embroidered in crimson and gold. On it would move, I thought, through the Lamb of God, the Gloria, and the Benediction, until the last amen shut like a door on this verbal pomp. But then I sensed something strange and wrong. The priest's speech was theatrical, but what was more noticeable was a pose of suavity, a bored and haughty approach to the holy words for which Cranmer had burned. As he turned to the altar to pray, I saw him sway and grab at the lace for support. Was he sick? Was he feeble? The woman with the lights on her hat turned to me and hissed, "He's drunk again." He was. He fired the Mass at us with scorn and contumely, as if his besottedness was a form of wisdom. He lurched around the altar, got the general confession mixed up with the order for morning prayer, and kept saying, "Christ have mercy upon us. Let us pray," until it seemed that he was stuck. There is no point in the formalities of Holy Communion where, in the case of such a disaster, the communicants can intervene, and there was nothing to do but watch him flounder through to the end. Suddenly he threw his arms wide, fell to his knees, and exclaimed, "Let us pray for all those killed or cruelly wounded on thruways, expressways, freeways, and turnpikes. Let us pray for all those burned to death in faulty plane landings, midair collisions, and mountainside crashes. Let us pray for all those wounded by rotary lawnmowers, chain saws, electric hedge clippers, and other power tools. Let us pray for all alcoholics measuring out the hours of the days that the Lord hath made in ounces, pints, and fifths." Here he sobbed loudly. "Let us pray for the lecherous and the impure. . . ." Led by the woman with the flashing hat, the other worshippers left before this prayer was finished, and I was left alone to support the drunken priest with my amen. He got through the rest of it, divested himself, extinguished his order lights, and hurried back to his gin bottle, hidden among the vestments.

The rest of Sunday passed swiftly and pleasantly in a round of cocktail parties, but that night I had another dream. I dreamed that I was standing at the bedroom window of the cottage in

Nantucket that we sometimes rent. I was looking south along the fine curve of the beach. I have seen finer, whiter, and more splendid beaches, but when I look at the yellow of the sand and the arc of the curve, I always have the feeling that if I look at the cove long enough it will reveal something to me. The sky was cloudy. The water was gray. It was Sunday — although I couldn't have said how I knew this. It was late, and from the inn I could hear that most pleasant sound of dishes being handled, while families would be eating their Sunday-night suppers in the old matchboard dining room. Then I saw a single figure coming down the beach. It seemed to be a priest or a bishop. He carried a crozier, and wore the mitre, cope, soutane, chasuble, and alb for high votive Mass. His vestments were heavily worked with gold, and now and then they were lifted by the sea wind. His face was clean-shaven. I could not make out his features in the fading light. He saw me at my window, raised his hand, and called, "Porpozec ciebie nie prosze dorzanin albo zyolpocz ciwego." Then he hurried along the sand, striking his crozier down like a walking stick, his stride impeded by the voluminousness of his vestments. He passed the window where I stood and disappeared where the curve of the bluff overtakes the curve of the shore.

I worked on Monday, and on Tuesday morning woke at about four from a dream in which I had been playing touch football. I was on the winning team. The score was six to eighteen. It was a scrub Sunday-afternoon game on somebody's lawn. Our wives and daughters watched from the edge of the grass, where there were chairs and tables and things to drink. The winning play was a long end run, and when the touchdown had been scored, a big blonde named Helen Farmer got up and organized the women into a cheering section. "Rah, rah, rah," they said. "Porpozec ciebie nie prosze dorzanin albo zyolpocz ciwego. Rah, rah, rah."

I found none of this disconcerting. It was what I had wanted, in a way. Isn't the unconquerable force in man the love of discovery? The repetition of this sentence had the excitement of discovery for me. The fact that I had been on the winning team made me feel happy, and I went cheerfully down to breakfast, but our kitchen, alas, is a part of dreamland. With its pink, washable walls, chilling lights, built-in television (where prayers were being said), and artificial potted plants, it made me nostalgic for my dream, and when my wife passed me the stylus and Magic Tablet on which we write our breakfast orders, I wrote, "Porpozec ciebie nie prosze dorzanin albo zyolpocz ciwego." She laughed and asked me what I meant. When I repeated the sentence — it seemed, indeed, to be the only thing I wanted to say — she began to cry, and I saw in the bitterness of her tears that I had better take a rest. Dr. Howland came over to give me a sedative, and I took a plane to Florida that afternoon.

Now it is late. I drink a glass of milk and take a sleeping pill. I dream that I see a pretty woman kneeling in a field of wheat. Her light brown hair is full and so are the skirts of her dress. Her clothing seems old-fashioned — it seems before my time — and I wonder how I can know and feel so tenderly toward a stranger who is dressed in clothing that my grandmother might have worn. And yet she seems real — more real than the Tamiami Trail four miles to the east, with its Smorgorama and Giganticburger stands, more real than the back streets of Sarasota. I do not ask her who she is. I know what she will say. But then she smiles and starts to speak before I can turn away. "Porpozec ciebie . . ." she begins. Then either I awake in despair or am waked by the sound of rain on the palms. I think of some farmer who, hearing the noise of rain, will stretch his lame bones and smile, feeling that the rain is falling into his lettuce and his cabbages, his hay and his oats, his parsnips and his corn. I think of some plumber who, waked by the rain, will smile at a vision of the world in which all the drains are miraculously cleansed and free. Right-angle drains, crooked drains, root-choked and rusty drains all gurgle and discharge their waters into the sea. I think that the rain will wake some old lady, who will wonder if she has left her copy of "Dombey and Son" in the garden. Her shawl? Did she cover the chairs? And I know that the sound of the rain will wake some lovers, and that its sound will seem to be a part of that force that has thrust them into one another's arms. Then I sit up in bed and exclaim aloud to myself, "Valor! Love! Virtue! Compassion! Splendor! Kindness! Wisdom! Beauty!" The words seem to have the colors of the earth, and as I recite them I feel my hopefulness mount until I am contented and at peace with the night.

CECIL DAWKINS

A Simple Case

(FROM SOUTHWEST REVIEW)

IN THE LAST HALF of August when the days begin almost imperceptibly to shorten, at around dusk in the Great Plains states the light sometimes gets a blue fall cast to it, and in this blue cast of light when the sun's gone down things take on an unearthly, strange appearance and one has to look carefully, and look again, to be sure of what he sees. It was, to Harold Widkins, a favorite time, not only because he could freely admit to having quit work for the day, but also because of the light itself that seemed to put things in a kind of distant perspective that rendered life a bit closer to his ideal of it.

When Harold walked from the outdoor light into the dim kitchen, he did not at first believe that he saw, standing with his back turned at the sink, a man peculiarly dressed and wearing a mask. His first impulse was to call his wife, who was in the henhouse, to see for herself, for he knew that she would never take his word for it.

But before he did anything at all, the masked man whirled around and grabbed up an oddly shaped gun from beside the cooling pie on the sideboard. It was this action, more than anything else, that convinced Harold Widkins that his eyes, in the blue dusk light, did not deceive him, and he felt a stir of excitement in his breast. He looked from the gun, which he classified as "foreign made," to the mask. It was a small black mask such as children wear at Halloween and ladies in the movies wear to gala masked balls. It had little slits in it that made the burglar's eyes look oriental, lidless and surprised, under the wide brim of the black felt hat.

The masked man stood there, an exotic thing in that familiar kitchen, and shook the gun like a finger at Harold. And Harold, in the midst of his fear and surprise, felt something like delight run through him, as though he were not just watching, but taking part in a kind of performance.

The burglar (as Harold designated him) didn't say anything. He kept casting his lidless eyes about the kitchen as if in some confusion as to what came next. And Harold, like a member of an audience watching an actor forget his lines, strained forward a little, as though he would like to prompt the man, toward whom he already felt a kind of proprietorship. He thought, in a momentary disappointment, that the burglar might be looking for a place to hide.

At that instant, Mildred Widkins came in from the henhouse and stopped abruptly beside Harold, who had not moved from the door.

"See!" Harold said, as though he intended "See, I told you!"

His wife's sharp gasp was the final confirmation of the burglar's real presence.

Then the muzzle of the pistol wavered between them as he said, clearly and unmistakably, "This is it!" The fright in Harold was mixed with a kind of satisfaction at the rightness of the expression.

Then the gun steadied, its aim coming to rest on Harold, singling him out. In the pure and empty silence, they heard the loud Click!

For the first time, Harold moved. He drew open the long drawer in the silver chest beside him on the cabinet, took out his own .38, and turned back in time to see the other man's finger squeeze again.

Harold fired.

The bullet hit the burglar below the left eye, just under the mask, and he fell back with the impact against the sink and slithered slowly to the floor where he sat, dead, propped against the plumbing.

Harold stood looking down at him, feeling, in spite of the accuracy of his shot, in some vague way disappointed. He tiptoed across the bright linoleum as if the man were asleep and bent from the waist to look down at the burglar's face. The left eye was becoming bloodshot, but the right one stared back at Harold in a kind of conspiracy. It was, Harold saw, a blue eye, and that came as a shock to him. Below the mask, the cheeks were shaven and unmarked, except for the clean hole of the bullet. Harold stroked his whiskers and noted the sand color of the sideburns that showed, long and curved, beneath the black felt hat that was still set firmly down on the burglar's head.

Then Harold understood his reason for thinking the man was peculiarly dressed. He was wearing a dark suit of winter clothes on a day when the temperature at noon had gone well over a hundred degrees in the shade.

As he bent there over his victim, Harold seemed to hear his voice telling the story to an audience indistinct but large, pausing for weight while his hands gestured effectively. Then he saw it as if it were on a screen and he could watch himself. He had grown taller and was wearing boots. The gun, when he whipped it out, came from a holster on his hip, and the woman he swept behind him was Mildred as she had been when first he courted her. In the picture, he was as obviously a hero as the burglar, in reality, was obviously a burglar.

Mildred Widkins, her fingers held tightly to her mouth, crept up beside her husband, and together, in silence, for another moment they looked down. Then she removed her fingers from her mouth and whispered, "Don't touch anything. They tell you not to go touching everything."

"I ain't laid a hand on him," Harold said in a loud, argumentative voice.

"Look there!" she said, her voice little more than a whisper.

He looked where she was pointing. The man's right hand, open but with the gun lying loosely on his palm, was missing the tip of its index finger.

"I seen that," Harold lied.

"You never no-such-of-a-thing," his wife said.

But Harold had come to feel so full of an inexplicable sadness that he didn't answer her back. He thought it was because Mildred had a natural capacity for spoiling things.

*   *   *

Harold Widkins was a straggle-haired man with a long trunk and exceptionally short legs. His mouth had deep creases enclosing it on either side like parentheses, and his eyebrows were perpetually raised, as though the whole of his life had turned out to be a surprising disappointment to him.

He was a man who had secretly always waited for something extraordinary to happen to him — love at first sight, discovery of buried treasure, guerrilla warfare, the ability to speak in tongues, wild public acclaim — anything to lift up his life and give it the kind of reality he had, even as a boy, come to expect. He had always loved a circus or a parade. When circuses and parades came to be all but extinct, he attended in place of them several auction sales a week. He had not for years missed a single movie that had come to the Picture Palace in Grand Junction, and his house was the first on that rural route to display, amid anachronistic lightning rods, the aluminum cross that heralded the awesome mystery of television. So Harold knew very well how life ought to be.

The trouble with life, he had often felt, was that you never had any practice for the big things, and that was why it was so easy to make a fool of yourself. When his father died he hadn't known how to act, though it had seemed to him that everybody else knew very well. He thought it must have been because he was young at the time. The others were older and had gone through it all before. Harold had made a fool of himself by weeping until an uncle had pointed out to him that tears were womanish. And then he'd taken it into his head to talk. He didn't seem to be able to stop talking, so the same uncle had been forced to hit him across the face in order to make him act in a more seemly fashion. He envied the burglar his rightness in all that he had done, for he himself had never been able to carry off a big moment, not that there'd been many such opportunities in his life.

For one thing, he usually talked too much for a man. At mealtime, while the women — his wife and his sister-in-law — ate, silent, their eyes on their plates, Harold would talk about his " 'quipment," about the new heavy tractor he planned to trade for, and how if he'd had a corn picker he could have made "several thoud'n dollars" on corn. The truth was, Harold had, here and there about the farm, two tractors, a baler, a mower, a wagon, two rakes, miscellaneous attachments — plows, disks, cultivators — not all of them completely paid for, and at least half of them out of commission in some way, and of the other half at least one or two big pieces that, if the truth were known, Harold either did not know how to operate or was afraid of. One tractor had been parked out of sight behind the barn since a year ago last May. It had a broken motor, and once broken, a motor was of no use to him thereafter. For, to Harold, a motor was as much of a mystery as the workings of the government. But he could talk about both in a knowledgeable way to the womenfolk.

"Cylinder's busted," he would say. "Take a hunnert dollars to fix it." Or, "Long's them dang Reds are in the White House, the farmer's gone to suffer. No use to talk about it. Take a hunnert thoud'n dollars to make a dime the way things are." So Mrs. Widkins raised fryers and hens, fattened calves and butchered hogs, and sold her eggs and butter.

Harold was actually a wise man, but he didn't trust his wisdom. He knew, for instance, that he talked too much and in figures too extravagant, and that people distrust a man who talks overmuch. He knew that his father had drunk, had beaten the children, had not been above taking a hand to his wife. But his father had been a silent man and people all woke up and took notice when he spoke his meager words. He could say "Rain tonight," and if the sky stayed clear they thought the Lord had made an oversight.

Harold knew as a child that he'd never be as big a man as his father, and his growth had borne him out. It wasn't that he was really a smaller man. In his chest and arms and back he was as strong and as big as his father had ever been. It was just that his legs were so stumpy. He realized, in his wisdom, that if he hadn't taken the trouble to explain it, they might all have seen this for themselves. But he would go ahead and explain it, time and again. He'd make up his mind in the morning to start holding his tongue, but by noon something would have to be explained, so talk he would, and see the guarded, polite faces. Or he'd hold his tongue awhile, hoping that his wife or his sister-in-law would speak up for him, tell them that he worked hard, that he tried, did the best he could, that his father had sons to help while he had none, that his father lived before there was " 'quipment" to cope with, and the "gover'ment" and the drought. But the women never did speak for him, so, explaining himself to polite faces, he would know the anguish of the lonely in defense of themselves.

He longed for a team to talk to. Who could talk to a sputtering tractor? He longed for a dog to follow him about from one chore to the next, but the pups, despite his coaxing, always stayed close to the kitchen waiting for a handout. Then, insulted by their indifference and to salvage his pride, he further alienated them by abuse.

He didn't have a way with animals like his father'd had, or a green thumb with crops, or the favor of the Almighty in the weather. Old Sam Widkins had always prayed the blessing at meals, spoke right up to God as His equal. But Harold couldn't pray. His wife was a church woman with a thoroughgoing knowledge of righteousness, and she knew his lusts and failures, his weaknesses and his sins. How could he pray with his wife at the table listening?

But Harold was proud of his wife, proud to have got her foolish long enough to win her, proud to have begot two daughters on her. And he would tell over and over how he'd won her, hoping someday to hit on the truth about it. But truth was mixed up in his mind with what ought to have been, with what he wanted to believe, and with what lore and the television preached at him about courtship and love and family life. And Harold tried to hold onto his faith in those things, even though television itself sometimes troubled his peace of mind. For interspersed in half-minutes between the Western heroes, loving mothers, precocious children, kindly, comic fathers, and singing lovers, spaced here and there amid a world that seemed to Harold all that was good, came the commercials appealing to his wisdom. With constricted breast he watched the white-coated man demonstrate the congestion of sinus; saw the silhouette of the human body, the digestive tract suddenly illumined; listened to all the ills of man; saw pills trickle down the diagramed gullet and fall into the stomach to be rushed to an ailing bloodstream; watched the scientific delineation of a headache — a hammer on the skull. Headache, neuralgia, neuritis, the common cold, sinusitis, indigestion, constipation, diarrhea, hemorrhoids, arthritis, tooth decay, bad breath from gastritis, from mouth germs, body odor, piles, rheumatism and its accompanying ills, iron deficiency anemia, tired blood, acne, broken hair ends, brittle nails, chafed hands, corns, fallen arches, nausea, insomnia, malfunctioning kidney, excess fat. And Harold's breathing would come in short gasps as he gripped the arms of his chair and his wisdom tried to respond, to shout "True! True! All of it true!"

But then the smiling man came on and told him to rest assured, that science had found a way, a miracle medicine, a pill or lotion, plaster, vapor, ointment, a syrup that not only cured but tasted good as well. This filter, that formula added to an herb used by the Indians in older times, and youth, perpetual, can be yours, Harold Widkins. He seemed so genial, so sure of himself, so kind in what he offered to share, this latter-day medicine man, that Harold instantly relaxed. And then the music came and on the screen again the hero battled evil in the form of recognizable villains, and always won. Wives honored husbands, children loved parents, and lovers were always true. The day was saved, and with it Harold's faith.

Along with his faith, he had a great deal of hope. He usually whistled in the morning and found good omen in whatever the sky promised, sun or rain. He'd talk at breakfast about all he intended to do that day, and he would eat hearty, for he was still naïve enough to believe that there was no sight softened a woman's heart and temper quicker than the sight of a man gorged on her own cooking. His wife's heart never softened, nor her temper either. The truth was she had a frugal bent and a meager appetite herself, and the sight of Harold stuffing himself shocked her sense of decency.

And Harold usually summoned hope again as he came back from the fields at night. He would talk at supper about the world, the farm, the 'quipment, again under the impression that women like to be instructed, that they felt safer knowing that he knew so much, that they trusted and respected his patience with their natural ignorance. His wisdom told him better, but he did not trust his wisdom, it being so contrary.

In answer to his wife's telephone summons, the sheriff of Grand Junction came squealing down the highway in a patrol car driven by an officer named Hemingway — a large man strapped and belted, with a pistol at his hip, a visored cap, and a pair of black boots that hugged his shapely legs. Behind them, driving his own dusty Ford, came the newspaperman, who took a picture of Harold looking startled by the events that followed one another too fast and by the flash of the camera.

The light of the flash, flaring and dying the same instant, made the kitchen seem, by contrast, very dim. So Mildred Widkins reached up and pulled the chain on the bulb that hung naked and free from the ceiling. The light came on, yellow and faint after the white splash an instant before. And the electric cord swung in a wide arc when she let it go, so that everything seemed to move in the swaying light, even the corpse, though except for the bulb swinging there over their heads nothing really moved at all.

The sheriff asked Harold how the shooting had come about.

"Well," Harold began, looking from newspaperman to lawmen, all of whom turned curious, impersonal eyes upon him, "I cut hay all morning and raked it around the pond before lunch and this afternoon I was baling and planned on baling until dark but the baler wasn't picking up just right. It'd kick out a forty pounder and then a hunnert pounder, and then the threader broke down and the danged machine was spitting out loose bundles and not cleaning up the windrows and finally I give up and come to the house, tired as I could be, and I opened the back door and seen this burglar standing there . . ." He pointed, realizing as the heads turned to look that he'd gotten a bum start, that they were impatient with his too many words, that they wanted it all in a sentence, explained away. But he'd wanted them to see it just as he had seen it in the blue fall light, wanted them to understand his weariness and delight, his fear and his sudden sorrow.

Hemingway looked at the burglar still sitting there against the pipes, his head at an uncomfortable angle, the blue eye and the red eye staring back at them, and said, "It looks like he was especially made up for this type of an evening."

"Well, get on," the sheriff said. "How'd it happen?"

While Harold took a breath, preparing to speak, his wife shoved in ahead of him and, in a brief statement or two, told it all. Harold was not listening. He was thinking that this was the first time she'd spoken up for him, explained for him. And it was also the very time he could not appreciate it. His face turned warm and dry with the knowledge of his own ingratitude.

When she finished, the sheriff nodded and Hemingway's one

long stride took him to Harold's .38 lying on the cabinet. He handed it to the sheriff and then knelt and picked up the burglar's gun from out of the limp and lifeless hand. He looked at it, holding it under the light, and grunted, "German made." And Harold felt the stir of satisfaction only faintly. He was beginning to realize some vague premonition.

Hemingway clicked the burglar's gun and shook it against his palm. He looked at Harold and then at the sheriff and he said one word, "Empty!" Harold felt a sinking sensation in his stomach as they turned to look at him.

"This gun is empty," Hemingway repeated. "You kilt a man had an empty gun." And for an instant Harold was afraid the patrolman was going to laugh.

Automobile lights swept across the window and brakes squeaked as a third vehicle stopped in the yard and joined its headlight beams to the other two pairs remaining on out there, illuminating the geraniums. The sheriff shrugged. "That'll be Javits." Javits was the coroner and undertaker and funeral parlor operator in Grand Junction. And before Harold had time to come out of his state, they swarmed for a moment around the kitchen and then they were gone, taking the dead man with them.

It seemed cruel to Harold that the gun was empty. And how was he supposed to have known? His wife said it was a clear case and that was all there was to it. In bed that night, Harold went over it all time after time from beginning to end until he had it firmly fixed — the mask, the black felt hat, the winter suit of clothes ("It looks like he was especially made up for this type of an evening"), the foreign-made gun, the words "This is it!" The burglar was obviously The Burglar, as anyone could plainly see. And when he finally slept, he dreamed about the inquest. He'd never been to an inquest, and in his mind he'd confused it with a courtroom trial complete with a poker-faced jury, a black-robed judge, and a very suave lawyer who looked like Melvyn Douglas. And he, Harold Widkins, was on trial for his life. The decision turned on one point. He produced detail after detail — hat, suit, gun, mask — all marked on tags as exhibits A, B, C, etc. But he seemed unable to convince them that The Burglar was indeed The Burglar. The courtroom grew tense. The judge was ready to lower his gavel with a pound. Then Mildred burst loose from the officer holding her back, ran weeping to fall at Harold's knees where he sat in the witness box, and said, "Bring in the corpse and look. You'll find" — pause — "you'll find that, on his right hand, the tip of his index finger is missing."

"I tried to keep my wife out of this," Harold said in a voice with a manly ring to it.

But it was over. He'd won. Everybody crowded in to shake his hand and pound him on the back. And Melvyn Douglas, his face black with anger, muttered something that Harold thought must have been, "I'll get you for this if it's the last thing I do . . ."

He was feeling gravely important, dressed in his blue serge suit with a white shirt and black tie, as he drove himself into town to go to the inquest. He tried to imagine his picture with the story in the newspaper, and the headlines — Hal Widkins Vanquishes Desperado. He liked to think of himself as Hal instead of Harold, but it was seldom any more that he could manage it, though when he was a boy in school he had signed all papers that way — Hal Widkins — with as much of a flourish as he could manage in his naturally crimped hand. The teacher, handing papers back, usually paused and squinted at the name and then said, "Oh, Harold," leaving him somehow mortified.

The inquest was a disappointment. It was in a small office on the balcony floor of the courthouse, where they all sat bunched in a circle on folding chairs. Harold never got it quite straight in his mind just what was the function of each of those in attendance. He wasn't given much of a chance to talk, and it seemed that most of what was necessary had already been written down. The man in charge said it was a simple case.

The Burglar had been identified. His name was Vernon Smith, and the name, taking the place of Burglar, came as a shock to Harold. Not only did the dead man have a name, he also had an address. It was in a town not fifty miles away, a town by the name of Rapids City up on the river. And he was being taken back home on the afternoon train for burial. This stranger, Vernon Smith, also had relations, and they'd already been notified and were expected at any time.

All that seemed to be left for Harold to do was to look once more at the body and to sign something. He followed the sheriff

across the street to the morgue, where they took him to a cool
back room and showed him a body that was lying on a table.

Harold walked up to it and looked down. The face, without
the mask, looked familiar to him. It must have been, he thought,
that it looked like so many other faces — round and ruddy, with
a mouth that seemed to be bruised. He did not remember that
mouth. And the hair that he had not seen before was limp and
fine, light brown and with a cowlick over the forehead. The
rakish sideburns had been shaved off and nowhere did Harold see
the black felt hat.

"That's him," Harold said, but it came out more as a question.

"Well?" the sheriff said, just a little bit impatient.

So Harold looked again. And now he saw that the body was
no longer wearing the dark winter suit of clothes, but blue serge
such as farmers wear on Sunday, such as Harold at this moment
had on.

He swallowed. Nothing about this corpse lying with a certain
decorum on the table identified him as The Burglar, and the
smell in the room was making Harold a little bit sick at his
stomach.

"They done a good job on the wound," the sheriff said, and,
grateful, Harold bent to look. But the patch on the left cheek
looked as if it might have been put on with makeup. Then he
remembered something. He looked at the hands, crossed there
over the chest. The left hand covered the right one, and Harold
had to lift it off in order to see what he was looking for. The
feel of it, cold and stiff as the hand of a wooden image, further
confused him and he almost forgot what he was after. He felt
the sheriff's eyes upon him, curious. "There!" he said, pointing to
the index finger with its tip missing. The sheriff looked and
grunted.

Harold straightened up and reached for the paper in the sheriff's
hand. The sheriff handed it to him and obligingly turned his
back for him to write against. Harold felt a wave of gratitude.
Then the sheriff shook his hand and went out, leaving him done
with and alone.

It was wrong. All of it, wrong. It was not as it should be. But
as Harold turned to leave, he could no longer have said how it
should have been. He only knew that he was unsatisfied, and

empty, and confused, as if he'd heard a song go off-key, or had a tube go out in the final reel and was never to know the ending, or listened to the greatest joke of his life only to have the teller forget the punch line, so that he could not laugh. And this expectation, of tears or laughter or knowledge like a burst of light, built to a force inside him that now might never be released, like a mighty bubble of gas pushing fatally against his heart.

He didn't at once see the people waiting for him to step aside so that they could enter. The sight of the man and woman dressed in their best for some occasion gradually focused out of the blur the world had come to be. They nodded, timid and unsure of themselves, and he returned their nods. The sheriff was out of sight and the undertaker, who'd brought them to the door, now turned his back and walked sedately toward the front of his establishment.

The man glanced around and, when his eyes lighted on the table with its burden, he looked quickly back to Harold. The woman, her face swollen-looking under the self-contained round hat, walked past Harold without looking at him again. But the man stayed in the door and put out his hand. "Smith. Vernon Smith," he said.

Harold felt as if he'd like to run, but he could not move. He remembered the sensation from a certain recurring dream he'd had as a child. Fighting the impulse to hide his hand behind his back, he reached out and shook the offered hand. But though he opened his mouth, he could not seem to think of his own name. Behind him he heard a sob break from the woman like a gasp of fright.

Vernon Smith Senior was a pink-faced man with pale watery eyes that looked as if he were perpetually prepared to weep. "He wasn't quite right," he said. "The boy never was quite right. A mule give him a lick in the head when he was a youngun." He glanced toward his wife and lowered his voice. "It wasn't that he was born thataway. There never was any — any kind of a taint in the family." He looked at the floor, cleared his throat, and brought his eyes up. The watery blue eyes jerked over Harold's face with the persistence of water bugs moving on the face of a pond. "His mother doted on him, though. Grieved over him. She always grieved over him."

He made no move to cross the room to look at his dead son, but seemed rather like a man waiting for a woman to finish with womanish things.

"A woman," he said, his eyes darting to Harold's mouth, forehead, chest, "a woman don't accept things."

Harold nodded.

"I kilt the mule," Mr. Smith said.

Harold nodded again, waiting. But that seemed to be all, the whole of it, and the man, seeing Harold wait for more, looked to oblige him.

"Are you the law?" he asked.

Fear and uncertainty gripped Harold in the intestines, and when it let go he felt that he had to hurry and find a men's room.

The man looked puzzled when Harold didn't answer. "He was a good boy," he said. "Never give us no trouble till now. No taint in the family. At heart he was as good a boy as you would hope to find. Simple, that's all. Just simple." Then he added, "He was named after me," in a voice that implied "the best of everything" and "every opportunity under the circumstances." He cleared his throat as if the gurgle were an old habit, as though something were stuck there that he'd given up hope of ever being rid of.

It was not until Harold was repulsed that he could fully recognize this man who stood before him as a man certain of his innocence stands before justice.

"I'm sorry as I can be," Harold said.

The man nodded, accepting this as only right and due.

"You shouldn't have bothered," Mr. Smith said, "if it was hard for you to get away this morning."

"It wasn't nothing," Harold said, glancing quickly around the room to see if there might be another exit. But when his eyes came to the woman doubled up with grief beside the table, he turned back to the man barring his way.

"I known he had that gun," Mr. Smith said. "But I never thought he'd get into trouble with it long's he had no bullets."

Harold said "Excuse me," and tried to move around Mr. Smith, but his words were not clear, and the man did not make room for him to pass.

"He tried to join the army," Mr. Smith said, and Harold, for one awful moment, thought the man might be going to smile, or might be expecting *him* to smile. When Harold simply stood staring at him, Mr. Smith continued, "He was always dressing himself up one way or another, but I never dreamed it would get him into any trouble. I known there wasn't a place for him anywheres in this life, but I tried to make him keep his eye on the hereafter." His eyes shifted across Harold's face. "I give a lot of my time to the church," he said. "I make calls every Sunday morning and pass the word along, for us that has it's got no right to hoard it to ourselves."

"Are you a preacher?" Harold choked the words out.

Mr. Smith shook his head. "I myself am not. But any questions you might have I can get an answer to. And every answer comes smack from the Bible, the word of God. Listen, if you ain't yet saved, there's not a whole lot of time." He leaned toward Harold, lowering his voice. "Read Revelations. It tells you right there." He pointed a finger at his open palm as though his text might be transcribed upon it. "Armageddon is upon us! 'There shall be wars and pestilence.' Now I don't have to tell you nothing about wars, for you know for yourself as well's I do there's been more wars in our lifetime than you could shake a stick at. And pestilence! Listen, do you keep a garden?"

Harold said his wife kept a garden.

"Have you ever before had more pests to cope with than you had this year?"

Harold agreed there'd been a plague of them.

Mr. Smith straightened up and crossed his arms, satisfied he'd made his point. "Well, there you have it."

Harold waited, not at all sure of what he had. But Mr. Smith had finished, was gazing across Harold's shoulder at the body of his son. His eyes swam and Harold thought that now he would break down, and his sympathy began to rise.

Mr. Smith said, "I give a lot of my time to the church, and I give to the poor, and I believe I'm saved."

Harold knew he had to get out, escape to some place where he could be by himself. He touched Vernon Smith's elbow and moved him aside.

"Pleased to have met you," Mr. Smith said. But Harold was stumbling through the curtained door, hurrying away.

Alone in the street, he stood a minute to get his bearings, lost in this town he'd grown up in. He spent some minutes studying the clock on the front of the courthouse facing out over the square, but he didn't read the time.

Then he walked to the café across the street, though he was not hungry, and entered the long, narrow room lined on one side by dark, old-fashioned booths and on the other by a modern, chrome-lined counter and bright plastic-covered stools. He took a seat in the first booth he came to. The place was empty except for a tall, hump-shouldered waitress reading a copy of *Silver Screen.* Some-one had left a coffee-stained morning paper lying on the table, and his own face stared up at him, unshaven and surprised. The picture cut him off just across the chest, and the galluses of his overalls showed.

It was a shock to see himself lying there defenseless on the table, obviously unprepared. He gave the paper a shove and it slid off onto the seat opposite him.

The waitress came with her pad and pencil, and when he said "coffee" she sniffed, pushed an end of hair back behind her ear, and went away without writing anything.

While he waited for the coffee, he couldn't keep from stretching his neck a little to see the paper. It was cupped against the back of the booth, and his face, somewhat distorted by the bend, looked back at him across the table.

He stared at the face. It was the face of a stranger. He felt that it was the way he had looked, but would never look again, as if the self that he'd been were now gone out of him, transferred to the image on the thin sheet of paper to stare back accusingly at his strange self across the table. He thought of his name, and it seemed to him to be the name of someone he had once known, a long time ago. After a time he recognized his feeling. It was the feeling he'd had as a boy coming out of a Tom Mix picture, as the horse shrank and disappeared, the gun became a toy, the chaps fell off of him and the spurs lay on the street, limp twists of dirtied foil, and he was alone in the late afternoon, in the dying light weak after the bright night of the Picture Palace, alone on an earth contrary, in a world he did not want to know. He saw that Harold had been a fool and Hal but an illusion, and, preparing to rise and leave the booth, he took out his purse, opened it, and read the identification — White, Male, Age 52, brown hair, blue eyes, 5 feet 9 inches tall, weight 162 pounds. He held the card closer, read it again, and carefully refolded the purse and placed it in the inside pocket of his coat as if it might be precious. Then he put a dime on the table, took up his hat, and walked out.

The waitress, stopping so suddenly to see him go that the coffee slopped over the side of the cup, was angered until she remembered that she'd seen him come out of the funeral parlor. She drank the coffee herself, absentmindedly, as she found her place again.

The sunlight seemed too bright to Harold that August day, both blinding and illuminating. On top of the First National Bank a twenty-foot signboard urged him to Insure the Future for Your Loved Ones, Rest in Peace That They Shall Know No Want, The Future Need Not Be Unknown, For Cents a Day — And in front of the First Baptist Church the board advertised Christian Fellowship Each Friday Night at Eight. The drugstore window held the remedy for every ill. But Harold was not reassured.

He turned slowly in the empty square, a lone man, stranger to himself, in suit and vest prescribed, yet naked in the light of this high noon, naked but for the weight that he now felt, heavier than any burden he had known. For previous burdens had all been personal, hence small, like the flu when there is not an epidemic. Now he felt that he was victim of a plague that raged the streets, invisible to all but him. And he must spread the word against it. What was it? What word would he say? To whom would he say it? For once in his life, Harold had no word at his command. He felt that he must find Mr. Smith.

He stumbled like a man in heatstroke to the funeral parlor and found it now deserted. The curtain hung down, unstirred, between himself and that back room. He went toward it, laid hands on it, and drew it aside. The body was gone, the table bare.

"He's gone. He's not here." It was the voice of Javits, the undertaker, behind him. Harold turned, without seeing the man, and went out again. From the station at the end of the street, the train bell tolled for the crossing. He came into the sun in time to see the long cars moving slowly out. And Vernon Smith, struck once by the mule and once by him, was going home. "I kilt the mule," Vernon Smith Senior said again to him. And what was it he had wanted to say to **Vernon Smith, Junior** or Senior, too late? "I kilt us both and now the two of us are dead and I don't know whether to be glad or sorry. We're in this together, Vernon Smith."

He felt that he'd been blinded that he might see, crippled that he might walk, had killed and died that he might be born, become a fool in order to learn to trust his wisdom. He didn't know yet what he was — a giant among giants or a pygmy among pygmies. But at least he felt he was onto it at last, had it in his reach. And as he watched the train disappear, he hoped that the kick of the mule and the kick of the .38 had equaled out for Vernon Smith and that now he was no longer not quite right but right again at last, devoid of gun and mask and winter suit of clothes, in no more need of defense, taint of the father gone, joke told, life spent and innocence recaptured.

There in the direct light of the sun, in the center of Grand Junction's namesake corner, Harold Widkins took off his hat and pledged himself to something as yet unknown.

GEORGE DICKERSON

Chico

(FROM PHOENIX)

I

I WAS hollow-standing before the door. The door was a greenness and had a thick rectangular small glass-window eye. The Eggshell pushed the button again and I could hear it ringing far off. The Eggshell, pushing hard on his white eggshell M. P.'s helmet, as a young chicken hatches into crowing, held his bolt of sudden lightning carbine in his tight hands. He pointed the open mouth of nothingness at me, daring me to run down the long length of the hospital corridor. I did not move.

He fingered the button again and the button created an eye in the rectangular glass eye of the door. The eye looked at me and then at the Eggshell, then back at me. I didn't like the eye. The eye disappeared and I heard the lock click—exploding and my eyes felt the door green falling away, swinging back. The eye belonged to a mountain of flesh and a mop of red hair. I knew his name was Shorty-eye.

Shorty-eye looked at me and said he was the corpsman. He asked me if I had ever existed in an Army neuro-psychiatric ward before. I said, "No, I did not care where I existed." It did not matter.

Shorty-eye took me to a room that was almost empty, with a desk and a scale to weigh my pound fleshness. He took me from my Army uniform and gave me sky-blue pajamas with no buttons, that I might have the pleasure of knotting them at my belly-button. He gave me cloth slippers with no strings, that I could enjoy their flap-flapping, without tearing the strings off to knot together, to strangle myself. I found out that everything was not given to us.

Glass and pencils, buttons and strings, knives and forks, razor blades
and identities were denied. It is wonderful how many tiny every-
things a once-upon-a-time-man can use to suddenly non-exist himself.

Shorty-eye took my clothes and with them locked up the statistical
data of my existence: my birthplace, age, name — Tom, and my
one false tooth.

Across the corridor from the room I was occupying were the
doors, holding cells together. Shorty-eye led me toward them and
then left-turned onto the corridor-long-running-tunnel. As I barely
walked I could hear the tearing of rose petals. They cut my feet
when I walked on them. I closed my sight, and Shorty-eye pulled
me firmly through my arm down the corridor.

When I opened my sight, a bug of a doctor stood before me,
with a grin reaching out to grab his recorder ears and dissecting
microscopic glasses. I later knew his name. Specs asked me why
I had been chain-dragged here. I tried to tell him simply that I had
a loneliness. I told him I was crazy and that I saw people walking
down the long black of streets, carrying their walls with them.
When I tried to touch them, I broke my fingers on their walls; and
once I had cried because I had known a girl with inverted breasts
and rouge caked into her jawbone. I told him that I could hear
shouting and crying behind their slate faces and I had tried to
save them, but I had failed. Now when I walk, I hear rose petals
tearing, and they cut my feet. I told him that I tried to drain the
blood by razor-blading my wrist, and I would gladly relieve him
of my eternal presence by doing it again.

His grin reached up and grabbed his ears, then fell down, and
he said quietly that he would try to help me, that everything they
would do would make me feel better. I later had many little meet-
ings with Specs, but I never could remember from one word to one
word what his mouth was moving about.

I occupied the same room with Specs for a non-remembered no-
timeness; and then Short-eye pulled me through another falling
away door-green and I was in the ward, the long cross of this world.
The ward fell away between two rows of beds, and on either side
it dangled its hands: the latrine and the bullpen. I see the burnished copper almost-mirrors of the latrine, denied glass, riveted to
the texture of the wooden walls. I see the bullpen in blind hot

sunlight, guarded securely by a steel barbed-wire fence, keeping the outside world from getting at me. And I see the heavy screens on the windows and the large shovel tablespoons, with which we eat our fuel on the tables at the far end of the cross.

But mostly I see the Sky-blues. I see them standing in their sky-blue pajamas staring at me with sucking eyes from the far end. I do not want to see them. I do not want my sounds to be taken into their ears. I do not want my sweat to be taken into their noses, nor my fingers to touch their feel. I just want myself alone, crouching behind my ribs. But I find myself liking them because they have no stone in their cheeks, nor slate for skin. I create them as they approach me, and they become grotesque truths to me.

I know them in a few days. One is Rubberjaws, a prisoner. I find out he is a prisoner by a mistake of the legal system. Rubberjaws finds himself existing here because he has been in the stockade and someone kicked him, his jaws broken into unconsciousness. Now he snaps his jaws with rubber bands, holding them in place, and the army has no better place to keep him than here.

Shaky simply shakes. That is a simple enough existence and Shaky loves simplicity and alcohol. I think mostly he shakes because he has afraidness. Shaky shakes most when he sees Monster. Monster is six-foot-five and silent. Monster hates himself. "I am a monster," he says quietly, with a hidden explosion. No one knows why he hates the strength that is him. Somewhere down inside the tall blond pillar that he is, red-hot-riveted his soul shouts, and someone has forgotten to put out the fire. The corpsmen are afraid of Monster. When they gently walk him, two or three of the biggest of them with their arms padlocking his, I see Monster stop, with a sudden stillness — perhaps trying to catch something that flickered inside — and two or three corpsmen whipcrack back on their armchains. But always Monster is just there and I can feel him. He paces up and down, looming great in the ward or in the bullpen, or standing pillar-like, staring somewhere-nowhere out the distance through the heavy steel screens.

There are others, including the Professor who is always nose buried in the thin transparency of words; and I can touch them all. I can put my finger right through and around them and hold them inside my ribs. I do not want to know or taste or feel them, but I have them poured into me by Chico. Chico is like some

miracle, some untouchable fantasy in the broken sunlight of my
childhood. He picks me up in the tremble of his fingers, caress-
pushing the craziness out of me, picking up the rose petals and
making them suddenly soft. He stops the brittle beating of my
fists and he is so large that he sucks me away from the ribcage.
Specs is giving me shock-electric salvation, but Chico forgets me
my craziness whenever I feel him. And I fear Chico because he
makes me church tremble, because I think I heard him singing in
the shadows, opening everything bright and clear.

II

Chico is the sunshine and the earth and the tree. He is the shortest of the Sky-blues, the friendliest, and the most mistreated.

In size he can tower to five-feet-three flexing gigantically every
one of his wiry muscles. He talk broke Eeenglish bout Puerto Rico
and his home, bout sea and children, small — they run round reel
queek and boom-boom fat tommies steeck out.

Chico has no other name, or if he does, I never know it. To the
corpsmen he is Chico, and to the other Sky-blues he is Chico-under-
the-bed.

Chico is there when I come. The first morning I get up in the
ward with the other Sky-b's, he is asleep under his bed on the floor.
The corpsman, Gastro (the big-belching-stomached-one), is yelling
at Chico.

"Chico! What are you doing under the bed again? I'll have to
report you to the doctor. You're just like everyone else." (Gastro
getting red around the gills.) "You have no special privileges!"
(Louder. Chico lying with hands behind head, looking into Gastro
with child-blue-eyes.) "Get up from there and make your bed."

"You-Coorpsman," Chico says. "I got wreenkles here (pointing
to face) — am thurty-fie. Go boom-boom at Gooooks een Krea.
Gooooks fall boom-boom and no go run round fat boom-boom
tummies out. You-Cooorpsman, I sleep on groun, no sleep een bad
when een Krea. Can no sleep een bad. B-b bad ees bad to sleeep
een. Floor ees gooo to sleep. Keeep tough."

Then Gastro takes Chico by the arm and pulls him out from
under his bed. Gastro is brave. He is six feet and has keys to the
door. Chico is large. He is five-feet-three-smiling-child-blue-eyed.
He remembers sometime when the Praysident of the You-knighted

States stands and geev heem cooongrees medal honor. He remember he stand crying and Praysident stand and tell bout goooks he go boom-boom at (no go run round no) in Korea and bout grenade peeces een his legs.

Gastro is pulling him and large Chico is going limp-silly with him because Gastro is brave and has never seen war and Chico has a disease that is eating the brave out of his mind and body and has left him childlike from shooting goooooks eeeen Krea.

"You-Coorpsman, I come. No pull, I come." (Smiling child-blue.) You-Cooorpsman, hurt." (Then giggling, shake-shaking, remembering Praysident, shake-shaking his hand.)

Chico is on his two flap-flapping feet, shuffling easily before Gastro. Gastro looks at Chico's magnificent crop of almost no-hair and then his smile-wrinkles and the child-blue innocent eyes.

"Don't sleep under the bed anymore!" Gastro belches.

Chico is shuf-shuffling. "Thank you-Coorpsman for waking me up." And Gastro turns and goes away because he will find Chico smiling from under his bed tomorrow — thank you, Coorpsman.

(Chico is hop-looking at me. I am floating somehow in the floor middle, trying to grab hold, trying to pull my ribs together. I try shutting my sight, squeezing it, hand-push-hard. I shut my sight, but he is somehow there, pulling my insides open with his gentle eye-fingers. I feel sick. My insides run up my throat — out. I weakly and woobly. Chico is eyeing me and it is open blueness. It is stained windows, stained hands with blue. Chico touches and I do not have to break my fingers on his stucco face, my fingers go right through to where I am not dirty. I floating in a thin strand of sunlight airness, I feeling his simple, feeling the stretch out reach touch of a child-flower. Chico runs into my ribs and sing shouts there.)

Chico loves all small things. He loves to stand in line. He loves the shaving or the eating or the shower lines. He will giggle in line. I see Chico shouting-giggle-shuffling. "Hey-you-Coorpsman. My turn nex? My turn nex? (Knowing it won't be his turn, knowing Coorpsman will get mad.) Lines are something special. They are each Christmas: waiting for the surprise package, can't sleep excitement waiting, finding the razor with the blade in it every morning. Surprised to find the blade always in it every morning. Surprised to find his face almost in the burnished copper riveted-

to-the-wall mirrors. Surprised when the razor with the razor blade
already in it takes away the rough ecstasy-feeling stubble from his
face almost in the mirror.

"You-Coorpsman. We shave thees morning. Yoo like to shave?
Shave after me." (Coorpsman is thinking how tedious it is to shave,
thinking how crazy Chico is.) Chico is in spasms of happiness and
hole worl ees wanderful.

The other Sky-blues, Monster (silently), and Shaky, and Rubberjaws, are watching and smiling inside at the sunshine of Chico
and the bubbling inside. They are watching Chico take the brush-
less shaving cream tube and squeeze it. He is watching the cream.
It is a white worm. It peeks out at him. He giggles and stops
squeezing. It sucks itself back. It peeks out. It backs in. It is
wonderful. Then he squeezes it all long-squirm out laughing. He
doesn't use it to shave with. He just likes to watch it squirm out.
He is laughing. Monster is almost laughing inside and Shaky is
roaring and Rubberjaws is hurt-stretch-laughing. The corpsman
is angry and shouting at Chico, who is laughing. Chico is special
sunshine for us and because people from the outside, like the corpsman, do not understand special sunshine, they lock Chico up and
save him for us.

(I am beginning to feel still. There are not so many rose petals
when I walk, ripping up through my knees. I am quieting, soft-
feather-down inside. I take Chico up into my sight, holding — I
can't let go. Suddenly I am piece-broken again. Inside I corrode,
rust-rotten, because Chico is so circular, so non-breakable. He is
almost — but I hyena laugh into myself. I do not take him into
my eyes. I step him out of my think, but he pops in eel-slippery.)

Chico is also evil. One morning after being pulled out from
under his bed and stand-shuffling in line, Chico gets before the almost mirror and looks slyly at the coorpsman. Coorpsman is not
seeing. Chico quickly unscrews razor and takes the blade out.
Sin!! Chico holds blade out at coorpsman. "Here Coorpsman,
blade is no een razor thees morning? What ees wrong?" Chico
stands on one foot with his tongue in his cheek. Chico is suddenly
roar-laughing. The coorpsman is suddenly roar-shouting scared-
mad. The corpsman tells Chico to lay the razor blade on the sink.
Chico stands there laughing, hopping faster on one foot. The
corpsman is shouting louder. Another corpsman comes and is

talking to Chico. Chico is laughing hysterically, hist-erackacka-ackalylyly. They call the corpsman Short-eye, whom Chico likes to talk to about his boom-boom tummied children. Short-eye comes and tells Chico to put the blade down. Chico looks at Short-eye and then at large Gastro, who stands behind the other two. Chico is roaring, and then he puts down the blade and walks toward the door, unable to contain his bubbling.

Gastro jumps for the dangerous blade. Short-eye and the other corpsman grab hold of great Chico. They tell Chico that he is going into solitary confinement for this. They try to act tough.

"Chico, you are going into the cell by yourself. If you do that again, we'll put you into a cell and never let you out."

"You-Coorpsman, I go, okay."

Chico looks almost sad, as if he were going away for good. He walks up the aisle between the beds towards the door. Softly he says, "Gooby Toemmee, Gooby Ruuuberjas, Gooby Moonster — Chico go away — Gooby." The door closes behind his greatness and we are saddest because our special sunshine is gone. But I am smiling inside because I know he will find something special. He will be surprised at being suddenly alone. He will like the sound of nothing. He will watch the sun rectangles move on the floor and have lots of time to dream about his boom-boom kid tummies. Best of all, he will be laugh-bubbling back among us, suddenly surprised at not being alone.

III

Chico has a tree. It is not so much of a tree, but to Chico it is a giant tree, and he climbs to the sky on it. Each day when we go out to the bullpen there is the pinochle game or the basketball or Professor reading a book. But Chico does not understand complex things like basketball. He watches the flap-flap of slippers on the dirt court and the big roundness of the ball as it flies from one Sky-blue to another. It is not important the beeg rounness go through circle een sky. It is too hot to be important. He watches the flap-flap of cards: kings queens aces. It is not important. He does not understand why Shaky gets so nervous when he doesn't win. He watches the flap-flap of Professor reading a book, turned-over pages. It does not matter what is written. They look nice — words. Streeeeetch waaaaaaay ooooooooooooouuuuuuuuuuuuut or

short wuds. He likes simplicity. *That,* he can understand: like the
word "tree." Chico likes tree, so he goes around boolpain and finds
a tree. Nobody noticed the tree before. It seems it must have suddenly grown there overnight. It is a giant tree — perhaps twelve
inches high.

"Seee, You-Chico, find heem treee. You-Tree, Treee." (Softly.)
Bubbling: "Hey, You-Toemmee, Chico find heem Tree."

Chico comes over to me where I am in the shade and pulls at my
arm. "You-Tree." I have to go over and see Chico's tree. It is a
maple tree over in the far corner of the bullpen. It comes only
halfway up Chico's calf. Chico is bubbling and hopping up and
down on one foot. "I haav treee."

Whispering, he says: "How eet say in Bibull — God make a
tree but cannot eat treee or geet keeecked out Pardice? Well, thees
ees good tree! Theees ees Chico's treee."

(I start to think his tree is silly. I start to try to run solitary into
myself, but Chico has me wide open and I can feel open chairs and
windows, and there is only present timeness. I am no past and no
ahead. He is warming me.)

I nod and smile quietly at Chico's tree.

Chico child-blues me. "I tell you bout treees." Chico tells me
bout trees in darkness and how trees, he thinks, are very lonely.
"Arrr you loonely?" He child-blue eyes me. "Yees, I theenk so."
Trees arr loonely. They geet loonely cause have stay een wan place.
They like people talk weeth them. I play een them when I waas
boom-boom tummy kiddie. Then they lak mee and they no loonger
loonely." He pouts a little. "Yooo understan, thees treee ees my
Pardice treee."

(I fall inside of myself and swim back out. It is easy to swim
out now, floating up the waves of sunlight. I look at the scar on
my wrist-dangle. I laugh-bubble inside. "Paradise.")

"I understand, it is your Pardice tree. — Pardice."

Then I go back over to the wall and the shade, and I watch
Chico and his tree. Chico is all lost in his tree. His mind is hiding
up in the leaves somewhere. He remembers falling boomp down
from a tree and he smiles. He touches gently one of the leaves,
making it real, and then he sits on the ground and smiles at Paradise. Everyday in the bullpen it is like this, and Chico carries out
a paper cup full of water to grow his tree sky high. Sometimes:
"Tree ees noo loonely now, hey you-Toemmee."

Chico is happy with his tree until the day of the tree-riot. Jungle-bunny starts the trouble. Junglebunny is a marine who did not like his duty assignment, and so he went in one day and pissed on his commanding officer's desk. Junglebunny is about eighteen, and he does not understand the simplicity and the sunshine of Chico-under-the-bed. He understands only stubborn. He has a scar on his left cheek, where he got into a fight about who was going to take a whore home. Junglebunny is one of the few Sky-blues I do not find in my ribcage. He yelps and howls and bites my feel, preying on Chico. But Chico never pays any attention to Jungle-bunny when he kids Chico about his sleeping under the bed. "Hah! Chico is a dog. He sleeps on the ground like a dog!"

Chico does not understand meanness and so he hangs his hands doglike in front of him and pants his tongue out doglike. I laugh and Shaky laughs and then Junglebunny does not understand that it is funny. "See! Chico knows he is a dog. Here doggy! Here doggy!"

Then we take Chico by the arms and laugh with him down to the tables for chow and leave Junglebunny hurt-mad inside. He does not understand why we like Chico better than him.

Junglebunny hates Chico's tree. When he finds out about Chico's tree, he runs around to all the Sky-blues in the bullpen and tells them about it. "Chico thinks he has a tree. It's only a foot high. He thinks he's going to grow the tree overnight so he can escape over the roof. Ha! Ha! He thinks he can escape."

The Professor does not even look up from his book.

"Corpsman! Chico's got a tree that he thinks he will escape on. Ha! Ha! He's crazy." The Corpsman smiles at Chico. Chico comes running over to the Corpsman. "Dooono take my treee. You-Joooonglebooonie." Chico spits. The Corpsman tells him they will not take his tree and then Chico is happy again, and he goes back to guard his loneliness.

Junglebunny sits over in the corner by the fence and scowls. He waits for his chance to make fun of Chico, and Chico sits over by his tree, guarding it from Joooonglebooonie.

It is two days after Junglebunny discovers Chico's tree that Jun-glebunny gets his revenge and the tree riot precipitates. Chico sleeps under his bed as usual, and Gastro has to pull him out as usual, but Chico does not want to stand in line this morning. He does not want to shave. It is visitor's day and Chico's family is coming to see him. Chico says, "Me noo shave tooday. My woooman coom. My woooman like me weeth beerd. Noo like mee all smoooth. No shave."

Gastro tells him he has to shave. It is a ward regulation.

"No shave!"

"We'll have to put you in solitary if you don't shave."

"No shave!"

"You won't be able to see your visitors."

"No shave! Dooono want too seee wooman eef I haav tooo shave."

Junglebunny laughs when they take Chico away to his cell.

"Goooby Toemmee, Gooby Shakee, Gooby Ruubberjas — Chico no shave."

(Shorty-eye walks me in to see Specs. Specs puts the electric salvation shock on me and I feel it tingle deeply. I sit quite in the stiff wood of chair. I see myself run up against the hollow bones of sunlight, then I spill on the floor with a clatter. I do not want to talk to the other Sky-blues. I try to reach out and touch Chico, but he slips far-greased away. I see Junglebunny smirking down the long length of a hollow. I want to be myself and sit. I sit stiff in the quite wood chair, clattering bounce on the floor. Junglebunny smirks near and leers that he has fixed Chico, torn Chico out on the wood tight of the ward. "Ha. Ha. I fix Chico. Ha. Ha. Ha. Ha. Ha. Ha. Ha. Ha. Ha." I push him back with my brittle fists, and quite wood the chair sits in me.)

Gastro brings Chico out to see his visitors. "No shave."

(I am knocked suddenly off my chair, but I feel a little elastic-stretched from Chico.)

When we are ushered out to the bullpen after dinner, the storm breaks. Chico goes to water his lovely tree. Suddenly: "You-Treeeeee. Soomboodie hurt You-Treeeeee." Chico is tear-crying and water-spilling down-falling on his sky-blue, and he is down-falling inside. "You-Tree" is torn up out of the ground, and broken-bodied leaf-bleeding. Torn Paradise.

Junglebunny makes the mistake of laughing. "What happened, Chico? Can't you escape now? Ha! Ha!" Suddenly Chico spins and is running fullspeedahead-bullfashion at Jooongleboooonie. Booom! Joongleboooonie is crashed down when Chico bull-butts him in the belly with his almost no-hair head. Chico is child-cry-

ing. Junglebunny is yelling, "Murder!" The corpsman runs over
to grab Chico, and Chico butts him suddenly crash landing in the
belly. Chico is laugh-crying now and runs for Joooongleboooooonie,
who accidentally gets up. Down falling is j-b. Back to the
cooooooorpsman, who accidentally gets up. Down bouncing is c-m.

Chico suddenly stops. He remembers the tree and runs over to
it. He kneels by it and touches the broken-bone tree. He feels the
wound in the ground and tries to stick the tree back in. It falls
over jaggedly.

Later, Specs talks to Chico, and then Chico and I go out with a
new corpsman to bury Chico's tree. Chico is sad and is like a priest.
He folds all the torn branches up together and caresses the leaves
with his soft-feeling hands. He lays them all in a pile and scuffs
some dirt over them with his hand-grenade legs. Then he mum-
bles something over the tree which I cannot understand, and I am
glad because I do not want to remember that much.

The corpsman is shuf-shuffling. Chico looks softly down and then
says, "You-Toemmee, you know. Sooomboodie breaks my treee
oop. Sooombooodie no go Pardice." Then he smiles surprised.
"Treee is no loooely mooore."

(I am looking at Chico, and he is fading a little. I stretch-feel
him die at my finger trembles. I grab, try to hold, but he slipping
greasely away — a little out . . .)

IV

(Gray this morning. Torn I twisted under Spec's touch — Specs
poking and pressing Chico from the shadows secret. Chico fading
and I stiffening, Specs Christing Chico, and I tearing and lonely.)

Sometimes Chico is almost what people in the outside world
would call rational. Even when he is almost-rational, he is never
quite like anyone else. One day Chico comes to me and says, "I
am going die veree sooon, hey-Toemmee." I am not sure whether
he is asking me or telling me. "Yes, I goona die. Doctor says I no
goona die. But I knoow. Doctor come roun in mooorning. Looook
at mee. Heee say: Why you-Chico sleeep unnder bad? I say, cause
I lak sleep unnder bad. He no ask meee: Why you-Chico goona
die? I nooo can say: cause I wanna die. He say I noo goona die!
He lie tooo mee. I can tell. I feeel. Soometime I lay wake night
and knooow. Sooometime whan I weeth my woooman sheee knoow

and shee cry. Doctor noo ask why my woooman cry. He oonly ask why you-Chico sleep unnder bad. Gooood Doctor." Chico stares down at his feet and follows a crack in the floor with his toe.

I try to tell Chico that he is not going to die, and he looks up at me into my eyes and sees that I am lying to him. He can see that I know he has a disease that is eating his brain up and that some-day he will wake up to find himself not here. Still, I have trouble believing it myself, and I am lying to myself more than I am trying to lie to him. I cannot picture him being anywhere but here on this ward with us. But Chico is hurt because he thinks I am like the Doctor who does not care about him.

"Doona lie to meee, you-Toemmee." (Far away.) "Yooo knoow, don yooo-Toemmee? I knoow whan I wake up, and I knoow I have not beeen membering where I am. Yoooo knoow where yooo arr all time, hey you-Toemmee?"

I want to tell him that sometimes I do not know where I am, that sometimes I feel all crazy inside, but I know that he will under-stand, and I do not expect him to understand, so I nod my head and follow a crack in the floor with my toe.

Quietly, he is speaking, — quietly so the others cannot hear, be-cause he is giving his insides to me, and I do not want them because they remind me of my insides, and I want them because I do not want to forget my insides.

(I am diving inside, but it is hard to swim back. Hyena laugh-like, I swing jaggedly at the end of my elastic. Specs is grin-catching at his ears, finger-tappings together. I feel dying. I try. I up-diving. Chico talking.)

"I have a wooman. Thass why I noo wanna die. Shee coom see meee here. Yooo have a woooman?" I do not answer him. He is gentle and goes on anyway.

He tells me about his woman. His woooooooman wears red be-cause he likes red. His woman makes kiddies for him, makes him three kiddies. His kiddies have nice teeth, and they like to listen to seashells. They hold them by their ears, and they show their white-teeth-smiling at the roar. Then they hold the shell up to Chico's ear and he hears the roar, the roar of sea, of blood-pound-ing-life in the ear. I feel the roar a little, too.

(Junglebunny leers near nowhere out of sudden space and we are dead, then his slope-shouldered grinning back disintegrates, and we are alive again.)

He tells me about his woman comes to see him. He wants to go to bed with her but cannot go to bed with her because he is here, because there is no aloneness with her, because Gastro is looking or Shorty-eye is eyeing. He waits until he thinks Shorty-eye is not looking, then he touches her breast, and he goes all crazy hot inside. Shorty-eye is looking, and Chico can see him smiling.

"Eet ees no fooonny, noo Toemmee?"

"No, it's not funny." I think of Shorty-eye thinking it funny and laughing over it. I think of him laughing when Chico and his woman are crazy-hot inside to be oneness with each other, and Shorty-eye laughing, and Junglebunny leering. Why can't they let him go home to his wife and his seashell-roar-loving kiddies? If he is going to die, why can't they let him die in floating-down one with his woman?

He is still talking. "Eeet ees no foonny — I like play kiddies games weeth my kiddies. Play Gian Steep: Leetle Steep. I goo to kiddies: You-kiddies may take twooo Gian steeps foowad. They geegle all hoppiness. I like my woooman too kees een my ear. Yooo like that? I tell kiddies: You—kiddies may take twoo Leetle Steeeps backwud. They go cry-cry een no hoppiness."

Chico is thinking about Gian Step–Little Step, when he suddenly is the other Chico, the no-membering Chico. He walks away grenade-legged, as if he has not been talking to me, and goes over to the window. It is raining, and I can see by the way that he looks out the screens that he has never seen it rain before. I can see that he wants to be let out in it suddenly, to feel it newly running down his child-face and into his wooman-keesed ears.

"Hey you-Toemmee, eet rains."

Now he is Chico-under-the-bed again. He is the director with his child-blues going: You may take two Giant Steps into happiness, Tommy. You may take one Giant Step into remembering yourself, Monster. You may take two baby steps back into hurtness, Junglebunny. — I am sorry, Junglebunny, I do not mean it, but you break up my tree — Coooorpsman, you cannot play because you do not understand the game.

V

Chico was to me all this leafness and all this tree. He was the sudden hopping inside of me. One dark I was sinking on the hard of my bed-forgetting, sweat-crying on my forehead. He says to me:

"Hey yoo-Toemmee — you sleep — noo?" I can hear his whisper crawl — stumble through the night.

"No. I'm not sleeping," I say, sweating, to him.

"Thaas baad," he stumbles to me. "Sooomday wee all sleeep. Noo, Toemmee?" He is telling me he will die down floating soon. I do not want to hold it in my ears. He is telling that I will forget him when he is die floating down. I tell him he will not die, and I know I am lying. He is going away sadly, nod nod his tired no-hair. I know he going to die down soon.

In the sunrise, I remember Specs calling me to his room. I remember tight sit in that room, staring at the round flesh of his face — the microscopic pierce of his thin sharp eyes behind his glasses.

The tight of that tomb room shone glare-white on the walls, stiff-lined on the sharp wood of his desk. Specs is hum-mumbling something to my forgot-conscious. I feel stiffening in me. I feel the daylight become hard glass.

He is saying, "You don't really think that Chico is Christ." He says it softly, understandingly with his complex rational. "He has flesh and blood just as you do, doesn't he? You don't really believe he's Christ?"

I stumble. "I guess not."

"If he were Christ, then he wouldn't be made of flesh or blood, — and he wouldn't be here unless it were Judgment Day. And if it were Judgment Day, we wouldn't be as we are now — sitting here as we are."

"I — I don't know." I said. "I didn't mean he is Christ. I don't know what I thought. I mean he is like Christ. He is simple and — oh, God!! ! — I can't explain. I don't know. I don't know."

I talk with Specs and he makes me know that Chico is not Christ, that I am all right, and I am not crazy. And when I am leaving his office, I feel strange. I feel as if I had been away from my body for a long time. I feel strange standing there in the suddenly length of the ward. I suddenly want to leave there. I suddenly am ashamed I am there. I can feel a stretching at my throat. The other patients are out in the hot sunlight of the bullpen and I do not want to go out there with them. I am ashamed to look at them. I feel funny about Chico. I am afraid to look at him. I go out to the sharp sunlight of the bullpen and I see Chico.

Chico runs human fashion up to me and says, "Hey yoo-Toemmee. Hey-yoo-Toemmee. Hey-yoo-Shakee, Toemmee ees heere. Toemmee cooms back from Doctor. How yoo, hey-Toemmee?"

He looks like a jiggling tired idiot. Except I know that he is not. But I am not sure, and I do not know what to say to him. I am ashamed for his jiggling and his no-hairness. "I'm all right, I guess." That is all I can say, and I go and sit down by the fence, feeling the hot steel wire through my pajamas, feeling very fatigued.

Chico looks hurt and puzzled for a moment, then he smiles sudden-brightly white in the sunshine and goes to talk to another patient. I do not know what to think. I am all mixed up, and I am ashamed I am here. I can see two soldiers talking as they walk down the road past the ward, and I turn my face away from them so they cannot see it.

(I am sitting in the sunlight steel hot fence on my back, and feeling Chico run out to the stretch end, then back and out, and I am a little slate-faced. I want to forget about him. I want to feel soldier-talking down the road. I look up at the wax sky, melting in the sun, and want to be outside.)

That night Chico died. I was lying on my bed in the dark, smoking a cigarette, feeling the smoke of it go down into my lungs, feeling it go slowly out of my nose and mouth. Chico gave a call from under his bed to the corpsman, they pulled at his arm and leg, trying to get him off the floor. He resisted them. I did not go near him, because I did not want to see him die. I saw the doctors standing over him, and the rush of the corpsmen back and forth, like little white bugs devouring something. I saw Shaky sitting afraid in his bed. I saw Monster looking down questionably at his large strong fingers. I heard Doctors talking among themselves, not quite saying loud enough to hear what had killed him.

They took him out on a cart, covered with the white grave of a sheet. I watched the whiteness move past my bed — out through the heavy steel door that closed after him with a dead click.

The next day, I saw the doctor again, and I felt better. He told me they would let me out pretty soon. I was glad about that. I didn't want to stay here anymore. I went back to the ward and couldn't talk to Rubberjaws or Shaky.

Three days later, they had a funeral for Chico in the hospital chapel. I didn't want to go, but the corpsman offered to take anybody that wanted to go. Shaky and Rubberjaws and Monster and Professor and even Junglebunny wanted to go, so I fell in at the back of the line.

We stood in the chapel, and I listened to the Priest saying something in Latin. I was watching Chico's wife, and she was crying softly. I was feeling the walls, dark-pressing in on me. After the Priest was finished, I went up to look at Chico. His face had the soft plasticity of flesh, but I was afraid to touch it. I wanted to touch it to make sure, but I couldn't. Suddenly I could feel him glowing. It was he floating out of his skywards body. I could see him hopping in front of me. He is smile-smiling in his child-blueness down into the deeply hot-riveted inside me. I am catch-quickening his sudden laughter. I want him to say "Hey-yoo. Hey-yoo– God, I coom to play seee-shell and Gian Steep weeth you. I coom to say, — take twoo Gian steeps eento worl. I coom flap-flap jig-jiggling. Hey-yoo–Gooooood."

Then there was nothing.

(He ran out and snapped the elastic.)

I was standing there, looking at the dead of a man, the dead flesh of a blind face. I did not know what to do. I was sorry I had doubted him. I could still feel him a little, moving in and out of that coffin. But I know now that it was my imagination, that I was only crazy for a little bit.

(I felt solid and well, brick plaster up against my once-filmsy ribs. I felt as if the something of Chico in my mind was soap-bubble burst. It was a hazy stinging film in the air.)

We went back to the ward, and I lay on my bed, and Chico and Junglebunny and Specs, Shaky and Monster, all bounced in and out of my mind like round balls of glass, brilliant complicated marbles. I played with them, and finally put them into my pocket. I laughed, not sure whether I had won or lost, and passed through the green door.

And now that I have left, I have almost forgotten about it all — but sometimes I think about the past and about Chico, and I turn around sometimes in the bright flowers of the sunlight and see him hop-happy smiling into me.

MAY DIKEMAN

The Sound of Young Laughter

(FROM THE ATLANTIC MONTHLY)

WHAT is *wrong* with him?" Victoria asked in a whisper when their hostess went up to look in on her husband.

"I don't know," murmured Kenneth. It was true, but he had the professional student's tightlipped way of expressing ignorance as if only being discreet. Victoria shrugged her shoulders, which were so luminously tanned that they looked wet, and stared off down the terrace.

Sometimes this was all it took to get Victoria sore at him. Ordinarily, it didn't get Kenneth down too much. From his mother, he was conditioned to nerves in women. And it was a sign of sensitivity. Also, he believed it could be that the more surface misunderstandings, the deeper the basic relationship, and that their getting married (it was set for fall) would relax Vicky. Besides, after a fuss, Victoria always gave in and told Kenneth she wasn't good enough for him, and that he was a much, much better *person* than she was, although Kenneth's roommate, Joe, who had called Victoria a terrific-looking tomato who would be hard to handle, said, "I do not regard it as a good sign when a girl tells me she is not good enough for me. When a girl tells me I am a much, much better *person* than she is, I say, man, watch *out*."

But Kenneth had banked a lot on this weekend at the Voerds'. He wanted to show Victoria and Erika Voerd, his philosophy chairman, off to each other. He wanted to get Victoria into the atmosphere of what he believed, although he hadn't met Axel Voerd yet, to be a mature marriage. Knowing that Axel Voerd was supposed to be convalescing from something, he had demurred a bit when Mrs. Voerd invited them, but she insisted it would do Axel good. "So come," she had exclaimed. "Bring Victoria, your fiancée — she is a good creature, your Vicky!" This description was so inept that it struck Kenneth as a possible unique insight.

Now, as he looked across at Victoria's narrow, bronzed, shield-shaped kneecaps under a tennis-anyone sort of getup so white it looked combustible in the sunshine, the very dazzle made him dread a fiasco — a quarrel the Voerds would notice, or even Victoria calling it off with him. The last idea gave Kenneth a joint-locking fear that made his own body seem constrictive, as if he were tied up. However, it was by this feeling, which he'd never had before, that he knew he was really in love with his fiancée.

Fiancée was a word he never expected to be throwing around, but Victoria, as he sometimes sang to her to "My Sugar Is So Refined," was the fiancée kind of girl. She was an ash-blonde, with an ash-blonde's gray eyes, so light that the pupils seemed set for distance, as if she were spotting a boat, the evening star, or the guest who just came in. Her suntan didn't give her that bumptiously sturdy look it gave some girls; it gave her eyes bigger shadows and made her arms and legs look fracturable as well as sinewy, so that Kenneth had to admit to all kinds of phony parlance involving thoroughbreds and so forth. She looked so weekend-in-Connecticut now; she had this quality of gracing the occasion, making the immediate present as nostalgic as a chorus of "Aurelie." And if this were a thing that went along with belonging to the when-daddy-overexpanded set, Kenneth felt that it was, as they said in the humanities, "valid."

Kenneth had real reasons for insecurity. The big one was that he was privately, helplessly aware, as if of impotence, that he was committed to never making any money in his life unless by fellowships or grants. This wasn't even as manageable as a case of deceiving himself, but rather as if some outer, obdurate self were deceiving *him*. Then, there was an almost cubist discrepancy in his looks. Front view he was handsome, theatrically so, because of bushy eyelashes; his profile was weak. If he had been integrally homely, he would have adapted, handled it with flair. As it was, caught by a side-view mirror, he would think, Here I was being Byronic when I was looking like an ostrich swallowing a golf ball.

Finally, it had been while he was hospitalized (it turned out to be mononucleosis) that they got engaged. Joe, whose field was mechanism, electronic and female, once remarked that lookers like Victoria had an instinct for being in at the kill. And in rare bad moments, Kenneth wondered if the disappointment Victoria sometimes showed in him was that he hadn't died.

So far, except for the delay in meeting Axel Voerd, the weekend seemed to Kenneth marvelous in its simplicity. They played a little croquet, and Erika Voerd baked; she baked kuchen, torten, and strudel. The house was a push-button colonial, and Kenneth found something very gracious in this scholarly European couple's impartial zeal for American gadgets, both antique and modern, although ordinarily he held the correct derision for both. But their apparent equal pleasure in rush candle dippers and automatic dishwashers made them seem more vital than if they'd bought a ruin and furnished it with old Hapsburg-style pieces. "They're unselfconscious," he would describe it, back at school. "They're not snobs about conveniences. No tearing out the central heating. It was an experience of royalty in the kitchen, so to speak."

"Axel again apologizes, he says how he welcomes you," cried Erika Voerd, lugging the oil paintings she had promised to bring out, her astronomer husband's hobby. "He hopes maybe to be well to come down for dinner." Her resolute diminutiveness, strident voice, amenable smile, the elegance of ideal balance between frills and butchiness, her flag-blue eyes and swan-blonde hair aged to the shade many younger women bleached to, made undergraduates ask, "Terrific?" and their girls cry, "Isn't she the great old *end?*"

"I was just saying to Vic," said Kenneth, "I love the way you don't affirm a kind of Freud-Strauss synthesis in Connecticut."

"Oh, we don't like to do that," said Mrs. Voerd, surprised, "because why." Like an ordinary suburban matron, she talked decor on the conventionally rueful note. She told them how she had been penny-wise, pound-foolish, trying to put the expression into American money, and enjoying their laughing at her. "So I made for the entrance hall the economy of the pattern of daisies. It is too moving." "Busy," suggested Kenneth. "Busy! Busy!" Mrs. Voerd thanked him. "And the decorator had told me, for a house of scale, baronial, sumptuous, a pattern of" — she made gestures of draw-

ing thread from a needle — "high feathers." "Plumes?" Victoria
offered timidly, and they all exclaimed triumphantly, "Plumes!
Plumes!"

Mrs. Voerd stood her husband's paintings against the low stone
wall of the terrace. They were very small canvases showing tiny,
globby cadmium-yellow suns and nebulas on scrubbed-in ultra-
marine backgrounds. "They're certainly very interesting," said
Kenneth, swallowing. "They've got a certain very definite quality."

A special sweetness of Mrs. Voerd's (in her work, she was such
a mordant critic) was that she took social remarks at respectful
face value. "*I* think they are!" she said. "*I* think they do!"

Victoria said, "He must be a terribly good *astronomer*." Because she appeared cool and poised, these faux pas of hers sounded
intended. Kenneth murmured, "Oh, Victoria!", which made her
give him a resentful blink and look away.

"But Axel is authority!" agreed Mrs. Voerd, in a fierce tone of
joy. She pronounced it o-*tor*-ity, so that it sounded like a classical
title. She told them things Axel had done with azimuths and
asteroids and equinoctials. Kenneth loved the way she said the
word "colure" in a deep purr, pursing her mouth in a kiss.
Victoria, in the rather flat voice in which girls talk to older women,
remarked, "I thought it was all *radar* now."

"*It* is all radar now!" Mrs. Voerd agreed, still more proudly.
"*Stars* is not practical! Axel always says, *is* not practical!" She
propped up a little canvas. Suddenly she looked up, shading her
eyes. Although there hadn't been a sound, Kenneth realized that
Axel Voerd was actually with them. But how had she known?
The man in the living-room photograph, in seaman-like black, so
close up he seemed larger than life, was out on his sundeck, almost directly above them. Kenneth heard him give a short cough
and take a breath. They weren't noises of a sick old man. Even
in these solitary, respiratory little sounds, the voice was alert and
virile. Mrs. Voerd's upraised face constricted in the sunshine and
looked powdery, as if it could flake into the air. Kenneth felt a
pang like jealousy, the feeling he got at a concert with a musician.
"This is senseless," he thought. "She's a woman who loves her
husband. Which is very marvelous." But as if to throw himself
between them, he said, almost in a shout, "I love the way he isn't
afraid of *color*."

"I was saying to Ken," said Victoria, also throwing her voice, "your husband looks like Tolstoy. Or — or some Baltic *captain*."

"Oh, the picture, that is by the Stamford Yacht Club," explained Mrs. Voerd. She indicated another canvas. "That is Betelgeux." She lingered lovingly over the *geux*. "I think Betelgeux."

As he recalled some cataclysmic perception from Mrs. Voerd's last book, her refuge in her husband's tiny, crudely painted heavens seemed to Kenneth her source of power; instead of relaxing by playing four-hand arrangements for pipe organ, or championship chess, this scholarly old couple got lost in the stars.

Mrs. Voerd turned the talk to the young couple's plans. With the rapt smile of a classic mother, as if these held a glory they were unaware of, she questioned Victoria, ducking her head to follow the girl's face as she would shift to knock her cigarette. "Well, Ken, of course, will go on with his doctorate, and I'll have to get some sort of *job*." Victoria laughed and added, beseechingly, "I majored in history sort of by *accident*."

"How? How do you mean this, you major in history by accident?" Mrs. Voerd asked eagerly, as if told of an academic distinction, and Vicky told her the story, probably slightly doctored, but cute, about how she told her deaf major-field adviser she was crushed over her D in a physics quiz, and he understood her to have announced she wanted to major in history. Most of Victoria's anecdotes described her fulfillment of misapprehensions she had accidentally given people. But she got the story off charmingly without making herself sound like a dimwit, and it brought up her vulnerable quality. "She's so vulnerable," Kenneth often explained to Joe. Joe replied, "Man, you're hooked."

Mrs. Voerd went up again to look in on her husband, and from the windows, they heard the rich, gargling sounds of German. Neither of them knew any German except for some philosophy, cookery, and operetta words. It sounded to Kenneth as if the Voerds were intensely and joyously planning weltschmerz, sauerbraten, and gestalt for *Die Fledermaus*. He and Vicky had to look at each other, and they started to laugh silently, whispering "Shut up!" One word kept recurring in Axel's talk, which sounded like Nutsy, or Mootzie, and they realized that this was some kind of pet name he called his wife, which shocked them.

"Axel is so disappointed!" reported Mrs. Voerd. "He is much

better, but not yet for tonight, but tomorrow for surely! He wishes again I should tell you once more how he welcomes you, it does him good that you are here, your presence in the house, and the sound of your young laughter."

Until dinner, she showed them her Early American collection, which looked to Kenneth like discarded plumbing parts. As she showed them jagging irons and jagger wheels for doing things to pastry, the idea of people's forging weapons for dealing with pastry, and of a great modern philosopher hunting them in barn auctions and paying big prices for them, gave Kenneth a sense of the majesty of the mundane. He looked at Victoria, who was examining a silver-luster Toby with a bemused expression, and thought, "Ancestors! We're going to be ancestors."

That night Kenneth got a few minutes alone with Victoria. It had the stolen savor most of his times alone with her had, with her telling him her mother's warnings. Tonight she told him her mother said not to stay up with Kenneth after the Voerds went to bed because "it would *look* so bad." "You know, never mind if I got *pregnant,* just it would *look* so bad," said Victoria. The reference to pregnancy she tossed off, but her bitterness about her mother's concern for appearances was passionate. Am I jealous of her mother? thought Kenneth. That's senseless. *"My* mother wouldn't worry about my getting you pregnant," he said, consolingly. "She'd worry about my not getting my eight hours. We must face it, honey. Our mothers trust us morally."

Even saying good night, they had two short fights and reconciliations. Victoria didn't want Joe to be best man. "I think Joe is a marvelous *person* with marvelous *qualities,"* she said. "It's just that he just isn't terribly *presentable."* "I'm afraid I don't pick my friends on the basis of how they look in cutaways," said Kenneth, stiffly. Then Victoria said his loyalty to his friends was what she loved about him. She said, "I just was brought up in these phony, disgusting criteria, and it makes me hate myself and hate everybody." Kenneth felt that she wanted him to rake her mother over the coals with her, but that this would be getting on dangerous ground. Also, from his own mother, he knew how to handle this dressy, girl-sized, hypertensive type of matron. You just kidded them along.

They lounged back on his bed. The white mattress in the screened sleeping porch had a movie-safari look. Victoria's suntan in the golden, insect-repellent-bulb light made her look anointed. Her neckline V of tan made all the white below it seem doubly bare. She smelled like the main floor of a fancy department store, like new ironing. Over their breathing and the bumping of white millers on the screen, some kind of insect kept pronouncing, "Nanette, Nanette," and another made fast irregular clicks like a typewriter. She giggled and whispered, "But, darling, this *looks* so bad," and he said, "My eight hours! I must have them! I must have them tonight!"

From upstairs, they heard the Voerds talking. The distance blurred it so that the German all sounded like indignant noises of strangling, *"Hoot, oot, woot, woot!"*, and they started to giggle, shushing each other. They got pensive about the Voerds. "I hope to God we get to meet Axel tomorrow," said Kenneth. "You know, they'd be terrific material for a profile. A double profile hasn't been done too often. I see them as a kind of transcended latter-day Sidney and Beatrice Webb. But," he added sternly, "I'm not a journalist."

"Of course, if you regard it as prostituting yourself to compromise at all, how are we going to support our *children?*" said Victoria.

"Would you want too *many* children?" asked Kenneth. Victoria, jerking upright, in an angular, tomboyish position, and yanking back her hair, so that her clear features shone like a fourteen-year-old boy's, said rapidly, as if reciting, that to her marriage was meaningless if it did not contain children, and Kenneth pointed out that you should not have children in a marriage that was otherwise meaningless. Since this was an abstract problem, it did not interest them long, and Victoria did one of her passionate about-faces which Kenneth had come to depend upon and said his dedication and single-mindedness were what she loved about him. "I loathe gray-flannel rat-race types," she said. "My roomie's mahogany magnate would drive me *mad.* Just from his letters to her I *know* he has fat *hands.*"

They said another good night, standing at the screen. The country darkness seemed cubic, as if the sleeping porch were a golden cage blocked up by the night. A white miller, the bean-

like bug body and Kleenex-scrap wings, bumped in front of their
eyes. "Betelgeux!" Victoria whispered, pointing to the dark. They
laughed and clutched each other. Kenneth said, "Darling, we're
going to be ancestors." She gave a submissive little shudder that
he felt run down her legs.

After she went up to her guest room, Kenneth was too jumpy to
sleep. He started a letter to Joe, but it was a "You should see me
now" letter, and he destroyed it. The frustration of a sense of
exaltation was that friends received it apprehensively, as if they
knew you were going to die. The night had a crisis quality before
he did get sleepy, and then he slept hard till morning.

Set on a tray on Axel Voerd's desk in the office adjoining the
sleeping porch Kenneth found juice and coffee cake for himself
and Victoria, the car keys, a locker key, and a note from Erika
propped against the celestial globe which asked if he "would
mind to" drive to the deep-freeze lockers and get a couple of nice
broilers for lunch, before it got too hot. She had drawn a little
road map of the route to the lockers, with the turnoff on the highway and the lockers marked by stars.

Exultantly Kenneth got Victoria, and they went out through
the breezeway to get the car. "Hey," said Kenneth. "We're eloping!"

"I never knew dew got things so wet," said Victoria.

To Kenneth this was the best part of the weekend, the chance
to drive Victoria in a good car in the early-Sunday country. The
car handled so powerfully it seemed to burn its own swath and
compose views no one had ever seen before. The country looked
like a garden, the scrubby trees of the low second-growth woods
singled out like ornamental plantings. Under this annunciatory
A.M. glaze, it became an ordered setting, a full palette of greens
shone in deliberate probity, little Fra Angelicos with beveled wings
and nimbuses seemed possible, and only expressions like "grand
design" and "creation" seemed to apply. The morning was proclam-
atory; if later would be glaring and humid, this present was all
the more — Kenneth could only think *valid.* Down an open swath
he saw oil-white patches of houses against the blue Sound, calendar
art come true at both ends in a chronicle writing in him and Victoria. "Why not *settle,* ultimately?" he thought. Being city-bred,

to *settle* was the most radical adventure. "What's so impossible?" Because she was his partner in this freedom, he felt deeply tender for Victoria, and her moodiness got through to him very faintly at first.

But she was in one of her most difficult moods. She got on the subject of British accents. She said British accents did something fantastic to her. In a tone of desperation, she said, "I forget British accents *exist*, and then I hear a British accent and I get weak in the *knees*." She suddenly asked Kenneth what his neck measurement was. He told her dryly he could probably cultivate a British accent and a bull neck, but then he looked at her and thought she looked like one of those wedding-stagefright girls in the newspapers who ride a cross-country bus and sit through six movies. She had bride nerves, that was all. And being a delicate-featured ash-blonde, her getting a little mussy looked touching. The rising heat had fuzzed her hair slightly at the temples, deepened the shading of her eyes, and creased her gray dress across her narrow groin. "She's so vulnerable," he thought, again.

They drove past an ivy-grown small stone church as the bell was ringing. "Oh," cried Victoria, as if wounded. "I wish I could go to church."

"I'll take you to church!" said Kenneth. He slowed the car and felt at the open neck of his sport shirt. "I'd need to go back for a tie."

"No, I don't have a hat," she said.

"A scarf?" suggested Kenneth, but evidently this was too stupid to get an answer. With the sun fuller, the morning got weightier, the trees rose out of darkening pools of shade like the landmarks that ratify in the memory the bad news that came just then.

Then, as usual after being difficult, she switched to her mother. "Ken," she asked, in an almost entreating voice, "does your mother embarrass you to absolute *tears*?"

"Well," said Kenneth, "I mean, I just wouldn't *take* her to a party for Allen Ginsberg — "

"No, no, no, no, *no!*" Victoria interrupted. "I mean, when she says you don't love her. I mean, when she wants to go deeply, deeply into — oh — "

"My mother is essentially a materialist," said Kenneth. "I mean, my eight hours is the extent — " Victoria didn't seem to listen, and for a while she didn't talk. Kenneth reached his right hand across the car seat and gently gripped her thigh. As if his caress prompted her, Victoria burst out again. "I've got something figured out about my mother. My mother's got a *myopia* neurosis."

"Oh?" said Kenneth. The interrogative *oh* was a mannerism he knew annoyed her, but it still came out. She started to expound her theory. This broke the flow of the country drive more jarringly than all the capricious business had. She sat forward and talked against the hum of the motor. Concentrating on her vulnerable quality got harder and harder for Kenneth. "Mother was, of course, *the* celebrated beauty of her day, unquote, and she would *not* wear glasses. I seriously doubt that my mother has ever in her life seen anything beyond her own manicured hand before her celebrated *face*. I really and truly believe my mother almost literally doesn't know other people *exist!*"

"I had an uncle who was very deaf — " said Kenneth, but to his relief, they got to the turnoff for the lockers.

He parked in the gravel area, and they went up a flagstone walk screened by a beachy translucent turquoise plastic partition. The factual intimacy of this bathhouse connotation made Kenneth only able to think about touching her. He had the burdened feeling he ought to straighten out a lot of things with her, but now it seemed a waste of this privacy. When he kissed her she kissed back, and when he touched her she seemed the smoother through the scratchy gray summer-suit stuff. She smelled like surf swimming, of lotion and washed hair. After all the little complications that seemed to beset her, the idea of physical love appeared to Kenneth as vastly healing, like glorious weather, and he could believe that once they really got together everything would be all right.

Driving back in now drilling sunshine that dug the landscape in shovelfuls of shade and glare, they got very gay. They talked about some of the same things as before, but now they laughed at them. They imitated their mothers complimenting each other's hats by saying how terrible they themselves would look in the hat. "*I* look like a *clown* in a high crown," squealed Victoria. "I look like *death* in a veil. I look like a racehorse in flowers. I'd look as if I'd had a few too many!" "I'd look like a whore!" yelled Kenneth. "A corpse!"

They were laughing when they drove into the Voerds' driveway. Two cars were parked in the circle. "Sunday hordes!" said Kenneth. "This early. Damn. Buzzards." He took the package of frozen broilers, and they went up the path to the front door, which stood wide open.

The hall was as bright as outdoors. All the daisies on the wallpaper, Mrs. Voerd's penny-wise daisies, looked as if they were growing. The house looked turned inside out, for painters, movers, or for sale. Sign-shapes of sunshine stood on the stairs. Kenneth saw that the sunshine came from the two open doors at the top. Both of Axel Voerd's doors, the two doors to the master bedroom suite, stood wide open. "They've taken him to the hospital," thought Kenneth. For some reason he was ashamed of himself and Victoria. The real-estate brightness of the hall resounded; it struck him that haunted houses were sunny, bright, and open.

Then, from the dining room he heard Erika Voerd's voice say, "But it is my young guests." She came along the hall. The sunshine made her face a drawn-up mask of the type in which the features are cut out of the metal. Even while already trying to change it to dismay, Kenneth felt his face smile in involuntary response to her own smile. "It is all over for Axel," she said. She held her hands as if offering them a treasure, in the gesture with which people tell their loss. At his side he heard Victoria give a low cry, but as if repelled by a story of sadism or a disgusting sight. "But it is all *right!*" said Mrs. Voerd. "Only you must forgive I make your errand, because I know you would feel, and what could you do. But it is all *right,* it is all right! He was made glad hearing your voices, and your young laughter."

A man who looked like some kind of professional family friend, a doctor or lawyer, came up. Silently he shook hands ceremoniously with Victoria and Kenneth and said, "You don't speak Hungarian?" It became apparent that this was the only English he knew. A brazen-haired woman in slacks so tight her hips looked crisscrossed by many cords underneath came up and made Erika Voerd sit down on a chair. With her voice breaking for the only time, Mrs. Voerd said, "But my young friends have had no meal!" The woman made a crooning noise and started to rub Mrs. Voerd between the shoulder blades like a masseuse. She had the almost drunkenly sullen expression many people wear in the presence of bereavement. Kenneth thought how round-shouldered Mrs. Voerd looked. Her upper back formed a small dome. What had her husband called her, Nootzie, Mootzie? She looked to him so diminished that he got the feeling that it was he who was growing, maladroit as a clown on stilts, and might at any moment hit his head. This sense of a ludicrous disparity of size struck him dumb. To speak was so impossible he held his teeth set.

Soon the people started to come. A son and daughter, with the wife and husband, arrived, but Kenneth didn't know which were the real children and which were the in-laws. The bleached woman in the slacks turned out to be the wife of a great poet. The Lutheran pastor from Westport came, explaining, as if this were his reason, that the Voerds hadn't "belonged." Everyone ignored Kenneth and Victoria. Erika was borne away among them all. There was a lot of mention of "heavy sedation." The poet's wife started to tell Kenneth that Axel had had his previous heart attack at her party, but when someone spoke to her, she dropped Kenneth and her story. After a while, Kenneth and Victoria got their things together, called their cab, and left without anyone speaking to them.

As they tore at country-taxi speed down the shining blue highway with the green banners of countryside flying off on each side, Kenneth said, "Ultimately, the question is what will this do to Erika Voerd as a *thinker*."

He addressed this to the heavy neck of the cab driver. Also throwing her voice for the benefit of the driver, Victoria said, "She seems to have transcended terrifically." The driver immediately spoke. Kenneth lurched in his seat before he realized that the driver was talking into his phone. "Party to the station," he said. "No, I'm still working on it."

They came up against a huge ink-brushed can-can girl on pink, a poster for a Broadway show, over a big empty luggage cart. A desert-like sun isolated the station. The train came in in a jet of steam that smelled like a men's room. "I'll have to notify people," said Kenneth, a little cheered. "The entire faculty. I'm obligated. I'll have to call their homes even though it's Sunday. It's a responsibility." Just as they boarded the train, he got a strange impression of a deadly flash of her eye and the words, *"Fun, though!"*

*   *   *

In the train, she got impossible. If he had wanted to say it, been the type who could, what would have been the Noel Coward sound of "Victoria, you're a bitch" almost made tears come into his eyes. He prayed that soon she would stop and say she didn't know what was the matter with her, and say she was sick. A few other times, after being bitchy, she pleaded being sick, or, after a party, not remembering what had happened, and these were certainly shabby tricks he disliked, but now he prayed she would pull all her shabby tricks.

She did takeoffs of him telling about the tragedy. Like many shy, aloof girls, she was an abandoned mimic when the mood was on her. Seeing himself played by someone he had been so close to, like seeing his profile in a side mirror, made him sit so still that small twinges and tickles of circulation needled his body all over.

First she did him doing the story for the grotesque. "So we come in with the frozen chickens. A lawyer comes up and asks if we speak Hungarian. The chickens are defrosting all over the floor. ——'s wife (what a tramp!) starts a masseur job on the widow. Mrs. Voerd says it's all right because he was happy hearing our young laughter."

Then she did his mood change. She shifted position and wrinkled her forehead as she did his trying for powerful effect with understatement. "It seems she had been occupying the same bed as himself. (It was a double bed.) They were a terrifically devoted couple. So in the morning she wakes up. She finds him. I mean, it was kind of rough. But it was essentially ritualistic the way she preserved the forms. Admetus, so to speak. I mean, it was an essentially *Greek* experience."

Exploratory horror, as if he had gotten a wound he had not been able to look at closely yet, made Kenneth feel a fullness of dread; something had happened in which the only certainty was that it would be worse when he looked at it.

She didn't say she was sick; she cried, trying not to (mastering herself completely when the conductor came through), and said she was sorry, she was sorry she couldn't marry him. In a terrified whisper, as if she were confiding that she had had an abortion or a prison record, she said she actually somewhat doubted that she had ever actually been really and truly in love with him.

Kenneth kept his eyes fixed on their two red tickets clamped in the seat-back slot at a thirty-three-and-a-third-degree angle apart, as if from the patness of this image he could draw a counterpoison. He realized he hadn't believed he would really get away with marrying Victoria; he had hoped they could push it through before she noticed the mistake. He would marry a wool-haired little girl named Yetta or Blanche, in a drawstring blouse falling off and a skirt painted on, who would support him by researching for Wilfred Funk, and not the idea of marrying her, but the idea that he would come to want to, made him shut his eyes; that the compatible would become desirable made death seem real.

Probably his and Victoria's mothers would remain friendly. It made him cold to the quicks of his fingernails to think that matrons' rapport over hats would flourish when grand passion had drowned to a tear in the beer over a closing-time chorus of "Sunshine came along with thee, and swallows in the air."

In a child's reciting voice as she talked against her crying, Victoria said the self-excoriating banalities. She said again that she wasn't good enough for him, and this time Kenneth knew immediately that this had always meant she didn't love him. She also said, "I very, very seriously doubt that I have ever in my life really loved anyone except myself," and this second banality now seemed to Kenneth simply literally true, and equally true of himself.

He wanted Victoria, the idea of it, and having everybody know; but the things that bothered her, her mother-thing, her apparent yen for a nineteen-inch-neck Britisher, didn't move him, and the idea of things ever happening to her looks, to her bronzed miniature-shield kneecaps, or her conical breasts, was an affront. He knew his pang at the sight of Erika Voerd's face, as she looked up toward her husband's sundeck, knowing she couldn't see him, was jealousy of her ability to love.

But, even now, he thought, there was a chance for him and Victoria, if he could get rid of caring about himself, if he could say to her, "It is all over, but it is all right!"

With a cold feeling, as if facing noble danger, he wondered if he could get rid of caring in the least how he himself felt, if he could possibly stop mattering to himself at all; but it all stuck to him, fear of getting hurt, as he was hurt now, and wanting her, the strongest self-love of all, desire, the centaur's blood that soaked Heracles' cloak — it burned through him as he tried to tear it off and think only about her herself. He tried to concentrate on how all of this was tough on her as well, on her problems, on her mother-ambivalence thing; but he thought of what she did to him and of what she had done to him, and the more he tore all that away, the more it stuck to him, the Deianiran robe, it burned into his flesh.

Only when a lot of time had passed, he thought, and he looked through the funeral-lace dirt of the window at the flying green country as if the trees were milestones, each sword of shade knighting him with a year's time, only after many stunning accolades of age, might he know this love which could say, "But it is all right! It is all right!" on the very morning of death.

STANLEY ELKIN

I Look Out For Ed Wolfe

(FROM ESQUIRE)

HE WAS an orphan, and, to himself, he seemed like one, looked like one. His orphan's features were as true of himself as are their pale, pinched faces to the blind. At twenty-seven he was a neat, thin young man in white shirts and light suits with lintless pockets. Something about him suggested the ruthless isolation, the hard self-sufficiency of the orphaned, the peculiar dignity of men seen eating alone in restaurants on national holidays. Yet it was this perhaps which shamed him chiefly, for there was a suggestion, too, that his impregnability was a myth, a smell not of the furnished room which he did not inhabit, but of the three-room apartment on a good street which he did. The very excellence of his taste, conditioned by need and lack, lent to him the odd, maidenly primness of the lonely.

He saved the photographs of strangers and imprisoned them behind clear plastic windows in his wallet. In the sound of his own voice he detected the accent of the night school and the correspondence course, and nothing of the fat, sunny ring of the world's casually afternooned. He strove against himself, a supererogatory enemy, and sought by a kind of helpless abrasion, as one rubs wood, the gleaming self beneath. An orphan's thinness, he thought, was no accident.

Returning from lunch he entered the office building where he worked. It was an old building, squat and gargoyled, brightly patched where sandblasters had once worked and then quit before they had finished. He entered the lobby, which smelled always of disinfectant, and walked past the wide, dirty glass of the cigarette and candy counter to the single elevator, as thickly barred as a cell.

The building was an outlaw. Low rents and a downtown address and the landlord's indifference had brought together from the peripheries of business and professionalism a strange band of entrepreneurs and visionaries, men desperately but imaginatively failing: an eye doctor who corrected vision by massage; a radio evangelist; a black-belt judo champion; a self-help organization for crippled veterans; dealers in pornographic books, in paper flowers, in fireworks, in plastic jewelry, in the artificial, in the artfully made, in the imitated, in the copied, in the stolen, the unreal, the perversion, the plastic, the *schlack*.

On the sixth floor the elevator opened and the young man, Ed Wolfe, stepped out.

He passed the Association for the Indians, passed Plasti-Pens, passed *Coffin & Tombstone*, passed Soldier Toys, passed Prayer-a-Day. He walked by the opened door of C. Morris Brut, Chiropractor, and saw him, alone, standing at a mad attention, framed in the arching golden nimbus of his inverted name on the window, squeezing handballs.

He looked quickly away but Dr. Brut saw him and came toward him, putting the handballs in his shirt pocket where they bulged awkwardly. He held him by the elbow. Ed Wolfe looked at the yellowing tile beneath his feet, infinitely diamonded, chipped, the floor of a public toilet, and saw Dr. Brut's dusty shoes. He stared sadly at the jagged, broken glass of the mail chute.

"Ed Wolfe, take care of yourself," Dr. Brut said.

"Right."

"Regard your posture in life. A tall man like yourself looks terrible when he slumps. Don't be a *schlump*. It's not good for the organs."

"I'll watch it."

"When the organs get out of line the man begins to die."

"I know."

"You say so. How many guys make promises. Brains in the brainpan. Balls in the strap. The bastards downtown." He meant doctors in hospitals, in clinics, on boards, nonorphans with M.D. degrees and special license plates and respectable patients who had Blue Cross, charts, died in clean hospital rooms. They were the bastards downtown, his personal New Deal, his neighborhood Wall Street banker. A disease cartel. "They won't tell you. The white bread kills you. The cigarettes. The whiskey. The sneakers. The high heels. They won't tell you. Me, *I'll* tell you."

"I appreciate it."

"Wise guy. Punk. I'm a friend. I give a father's advice."

"I'm an orphan."

"I'll adopt you."

"I'm late to work."

"We'll open a clinic. 'C. Morris Brut and Adopted Son.' "

"It's something to think about."

"Poetry," Dr. Brut said and walked back to his office, his posture stiff, awkward, a man in a million who knew how to hold himself.

Ed Wolfe went on to his own office. He walked in. The sad-faced telephone girl was saying, "Cornucopia Finance Corporation." She pulled the wire out of the board and slipped her headset around her neck where it hung like a delicate horse collar. "Mr. La Meck wants to see you. But don't go in yet. He's talking to somebody."

He went toward his desk at one end of the big main office. Standing, fists on the desk, he turned to the girl. "What happened to my call cards?"

"Mr. La Meck took them," the girl said.

"Give me the carbons," Ed Wolfe said. "I've got to make some calls."

She looked embarrassed. The face went through a weird change, the sadness taking on an impossible burden of shame so that she seemed massively tragic, like a hit-and-run driver. "I'll get them," she said, moving out of the chair heavily. Ed Wolfe thought of Dr. Brut.

He took the carbons and fanned them out on the desk. He picked one in an intense, random gesture like someone drawing a number on a public stage. He dialed rapidly.

As the phone buzzed brokenly in his ear he felt the old excitement. Someone at the other end greeted him sleepily.

"Mr. Flay? This is Ed Wolfe at Cornucopia Finance." (Can you cope, can you cope? he hummed to himself.)

"Who?"

"Ed Wolfe. I've got an unpleasant duty," he began pleasantly. "You've skipped two payments."

"I didn't skip nothing. I called the girl. She said it was okay."

"That was three months ago. She meant it was all right to miss a few days. Listen, Mr. Flay, we've got that call recorded, too. Nothing gets by."

"I'm a little short."

"Grow."

"I couldn't help it," the man said. Ed Wolfe didn't like the cringing tone. Petulance and anger he could meet with his own petulance, his own anger. But guilt would have to be met with his own guilt and that, here, was irrelevant.

"Don't con me, Flay. You're a trouble-maker. What are you, Flay, a Polish person? Flay isn't a Polish name, but your address . . ."

"What's that?"

"What are you? Are you Polish?"

"What's that to you? What difference does it make?" That was more like it, Ed Wolfe thought warmly.

"That's what you are, Flay. You're a Pole. It's guys like you who give your race a bad name. Half our bugouts are Polish persons."

"Listen. You can't . . ."

He began to shout. "*You* listen. You wanted the car. The refrigerator. The chintzy furniture. The sectional you saw in the funny papers. And we paid for it, right?"

"Listen. The money I owe is one thing, the way . . ."

"We paid for it, right?"

"That doesn't . . ."

"Right? Right?"

"Yes, you . . ."

"Okay. You're in trouble, Warsaw. You're in terrible trouble. It means a lien. A judgment. We've got lawyers. You've got nothing. We'll pull the furniture the hell out of there. The car. Everything."

"Wait," he said. "Listen, my brother-in-law . . ."

Ed Wolfe broke in sharply. "He's got some money?"

"I don't know. A little. I don't know."

"Get it. If you're short, grow. This is America."

"I don't know if he'll let me have it."

"Steal it. This is America. Goodbye."

"Wait a minute. Please."

"That's it. There are other Polish persons on my list. This time

it was just a friendly warning. Cornucopia wants its money. Cornucopia. Can you cope? Can you cope? Just a friendly warning,
Polish-American. Next time we come with the lawyers and the
machine guns. Am I making myself clear?"

"I'll try to get it to you."

Ed Wolfe hung up. He pulled a handkerchief from his drawer
and wiped his face. His chest was heaving. He took another call
card. The girl came by and stood beside his desk. "Mr. La Meck
can see you now," she mourned.

"Later. I'm calling." The number was already ringing.

"Please, Mr. Wolfe."

"Later, I said. In a minute." The girl went away. "Hello. Let
me speak with your husband, madam. I am Ed Wolfe of Cornucopia
Finance. He can't cope. Your husband can't cope."

The woman said something, made an excuse. "Put him on, goddamn it. We know he's out of work. Nothing gets by. Nothing."
There was a hand on the receiver beside his own, the wide male
fingers pink and vaguely perfumed, the nails manicured. For a
moment he struggled with it fitfully, as though the hand itself were
all he had to contend with. He recognized La Meck and let go.
La Meck pulled the phone quickly toward his mouth and spoke
softly into it, words of apology, some ingenious excuse Ed Wolfe
couldn't hear. He put the receiver down beside the phone itself and
Ed Wolfe picked it up and returned it to its cradle.

"Ed," La Meck said, "come into the office with me."

Ed Wolfe followed La Meck, his eyes on La Meck's behind.

La Meck stopped at his office door. Looking around he shook his
head sadly and Ed Wolfe nodded in agreement. La Meck let Ed
Wolfe pass in first. While La Meck stood, Ed Wolfe could discern
a kind of sadness in his slouch, but once La Meck was seated behind
his desk he seemed restored, once again certain of the world's sound-
ness. "All right," La Meck began, "I won't lie to you."

Lie to me. Lie to me, Ed Wolfe prayed silently.

"You're in here for me to fire you. You're not being laid off. I'm
not going to tell you that I think you'd be happier someplace else,
that the collection business isn't your game, that profits don't justify
our keeping you around. Profits are terrific, and if collection isn't
your game it's because you haven't got a game. As far as your being
happier someplace else, that's bullshit. You're not supposed to be
happy. It isn't in the cards for you. You're a fall-guy type, God

bless you, and though I like you personally I've got no use for you in my office."

I'd like to get you on the other end of a telephone some day, Ed Wolfe thought miserably.

"Don't ask me for a reference," La Meck said. "I couldn't give you one."

"No, no," Ed Wolfe said. "I wouldn't ask you for a reference." A helpless civility was all he was capable of. If you're going to suffer, *suffer,* he told himself.

"Look," La Meck said, his tone changing, shifting from brutality to compassion as though there were no difference between the two, "you've got a kind of quality, a real feeling for collection. I'm frank to tell you, when you first came to work for us I figured you wouldn't last. I put you on the phones because I wanted you to see the toughest part first. A lot of people can't do it. You take a guy who's down and bury him deeper. It's heart-wringing work. But you, you were amazing. An artist. You had a real thing for the deadbeat soul, I thought. But we started to get complaints, and I had to warn you. Didn't I warn you? I should have suspected something when the delinquent accounts started to turn over again. It was like rancid butter turning sweet. So I don't say this to knock your technique. Your technique's terrific. With you around we could have laid off the lawyers. But Ed, you're a gangster. A gangster."

That's it, Ed Wolfe thought. I'm a gangster. Babyface Wolfe at nobody's door.

"Well," La Meck said, "I guess we owe you some money."

"Two weeks' pay," Ed Wolfe said.

"And two weeks in lieu of notice," La Meck said grandly.

"And a week's pay for my vacation."

"You haven't been here a year," La Meck said.

"It would have been a year in another month. I've earned the vacation."

"What the hell," La Meck said. "A week's pay for vacation."

La Meck figured on a pad and tearing off a sheet handed it to Ed Wolfe. "Does that check with your figures?" he asked.

Ed Wolfe, who had no figures, was amazed to see that his check was so large. Leaving off the deductions he made $92.73 a week. Five $92.73's was evidently $463.65. It was a lot of money. "That seems to be right," he told La Meck.

La Meck gave him a check and Ed Wolfe got up. Already it was

as though he had never worked there. When La Meck handed him
the check he almost couldn't think what it was for. It was as if there
should have been a photographer there to record the ceremony.
ORPHAN AWARDED CHECK BY BUSINESSMAN.

"Goodbye, Mr. La Meck," he said. "It has been an interesting
association," he added foolishly.

"Goodbye, Ed," La Meck answered, putting his arm around Ed
Wolfe's shoulders and leading him to the door. "I'm sorry it had to
end this way." He shook Ed Wolfe's hand seriously and looked into
his eyes. He had a hard grip.

Quantity and quality, Ed Wolfe thought.

"One thing, Ed. Watch yourself. Your mistake here was that you
took the job too seriously. You hated the chiselers."

No, no, I loved them, he thought.

"You've got to watch it. Don't love. Don't hate. That's the
secret. Detachment and caution. Look out for Ed Wolfe."

"I'll watch out for him," he said giddily and in a moment he was
out of La Meck's office, and the main office, and the elevator, and
the building itself, loose in the world, as cautious and as detached
as La Meck could want him.

He took the car from the parking lot, handing the attendant the
two dollars. The man gave him fifty cents back. "That's right," Ed
Wolfe said, "it's only two o'clock." He put the half dollar in his
pocket, and, on an impulse, took out his wallet. He had twelve
dollars. He counted his change. Eighty-two cents. With his finger,
on the dusty dashboard, he added $12.82 to $463.65. He had
$476.47. Does that check with your figures? he asked himself and
drove into the crowded traffic.

Proceeding slowly, past his old building, past garages, past bar
and grills, past second-rate hotels, he followed the traffic further
downtown. He drove into the deepest part of the city, down and
downtown to the bottom, the foundation, the city's navel. He
watched the shoppers and tourists and messengers and men with
appointments. He was tranquil, serene. It was something he would
be content to do forever. He could use his check to buy gas, to take
his meals at drive-in restaurants, to pay tolls. It would be a pleasant
life, a great life, and he contemplated it thoughtfully. To drive at
fifteen or twenty miles an hour through eternity, stopping at stop-
lights and signs, pulling over to the curb at the sound of sirens and

the sight of funerals, obeying all traffic laws, making obedience to
them his very code. Ed Wolfe, the Flying Dutchman, the Wandering Jew, the Off and Running Orphan, "Look Out For Ed Wolfe,"
a ghostly wailing down the city's corridors. What would be bad? he
thought.

In the morning, out of habit, he dressed himself in a white shirt
and light suit. Before he went downstairs he saw that his check and
his twelve dollars were still in his wallet. Carefully he counted the
eighty-two cents that he had placed on the dresser the night before,
put the coins in his pocket, and went downstairs to his car.

Something green had been shoved under the wiper blade on the
driver's side.

YOUR CAR WILL NEVER BE WORTH MORE THAN IT IS WORTH RIGHT
NOW! WHY WAIT FOR DEPRECIATION TO MAKE YOU AUTOMOTIVELY
BANKRUPT? I WILL BUY THIS CAR AND PAY YOU CASH! I WILL NOT
CHEAT YOU!

Ed Wolfe considered his car thoughtfully a moment and got in.
He drove that day through the city playing the car radio softly. He
heard the news each hour and each half hour. He listened to Arthur
Godfrey far away and in another world. He heard Bing Crosby's
ancient voice, and thought sadly, Depreciation. When his tank was
almost empty he thought wearily of having to have it filled and
could see himself, bored and discontented behind the bug-stained
glass, forced into a patience he did not feel, having to decide
whether to take the Green Stamps the attendant tried to extend.
Put money in your purse, Ed Wolfe, he thought. Cash! he thought
with passion.

He went to the address on the circular.

He drove up onto the gravel lot but remained in his car. In a
moment a man came out of a small wooden shack and walked
toward Ed Wolfe's car. If he was appraising it he gave no sign. He
stood at the side of the automobile and waited while Ed Wolfe
got out.

"Look around," the man said. "No pennants, no strings of electric
lights." He saw the advertisement in Ed Wolfe's hand. "I ran the
ad off on my brother-in-law's mimeograph. My kid stole the paper
from his school."

Ed Wolfe looked at him.

"The place looks like a goddamn parking lot. When the snow

starts falling I get rid of the cars and move the Christmas trees right onto it. No overhead. That's the beauty of a volume business."

Ed Wolfe looked pointedly at the nearly empty lot.

"That's right," the man said. "It's slow. I'm giving the policy one more chance. Then I cheat the public just like everybody else. You're just in time. Come on, I'll show you a beautiful car."

"I want to sell my car," Ed Wolfe said.

"Sure, sure," the man said. "You want to trade with me. I give top allowances. I play fair."

"I want you to buy my car."

The man looked at him closely. "What do you want? You want me to go into the office and put on the ten-gallon hat? It's my only overhead so I guess you're entitled to see it. You're paying for it. I put on this big frigging hat, see, and I become Texas Willie Waxelman, the Mad Cowboy. If that's what you want, I can get it in a minute."

It was incredible, Ed Wolfe thought. There were bastards everywhere who hated other bastards downtown everywhere. "I don't want to trade my car in," Ed Wolfe said. "I want to sell it. I, too, want to reduce my inventory."

The man smiled sadly. "You want me to buy *your* car. You run in and put on the hat. I'm an automobile *salesman,* kid."

"No, you're not," Ed Wolfe said. "I was with Cornucopia Finance. We handled your paper. You're an automobile *buyer.* Your business is in buying up four- and five-year-old cars like mine from people who need dough fast and then auctioning them off to the trade."

The man turned away and Ed Wolfe followed him. Inside the shack the man said, "I'll give you two hundred."

"I need six hundred," Ed Wolfe said.

"I'll lend you the hat. Hold up a goddamn stagecoach."

"Give me five."

"I'll give you two fifty and we'll part friends."

"Four hundred and fifty."

"Three hundred. Here," the man said, reaching his hand into an opened safe and taking out three sheaves of thick, banded bills. He held the money out to Ed Wolfe. "Go ahead, count it."

Absently Ed Wolfe took the money. The bills were stiff, like money in a teller's drawer, their value as decorous and untapped as a sheet of postage stamps. He held the money, pleased by its weight. "Tens and fives," he said, grinning.

"You bet," the man said, taking the money back. "You want to sell your car?"

"Yes," Ed Wolfe said. "Give me the money," he said hoarsely.

He had been to the bank, had stood in the patient, slow, money-conscious line, had presented his formidable check to the impassive teller, hoping the four hundred and sixty-three dollars and sixty-five cents she counted out would seem his week's salary to the man who waited behind him. Fool, he thought, it will seem two weeks' pay and two weeks in lieu of notice and a week for vacation for the hell of it, the three-week margin of an orphan.

"Thank you," the teller said, already looking beyond Ed Wolfe to the man behind him.

"Wait," Ed Wolfe said. "Here." He handed her a white withdrawal slip.

She took it impatiently and walked to a file. "You're closing your savings account?" she asked loudly.

"Yes," Ed Wolfe answered, embarrassed.

"I'll have a cashier's check made out for this."

"No, no," Ed Wolfe said desperately. "Give me cash."

"Sir, we make out a cashier's check and cash it for you," the teller explained.

"Oh," Ed Wolfe said. "I see."

When the teller had given him the two hundred fourteen dollars and twenty-three cents, he went to the next window where he made out a check for $38.91. It was what he had in his checking account.

On Ed Wolfe's kitchen table was a thousand dollars. That day he had spent a dollar and ninety cents. He had twenty-seven dollars and seventy-one cents in his pocket. For expenses. "For attrition," he said aloud. "The cost of living. For streetcars and newspapers and half gallons of milk and loaves of white bread. For the movies. For a cup of coffee." He went to his pantry. He counted the cans and packages, the boxes and bottles. "The three weeks again," he said. "The orphan's nutritional margin." He looked in his icebox. In the freezer he poked around among white packages of frozen meat. He looked brightly into the vegetable tray. A whole lettuce.

Five tomatoes. Several slices of cucumber. Browning celery. On another shelf four bananas. Three and a half apples. A cut pineapple. Some grapes, loose and collapsing darkly in a white bowl. A quarter pound of butter. A few eggs. Another egg, broken last week, congealing in a blue dish. Things in plastic bowls, in jars, forgotten, faintly mysterious left-overs, faintly rotten, vaguely futured, equivocal garbage. He closed the door, feeling a draft. "Really," he said, "it's quite cozy." He looked at the thousand dollars on the kitchen table. "It's not enough," he said. "It's not enough," he shouted. "It's not enough to be cautious on. La Meck, you bastard, detachment comes higher, what do you think? You think it's cheap?" He raged against himself. It was the way he used to speak to people on the telephone. "Wake up. Orphan! Jerk! Wake up. It costs to be detached."

He moved solidly through the small apartment and lay down on his bed with his shoes still on, putting his hands behind his head luxuriously. It's marvelous, he thought. Tomorrow I'll buy a trench coat. I'll take my meals in piano bars. He lighted a cigarette. "I'll never smile again," he sang, smiling. "All right, Eddie, play it again," he said. "Mistuh Wuf, you don' wan' ta heah dat ol' song no maw. You know whut it do to you. She ain' wuth it, Mistuh Wuf." He nodded. "Again, Eddie." Eddie played his black ass off. "The way I see it, Eddie," he said, taking a long, sad drink of warm Scotch, "there are orphans and there are orphans." The overhead fan chuffed slowly, stirring the potted palmetto leaves.

He sat up in the bed, grinding his heels across the sheets. "There are orphans and there are orphans," he said. "I'll move. I'll liquidate. I'll sell out."

He went to the phone and called his landlady and made an appointment to see her.

It was a time of ruthless parting from his things, but there was no bitterness in it. He was a born salesman, he told himself. A disposer, a natural dumper. He administered severance. As detached as a funeral director, what he had learned was to say goodbye. It was a talent of a sort. And he had never felt quite so interested. He supposed he was doing what he had been meant for, what, perhaps, everyone was meant for. He sold and he sold, each day spinning off, reeling off little pieces of himself, like controlled explosions of the sun. Now his life was a series of speeches, of nearly earnest pitches. What he remembered of the day was what he had said. What others said to him, or even whether they spoke at all, he was unsure of.

Tuesday he told his landlady, "Buy my furniture. It's new. It's good stuff. It's expensive. You can forget about that. Put it out of your mind. I want to sell it. I'll show you bills for over seven hundred dollars. Forget the bills. Consider my character. Consider the man. Only the man. That's how to get your bargains. Examine. Examine. I could tell you about inner springs; I could talk to you of leather. But I won't. I don't. I smoke, but I'm careful. I can show you the ashtrays. You won't find cigarette holes in *my* tables. Examine. I drink. I'm a drinker. I drink. But I hold it. You won't find alcohol stains. May I be frank? I make love. Again, I could show you the bills. But I'm cautious. My sheets are virginal, white.

"Two hundred fifty dollars, landlady. Sit on that sofa. That chair. Buy my furniture. Rent the apartment furnished. Deduct what you pay from your taxes. Collect additional rents. Realize enormous profits. Wallow in gravy. Get it, landlady? Get it? Just two hundred fifty dollars. Don't disclose the figure or my name. I want to remain anonymous."

He took her into his bedroom. "The piece of resistance, landlady. What you're really buying is the bedroom stuff. I'm selling you your own bare floor. What charm. Charm? Elegance. Elegance! I throw in the living-room rug. That I throw in. You have to take that or it's no deal. Give me cash and I move tomorrow."

Wednesday he said, "I heard you buy books. That must be interesting. And sad. It must be very sad. A man who loves books doesn't like to sell them. It would be the last thing. Excuse me. I've got no right to talk to you this way. You buy books and I've got books to sell. There. It's business now. As it should be. My library—" He smiled helplessly. "Excuse me. Such a grand name. Library." He began again slowly. "My books, my books are in there. Look them over. I'm afraid my taste has been rather eclectic. You see, my education has not been formal. There are over eleven hundred. Of course many are paperbacks. Well, you can see that. I feel as if I'm selling my mind."

The book buyer gave Ed Wolfe one hundred twenty dollars for his mind.

On Thursday he wrote a letter:

American Annuity & Life Insurance Company,
Suite 410,
Lipton-Hill Building,
2007 Bevero Street, S.W.,
Boston 19, Massachusetts

Dear Sirs,

I am writing in regard to Policy Number 593-000-34-78, a $5,000, twenty-year annuity held by Edward Wolfe of the address below.

Although only four payments having been made, sixteen years remain before the policy matures, I find I must make application for the immediate return of my payments and cancel the policy.

I have read the "In event of cancellation" clause in my policy, and realize that I am entitled to only a flat three percent interest on the "total paid-in amount of the partial amortizement." Your records will show that I have made four payments of $198.45 each. If your figures check with mine this would come to $793.80. Adding three percent interest to the amount ($23.81), your company owes me $817.61.

Your prompt attention to my request would be gratefully appreciated, although I feel, frankly, as though I were selling my future.

On Monday someone came to buy his record collection. "What do you want to hear? I'll put something comfortable on while we talk. What do you like? Here, try this. Go ahead, put it on the machine. By the edges, man. By the edges! I feel as if I'm selling my throat. Never mind about that. Dig the sounds. Orphans up from Orleans singing the news of chain gangs to café society. You can smell the freight trains, man. Recorded during actual performance. You can hear the ice cubes clinkin' in the glasses, the waiters picking up their tips. I have jazz. Folk. Classical. Broadway. Spoken Word. Spoken Word, man! I feel as though I'm selling my ears. The stuff lives in my heart or I wouldn't sell. I have a one-price throat, one-price ears. Sixty dollars for the noise the world makes, man. But remember. I'll be watching. By the edges. Only by the edges!"

On Friday he went to a pawnshop in a Checker Cab.

"You? You buy gold? You buy clothes? You buy Hawaiian guitars? You buy pistols for resale to suicides? I wouldn't have recognized you. Where's the skullcap, the garters around the sleeves? The cigar I wouldn't ask you about. You look like anybody. You look like everybody. I don't know what to say. I'm stuck. I don't know how to deal with you. I was going to tell you something sordid, you know? You know what I mean? Okay, I'll give you facts.

"The fact is, I'm the average man. That's what the fact is. Eleven shirts, 15 neck, 34 sleeve. Six slacks, 32 waist. Five suits at 38 long. Shoes 10-C. A 7½ hat. You know something? Those marginal resturants where you can never remember whether they'll let you in without a jacket? Well the jackets they lend you in those places always fit me. That's the kind of guy you're dealing with. You can have confidence. Look at the clothes. Feel the material. And there's one thing about me. I'm fastidious. Fastidious. Immaculate. You think I'd be clumsy. A fall guy falls down, right? There's not a mark on the clothes. Inside? Inside it's another story. I don't speak of inside. Inside it's all Band-Aids, plaster, iodine, sticky stuff for burns. But outside—fastidiousness, immaculation, reality! My clothes will fly off your racks. I promise. I feel as if I'm selling my skin. Does that check with your figures?

"So now you know. It's me, Ed Wolfe. Ed Wolfe, the orphan? I lived in the orphanage for sixteen years. They gave me a name. It was a Jewish orphanage so they gave me a Jewish name. Almost. That is they couldn't know for sure themselves so they kept it deliberately vague. I'm a foundling. A lostling. Who needs it, right? Who the hell needs it? I'm at loose ends, pawnbroker. I'm at loose ends out of looser beginnings. I need the money to stay alive. All you can give me.

"Here's a good watch. Here's a bad one. For good times and bad. That's life, right? You can sell them as a package deal. Here are radios. I'll miss the radios. A phonograph. Automatic. Three speeds. Two speakers. The politic bastard shuts itself off. And a pressure cooker. It's valueless to me, frankly. No pressure. I can live only on cold meals. Spartan. Spartan.

"I feel as if I'm selling—this is the last of it, I have no more things — I feel as if I'm selling my things."

On Saturday he called the phone company: "Operator? Let me speak to your supervisor, please.

"Supervisor? Supervisor, I am Ed Wolfe, your subscriber at TErrace 7-3572. There is nothing wrong with the service. The service has been excellent. No one calls, but you can have nothing to do with that. However, I must cancel. I find that I no longer have any need of a telephone. Please connect me with the business office.

"Business office? Business office, this is Ed Wolfe. My telephone number is TErrace 7-3572. I am closing my account with you. When the service was first installed I had to surrender a twenty-five-dollar deposit to your company. It was understood that the deposit was to be refunded when our connection with each other had been terminated. Disconnect me. Deduct what I owe on my current account from my deposit and refund the rest immediately. Business office, I feel as if I'm selling my mouth."

When he had nothing left to sell, when that was finally that, he stayed until he had finished all the food and then moved from his old apartment into a small, thinly furnished room. He took with him a single carton of clothing—the suit, the few shirts, the socks, the pajamas, the underwear and overcoat he did not sell. It was in preparing this carton that he discovered the hangers. There were hundreds of them. His own. Previous tenants'. Hundreds. In each closet on rods, in dark, dark corners was this anonymous residue of all their lives. He unpacked his carton and put the hangers inside. They made a weight. He took them to the pawnshop and demanded a dollar for them. They were worth, he argued, more. In an A&P he got another carton free and went back to repack his clothes.

At the new place the landlord gave him his key.

"You got anything else?" the landlord asked. "I could give you a hand."

"No," he said. "Nothing."

Following the landlord up the deep stairs he was conscious of the $2,479.03 he had packed into the pockets of the suit and shirts and pajamas and overcoat inside the carton. It was like carrying a community of economically viable dolls.

When the landlord left him he opened the carton and gathered all his money together. In fading light he reviewed the figures he had entered in the pages of an old spiral notebook:

$$
\begin{array}{lr}
\text{Pay} & \$463.65 \\
\text{Cash} & 12.82 \\
\text{Car} & 300.00 \\
\end{array}
$$

Savings 214.23
Checking 38.91
Furniture (& bedding) 250.00
Books 120.00
Insurance 817.61
Records 60.00

Pawned:
Clothes $110.00
2 watches 18.00
2 radios 12.00
Phonograph 35.00
Pressure Cooker 6.00
Phone deposit (less bill) 19.81
Hangers 1.00
_____
Total $2,479.03

So, he thought, that was what he was worth. That was the going rate for orphans in a wicked world. Something under $2,500. He took his pencil and lined through all the nouns on his list. He tore the list carefully from top to bottom and crumpled the half which inventoried his ex-possessions. Then he crumpled the other half.

He went to the window and pushed the loose, broken shade. He opened the window and set both lists on the ledge. He made a ring of his forefinger and thumb and flicked the paper balls into the street. "Look out for Ed Wolfe," he said softly.

In six weeks the season changed. The afternoons failed. The steam failed. He was as unafraid of the dark as he had been of the sunlight. He longed for a special grief, to be touched by anguish or terror, but when he saw the others in the street, in the cafeteria, in the theatre, in the hallway, on the stairs, at the newsstand, in the basement rushing their fouled linen from basket to machine, he stood, as indifferent to their errand, their appetite, their joy, their greeting, their effort, their curiosity, their grime, as he was to his own. No envy wrenched him, no despair unhoped him, but, gradually, he became restless.

He began to spend, not recklessly so much as indifferently. At first he was able to recall for weeks what he spent on a given day. It was his way of telling time. Now he had difficulty remembering

and could tell how much his life was costing only by subtracting
what he had left from his original two thousand four hundred
seventy-nine dollars and three cents. In eleven weeks he had spent
six hundred seventy-seven dollars and thirty-four cents. It was almost
three times more than he had planned. He became panicky. He
had come to think of his money as his life. Spending it was the
abrasion again, the old habit of self-buffing to come to the thing
beneath. He could not draw infinitely on his credit. It was limited.
Limited. He checked his figures. He had eighteen hundred and one
dollars, sixty-nine cents. He warned himself, "Rothschild, child.
Rockefeller, feller. Look out, Ed Wolfe. Look out."

He argued with his landlord, won a five-dollar reduction in his
rent. He was constantly hungry, wore clothes stingily, realized an
odd reassurance in his thin pain, his vague fetidness. He surren-
dered his dimes, his quarters, his half-dollars in a kind of sober
anger. In seven weeks he spent only one hundred thirty dollars,
fifty-one cents. He checked his figures. He had sixteen hundred
seventy-one dollars, eighteen cents. He had spent almost twice what
he had anticipated. "It's all right," he said. "I've reversed the trend.
I can catch up." He held the money in his hand. He could smell
his soiled underwear. "Nah, nah," he said. "It's not enough."

It was not enough, it was not enough, it was not enough. He had
painted himself into a corner. Death by *cul-de-sac*. He had nothing
left to sell, the born salesman. The born champion, long-distance,
Ed Wolfe of a salesman, and he lay in his room winded, wounded,
wondering where his next pitch was coming from, at one with the
ages.

He put on his suit, took his sixteen hundred seventy-one dollars
and eighteen cents and went down into the street. It was a warm
night. He would walk downtown. The ice which just days before
had covered the sidewalk was dissolved to slush. In darkness he
walked through a thawing, melting world. There was, on the edge
of the air, something, the warm, moist odor of the change of the
season. He was, despite himself, touched. "I'll take a bus," he
threatened. "I'll take a bus and close the windows and ride over
the wheel."

He had dinner and some drinks in a hotel. When he finished he
was feeling pretty good. He didn't want to go back. He looked at
the bills thick in his wallet and went over to the desk clerk. "Where's

the action?" he whispered. The clerk looked at him, startled. He went over to the bell captain. "Where's the action?" he asked and gave the man a dollar. He winked. The man stared at him help-lessly.

"Sir?" the bell captain said, looking at the dollar.

Ed Wolfe nudged him in his gold buttons. He winked again. "Nice town you got here," he said expansively. "I'm a salesman, you understand, and this is new territory for me. Now if I were in Beantown or Philly or L.A. or Vegas or Big D or Frisco or Cincy, why I'd know what was what. I'd be okay, you know what I mean?" He winked once more. "Keep the buck, kid," he said. "Keep it, keep it," he said, walking off.

In the lobby a man sat in a deep chair, *The Wall Street Journal* opened widely across his face. "Where's the action?" Ed Wolfe said, peering over the top of the paper into the crown of the man's hat.

"What's that?" the man asked.

Ed Wolfe, surprised, saw that the man was a Negro.

"What's that?" the man repeated, vaguely nervous. Embarrassed, Ed Wolfe watched him guiltily, as though he had been caught in an act of bigotry.

"I thought you were someone else," he said lamely. The man smiled and lifted the paper to his face. Ed Wolfe stood before the man's opened paper, conscious of mildly teetering. He felt lousy, awkward, complicatedly irritated and ashamed, the mere act of hurt-ing someone's feelings suddenly the most that could be held against him. It came to him how completely he had failed to make himself felt. "Look out for Ed Wolfe, indeed," he said aloud. The man lowered his paper. "Some of my best friends are Comanches," Ed Wolfe said. "Can I buy you a drink?"

"No," the man said.

"Resistance, eh?" Ed Wolfe said. "That's good. Resistance is good. A deal closed without resistance is no deal. Let me introduce myself. I'm Ed Wolfe. What's your name?"

"Please, I'm not bothering anybody. Leave me alone."

"Why?" Ed Wolfe asked.

The man stared at him and Ed Wolfe sat suddenly down beside him. "I won't press it," he said generously. "Where's the action? Where *is* it? Fold the paper, man. You're playing somebody else's gig." He leaned across the space between them and took the man by the arm. He pulled at him gently, awed by his own boldness. It was the first time since he had shaken hands with La Meck that he had touched anyone physically. What he was risking surprised and puzzled him. In all those months to have touched only two people, to have touched even two people! To feel their life, even, as now, through the unyielding wool of clothing, was disturbing. He was unused to it, frightened and oddly moved. The man, bewildered, looked at Ed Wolfe timidly and allowed himself to be taken toward the cocktail lounge.

They took a table near the bar. There, in the alcoholic dark, within earshot of the easy banter of the regulars, Ed Wolfe seated the Negro and then himself. He looked around the room and listened for a moment. He turned back to the Negro. Smoothly boozy, he pledged the man's health when the girl brought their drinks. He drank stolidly, abstractedly. Coming to life briefly, he indicated the men and women around them, their sun-tans apparent even in the dark. "Pilots," he said. "All of them. Airline pilots. The girls are all stewardesses and the pilots lay them." He ordered more drinks. He did not like liquor and liberally poured ginger ale into his bourbon. He ordered more drinks and forgot the ginger ale. "'*Goyim*," he said. "White *goyim*. American *goyim*." He stared at the Negro. "These are the people, man. The mothered and fathered people." He leaned across the table. "Little Orphan Annie, what the hell kind of an orphan is that with all her millions and her white American *goyim* friends to bail her out?"

He watched them narrowly, drunkenly. He had seen them before —in good motels, in airports, in bars—and he wondered about them, seeing them, he supposed, as Negroes or children of the poor must have seen him when he had had his car and driven sometimes through slums. They were removed, aloof—he meant it—a different breed. He turned and saw the Negro and could not think for a moment what the man could have been doing there. The Negro slouched in his chair, his great white eyes hooded. "You want to hang around here?" Ed Wolfe asked him.

"It's your party," the man said.

"Then let's go someplace else," Ed Wolfe said. "I get nervous here."

"I know a place," the Negro said.

"*You* know a place. You're a stranger here."

"No, man," the Negro said. "This is my hometown. I come down here sometimes just to sit in the lobby and read the newspapers. It looks good, you know what I mean? It looks good for the race."

"The *Wall Street Journal?* You're kidding Ed Wolfe. Watch that."

"No," the Negro said. "Honest."

"I'll be damned," Ed Wolfe said. "I come for the same reasons."

"Yeah," the Negro said. "No shit."

"Sure, the same reasons." He laughed. "Let's get out of here." He tried to stand, but fell back again in his chair. "Hey, help me up," he said loudly. The Negro got up and came around to Ed Wolfe's side of the table. Leaning over, he raised him to his feet. Some of the others in the room looked at them curiously. "It's all right," Ed Wolfe said. "He's my man. I take him with me everywhere. It looks good for the race." With their arms around each other's shoulders they stumbled out of the room and through the lobby.

In the street Ed Wolfe leaned against the building and the Negro hailed a cab, the dark left hand shooting up boldly, the long black body stretching forward, raised on tiptoes, the head turned sharply along the left shoulder. Ed Wolfe knew he had never done it before. The Negro came up beside Ed Wolfe and guided him toward the curb. Holding the door open he shoved him into the cab with his left hand. Ed Wolfe lurched against the cushioned seat awkwardly. The Negro gave the driver an address and the cab moved off. Ed Wolfe reached for the window handle and rolled it down rapidly. He shoved his head out the window of the taxi and smiled and waved at the people along the curb.

"Hey, man. Close the window," the Negro said after a moment. "Close the window. The cops, the cops."

Ed Wolfe lay his head along the edge of the taxi window and looked up at the Negro who was leaning over him and smiling and seemed trying to tell him something.

"Where we going, man?" he asked.

"We're there," the Negro said, sliding along the seat toward the door.

"One ninety-five," the driver said.

"It's your party," Ed Wolfe told the Negro, waving away responsibility.

The Negro looked disappointed, but reached into his pocket to pull out his wallet.

Did he see what I had on me? Ed Wolfe wondered anxiously. Jerk, drunk, you'll be rolled. They'll cut your throat and then they'll leave your skin in an alley. Be careful.

"Come on, Ed," the Negro said. He took him by the arm and got him out of the taxi.

Fake. Fake, Ed Wolfe thought. Murderer. Nigger. Razor man.

The Negro pulled Ed Wolfe toward a doorway. "You'll meet my friends," he said.

"Yeah, yeah," Ed Wolfe said. "I've heard so much about them."

"Hold it a second," the Negro said. He went up to the window and pressed his ear against the opaque glass.

Ed Wolfe watched him without making a move.

"Here's the place," the Negro said proudly.

"Sure," Ed Wolfe said. "Sure it is."

"Come on, man," the Negro urged him.

"I'm coming, I'm coming," Ed Wolfe mumbled, "but my head is bending low."

The Negro took out a ring of keys, selected one, and put it in the door. Ed Wolfe followed him through.

"Hey, Oliver," somebody called. "Hey, baby, it's Oliver. Oliver looks good. He looks *good*."

"Hello, Mopiani," the Negro said to a short black man.

"How is stuff, Oliver?" Mopiani said to him.

"How's the market?" a man next to Mopiani asked, with a laugh.

"Ain't no mahket, baby. It's a *sto'*," somebody else said.

A woman stopped, looked at Ed Wolfe for a moment, and asked: "Who's the ofay, Oliver?"

"That's Oliver's broker, baby."

"Oliver's broker looks good," Mopiani said. "He looks *good*."

"This is my friend, Mr. Ed Wolfe," Oliver told them.

"Hey, there," Mopiani said.

"Charmed," Ed Wolfe said.

"How's it going, man," a Negro said indifferently.

"Delighted," Ed Wolfe said.

He let Oliver lead him to a table.

"I'll get the drinks, Ed," Oliver said, leaving him.

Ed Wolfe looked at the room glumly. People were drinking

steadily, gaily. They kept their bottles under their chairs in paper bags. Ed Wolfe watched a man take a bag from beneath his chair, raise it, and twist the open end of the bag carefully around the neck of the bottle so that it resembled a bottle of champagne swaddled in its toweling. The man poured into his glass grandly. At the dark far end of the room some musicians were playing and three or four couples danced dreamily in front of them. He watched the musicians closely and was vaguely reminded of the airline pilots.

In a few minutes Oliver returned with a paper bag and some glasses. A girl was with him. "Mary Roberta, Ed Wolfe," he said, very pleased. Ed Wolfe stood up clumsily and the girl nodded.

"No more ice," Oliver explained.

"What the hell," Ed Wolfe said.

Mary Roberta sat down and Oliver pushed her chair up to the table. She sat with her hands in her lap and Oliver pushed her as though she were a cripple.

"Real nice little place here, Ollie," Ed Wolfe said.

"Oh, it's just the club," Oliver said.

"Real nice," Ed Wolfe said.

Oliver opened the bottle and poured liquor in their glasses and put the paper bag under his chair. Oliver raised his glass. Ed Wolfe touched it lamely with his own and leaned back, drinking. When he put it down empty, Oliver filled it again from the paper bag. He drank sluggishly, like one falling asleep, and listened, numbed, to Oliver and the girl. His glass never seemed to be empty anymore. He drank steadily but the liquor seemed to remain at the same level in the glass. He was conscious that someone else had joined them at the table. "Oliver's broker looks good," he heard somebody say. Mopiani. Warm and drowsy and gently detached, he listened, feeling as he had in barbershops, having his hair cut, conscious of the barber, unseen behind him, touching his hair and scalp with his warm fingers. "You see Bert? He looks good," Mopiani was saying.

With great effort Ed Wolfe shifted in his chair, turning to the girl.

"Thought you were giving out on us, Ed," Oliver said. "That's it. That's it."

The girl sat with her hands folded in her lap.

"Mary Roberta," Ed Wolfe said.

"Uh huh," the girl said.

"Mary Roberta."

"Yes," the girl said. "That's right."

"You want to dance?" Ed Wolfe asked.

"All right," she said. "I guess so."

"That's it, that's it," Oliver said. "Stir yourself."

He got up clumsily, cautiously, like one standing in a stalled Ferris wheel, and went around behind her chair, pulling it far back from the table with the girl in it. He took her warm, bare arm and moved toward the dancers. Mopiani passed them with a bottle. "Looks good, looks good," Mopiani said approvingly. He pulled her against him to let Mopiani pass, tightening the grip of his pale hand on her brown arm. A muscle leaped beneath the girl's smooth skin, filling his palm. At the edge of the dance floor Ed Wolfe leaned forward into the girl's arms and they moved slowly, thickly across the floor. He held the girl close, conscious of her weight, the life beneath her body, just under her skin. Sick, he remembered a jumping bean he had held once in his palm, awed and frightened by the invisible life, jerking and hysterical, inside the stony shell. The girl moved with him in the music, Ed Wolfe astonished by the burden of her life. He stumbled away from her deliberately. Grinning, he moved ungently back against her. "Look out for Ed Wolfe," he crooned.

The girl stiffened and held him away from her, dancing self-consciously. Ed Wolfe, brooding, tried to concentrate on the lost rhythm. They danced in silence for a while.

"What do you do?" she asked him finally.

"I'm a salesman," he told her gloomily.

"Door to door?"

"Floor to ceiling. Wall to wall."

"Too much," she said.

"I'm a pusher," he said, suddenly angry. She looked frightened. "But I'm not hooked myself. It's a weakness in my character. I can't get hooked. Ach, what would you *goyim* know about it?"

"Take it easy," she said. "What's the matter with you? Do you want to sit down?"

"I can't push sitting down," he said.

"Hey," she said, "don't talk so loud."

"Boy," he said, "you black Protestants. What's that song you people sing?"

"Come on," she said.

"Sometimes I feel like a motherless child," he sang roughly. The other dancers watched him nervously. "That's our national anthem, man," he said to a couple that had stopped dancing to look at him. "That's our song, sweethearts," he said, looking around him. "All right, mine then. I'm an orphan."

"Oh, come on," the girl said, exasperated, "an orphan. A grown man."

He pulled away from her. The band stopped playing. "Hell," he said loudly, "from the beginning. Orphan. Bachelor. Widower. Only child. All my names scorn me. I'm a survivor. I'm a god-damned survivor, that's what." The other couples crowded around him now. People got up from their tables. He could see them, on tiptoes, stretching their necks over the heads of the dancers. *No*, he thought. No, no. Detachment and caution. The La Meck Plan. They'll kill you. They'll kill you and kill you. He edged away from them, moving carefully backward against the bandstand. People pushed forward onto the dance floor to watch him. He could hear their questions, could see heads darting from behind backs and suddenly appearing over shoulders as they strained to get a look at him.

He grabbed Mary Roberta's hand, pulling her to him fiercely. He pulled and pushed her up onto the bandstand and then climbed up beside her. The trumpet player, bewildered, made room for him. "Tell you what I'm going to do," he shouted over their heads. "Tell you what I'm going to do."

Everyone was listening to him now.

"Tell you what I'm going to do," he began again.

Quietly they waited for him to go on.

"I don't *know* what I'm going to do," he shouted. "I don't *know* what I'm going to do. Isn't that a hell of a note?

"Isn't it?" he demanded.

"Brothers and sisters," he shouted, "and as an only child bachelor orphan I used the term playfully you understand. Brothers and sisters, I tell you what I'm *not* going to do. I'm no consumer. No-body's death can make me that. I won't consume. I mean it's a question of identity, right? Closer, come up closer, buddies. You don't want to miss any of this."

"Oliver's broker looks good up there. Mary Roberta looks good. She looks good," Mopiani said below him.

"Right, Mopiani. She looks good, she looks *good*," Ed Wolfe called loudly. "So I tell you what I'm going to do. What am I bid? What am I bid for this fine strong wench? Daughter of a chief, masters. Dear dark daughter of a dead dinge chief. Look at those arms. Those arms, those arms. What am I bid?"

They looked at him, astonished.

"What am I bid?" he demanded. "Reluctant, masters? Reluctant masters, masters? Say, what's the matter with you darkies? Come on, what am I bid?" He turned to the girl. "No one wants you, honey," he said. "Folks, folks, I'd buy her myself, but I've already told you. I'm not a consumer. Please forgive me, miss."

He heard them shifting uncomfortably.

"Look," he said patiently, "the management has asked me to remind you that this is a living human being. This is the real thing, the genuine article, the goods. Oh, I told them I wasn't the right man for this job. As an orphan I have no conviction about the product. Now you should have seen me in my old job. I could be rough. Rough. I hurt people. Can you imagine? I actually caused them pain. I mean, what the hell, I was an orphan. I *could* hurt people. An orphan doesn't have to bother with love. An orphan's like a nigger in that respect. Emancipated. But you people are another problem entirely. That's why I came here tonight. There are parents among you. I can feel it. There's even a sense of parents behind those parents. My God, don't any of you folks ever die? So what's holding us up? We're not making any money. Come on, what am I bid?"

"Shut up, mister." The voice was raised hollowly someplace in the back of the crowd.

Ed Wolfe could not see the owner of the voice.

"He's not in," Ed Wolfe said.

"Shut up. What right you got to come down here and speak to us like that?"

"He's not in, I tell you. I'm his brother."

"You're a guest. A guest got no call to talk like that."

"He's out. I'm his father. He didn't tell me and I don't know when he'll be back."

"You can't make fun of us," the voice said.

"He isn't here. I'm his son."

"Bring that girl down off that stage!"

"Speaking," Ed Wolfe said.

"Let go of that girl!" someone called angrily.

The girl moved closer to him.

"She's mine," Ed Wolfe said. "I danced with her."

"Get her down from there!"

"Okay," he said giddily. "Okay. All right." He let go of the girl's hand and pulled out his wallet. The girl did not move. He took out the bills and dropped the wallet to the floor.

"Damned drunk!" someone shouted.

"That white man's crazy," someone else said.

"Here," Ed Wolfe said. "There's over sixteen hundred dollars here," he yelled, waving the money. It was, for him, like holding so much paper. "I'll start the bidding. I hear over sixteen hundred dollars once. I hear over sixteen hundred dollars twice. I hear it three times. Sold! A deal's a deal," he cried, flinging the money high over their heads. He saw them reach helplessly, noiselessly toward the bills, heard distinctly the sound of paper tearing.

He faced the girl. "Goodbye," he said.

She reached forward, taking his hand.

"Goodbye," he said again, "I'm leaving."

She held his, squeezing it. He looked down at the luxuriant brown hand, seeing beneath it the fine articulation of bones, the rich sudden rush of muscle. Inside her own he saw, indifferently, his own pale hand, lifeless and serene, still and infinitely free.

DAVE GODFREY

Newfoundland Night

(FROM THE TAMARACK REVIEW)

As SOON as the drinking started the Professor asked them to leave —
the children who were helping his daughter Grace celebrate her
twentieth birthday — and he went upstairs while she and her David
Saltzman cleaned up. He stopped once and leaned over the balustrade to say good night in his usual manner.

"Bon et amusant soir, mes enfants," he said, "and if Charlemagne
calls again, tell him I'm sorry I'm so swamped, but there's a man
called Alcuin at York who might take the job."

All three of them performed their duty and laughed. The Professor replaced one of the bulbs in the chandelier before he went
into the bedroom. He was the kind of man who used Mazda bulbs
for the name alone, even if they did cost a few cents more.

Ordinarily, on any other night of the year, he would have stayed
when the drinking started and poured all the children another
glass of wine, but this had as long been a deathnight as a birthday
for him and he had, tonight, no desire to be kind to the children of
St John's or any children.

In the morning he would become again his image of himself, a
spark of chaos in the traditional world of these wolf-eyed boys and
seal-bodied girls. They would wander in as always, night in and
night out, hours without end, each unto himself a searcher, listening
with caged wonder and going away with their questions refreshed;
Tony, Albert and Kung Fu, David and Shrevlin, and all the others.

Tonight, however, was the night he allowed himself to look at
the picture of Grace's mother and to read the letter. He could not
now pretend he was anything but an aging English teacher in a

Newfoundland fishing port, nor they anything more than a fresh layer of the ocean-mortised strata of St John's — only temporarily students, permanently the shadows and rebirths of their fathers; waiting with shallow draughted rebellion to follow those same sea-shaggy fathers into the dories and cat houses, the kitchens or garages or starving synagogues of St John's, where they would forget or twist everything he had made them straighten and remember.

The picture was stored in a velvet-lined pine case which, having once held his father's log, now held only that picture, the letter, and the coin. She had, as always, pinecone brown hair and storm black eyes and, as he remembered, a maiden's slow drifting body — nothing any judge would summon out from a crowd; only a simple star that might shine forth once and ever again be lost in the multitude. The Professor prided himself that he preferred to watch one star at a time.

Not that the Professor had any star-crossed illusions. If anything he would say that it was he who had doublecrossed the stars. But he saw her now only through that mist; that mist which he said was like the June fog off the Grand Banks, the product of two conflicting currents, a mist composed half of his thoughts and memories — this half warm and turgid and lazy like the great hammock drift of the Gulf Stream, and composed half of her revivified presence — this half cold and clear and crisp like the great glacial spear of the Labrador current. And because he saw her only through this intermingled mist and never expected nor wanted to do otherwise, he held separate this one night, this one night when the mist was thick enough to block out everything except his one drifting and glacial star.

He had not always known her. It was in the year he was fifteen that his father had moved them across the strait from Bounty Bay to Belle Isle, to a farm that was really and only a farm; really, because it was ten acres large and only because there was no question of deserting it just because the cod were running. It was a kind and warm year. The land had decided to give them a summer of a hundred days and the men were beginning to walk straight again and not run from every hint of frost nor curse every cool evening.

Grace came, one morning, into the barnyard and stared at his father and the four sons. She was like a whippoorwill come out too early at night and caught in a flock of crows, wildbird shy, her body quivering with fear and expectation, sure of the likeness between her and them, not sure in what amount they saw it.

"My name is Grace de la Salle. My father takes the farm between you and the Widow Jackson."

She quivered uncertainly after saying it, like the first whiskeyjack arriving uncertainly in May. Then she ran towards the Professor and tagged him and teased him after her. He followed her into the rocky meadows. He said afterwards that the appearance of a magnet is a wonderful thing to a boy who is looking for the way.

The family taunted him for a while and his mother threatened to change his name from *le Professeur* to *l'Amoureur Petit*. But by then Grace was his lodestar and he could not give a care for what he called the small, magic-lantern images of their mockeries.

They grew up together for five years. During the second and third years his father went after cod again because of the barrenness of the land and lost one son. During the fourth and fifth years the Professor went with him and learned his lessons by oil lamp in the cabin. During the fifth year he bought a camera and won a bursary to the university at St John's.

The picture was taken before he left. She was wearing red plaid shorts and a red blouse tied at the slight white bulge of her belly, standing in front of a green cedar with her tanned legs lost in the meadow of white weeds that surrounded their hiding place.

After he took the picture they ran inside. It was merely four walls of pine and cedar and one mountain ash. There were cedar boughs on the ground and among them grew pigeonberries, sheep laurel, red snakeberries, and the feather moss. She gazed at them with the air of a pagan to whom the contemplation of such was a holy and happy thing, greater than the possession of the richest cedar chest in town. The Professor saw her there with the air of a blue whiskeyjack drifting freely above a cageful of birds of paradise.

"Tell me a lie," she said, "before you go to your city."

"And what color lie are you looking for?" asked the Professor slowly. Even now he remembered with shame that he had been thinking of the unbelievably large library on Crosset Street in St John's.

"What color have you for to tell today?"

"Blue," he said.

"Blue will do very good," she said, "then you will remember saying it at me, for St John's is so smoky you will not often see the blue."

"Not blue like the sky," he said, "nor like the sea, but the kind there's never enough of, the kind like new snow on the flats in

January; the kind where you have to blink to look at it; and past
the farms it's bluer than the August sea, though it seems white as
chicken feathers where it lies close in the webbing of your snow-
shoes.

"That's not a lie yet. I'm doing better than that just by saying
nothing."

"And blue like it will be a hundred years from now when we
creep out of here, out of our *salle petite,* and laugh at the sad world
running on its crooked path below, and run back in for another
hundred years which will be like a day in our eyes or even less than
a day, like the length of that whiskeyjack's song."

"You lie much better than does he."

The bird seemed to be singing to the backwashed cliffs in the
Strait of Belle Isle. Widow Jackson was screaming at it for disturbing her awful contemplation of those scarred and lined rocks, for
interrupting her bitter comparison of how much longer those rocks
were given to accept their scars and lineaments from the sea than
was she.

"Forget her and tell me the red lie," said Grace, *"le mensonge
d'amour."*

Then she turned and he caught again, full face, the warm intensity of the two soft ellipses of her dark nostrils, the warm mother-
hood curve of her mouth.

"Love is a red thing forever against the great gray nets of sorrow
and the deep baited hooks of age. The love of a man for a patched
mackinaw, the red love of a man for a paintless and weatherworn
hull, the love of a man for a shark in his nets because a shark is
better, far better, than no fish at all."

"Beau menteur," she said, which means, at least, beautiful teller
of warm tales on a cold March night.

Then she seized the Professor's hand and pulled him down and
placed the hand over her breasts and circled the other hand over
the slight bulge of her belly which she had told him was only natural in women of eighteen and nothing he should worry himself into
the sea about.

"It happen to all the young women, even the ones who aren't having so good chance to be wicked as me. Do not worry yourself into
the sea about it, it is natural. Tell me now the lie of the love of a
boy for a woman and of the woman for the boy."

He had made the mist almost deep enough now, almost as warm

and lazy as a drifting dory, almost as clear and cold as a blue shark. He made it a little deeper.

"The saddest love of all and the greatest. The love of the wind for a rusty corn tassel, the love of the wind for the brown feathers of a mallard in flight."

Between them and the hamlet, Widow Jackson rose from her chair to scream at the scarred cliffs.

"You'll get et all ta hell same's me," she cracked, her arms flailing against the breeze. "You goan last some longer but they'll et you too. We be all ta same, it's no better ta be me than you, one bowl of ta same rotten meal and fish bones."

"Forget her," said Grace, "tell it to me again in one time and then you can. Then we can have each other again. Then you can go and leave me and learn whatever it is you do not already know. Only poet me first, poet me of the lodestar."

"If we are not one," he repeated, "we are two so made as fisherman and bright north star, never both reaching the same warm home, yet one following wherever the other must go."

The Professor's hand ebbed from Grace's breast slowly, as though reluctant to forsake the flowing.

"Poet again," she said, "please once more."

"I cannot poet you of love," said the Professor sadly, "because there is no rhyme for love. Nor can anyone. They who try are only harsh fishermen, fishermen with cracked boots pulling already dead cod out of the sea and slitting them for the salt. Love's pigment is too delicate for salt. Love is too wild to catch."

"Lie then," said Grace.

"I can lie some of feeling, which is neither salt nor the sea but is itself. I can feel then your arms and your breasts and your belly so fiercely that the cliffs will be ashamed of the tender touch of the storms."

"Touch me then," she whispered, "once more then before we go, touch me."

"Are you ready," he said.

"I am ready, slowly now, slowly; like a dory adrift."

They moved hand in hand on the boughs and rolled over with their time spent to watch the blue of the sky which changed slowly, for them, into the winter blue of deep blizzard snowdrifts so that neither of them saw Widow Jackson peeking in from the north side of the cedars as was her manner, for it was a happy thing and a beautiful thing to watch, even for a widow.

And if silence is a silver gift then blindness is gold fresh from the mines at Porcupine. For, when he had put the picture back into the pine case and before he had taken out the letter, it was the quiet rustle of white lace and brown woolen trousers which pried his ears open, but it was the harsh stare of the circle of five Mazda bulbs which broke into his eyes. By then he had opened the door back into the hall and stood below the chandelier, one hand on the balustrade. Reality shriveled the leapings of his mind like the coarse salt cast on a gutted cod. He croaked down at them.

"Grace! Tell that filthy little fisher of girls to get his paws off you and get himself back to his dory. Your mother didn't die to bring you into a goddamned bawdy house."

Then, his conscience salved by saying that, he started remembering again. He turned out the cluster of bulbs, shut the door and took out the letter so he could salve his imagination once more.

And when he saw the deepness of the mist which he knew would come out of that letter, he smiled sadly to himself, as if in apology to himself for having to have a conscience, and he whispered to himself, no my little Grace, not into a god-be-damned body house. Then he read the letter. Then he finally made the mist as deep as he wanted it, as deep as the June mauz off Newfoundland, as warm and lazy and turgid as the great dory drift of the Gulf Stream, as cold and clear and crisp as the great blue shark spear of the Labrador current.

"o love i know you are happy there in saint johns where you can be anight the men you have told me about so i am not sending you this letter ever but shall keep it until you are anight me again in our petite salle when the ice and the storms have gone and you can come again and then you can listen to me read it to you and i will listen to you tell me about your shakespear who you say would understand you and me and your rablais who you say would laugh at us but then would come and peek like we caught old widow jackson doing that time and your witman who i know would aid us and not leave the days as they are with you cast out from the roof of your pere because you have to be a professeur and me cast out from the roof of my pere because i have given you my flower and am carrying your fruit and will be delivered of it only by taking the charity of

strangers but i am happy love for most of the time i can see you
through the mauzy distance which keeps us one from the other and
i hope at times you think of me especially in the still of the night
when you are like me and lonesome as a gull on a rock and it is only
a small some of the time that i think at you and wish that the ice
and the storms were not between us so i could send you this letter
and wish that you were here anighst me so do not say i sin against
you for that small some of the time o my love for i cannot keep it
down to want you here and most at nights when i remember the
days when we were on belle isle with only the farm of widow jackson between us for always then i get to thinking how warm it would
be if you were here again o love but i do not mean to complain i
who have your coin and wear it around my neck for it is my crucifix
and my rosary since the father did cast me out and commanded my
pere to do likewise in the name of their god so now i do as i know
you would want and around my neck i wear the coin against my
skin and under all my clothes so that it can hear my heart beat and
i know the coin so well against my breasts which are swelling for
the little grace that i can tell which side is out either the side with
the picture of the bearded king and the four numbers one six nine
eight or the side with only the circle of leaves and the latin and the
name of your great grandpere cut into it so he could give it to his
love as you have given it to me and o love i am forty times happier
with my coin than they who have diamonds and walk to the other
side of the streets of bounty bay when they see me coming though
that is sometimes a bad thing for me as it is hard to remember in
the rays of the sun and on the streets of the town just how sweet and
strong your lies can be but at least i remember to forget them when
they change sides and look away from me for they are so often
bostoons and chuckleheads as you say and i go down then to the
cove where i can ly on the sand for it is early june now and i look
at the pictures you have sent me with the grenville men and at the
poems and i can see you so clearly especially when it is dusk and
the dark of the first stars is all around and dew seems to drift
everywhere between the leaves and the sand o love when did you
first show me that things are most clear when they are shadowed
or watered or branched so that the dark of the water or the leaves
let you see what is truly there because it is such a comfort to have
that and all the other things you have taught me when the nurse

comes and rolls me over and diagnoses me like i were a cod out
on the rack of a poor man so that i have never told her about you
my love but just let her think what she wants to think which is not
what i would want to have in my head for she is a bostoon and
a chucklehead and not at all like the doctor who i have told about
you for he is so warm when he talks and when he calls me grace
that i can almost think it is you and i have showed him your coin
and said as how you will marry with me when you are truly a
professeur so this morning i have hear him tell the nurse to be
more kind at me and i know they are worried into the sea about
me and that i will not be strong enough for at times the blood
rushes in me like a march tide and my whole body aches and
whirls like a dory in a storm at the ocean but i will fool them
both for i have so much to be strong for o love i who am always
in heaven and will always be so even when the day is arrive that
we must die and voyage where the petite salle is maybe waiting
for us o love i who am always in heaven even when you are not
here anighst me no no that is not true o love it is not vraiment
so for at times i am more lonesome than any gull on any lonely
rock and i want to tell you and i want you to come home somehow
and be here anighst me but it is always true in the way your lies
are true for i want always to be in heaven but seem to be in hell
and when the pains come hard like a storm and blood rushes all
through my body so i can see you only by pressing the coin hard
in my hands and peering through the black which is all my world
then staring like my pere must stare when the ship of his sons is
out late o love even then i remember that i want to be in heaven
and when the pain is gone then i go into purgatoire until i can
hear you again or see through the mauz or smell you again strong
like the warm breeze of the straits when the wind is blowing deep
from the south like the day when we first went into the petite
salle or the year when the sheep were so many that we could run
across their backs in the pen and their wool was almost as soft
as your eyes that day when we learned that the moon kept time
like me and the tides that flowed in the straits flowed also in me
o love you will come no so soon to me and will not need to walk
into purgatoire ever again o love we will walk to the shores of
the straits and see our belle isle and go there as i went this morning
with my eyes for this morning they left me for an hour when i told

them i needed to go to church you know what church i went to down by the sand i went walking and looking for the grass which you told me is the handwork of god and mountain ash who is my brother o love you must not be wrath with me that i could not make them kin and holy for the grass and the mountain ash are poor things to me love for they have not your lies to ring like the angelus in their ears and your face to shine like the lodestone in their eyes o love i saw you this morning before i came back coming to me o my love and walking grand and young off the packet as you will truly walk in a month and already you had forgiven me for hiding the little grace because you had to go away and i knew you had to go away but you had forgiven me and all was absolution for you were touching me o love you who are my handwork and my god warm and soft as the southern stream and my mountain ash and my brother cold and clear as the northern stream coming to me up the straits so that we may run bare across the wool backs of the sheep and hide again in the cedar boughs of our petite salle de la grace."

WILLIAM J. J. GORDON

The Pures

(FROM THE ATLANTIC MONTHLY)

A MYOPIC in a back-room lab hollers "Eureka" and stumbles out with some new hooligan of an alloy. Cheaper than mud and tougher than diamonds. Right away I'm supposed to have free samples for my clients. They figure I'm the sharpest metal-fatigue man in the business, so nothing new in metals should happen anywhere without me plugging right in. No kidding. Samples! There's only one way to plug into the latest technical poop. I take in every scientific symposium in my line. What a bind. Three days folded into one of those wooden camp chairs.

Not only that, but I have to watch myself every second or I'll get sucked into the running fight between the pures and the applieds. For instance, last week I was in South Station buying a magazine for the trip out to the Third Metallurgical Congress in Chicago when up comes Professor Keel.

"Hi, Fairley," he said.

Professor Keel is leader of the applieds. No formal election or anything. He's just the appliedest. He patted a small wrapped package.

"You'll need more than *Time* Magazine to sweat out a train trip with the 'good guys.'" He laughed. That's what the applieds call the pures. They refer to themselves as the "bad guys." Keel thought the pure-applied battle was a riot. He's a nifty dresser — he gets those big consultant fees. And he has a manicure every Saturday. No bull! He marches in there and holds out his hands so some bimbo can work on them. You can see him right through the window.

He patted his package again. "Look into the pewter pot, an
see the world as the world is not," he said. He raised up his eyes lik
a priest. "Give me strength to endure the pures, for they know no
what they do," he prayed and walked away humming.

I went back to picking out a magazine. You've got to be carefu
what you read on a train full of academic people. With *Fortune*
the pures call you a fascist. With the *Saturday Review,* the applied
figure you've gone high-hat. I was reaching for something with
bimbo on the cover when I heard a whisper in my ear like a com
bination special agent and pimp.

"Good afternoon, Dr. Fairley." It was Professor Sanborn, bo
of pures. Also no election. Just the purest. Dresses like a refuge
No big consultant fees, so he's a snob. "I see you're arming yourse
for the trip with the 'gadgeteers.'" That's what the pures call th
applieds, "gadgeteers." It's the worst thing they can imagine sa
ing, and they don't think it's funny. This trip was shaping up int
a real knockdown, drag-out. "See you on board," Professor Sanbor
hissed, and took off. I hung around fingering the magazines ti
train time and got on at the last minute. In fact, I thought of takin
a plane.

Guess what I had for a Pullman. One of those prewar babies wi
uppers and lowers and a big can at each end. I swung up on th
platform, and a bald guy with a box in his hand asked me for m
name. I told him, and he began hunting around in his little bo
Finally he pulled out a big red lapel button. On it was printe
"Dr. A. Morrison Fairley, Consultant," and on the bottom, "Ca
me SONNY." I gave the bald guy a look. He got the message.

"I thought I'd try to add a little informal dynamics," he sai
"Last summer we had the same trouble at Camp Highlife. Th
way I figure — "

"Did you get all the Metallurgical Congress members to put o
the buttons?" I asked.

"Oh, yes," the bald guy said. "I had a little mix-up with Profess
Sanborn. Had to help him pin it on. I got the feeling he was figh
ing it." This trip was going to be a beaut. I went into the car, an
sure enough, everyone was wearing his badge. But you could te
the pures from the applieds. The pures had scratched out the nic
names on theirs. I dropped my bag and began to make my way u
the car, talking science with pures and yukking it up with applied

The applieds went in for a lot of handshaking and backslappi and calling back and forth, like a bunch of alumni. The pures greeted each other quietly — "Nobody here but us pures." In five minutes, by the time we got to Back Bay Station, all the pures were correcting exams or writing technical papers.

There was one man in the car who was a stranger to me. He was scribbling in a notebok, so I figured him for a pure, even though I couldn't see if his nickname was scratched out. When I sat down beside Professor Sanburn, I asked about the scribbler. Sanborn pushed his lips right up against my left ear, his eyes rolling all over his head on the lookout for spies. He doesn't do top-secret work or anything, but he wants people to think he's in on something red hot.

"That's my new man," Sanborn hissed. "Brilliant — mathematical wizard — pure mathematics, that is. From Cambridge University. They have a certain style of science over there you know. Name's Professor Black."

"How lucky you are to have him," I whispered.

Sanborn nodded his head to show how lucky he was, and I got up and went down the aisle. From the others I learned that Professor Black was indeed a valuable piece of scientific merchandise. All had read his paper, "The Erosion of Metals and the Ballistics of the Upper Atmosphere." Black was, as Sanborn had promised, pure as the driven snow. Even Keel, leader of the applieds, respected him.

"It was a lucky day for Frank Sanborn when the university dug up the dough to buy Black away from the Cavendish," Keel told me. "Sanborn's department hasn't turned out anything significant for ten years, but Black will change all that. I hardly know the man, you understand. Sanborn keeps him under lock and key like a god-damn virgin."

Professor Black stayed in his seat, still scribbling in his notebook. He was a very small, round man, about thirty, cherubic face, pink and white, feathery blond hair. Every once in a while he would raise his face from his work to look out the window. His lips kept moving in some technological litany. Of course, being new, he hadn't any friends aboard, and his busy-busy attitude made it hard to strike up a conversation with him, or else I would have. What the hell? Everybody likes me.

The trip went along nicely. After supper the applieds pushed into the club car for highballs, the whole bunch of them. The pures were so damn churchy that it made the applieds extra noisy and gay. About eleven thirty I packed my traps and sloped for bed. When I entered the men's washroom I found Professor Black stripping lengths of toilet paper off a roll. Very carefully he was covering the floor with toilet-paper steppingstones. His underwear hung on a hook. He had five of those little Pullman towels knotted together and tied around his baby-fat waist. He smiled at me and went back to work. I said, "Hi," and began fiddling with my toilet kit. If some nut wants to lay down a bum-wad mosaic in a Pullman men's room, that's okay with me. He unrolled a path of toilet paper ahead of himself into the w.c. and shut the door.

Professor Black had just closed the door behind him when Professor Keel came in holding a pint of bourbon. He waved the bottle at me. I guess I didn't look too full of beans.

"It couldn't hurt you," he said. He poured a drink into one of those conical paper cups you find in trains. Then he made a drink for himself. I sat down next to him on the long black leather settee those old sleeper toilets have. What a room! The heavy faded green curtain blocking the entrance, the stained leather settee, the three metal washbasins lined up in a row; and at the far end was the door to the w.c. Even the cuspidor was there, squatting down under the empty metal matchbox container. I was taking my first sip of bourbon when Professor Sanborn slippered in. He was decked out in a woolen bathrobe with a Sears, Roebuck design on it. He went right up to a little basin, squeezed out a two-inch toothpaste worm, and began to brush his teeth.

"How about a little snort, Frank?" said Keel. He winked at Professor Sanborn, who worked up so much lather in his mouth that I thought he'd strangle. With his back to the door of the w.c., Sanborn didn't see Professor Black skip out in his Pullman-towel skirt. Black bumped into Sanborn.

"Oops!" said Black. "Sorry." Sanborn's mouth was too full of toothpaste for him to talk. He bobbed his head and stood aside for his bright young man.

"Drink?" said Keel to Black.

Black thought a moment.

"I'd be grateful to you," he said. Sanborn gave both of them a dirty look.

Keel pulled out another of those conical paper cups and filled it. Black took it in his infant fist and drank it in one gulp.

"Mmm — just the job," he said. "Queer, you know. I never developed a taste for Scotch, but I always loved bourbon, and I'm a Scotsman."

Keel refilled Black's paper cup. By this time the cup was so soggy that Black gripped it by the bottom vertex so as not to force out the booze. All the while he was turning on faucets in the three little shaving bowls. With one hand he pinched the papercup, and with the other he tested the water in the washbowls and added hot water or cold, according to his taste. Filling the bowls was quite a project — noisy, too. Sanborn watched Black with visible anxiety, Keel with delight, none of us with comprehension. I was afraid Keel was feeling his oats, and sure enough, he opened up the can of peas.

"Tell me, Professor Black," said Keel. "Where do you stand on the subject of pure as opposed to applied science?"

"Let me see." The little guy had filled three washbasins according to his recipe. He threw his Pullman-towel skirt on a hook and leaned against a basin, completely naked. He was real cute and relaxed. He sipped the bourbon that was forced to the top of the cup as it collapsed. He was thinking about his answer to Keel, working hard to understand how he actually felt.

"As a pure man yourself," Keel went on, "you must have some conviction, some constructive bias." That was the ball game, right there!

"Keel," Professor Sanborn interrupted, "I'm afraid it's impossible for your kind to understand how *we* function. Pure scientific investigation must have no purpose. It is research for its own sake. Furthermore, since Professor Black is a stranger in our country, it is an imposition to lure him into a private fight." Sanborn's knobbly bathrobe made me think of a down-South camp-meeting preacher on his way to the outhouse. As he talked, bits of forgotten toothpaste foam flicked out.

"Frank," said Keel to Sanborn, "I purposely directed my question to Professor Black hoping to get a new point of view. You see — "

"Could someone give me a leg up?" asked Black. The little guy was standing next to the middle washbasin, one hand on it and one hand holding his paper cup. He lifted one foot off the floor, and I leaned over and cupped my hands around his foot as if I were helping someone up on a horse.

"Thank you," said Black. "A wee bit more."

I gave a little hoist, and up he went into the three basins, fat little feet in one, round ass in the middle basin, head in the third. It seemed impossible that Black would fit into the three basins, let alone be grunting contendedly. He held his head way back in the last basin and sipped at his paper cup of bourbon by continuing to pinch the conical bottom in one hand. In his other hand was one of those tiny pieces of soap they give you in Pullmans. Finally Keel found his voice again. "I feel sure that Professor Black *does* have a new point of view," said Keel.

Black lost the piece of soap. He groped around in all the basins till he found it. Then he washed his feet with great difficulty. Finally, he lathered his behind and lay back again.

"Pure science," Black mused, "pure science. Let's work from analogy. With some people, if a mountain's there, they have to climb it. With me, if a typewriter's there, I have to start thumping. I love to slap the keys on the roll, particularly if I have nothing to say, which is the usual case. Pure typing, that's what! Typing for typing's sake!"

He paused a moment to pinch a little bourbon into his puckered mouth. In the interim, Professor Keel said that he was very interested and Professor Sanborn appeared to be in shock. I didn't know what to do or say. This pure versus applied business was something I had always avoided, and I wasn't going to get pulled in now. But Black looked like dynamite, and I figured there'd be fireworks.

"Pure typing is like pure art or pure science." Black picked up where he had left off. "Applied art is for advertisements — billboards, calendars. Applied science is for gadgets. Applied typing is too commercial for me, in like manner. Pure typing is sans the commercial blight of purpose. It does not soil its soul for gold. Its eyes are raised to the high *a priori* road of absolute essence. It's a kind of Zen within Zen."

He stopped a moment to hold out his limp paper cup to Keel. Like a zombie, Keel rose and filled it. By this time all the wet strength of the paper cup was gone. The bourbon began to leak out of the bottom in little tears. Black concentrated on this phenomenon as though it were a great discovery, then tucked the conical bottom into his mouth and sucked.

"Trouble with Joyce was he dropped his sights too low; next thing you know three professors made him coherent. As a pure typist he was all washed up. Personally" — Black raised his head a bit to tell us this in a confidential manner; he almost mimicked Professor Sanborn's pimp delivery — "personally, I believe that Joyce had the talent to be a great pure typist, perhaps the greatest. He simply couldn't tolerate the rarefied atmosphere of intensely concentrated ambiguity. The professors hammered a wedge into him by interpreting his reference to the Greek myths, and then the balloon went up, the flap was on. After that, the professors made sense out of everything. Joyce was a beaten man, applied and beaten."

All this while Black had been soaping himself with that midget piece of soap. He kept losing the soap and feeling around for it. By squirming into a sequence of contortions he managed somehow to lather his whole body. Then he picked his head out of its basin and his feet out of their basin. He left his bottom in the middle basin and swung down his legs. They were short and hairless, like an infant's. Professor Sanborn's skinny blue hands fidgeted in his toilet kit. Keel got up and filled Black's leaking cup, put some more booze in mine, and absentmindedly poured a cup for Sanborn.

Sanborn autnomically tossed off his drink in one swallow. For a moment his old eyeballs glazed over like candied apples. He didn't say anything. He just sat there and stared at Black's plump feet. Keel, too, seemed to be hypnotized by the plump pinkness. He sipped at his drink and kept his eyes on the feet dangling below the Pullman basin.

"Next time I have my hands done," Keel said quietly, "I think I'll have my feet done too."

Suddenly Sanborn snapped out of his trance and rose to go out. Immediately, Black jumped off his perch, hopped across the room on his bumwad steppingstones, and blocked the exit. There he was, the little cherubic bastard, standing stark naked against the green drape, soapy lather drying on his body in bubbles; smiling, not tough, kind of pleading.

"Professor Sanburn," he said, "I beg you to stay till I've finished my wee treatise."

Sanborn tried to duck under Black's outthrust arms, but Black crouched down and blocked him.

"It wouldn't be fair not to hear me out, now would it, sir?"

That drink of bourbon Sanborn had tossed off must have given

him some bezazz. He tucked his toilet kit under his arm and looked
Black right in the eye. Then he put his lips to Black's right ear.
"You are correct, sir," hissed Sanborn in his top-secret style. "It
would not be fair. But it's after midnight. I am growing tired. I
would appreciate your coming to the point of what you call your
'treatise.' " And he went back and sat down next to Keel.

Keel and Sanborn were being drawn closer through sharing this
guy Black's performance. They huddled together on that black
leather men's room settee like a couple of kids watching Dracula.

"If I understand you, Professor Black" — Keel was trying to plug
in — "you're saying that applied science is a lower order of activity
than pure science."

Keel is a good guy — jokes, drinks, and no question about com-
petence in his field. But he's trade school, no real intellectual. I at
least had heard of Joyce, a crazy writer. But I bet Keel didn't have
a clue. That narrow-gauge mind of his was glued to the pures-
applieds battle. If he could swing Black over to the applieds, it
would mean a lot of prestige to his position. Black had drained the
three basins and was putting in fresh water.

"Don't know where I stand. That's why I didn't want Professor
Sanborn to leave. If I can talk for a few more minutes, I think I'll
get somewhere!"

With that, Black waved a foot at me, and I boosted him into
the three basins again. Only this time, after lying down, he splashed
water all over himself, rinsing off the soap. The soap had dried, and
he had a hell of a time.

"Always have a wash before going to bed — every night — never
miss — sleep better."

He ducked his head backward into the basin and thrashed around
till I thought he'd bust something. Finally he lifted out his head
and rested his cheek on the side of the bowl.

"Take Da Vinci. What kind of pure typist would he have made?
Mediocre. Too much control. Gertrude Stein? She talked a good
game of typing — 'Pigeons on the grass, alas' — but when it came
right down to it, she tightened up. The unanalyzed music of the
spheres, that's the symbol of your best kind of pure typist. How
about this? Jazz typing — hot typing, cool typing, or whatever you
Americans call it. A cocktail-bar combo of organ, cornet, and IBM
electric! Now there's pure typing for you! No words, no poems,
pure percussion. Wouldn't be half bad."

"Professor Black," Sanborn interrupted, "if you carry out your excellent logic to a systematic limit, you are forced to admit that even your quaintly conceived notion of pure typing breaks down in your last example."

"Which example, sir?" asked Black.

"In your musical example," said Sanborn, "which I enjoyed very much."

You have to hand it to Sanborn. He's sharp. He'd been following Black all the while. I'd thought he was scared stiff.

"Pursuing your train of thought a moment: you invented a form of typing so pure that its only use would be as part of some kind of jazz band. Right?"

"Combo — yes, sir."

"Fine. As you say, 'combo.' Very well. The fallacy in your logic derives from the fact that the purest typing you could invent has a use — namely, in a jazz combo."

Sanborn had been leaning foward to deliver his critique. Now he relaxed back on the settee. Keel shook the last drink out of his bottle, sighted over the spitton like a bombardier, and let go! Crash!

Black skidded out of his three bowls and stood dripping in front of Sanborn. He danced around, sending little drops of water all over Sanborn and Keel. He was so excited he forgot to use his toilet-paper steppingstones.

"You're right," he cried. "By George, you're right!"

He grabbed for his string of knotted Pullman towels and began rubbing himself down with them. He stopped.

"But what is the final implication, sir, would you say?"

Sanborn closed his eyes in thought. "I would hold that the systematic resultant of your dissertation is that jazz typing is not pure typing. There's your fallacy, right there."

"I would query that point, sir," said Black. "I would say that my argument implies that the difference between pure and applied has been overemphasized."

Keel finally plugged in, at least to the fact that the old battle was on. "I say something different from both of you," Keel said. "Professor Black has shown that nothing is truly pure, that nothing exists until it is applied."

"Professor Keel," said Sanborn, "that's a typical biased resultant, worthy of your usual intellectual conduct."

Black had by this time put on his underwear. Without saying

good night Sanborn pushed his way out through the green curtain. Keel followed, arguing, and Black and I were left alone.

"Maybe only one thing is pure," Black said to me. "Spontaneous war!"

"Professor Black," I asked, "was that bath really satisfying?"

"Oh, my, yes," said Black. "But even war is not perfectly pure; it's such an ends-and-means mix-up. Over in Moscow they've got a huge cigar pointed toward New York. In New York there's a great thing pointed toward Moscow. Each missile is filled with special instruments to get on target. And all that fuel — very inefficient, very gadgety, not pure at all."

"It didn't look very comfortable," I said, "with your knees bent up and all."

"But it could be made pure," Black went on. "Let's say the two missiles, in Moscow and New York, were directed straight up and just had a tiny bit of fuel, or no fuel at all, just a great big spring, no complicated gadgets that might go wrong."

"I might try a tub like yours myself," I said. I began to take off my pajamas. "Trains always make me feel dirty."

"At a given signal Moscow and New York could blow themselves up with an elegance and certainty unattainable under present gross gadgetry conditions. Each missile would go straight up for a few feet, then *down!* And *bang!* Here, let me show you. If your feet aren't placed just so in that last basin, it throws off the whole wash."

JOHN HERMANN

Aunt Mary

(FROM PERSPECTIVE)

I REMEMBER Uncle Josie because his wife, Mary, long-nosed, em-
bittered, came weekly when I was a child to visit my mother, sitting
at the round, dining-room table telling her about his other women.
When I came in from the porch, where I had been reading, on my
way upstairs to my room, the conversation halted above Aunt
Mary's hands folded tightly on the lace tablecloth. My mother would
be sitting on the edge of her chair across the table waiting to get
back to the kitchen and to the apple-peeling she had started for a
pie. Their condemnation filled the air above their heads like fly
spray. As I closed the door to the upstairs behind me, I heard Aunt
Mary's voice begin again: "And last night I told him . . ."

He must have been fifty then. To me, still in parochial school,
abashed by the nuns' eyes that looked to us as unswerving as railroad tracks from beneath their coifs, the white, bushy crest of Uncle
Josie's hair, uncovered even in the coldest of northern Wisconsin
winters when the snow squeaked underfoot, was a jaunty banner of
sin beside Aunt Mary's black cloche hat and shoulders hunched together. To others he might have been nothing. To me he was
an Attila, riding hard.

The year I was in the seventh grade, Aunt Mary came to stay at
our house for an entire week, and my father had to move upstairs
with us boys while she and my mother slept together in the bedroom
downstairs, where late into the night we heard them talking quietly
like executioners waiting for the dawn. At meal time, the pinched
face, slightly blue in the cold, like china, was held unbending over

the table, nibbling at the tiny portion of potato she had allotted
herself, as if she were making sure she were not imposing on us. She
wore perpetually, like a medal, a St. Sebastian look of martyrdom
and Uncle Josie, the Roman soldier shooting arrows into her, was
doomed to hell as surely as Gung Chisle, a farmer outside of town
who had hacked at his wife's head with his pig-butchering knife the
year before and who now sat in the county jail thinking about it —
and the maple sugar gathering that he was missing.

When Uncle Josie came to the house to see Aunt Mary, however,
he was clean, meek, and wearing a tie, which was more than my
other uncles did. Nevertheless, I knew from my mother's frozen,
unbending stance beside the flower box on the railing where they
talked that he was the closest image to Lucifer that I was likely to
encounter. He is dead now, along with Aunt Mary, both sifting
away in the Antigo Cemetery beneath their granite headstones
stained by water and teetering, as if one corner of the boxes had
given way first. But Uncle Josie doesn't stay there all the time. For
thirty years now he has followed me, and I can call him to me whenever I want and he comes, the head and hair at least, and the tanned,
sober face. Often he comes unasked for, when I read in the paper
about a woman who shot her husband, when I sit in church next to
a folded pair of hands. He says nothing when he comes, like the
statue of a saint. But I know he is hardly that, for Aunt Mary's
hands resting across the pew top where she knelt beside my mother
at church on Sunday were thin and strong and never stopped along
the circle of beads, and the long-suffering faces of both of them were
uplifted confidently to the altar through the rain of sorrow falling
upon the daughters of Eve — the sorrowful mysteries of being married to a man with hair like an aureole of light and, I envisioned,
with girls all over his lap where he sat in the bar of the Antigo Hotel
near the railroad tracks, girls whose laughter came up the steps to
the sidewalk and said: "Aunt Mary, you're an old bitch," and
laughed and giggled again and snuggled closer. Uncle Josie, Uncle
Josie, Uncle Josie. He drifts through my boyhood with all the elan
of iniquity and adventure while I listen to the clanging of the train
in the night as it gets ready to leave for Eland and Appleton and
Fondulac, all the towns downstate that glowed, it seemed to me,
brighter and warmer than those bleak station platforms of the north
where the freight wagons were backed up against the brick walls of

the depot and only a few flakes of snow, drifting down along the side
of the building, fell on the suitcases, the gray bags of mail. Someday
I too. And I had. I did. I am.

But whenever I take my family back to Wisconsin in the summer
to where my mother still lives, Uncle Josie is there also, most often
hovering around the place where the boardinghouse used to be, to
where Aunt Mary had banished him after they were separated. It
is a mortuary now that has petunias in geometric beds by the sidewalk and a lawn like a tablecloth and a sign like a placecard in one
corner with a single name on it — MacMillans — as if everyone in
Antigo knew what it meant, like Caesar, like Napoleon, like Sopho-
cles, like gray gloves and a cart with rubber wheels for the casket
in church. And on my way downtown to get a haircut I see him
from a distance sitting on the porch, but then as I come nearer, he
gets up and walks toward the door so that I glimpse only his head
moving into the dimness of the foyer. And in the next block I see
him over the half curtains of Martini's saloon leaning against the
bar in that limbo of debauchery and gloom spending Aunt Mary's
money, sliding it across the counter. And on Main Street when I
stop before Barney Jewel's music store with its white plaster dog
sitting on an island of green felt, its head cocked listening to all
those people underground, he joins me at the window, staring at
those refinements he never knew married to Aunt Mary, at that
sheet music whose notes he couldn't read, at the gleam of that
polished piano and the intricate levers of that clarinet's sweetness.
What then, Uncle Josie? What good are all the girls now?

There weren't any girls, he said.

Come now. I'm not that pink-jowled Kenneth of Aunt Mag's you
knew thirty years ago.

No girls, he said. I was fifty already.

Aunt Mary said . . . But he had slipped across the street into
Tomany's Pool Hall, and I could see him going past the spotlighted,
green baize tables toward the poker games in the back room.

Here me. At continuous pole of barber shop. Where hair plaster-
ing I endured as a youth. I enter. Mr. Yaeger. Without teeth.
Except him, all new. I choose — any, all, Mr. Yaeger himself. Sheet
thrown over, immobilized like a charm. Conversation begun, pin-
ning cloth around my neck.

"Where are you now, Ken?" As if defective, lotus-succumbing, I

had deserted that Main Street of his for softer climes. Hair hacked
at. Not white, not bushy, not aureoled. Hair.

"West Coast," I say.

"Still teaching?" As if I hadn't pitched oats all through the sum-
mers along the windrows with farmer cousins. Snip. Snap. Clicks
comb against shears in barbershop harmony while across the street
over the tops of the parked cars I see Uncle Josie emerge from
Tomany's and turn toward the tracks, toward Hoffman House, to
those Circe caves and board-creaking rooms.

"Yes. California," I say to annoy him. "College." And he pauses
to absorb what that means, his shears, his comb, resting against the
back of the chair.

"College, eh? How'd that happen?" Gums mash molars, pushing
out his lips. Stench blown, moist, past my ear.

"Ten years ago. Pleasant place." I add: "Should visit it sometime." He jacks down the chair. Take that for leaving Wisconsin
cut-over timberland for the idleness of Rose Bowl perfumery and
bathing-suit poses. I could play too: "Beautiful country. No snow
at all." As if June never knew where his barbershop was, and summer came and went like a ten-minute train stop between long
months of uninterrupted snow. But Uncle Josie and I have no
chance really, the close-cropped stubble of my own hair in the
mirror, tonsured, nun-like, denying his halo, with Aunt Mary's
pinched nose hanging over her upper lip, with my mother's potent,
five-hundred year indulgences against him, with Mr. Yaeger's mouth
like a munching sea anemone.

Dusted with talcum, mummied with pomade, I seek the street.
That way? This? Uncle Josie has disappeared, silent, evasive, to
rejoin his bella raggazza, those Hoffman House hanger-ons, to en-
tangle his handsome head with their disordered, tumbled, end-
frizzed ambiguities. Wrecker of family sanctity, roué of a main
street two blocks long, spender of Aunt Mary's church pence on a
schooner of beer. A ghost, he is more palpable than Mr. Yaeger
folding his cloth behind the window and his smile travels out of
town past the First National Bank's green-faced clock, past Krom's
Grocery, Miller's Poultry Market and Feed Store, Talarcyk's grain
elevator, and Jacobson's Hardware, to stop at those country taverns
outside of town, set like buoys in the second-growth poplars and
birches, where the tires of the car lurch sideways in the gravel, and

the net curtains are drawn primly across the windows upstairs. Oh naughty Uncle Josie. Oh naughty, happy boy, making fun of them all.

Until this year. One of the disadvantages of a small college is a coffee shop where profundities are proposed and epiphanies occur every week to apostles sitting around a table on the patio stirring their cafeteria coffee with a wooden spoon while the Holy Ghost descends. Student disciples. I succumbed to it, and most of my colleagues — preferring six sympathizers, we tell ourselves, to forty faces. *Hic venit in testimonium. Non erat ille lux; sed ut testimonium prehiberet de lumine.* Function. And most of the students know. Yet even in California sunshine, with the campus in green swells like a golf course rolling off toward the Pacific and with the sidewalks in January gold avenues of warmth between the banks of ivy, a gull on his way back to shore squawks in distress, the notes strung like lanterns over our heads. Among the students who gathered there between classes were Marjorie and Vic — a married couple who were attending college together. I admired them both: she a girl with close-cropped black hair, blue-black, knee-length stockings, and eyes that followed around your face as you talked as if she were listening not to what you said but to you; he with a smile and teeth so white you thought he had Douglas Fairbanked over from Hollywood. At times during the year he featured a beard so that I envisioned him occasionally standing beside a wagon train, his hat pushed back on his forehead, smiling at Indians and broken axles, and the smallpox that was ravaging his followers, gazing to that promise in the distance — an oasis, a drink, a college set on a hill near the Pacific. I had her first in class, a summer-school six weeks of vacation exuberance where all the students came back each morning progressively more tanned from an afternoon's swimming at the beach or at the college's outdoor pool. Mine was from tennis, but it didn't make any difference: healthiness flowed through the room as pervasively as a Mr. Yaeger talcum. Only she remained the same throughout the summer, her face from the back row as pale as the Virgin Mary's listening to the angel's first ave. Her work was intense; her comments in class, mystically perceptive.

I knew him at that time only casually — at the coffee shop where I would see them together in a formal transfer of change from his hand to hers, as if they had been married a long time already and talked now about thirty-five cents and a package of cigarettes rather than about Vico's influence on Joyce or Camus's solitarity. His reputation in the department was mixed. To some, he was brilliant, iconoclastic, provoking — all those qualities that draw attention like a lighthouse above the monotonous water. To others, he was a troublemaker who questioned whatever they said, and when they explained it further, called it mush, from the rim to the bottom of the bowl. When he signed up for my course that second fall, I was pleased. He cut apart banalities with a chuckle like Bluebeard's. He wrote vehement, inconclusive papers that he himself did not understand and before which the other students sat baffled and silent. He outshouted James Wilton, Esq., out dimpled Miss McKay, out-sobered Mrs. Connelly, out-laughed Mr. Lein. He was a protean champion of nimbleness hard not to admire.

At the coffee shop our table become a tepee of hilarity, its noise in gushers spilling over the surrounding tables, silencing them. Except that he and she were seldom together at those times. She, when I looked up from the circle of my cup, going by herself up the hill toward the classrooms; he, unnoticing, waving his arms, his teeth startling white back of his laughter, mimicking Wilder's timidity in sorting out objective complements. He was corrupting even me. Beside him sat the best poetess on campus, a placid girl with eyes that, buried beneath substantial eyebrows, seemed to pick up people, sights, and slowly whirl them like a cream separator until she knew what inscape held them together: 3.1 percent fat, .2 percent mineral, 96.7 percent water. She sipped her coffee like cognac. She said little. Until three months later we were pilloried, the afternoon extracted, in a poem appearing in the school's literary magazine.

"What do you know about the Holmeses?" I asked Stan Hubble who occupied half the office. He was a bushy-haired poet and painter whom when I first met I wanted to make into another Uncle Josie, but his wife was devoted and wore a ponytail beneath Aunt Mary's cloche hat.

"They're fine kids," he said. It was late afternoon, and from our third-floor office we could see the ocean with its fringe of palm trees in the distance, its colors, green, blue, as incredible as a travel poster's.

"That all? What about that other girl — Audrey?"

He snuffed out his cigarette in the ashtray that he had brought back from Mexico City. "She writes good poems." It was a *camino sinuoso* he refused to enter. It was none of my business either, I suppose. But in January my *Dombeya wallichii* in the backyard had burst out in pink blossoms as big as snowballs, deceiving even the butterflies into thinking it was spring, and Marjorie met me, was waiting for me I realized afterward, as I came from my afternoon class.

"Ah, hello," I said, pleased, when she stopped me. We all, I too, want to be Apollo.

"Can I see you. To talk with, I mean?" The edges of her nostrils were red, and the knuckles of her hand around her notebook held at her waist looked white and cold.

"Of course, of course, of course." Joviality, friendliness, sympathy — I had made them into an image. "Wait until I dump these in the office," I motioned to my books, "and I'll buy you a cup of coffee." She smiled, a quick parentheses taken out of her solemnity. When I returned, she was still waiting at the bottom of the steps where I had left her, an unchanged Ariadne, catatonic and dazed.

We started down the hill. "Now what can I do? You've got another idea about Dante? You've just uncovered the secret of Graham Greene?"

"No," she said. She held the notebook in the crook of her arm against her chest, following with her eyes, over its edge, the cracks of the sidewalk. "No," she said again, a question really. "Wait until we . . ."

I did. In front of us beyond the city rose the range of mountains, snowcapped, gully-streaked in the sunshine seventy-five miles away, shutting us off from the rest of the country like a fence. "You can see them," I said, pointing, and she looked up from the sidewalk briefly and then down again.

"It *is* clear, isn't it?" she said. But she didn't care.

I picked a table by itself in the sunshine. My wooden spoon clicked against the plastic cup.

She put her books on the table and folded her hands in front of her on the edge as if to steady them although it looked as if she were praying. "How does one keep from going insane?" she said without looking at me. And seeing that bowed head, I recognized that the blossoms of my *Dombeya wallichii* had lulled even me. I

shoved at the curling varnish on the table top with the tip of my
spoon, fumbling for a line of poetry that would explain all and yet
not be mine. The pieces came off in flakes as thin as cicada shells,
and I scraped them into a pile in front of me to toy with so that I
wouldn't have to look at her. Why me out of all the myriad fly
specks clustered between the range of mountains, the humping wash
of the ocean, and a sky that straight up from where I sat was a line
curling off the graph toward infinity? For a moment, sitting on the
edge of the bench across from her, I felt sorry for myself, as if army
headquarters had mixed up my MOS numbers, believing me to be
a squad leader when I was and always had been a 745 rifleman. You,
now, take this squad . . .

Without waiting for my answer she said: "I can't . . . He's . . .
Have you . . ." The words like snowflakes turned, skittered, fell
individually, disappeared with only the impression of bleakness left,
of the coming of winter when each of the houses in Antigo clapped
on storm windows and withdrew within itself.

I said something. I don't know what. "Each of us . . . Everybody doesn't always . . ." until she interrupted, her hands still
pressed on the table in front of her, the nails so short they looked
like circles instead of ovals on the tips of her fingers.

"I can't stand it any longer. He won't even speak to me." I was
no Father Saile. I had only pretended to be. There was no stole
around my neck. No pontifical grace in the signs I made. I had
been committed, I thought, to no more than some lines from Donne,
a handful from Herbert, a sentence from Shakespeare, an ambiguity
from Yeats, a Latin phrase or two from the liturgy: *locum refrigerii,
lucis et pacis ut indulgeas, deprecamur.* What then.

"But everyone . . ." I said.

She unfolded her hands and drew her books toward her as if she
recognized that the dinghy of her hope that she had sent out toward
me was useless too, that my profundities were no more than the
varnish flaking from the boards on the table, piled in front of my
cup like shards, like debris dumped into a garbage heap from the
plateau of an Indian cliff dwelling, centuries before.

"They'll give me back my money, won't they?"

I didn't realize for a moment what she was talking about.
"They . . . ?"

"For my registration. If I drop out now?"

This I knew. "Of course. Of course. All you do is to fill out a card and turn it in at the registrar's."

I met her two days later crossing the campus from the parking lot. I had a class. It was a moment. "I'm leaving," she said without stopping. She was purposeful at least. I had had my chance. Already we were moving apart.

"Where?" I followed a step after her, but she kept on.

"San Francisco." There was no recrimination in the face turned sideways over the shoulder, only a brittleness that made me see again the empty cocoons I had knocked down with a broom from the underside of the garage eaves that fall.

"Write me," I said, as if I still had the secret of success buried somewhere like a cache between the covers of a book that I just had not had the time to look up for her.

"We'll see," she said. "Goodbye." Black-stockinged, the belt of her jacket in back an illusion of neatness and control, she left — me, the pepper trees, the straight facades of the buildings honeycombed with cells of wisdom, the campus — walking through the parking lot to the bus stop on the street.

> "... Others because you did not keep
> That deep-sworn vow have been friends of mine ..."

It sounded inevitable and correct as I read it to my sophomores, and they liked it, thought it nice. But I doubt if Aunt Mary had heard of it at all.

Audrey, who had never seen the Antigo Hotel and never giggled, sat beside Vic, however, more and more that semester at the coffee shop, smoking her cigarette with a measured satisfaction, snuffing it out at always the same length in the ashtray, her round face as placid as a rose petal. The fountain of our laughter and rhetoric sprayed as high as before and like children we daringly ran into and out of its drenchings.

Stan added another note. His wife made jewelry, and two months later one of the pieces was an engagement ring. Vic had asked her to make it for him. A month later it was on Audrey's finger as she put down her coffee on the patio table and slid over next to Vic on the bench, both of them smiling at the secret, like a wrapped package, between them.

"Married?" I asked Stan, back in our office.

"I don't know," he said. "They can't be. It takes a year for a divorce and it's been only months."

They were the best students I had had, and when they graduated together that spring, I missed them — the Hollywood smile, the wagon-train beard, the mind ensconced assuredly in the placid girl body, as if she knew already what trees talked of and birds cried and flowers said. They settled in a little town not far from the college and came to see my wife and me on and off all through the summer and fall. Their satisfaction with each other, as they sat in our living room, surrounded them like sanctifying grace, anointed and safe, supporting the knowledge of their living together as easily as a cork riding untroubled up one side of the wave and down the other. I couldn't help but admire them. When they left, I even kissed my wife. They had that effect.

Last month for the four days of Thanksgiving holiday, my wife and I visited friends in Sausalito. Having gone one night to a Basque restaurant in North Beach, we later were sorting out foreign dolls in one of the shops on Green Avenue as a present for our daughter. I turned to show one to my wife and framed by the bric-a-brac of shelves at the end of the store was Marjorie paging through a magazine, picking up and putting down a book. I did not believe it. She moved to another counter of books, drifting like a piece of wood waiting to be caught in a corner of a rock, in a clump of weeds. When she saw us, her face dissolved like a child's parapet of sand at the beach. All three of us moved to the sidewalk outside to talk, leaning against the fender of a sports car, dodging the restive, hoping to be titillated groups of juveniles streaming past on the sidewalk. The blue eyes had sunk deeper as if only inward was the seed. Beside the tips of my black, polished shoes were her bare feet in sandals, purple, splotched, reddened. Cathy stood politely aside as we talked: about a friend we had known, about a magazine she had bought and held now in her hand like a class book. "We were just going to have some coffee," I said to her, motioning to Cathy. "Will you?" Marjorie nodded.

We found a coffee house that reminded me of Martini's saloon — LADIES ENTRANCE. We sat at a round, dining-room table, scarred and massive, with high-back kitchen chairs, spokes missing, one leg on mine shorter than the others. It was the kind of dining-room table my mother had banished to the attic when I was five years old as a disgrace to the family. My white collar, my tie, Cathy's black evening purse resting on the table were only embarrassing.

She wanted to know about the college. But not really. It was her husband that she wanted me to talk about. He's extremely happy. He's living with Audrey now. They're to be married as soon as they get rid of your blue eyes, Aunt Mary. I said nothing. Ashamed. She was going to school. She was flunking out, and the dog-eared quarterly on the table, smudged, second-hand, was the only life raft I had left her. I looked at it hopelessly. She left by herself, thanking us for the coffee, joining the stream of tassel caps, beards, sweaters, capri pants going past on the sidewalk outside.

Today I had a note from her with a poem, asking my opinion.

I've heard the grunting-rumbling of the beast
At feeding time the thirsty-throated cries
Of never-sated tongue once bloody feast
Is done. I've heard the necessary sighs
And seen the coupling in the forest shade.
I've watched it lope across a plain, and made
My feet to follow, though my hands were numb.
We are alone together, beast. I come.

Audrey would never have written it. Not this fall at least, with Uncle Josie's arm around her shoulder coming up the sidewalk to my house laughing into each other's faces beneath the acacia tree. And when I see them out the window, I lock the door on them and go back to my study where Aunt Mary sits on the couch looking at her sandaled feet. "The Lord?" she says hopefully, looking up. Behind her on the wall, framing her, are three shelves of my books. I sit down on the chair at my desk.

"I don't know, Aunt Mary," I admit. "I don't know, dear girl."

KATINKA LOESER

Beggarman, Rich Man, or Thief

(FROM MCCALL'S)

HE KICKED the back door open, slammed it shut behind him, jerked a kitchen chair to attention, sat down on it, propped his chin on his hand, and stared straight ahead. He was eight years old. His high white sneakers were filthy beyond comment; the tips of the laces had long since disappeared, and the laces themselves were getting frayed. His long khaki pants were baggy, and his white T shirt hung loosely from his drooping shoulders. His hair was lemon-colored, and his soiled face was the color, texture, and temperature of a sun-ripened peach just fallen from the tree of grace. He had achieved what the jam recipes call a rolling boil.

"Don't expect to see *me* in heaven," he said conclusively.

"All right," I said, turning on the cold water in the sink.

He sniffed. "You said everybody goes to heaven," he said. "Everybody means Sid, too. So if Sid goes, I don't."

"Oh, come on," I said. "We would miss you."

"*Sure* you would."

"Is there a reason for this?"

"That's what you always say. Is there a reason? I'll say there is," he said bitterly.

"Tell me what it is."

"Listen," he said. "I wouldn't go anywhere with that creep." He was still dangerously close to saying "cweep."

"There'll be plenty of other people in heaven," I told him. "You wouldn't have to play with Sid all the time."

"Ha! With my luck, we'll live right across the road from him again. *You* don't care."

"Of course I care," I said. "I'd want you around."

"Then why don't you listen?" he demanded.

"I *am* listening," I told him. "I can listen and wash the lettuce at the same time."

"*Sure* you can."

I put the lettuce down and turned and faced him. "All right. I'm listening."

He looked up at me without moving his head. "What's so great about heaven?" he said. "What does it look like?"

"You go to Sunday School," I said. "You ought to know."

"Oh, *sure.*"

"Well, haven't you heard anything about it there?"

"No," he said flatly.

"What do you do there?"

"Oh — " he sighed — "make angels out of pipestem cleaners. Color."

"Well. Heaven probably looks like some of the places you color."

"What else?"

"I expect it looks like the country. You know, like some of the country around here, when we go for drives."

"Sounds stupid. Where does everybody live? Aren't there any houses or anything, or any tall buildings?"

"Yes, I guess there are. Maybe there is a big city, like New York. That would be nice, wouldn't it?"

"New York. New York. Who wants to go to New York!"

"You do."

"Only if we take the train. New York is for oddballs."

"What's an oddball?" I said.

He squirmed impatiently. "An oddball is a fink."

I was curious about this renaissance of "fink" among the very young, as a term of general opprobrium, completely apart from its original meaning. "Do you know what a fink is?" I asked.

"Do I know what a fink is!" he said, throwing up both hands.

"It's a strikebreaker," I told him.

"A strikebreaker. If that's what they do, no wonder they call them finks. Sid is a fink. What are all those little holes in your face?"

"Those are the pores in my skin. You see, there are pores in your skin so the skin can breathe."

"Who cares about pores? That's all you ever talk about, pores,

pores, pores. I suppose pores go to heaven, too. Why does everybody have to go there even if they don't want to?"

"Well," I said, "a lot of people believe that everybody doesn't
have to. That some people aren't allowed."

"Who's not allowed?"

"Oh — people who have been bad."

"Ha!" he exclaimed. "That's what I believe, too. So Sid won't."

"Everybody," I said firmly.

"Even Bobby? He's a Jew. They don't believe in God."

"Who said?"

"Oh, who cares who said. I wish we could ever be Jews. They get
more time off from school than anybody. Anyway, I'm glad we're
not Christians, like Sid."

"But we are."

"That does it." He hit the table with his fist.

"You haven't told me yet," I reminded him, "why you're mad at
Sid."

He sat upright. "He stole my dime."

"What dime?"

"You know. The one I got this morning when I put that tooth
under my pillow last night."

"Oh, yes," I said. "By the way, how come you didn't tell me you
had a loose tooth? I didn't even know about it until you had it in
your hand and showed it to me before you went to bed last night —
and you still haven't let me see where it came from."

He sighed. "I don't have to tell you everything. I'm not a baby,
you know."

"Don't get mad. I was just wondering, that's all. How did Sid
steal your dime?"

"Took it right out of my hand when I showed it to him."

"Why didn't you take it back?"

"He's bigger than me. You know that."

"I guess I can't do anything about it. This seems to be your problem. I'm sorry."

"Sure," he said. "You're *sorry*. That's all you ever say. You're
sorry. But you don't do anything about it. You just stand around
and wash lettuce."

"You like to eat, don't you?"

"No. Not any more. What's for dinner?"

"Hamburgers."

"Ugh."

"Now may I go on with my work?"

He shrugged. "Listen," he said. "You know you said some people think that bad people don't go to heaven. Name some bad people. I thought they were all dead, like on television."

"I should say not. There are still plenty of bad ones around."

"How can you tell?"

"They lie and steal and hurt other people."

"Aha!" He pointed a finger at me. "Sid steals."

"Now, look," I said. "Sid seems like a nice little boy to me. I can't believe he would take your dime."

"You always think other kids are nice. You never think your own kids are nice, though. Oh, no. And you wouldn't get their dimes back for them, either."

"Now, you listen to me," I said. "I do think my own kids are nice. I know also that they wouldn't lie or steal or hurt other people."

"You do? You know that?"

"Of course. Why don't you run on out and go over to Sid's and ask him to give you your dime back?"

"Well," he said, "maybe I'll do that later."

"Later will be too late," I said. "You have to eat, and I'm sure you haven't finished your homework."

He slid off the chair and came and stood by me as I unwrapped the ground meat and began to shape it into patties. "I like you, Mom," he said, standing very close. "Hamburglars. Boy. Mom, what happened to that tooth I got the dime for?"

"It's gone," I told him. "You got the dime in place of the tooth."

"I know," he said.

"Now run on over and get the dime back. Just say to Sid, 'That was my dime that I got for my tooth, and please give it back!' "

"That's just the trouble," he said.

"What's the trouble?"

He looked up at me and smiled, but it was a smile beaded with tears. "See," he said, "it was Sid's tooth."

ST. CLAIR McKELWAY

The Fireflies

(FROM THE NEW YORKER)

I'M IN a position (he said) to take advantage of you, my brother; you're younger than I am, a lot younger. For the time being, I'm an elderly man. Not for another few years — maybe not for twenty years — will I be an *old* man. You never know, you see, just when it's going to hit you. There's the youth of life and the prime of life and, beyond that, the decline of life — all in the same life. And you, of course, know what comes after that. Or do you?

What's death? Can you tell me? Women? Do you know them? Did you know your mother? Not then, as you were then, but now, as you are now. And memory? How about memory? There are plenty of questions I could ask you, and you could tell me what you know, but that's not the proposition we have here. I'm going to tell you something *I* know.

When I get to be an old man instead of just an elderly one, I'll still go on talking to you, I suppose, but I'll talk in code. I'll talk in the code that can be understood only by other old men. Should you then get to be an old man yourself while I'm still able to talk to you, you'll get only a few words of any kind out of me. You've seen old men chatting and chuckling among themselves, but have you ever seen one old man really *talking* to another old man? Of course not. One old man has nothing to tell another old man. He wants to talk only to the young, and even to them he talks in code.

I'll tell you this straight. I haven't learned the code yet. And I'm on the mend, as you can see. I'm convalescing. And there's a word for you! It's boxed in, it's been made to smell of the sickroom, it' been shoved around on the shuffleboard courts, but the grandeur of it is still discernible if you look at it hard and dig to the root of it. *Valesco! Valeo! Valor!* Can you see the legions? Hear the trumpets? See the hillside in the dusk? See them falling back? See them having another try at it? And still another? See the banners waving? That's a man's word, my brother — convalescence. Look where it comes from. And where do all the words of men come from? I'm going to tell you. They come from women, from men's memory of women. As it was then and as it is now.

But it's about memory that I especially wish to speak to you. The terrain is deceptive and the maps are undependable. The lady who was in the room down at the other end of this corridor sent me a flashlight some days ago, when I was using damp matches in a cave. I saw her first when I was on my way to Penang. Oh, I know what that sounds like — and, in a way, that's what it *was* like. I was young. But youth's not what I'm telling you about. And I wasn't a seagoing man, as you know as well as I do. I was and am a Standard Oil man. And this lady down the corridor was never what our Aunt Mary would call one of my women. I saw her first on the boat going from San Francisco to Shanghai, and I saw her in a club in Shanghai — not a nightclub, a club. And then, later on, I saw a lot of her in Penang. After that, I never saw her again. And I didn't see her here in this place where we are now. She could only send messages to me by the nurses, and that was all I could do — send messages to her. By the time I was in good enough shape to write her a note or a letter, she'd left. Our acquaintanceship had never been anything but social, and I'd hardly even thought of her since that period in Penang forty years ago. I'd never realized she had a place in memory.

When I first got into this hospital, it was the memory of Nancy I was after, of course — not the Nancy you first met, after we got back from Penang with the two kids, but the Nancy you never saw. The memory I was after when I found myself in here was the Nancy I knew before all that, and, day or night, I was unable to get it. That's one of the troubles elderly men have, you see. We all have it. We try and we try to remember a woman we want to remember — we want all of her, we won't settle for fragments, and we go after it. We strip ourselves, we put aside all the paraphernalia we've collected in a long life, and we go after the memory as if we were what we used to be and as if there was just that memory of that woman, with nothing around it. It's a mistake to drop everything you've got when you go back into memory, because at any moment, in order to find your way through some woods you'd never known were there, you may require something you only picked up the day before yesterday. The trick is to take along everything you've got. I'm talking, of course, about the whole of memory. If it's just a man's own memory he's after, it's no problem. If that's all he wants, he can go look at one of his old battlefields with his son-in-law. That's just *his* memory.

But I was as ignorant as you or the next man when I first got into this hospital and started going after the memory of Nancy. I went after it like a bull terrier — white hair and pink eyes — as if I could grab what I was after and hold it between my paws. But the kind of memory I'm talking about isn't an object. It's part of something — a lot goes with it, there's a great deal around it. In a way, it's like the world, a part of the wide, wide world. And where it comes from is from everywhere. To get it, you've got to use a lot of things that are close to it and away from it. We think of memory — I mean memory like the memory of Nancy — as something that belongs only to us. But if that's all it is, it's not what we're after. It's not the whole thing. It belongs to a lot of people. That's part of what I mean when I say you've got to take everything with you that you can lay your hands on when you go after it. You need not only everything you've got but as much of what other people have got as you can borrow or steal. You need the eyes of other people as well as your own eyes, for one thing. You need what's behind their eyes, too.

It was after I'd been here in this bed a couple of days and nights and was beginning to feel fairly good for short flashes at a time that one of the nurses told me there was a lady down the corridor who thought she used to know me some years ago. "She said to ask if you weren't once in Penang. P-e-n-a-n-g — she spelled it out for me," the nurse said. "In Malaya."

I replied that I certainly was in Penang — for several years in the early nineteen-twenties.

The nurse said this lady's name was Mrs. Carter and that she'd said she thought maybe I was the Thomas K. Richards of Standard Oil she used to know in Penang, and that if I was, maybe I'd remember her — Betty Carter. "She said to tell you her husband's name was Jim — she seemed to think that might help you remember her," the nurse said.

"Tell her I remember all about her," I said. "Tell her to come in here and see me as soon as I'm feeling better. Tell her I don't need Jim or anybody else to remember her by."

"She can't come to see you," the nurse said, "any more than you can go to see her. But I'll tell her what you said. She's nice. She's a nice woman."

"Tell her I'll be down to see her when I'm better," I said. "Tell her I remember the launch party she gave for the American Minister to Siam on his way to Bangkok."

"Minister?"

"Like an ambassaor," I explained. "Mrs. Carter and her husband had this boat, you see, for giving launch parties on the river in Penang. What we'd call a cabin cruiser now. Tell her I can remember *all* her parties. Her dinner parties and her No. 1 boy, Ho Sing."

"I'll tell her," the nurse said.

"Is she very sick?"

"Not too bad. I'll give her your message before we get her to sleep. You can have another pill tonight if you need one, you know. And just put on your light if you want anything."

This was one of the good nurses, of course. Most of them are all right, but this one's young and not bad-looking, and she's bright, as well. If she'd been in Penang in 1921, before she was born, and was the way she is now, she would have been a very popular American girl.

I never asked for the second sleeping pill that night, because I didn't want to sleep or dream or do anything but lie here with the night light from the city streets coming in the window, remembering Mrs. Carter. I thought of her, and I still think of her, as Mrs. Carter — not as Betty — and that may be because, on the boat going from San Francisco to Shanghai, I first became aware of her as the Mrs. Carter who had all the children and the French governess. Her husband wasn't with her — he'd already gone out to Shanghai, to manage the branch that the Orient & San Francisco Bank had there in those days, and she and the children were joining him. They'd been with him in Paris before that. She just seemed like a kind of ordinary middle-aged American woman to me for part of that trip, but she was nowhere near middle-aged — she was probably not much over thirty. The thing is, of course, that I was exactly twenty-two, and she'd probably have seemed middle-aged to me even without all the children. Actually, there were only *three* children, and at the time I paid no attention to them. I was after the French governess. And can you beat this? I know now — just as I know a good many things I didn't know then, and yet I *did* know them then — that I was after the governess not so much because she was young and not unattractive but simply because she was French. I can't remember now just what that governess did look like.

Have you any idea how young men are at twenty-two? Does anybody have any idea? I'd never been anywhere, I'd gone to work for Standard Oil fresh out of Dartmouth, I wasn't a bad kid, as kids go, I wasn't even such a bad older brother, was I? But on that ship, that Dollar liner going to the Orient, I was insufferable, I was a snob, I was somebody I'd never been before and have never been since.

But I'm only going to touch on what *I* was. I'm trying to give you an idea of Mrs. Carter. Or, rather, I'm trying to give you my idea of Mrs. Carter. I know now — and I'd know this even if I'd never seen her later on in Penang — that she was just a nice woman and had these three children who tumbled around the ship. They were always playing around, and the French governess watched over them. Then, in the evening, the French governess would come on deck when they'd all three been put to bed, and I would moon at her and dance with her, and once or twice I lured her to my cabin. I never got that governess, but I scared her, I'm afraid, or confused her. One day, Mrs. Carter took my arm in a friendly way and walked up toward the bow with me and said in what I know now was a very tactful fashion that she was afraid I was turning the poor girl's head. Those were her words — old-fashioned words now. And do you know what I said to Mrs. Carter? I said, "I can see, Mrs. Carter, that you're not very accustomed to having servants." You can't believe it, I can't believe it, I hope nobody can believe it, but there it is! That's what I said. And *you* know how accustomed *I* was to having servants! I didn't choose to remember until years afterward that Mrs. Carter replied that day that of *course* she wasn't used to servants, that this one was the first she'd ever had, and I forgot as best I could that Mrs. Carter laughed at me in a way that wasn't at all derisive. I suppose it was sisterly — possibly it was sisterly. I did allow myself to understand eventually on that trip, though, that I might be making a fool of myself going after the French governess, because she'd turned out to be awkward and childish and her hands were large and rough-skinned. I'd presumed she was twenty-three or so, and experienced in addition to being French, but she was probably barely twenty and had come out of a convent. I spoke only inferior Dartmouth French, and she had very little English, and it dawned on me that the whole thing had got off on the wrong foot. So I convinced myself that I'd merely been being chivalrously democratic and worldly with the governess, and managed — at least in the mind's eye I was then using on myself — to rise above the situation.

Nevertheless, I was surprised and pleased when Mrs. Carter included me in a general invitation to the passengers who'd been in the cocktail crowd in the small ship's little bar — an invitation to join her husband (who'd met her at the dock, of course) at the Shanghai Club for drinks the next day, before the ship steamed on for Hong Kong and Singapore. I was surprised, but by the time I'd met her husband and we'd all had a pleasant hour or so at the Shanghai Club, I'd begun to realize that this middle-aged woman with the three children wasn't very old, after all; that her husband, Jim, looked like the sort of older man I'd like to get to know better; and that Mrs. Carter seemed to be at least as fond of me as she was of the other male members of the ship's cocktail crowd.

Whatever role it was I'd been playing for a good part of that voyage had vanished from my memory — at least, for years to come — like an unsuccessful costume rented for a fancy-dress ball and returned the next morning. The tumbling children came into the Shanghai Club with the governess while Mrs. Carter's little party was breaking up, and I think I probably saw those children distinctly for the first time then. Before that, on shipboard, they'd just been three small moving clumps of dresses and rompers, but now they were more or less motionless and were shaking hands with me and the other guests, one after the other — girls of four and three, and a boy of two. That night in the hospital those children's names came back to me, along with other things about that trip and about the years in Penang, and, as the days and nights in this bed went on, Mrs. Carter became an indispensable element in the chemistry of the memory of Nancy — the memory I'd been seeking. The children's names were Elizabeth, Katherine, and James, and all our crowd in Penang called them by their whole names after they arrived, later on that year, because Mrs. Carter said she thought it much nicer if grown people called children by their whole names and left it to other children to make up nicknames — if they had to have nicknames. Jim had been offered a better job at a new bank in Penang; they stayed there two or three years.

I can't tell you whether I began to know or to sense, or whether I was even vaguely aware of, what was going on in the memory department as I lay thinking about Mrs. Carter that first night, but what happened was that before I slept I knew I wanted to go on thinking about her and Jim and Elizabeth, Katherine, and James, and about all the people, small and large, who'd filled the days in Penang before I married Nancy.

As the hospital days proceeded, the messages went back and forth between Mrs. Carter down the corridor and myself in this room. The first thing in the morning, after that initial message, I asked the morning nurse about Mrs. Carter and how she was. But the nurse was one of the indifferent, overefficient ones, and her "Oh, she's doing nicely" meant nothing, and I didn't try to send a message by her to Mrs. Carter. The afternoon nurse was one I hadn't seen before and didn't much like the looks of, but while she was taking my pulse in a perfunctory way she told me, as if she were reciting a lesson, "The patient Mrs. Carter sent you her best wishes and said she'd forgotten all about the American Minister's launch party but remembered everything about it when you reminded her of it last night, and that she'd recalled exactly how he looked when his dignified, fat red face appeared above the muddy river water, once he came to the surface after falling in so unexpectedly with his pongee suit on."

"Did you take that down in shorthand?" I asked, and I suppose I asked it suspiciously.

"I can remember things I'm told," the nurse said, but when she looked at me — I probably tried to seem sicker than I was — she said, "Well, she's a very nice patient, and I'm not wild about *all* patients. This seemed important to Mrs. Carter, and she repeated it several times to me, and so I've done what she asked me to do, that's all."

"It was a long time ago, and we haven't seen each other for many years," I said. "I knew her — everybody knew her — very well in those days in the Far East. She had three cute little children. Her husband taught me to play chess."

"She's a widow," the nurse said, "and she's had no visitors, but she reads a lot, and, of course, she sleeps a good deal of the time. She told me she had two daughters and a son and seven grandchildren, but that they were scattered around in Europe and on the West Coast. She was on her way back from Italy to see the ones in Santa Barbara when she had this attack."

"It's her heart?"

"No, she'd had some surgery. And you're supposed to rest, you know. Anyway, she said to remind you of the Polo Club. 'The club,' she said, 'not the polo.' "

"Tell her I'd forgotten about the Polo Club but was thinking of Dr. Smith's particular way of putting out his cigarette," I said, and the nurse grinned as if she'd been in Penang herself, and nodded, and went away.

Dr. Smith was Nancy's father, of course, but I don't think I ever told you about his spitting fish. He was an ichthyologist and started out in the nineties from the Smithsonian Institution, in Washington, with his bride, when he was a young man. He was going around the world on his honeymoon, but he'd run across so many fantastic fish in Malaya and Siam that he'd stayed on there, first in one place and then in another, and Nancy was born out there, as you know, and they'd never gone back to the States except once in a great while, and to see Nancy graduate from school in Farmington. His spitting fish were the kind that spit up at insects on the branches of trees to make them fall in the water. Dr. Smith would hold his cigarette out over the pond at those garden parties when he was through smoking it, and one of these fish would come to the surface and spit out the light on the cigarette. But nobody else could get those fish to do that for them. Well, it's not much of a story — it's only that I knew Mrs. Carter would be seeing the whole scene, all those scenes there in the Smiths' garden in Penang at the same time I was seeing them in this room, and it's also that she'd know I'd know she'd heard about Nancy, or had read it in the paper somewhere. As a matter of fact, I think Mrs. Carter even knew what I was after. Mrs. Carter was that kind of woman.

She was the kind of woman people used to say was a wonderful hostess. In those days, you understand. Like so many other words, that word doesn't seem to mean the same thing now — not exactly. Maybe it takes servants to make a woman a wonderful hostess. Out there, even *I* became accustomed to servants. We all had servants, and Mrs. Carter had the French governess to start with, and she had a cook and a No. 1 boy and a coolie and a chauffeur and a gardener, and so on. But she knew how to handle them better than anybody else, and her dinner parties were always fun because, even with the little she had to go on as far as guests were concerned, she mixed people as perfectly as her No. 1 boy mixed drinks.

As the days in the hospital went on and I got better at it, there would be the whole scene, all those scenes in Penang — the parties at her house, at other houses there, the goings on at the Polo Club, and the young English faces and the young American faces, and the government people, the European diplomats and semi-diplomats and foreign advisers and financial advisers and the local princes. There were the white mosquito boots everybody wore in the evening — the men, that is — and the embroidered silk skirtlike bags the ladies would put their feet in and pull up over their knees as gracefully as possible when the mosquitoes got bad, and the tennis on the lawn courts in the afternoon, and the golf on the flat course, but with plenty of over-water holes to make that course tricky. We exchanged messages as the days went on, but, as I say, I never saw Mrs. Carter. Yet I had her eyes and the eyes of all those Penang people — and what was behind them — as well as what I had myself.

The night nurse who'd brought me the first message from her — it was she who finally told me about what was wrong with Mrs. Carter.

"It's C.A.," the nurse said one night when I kept on asking her.

Then the nurse had to tell me in the ugly word of two syllables what the third and the first letter of the alphabet mean in a New York hospital, because I'd never heard it called that. Did you know they call it C.A.? I hope I never hear anybody call it C.A. again.

I also found out from the good daytime nurse that it was cancer of the womb that Mrs. Carter had — that she still had after the surgery. I wondered why the son and daughters weren't there, but it seemed Mrs. Carter hadn't wanted to wire them or cable them at first, and now wasn't going to, because she knew it was only a matter of days. Or maybe hours. But in any case I couldn't think of the grown son and the grown daughters, but only of those tumbling children on the Dollar liner, and of where Elizabeth and Katherine and James had come from. When I found out from the nurse what the exact situation was, I expected, I suppose — oh, of course I expected! — to get some particular kind of message from Mrs. Carter. But I only expected it for a moment or two, I'll say that. She'd send no particular kind of message, I realized, and she wouldn't expect me to, and I didn't, thank Christ. She'd never sent any message at all about Nancy; she knew she didn't need to, and it wasn't what she'd have done even if she thought for a moment she ought to. And she'd send no message about herself or about Jim. Her last message to me was, "The fireflies that lit up all at once."

There were certain trees out there around Penang that a certain kind of lightning bug seemed to live in, or roost in at night — the way flocks of certain kinds of birds roost in certain kinds of trees, you see. Thousands, *tens* of thousands, of these fireflies would be in one of these trees, all over every branch and twig of it. And for some reason — nobody knows why, as I understand it — they would all light up at once on certain evenings. I don't mean they would all light up just once on one evening. I mean at intervals on certain evenings they would all light up. We used to see them most often on the boat rides we'd take sometimes along the *klongs,* the little canals, that ran through the paddy fields. They were ditches, actually, but in some seasons of the year they were deep enough and wide enough to hold four or five small boats in single file — the kind of boat that has an oarsman at the stern. The far eastern version of gondolas, I guess you might call them. Sometimes, after one of Mrs. Carter's dinner parties — it had to be clear and with no moon, only the stars — she'd have the boats and the oarsmen there at the dock where they kept the launch for the launch parties. The launch parties, you understand, were daytime affairs. And then, by fours and threes and sometimes by twos, her guests would get in the boats — long dresses and black ties and white mess jackets — and sit on cushions in the bottoms of the boats, and the oarsmen would take them a little way down the river and on into one of the *klongs.* It was always a long distance off, to the right or to the left across the paddy fields — the tree with the fireflies that lit up all at once. The whole dark shape of the tree would light up — not in a flash but in a glow, a golden glow. Then there'd be only the light of the stars. And after a while the same tree, or maybe another tree off on the other side in the distance, would light up all at once in a golden glow — all of it, like memory.

URSULE MOLINARO

The Insufficient Rope

(FROM PRISM)

THE APARTMENT was empty when she returned from work on Monday night. She decided to hang herself. Monday night was a good time to die, if one didn't like one's job. Not as good as Monday morning, or Sunday night, but they were always at home then. One of them was always at home. Her daughter asleep upstairs. Her mother tiptoeing from bathroom to kitchen to child's room, downstairs, upstairs, downstairs, an angelic shadow of insinuating selflessness; carrying a dirty diaper to the sink; peering over a gold-rimmed lorgnette to see if she disturbed. Her husband's cough in the hall, on working mornings, three hours before her alarm went off. His smell of printer's ink and steel-filled cavities when he slipped into her bed. His long nose purposeful as a dog's as he ran in and out of the house on Saturdays and Sundays, because the gambling club was just around the corner on rue Madame. He ran back to borrow from her when he lost, to pay her back when he won. She was glad *he* would find her, and not her mother. Her mother would have believed her back to life, somehow, pitting the power of her incredulity against the bluntest evidence: Impossible! Her daughter had *not* hanged herself! She had *not* left her mother! She had not wished to leave her . . . until the obedient filial heart began to beat again and she was again able to drag her hurt to the Library, every weekday morning, to earn money because she, too, was a mother now, and a mother sacrifices everything for her child except, of course, her mother. But her mother had been given a granddaughter, a ransom for the daughter, a baby still too young to walk. It would take years before it could run away from her love. At least it would be spared its own mother's love. Its own mother was withdrawing — early, before the resemblance set in; before jovial shopkeepers felt the urge to remark how much the daughter's nose was beginning to curve like her mother's; before sweet old ladies raised their teacups to toast the repetition of the mother's dainty waistline. Her daughter would be allowed a face of her own, a virgin future, unpredicted by liver-spotted hands and age-rinsed eyes. The grandmother's face would be too remote, harmless behind the wrinkle-fence of another generation. "A wise groom looks at the mother before he marries the daugher." Her mother's most cherished cliché, an unstated compliment she liked to pay herself since, at fifty-six, her breasts were firmer and rounder than her daughter's. It would have been unkind to make open comparisons . . . Did her mother realize that it was *not* to look at her that her husband spent his weekends gambling on rue Madame? He loves me by mistake, she thought. He is safe. He, too, would be glad to find her, glad to cut her loose, and bury her, and heap flowers on her grave, sure at last where her body was — or would be — every hour of the day, until he died himself, or found another, as her lover had. She would be buried before her mother came back. She had six hours before her husband came home. Everything was as though she had planned it. Although, had she really planned it, she would not have given them this extra day at the Library, reading galley proofs of The Budget in six point. She might have gone to the park and read. So many books she would not read now. Or she might have eaten extravagantly — a traditionally large, luxurious last meal, bribing the body's forgiveness for what one was about to do to it. Or she might have slept. Sleeping would have been best. She would not have had to feel her soul all day, hanging limply inside her like a worn-out garter, with tiny blackheads piercing through the pinkness. She went upstairs to bathe. The bathroom was on the second floor, across from the child's room. It had one stained-glass wall, guarded by a continuation of the stairs' firm wooden banister. At night, when her husband left the light on inside, the bathroom hung into the dark studio below like a giant magic lantern. He loved it, and went to sleep smiling up at the soft-colored confusion which reminded her of traffic lights and lower-class weddings. She would leave the light on for him, she thought. She would hang herself from the middle of the banister, between the seventh and the eighth bar. She emptied her perfume bottles over her thighs and shoulders. She put make-up on, and lipstick, and curled her hair over her forehead, the way her lover had liked it. She tied a piece of washline around the banister. She knotted the other end around her neck — which took a long time. She climbed over the banister and let herself drop. It was a short drop, less than half a story. Was that why nothing seemed changed, why everything remained as it had been? On all sides people were bumping into her, as though she were hanging on one simian arm from a strap in the subway, after work. Eyes stared at her, protruding with suspicion, creating the familiar uneasiness which made her shift her feet. She felt them flailing clumsily somewhere far below. The back of her tongue was pressing down on a raspberry seed. She remembered having eaten raspberry jam for breakfast — her mother's favorite jam. She should have brushed her teeth. She always forgot to brush her teeth. On her travels, the one thing she would leave behind was, unfailingly, her tooth brush. Her lover told her that the new woman used a silver tooth brush. He was so impressed, he had to tell her. She had dragged him into a pharmacy and shown him the model his new woman used: a cheap, gunmetal-colored handle with nylon bristles. But in her lover's mind it had remained a silver tooth brush, uncheapened by the proof — which proved nothing but her partiality, her unjust dislike of anything connected with the new woman. She should have brushed her teeth. Now they would lay her into the earth with this seed inside her. A bush would grow out of her sloppiness. First a daughter, and now a raspberry bush. Life, always life, more life, sly and infinite, and she had hoped to stop infinity with a piece of clothesline. Perhaps it had been too short. Perhaps she should have prepared herself differently. She had run into death the way she used to run into examination rooms: with a thorough knowledge of the wrong books. Relying on spontaneity and intuition to get her through. Perhaps she should have gone to the trouble of jumping from the Eiffel Tower, or from the Empire State Building, instead of heeding the suggestion of an empty two-story apartment with a firm wooden banister outside one bathroom wall. Again her impatience had trapped her, making her concentrate on perfume and curls, while the insidious seed was left to germinate between her teeth. She was no match for life. But life could afford to wait. It *had* time, because it *was* time. A patient monster, it hung around couples. All sorts of couples. The most unexpected couples, like an early-risen proofreader and a raspberry. But the raspberry had been cooked. They had boiled the seed when they made the jam, and what did it matter anyhow whether it germinated, or did not germinate? Her preoccupation with it was only pretense, offered by the pain in her tongue. When the pain stopped, she clung to the thought of the raspberry, elaborating on it, as a front, to help her ignore the staring eyes around her. They were dissecting her, with discreet nudges and snickers, pointing to her long fingernails, to the curls over her eyes. They excluded her. They made her feel different. But she *wanted* to be different! She didn't want to be like them, not even if being like them were the toll for everything she wanted. If acceptance, and acclaim, and being loved depended on cutting her fingernails, then she preferred to remain long-nailed, and unacceptable, and unloved. She *had* remained long-nailed, and unaccepted, and she was lying to herself. She would have cut her nails to be loved. But some *had* loved her. Her husband still loved her, by misapprehension, for something he thought she was and she knew she was not. Now he would think that she hanged herself because the gallery rejected all her paintings. They were leaning against the mantelpiece where her mother had stacked them. The bathroom light was slanting across their turned canvas backs, oblique as sunbeams before a thunderstorm. He would see them as soon as he opened the door. He would see them before he saw her. She did not mind his misunderstanding. It was full of admiration. It had not mattered, until her lover came and loved her as she really was: a female replica of his own self-involvement, another cocoon with whom he exchanged brilliant silken threads, until the unraveled ego could no longer stand its bareness. He had fled to the new woman then, a nice dull cotton-type of woman who was adoringly rewinding his ego for him. Cutting her nails would not have brought him back. He had his own nails to think about. He had always thought about his own nails when he looked at hers. They had become his nails, long and painted, digging into his palms. That's why she had thrown her body away when he rejected it. She had thrown it after him like a forgotten jacket. Let him drape the cotton woman in it, if he cared to. She didn't want it any more. Not any more than he did. She had slipped out of it before he made

her resemble the others. All the other rejected bodies in the world.
But the others, too, had slipped out of their bodies. They were
swaying around her, snickering and nudging. She envied them as
she always had, for their ready grins, their staring, their deeply
sincere hypocrisies. When she went to the washroom, at the Library, she used to tell herself: now, here, for once, I do as they do.
I am like them. But she was different. She didn't wear a slip,
and even if she had worn a slip, she would have lifted it in some
peculiar way of her own, a way of which the others would have
disapproved, could they have seen her. Now they could see her
everywhere, all the time. She had forsaken the privacy of her body.
She had undressed her soul. It shivered in the early morning draft
which blew in through the window and made her neck feel stiff.
She longed to be reborn a cow, in India, grazing on warm aromatic
meadows, gazing with bovine benignity upon a people of vegetarians. Her husband had thrown the windows open. That's why
it felt so cold in the apartment. Their neighbor was there, in his
pajamas, calling across the hall to his wife, urging her to go back
to bed, assuring her that nothing had happened. She felt gratified
that her tongue was sticking out so far. Her mother's education
had never permitted such a gesture, not even the thought of it.
The *concierge* was there, too, running back and forth between
the kitchen and the foyer, clattering through drawers for a knife
to cut the clothesline. Her husband was nipping at it with a pair
of scissors. He lay stretched out along the bathroom wall, reaching
through the banister, panting his morning smell on her face. The
neighbor was wobbling on the couch underneath, holding on to her
knees, to catch her when the rope was cut. He fell under her sudden weight. For a moment she lay in the neighbor's arms on the
couch, until her husband came running down the stairs and
pulled him away. They tried to push her tongue into her mouth,
but her tongue was too stiff, and her eyelids would not close. The
concierge found one of her scarves — the yellow silk scarf from
Florence. How fast she found it! How did the *concierge* know
where she kept her scarves? They covered her face and evened her
legs. The neighbor's wife was at the door again, but the neighbor
would not let her in. "My wife's too sensitive," he said. It wasn't
true. The neighbor's wife was as robust as a nurse, inside. She was
glad they didn't let her in. The *concierge* was woman enough,

peering under her skirt to see if there was any blood . . . as though
the immediate body functions explained everything, even her
lover, and why he left her. She had always preferred men. Men
were kinder, less matter of fact. They let her cheat a little, understanding her better for it, in the end. Except her lover. Her
lover had understood her like a woman. Why did she have to
give birth to a daughter, perpetuating the mother race, handcuffed
between two generations of mothers, like a murderer on his way
to jail? A son would have linked her to the present. Men were
the present. With a daughter, the future had merely reproduced the
past. She thought of her grandmother, large and flabby, seated on
her childhood like a satiated spider. At least her mother would not
sit on her daughter quite so heavily. Her mother was slight. She
was timid. Perhaps her daughter would grow up to resemble the
large, flabby grandmother. Perhaps she was resembling her herself
at this moment, with her bulging eyes and bloated face . . . Her
grandmother, wandering from room to room, preceded by a pointed
black-satin stomach, licking her forefinger, retracing table tops and
chair arms and picture frames to test the maids' dusting . . . The
concierge was making coffee for her husband and the neighbor.
For herself, too. She carried three cups in from the kitchen —
without the saucers — and three spoons. The cups were going to
leave rings on the table, once the hot coffee was poured into them;
three whitish rings for her mother to notice and grieve over when
she returned: "Mahogany is so delicate. None of this would
have happened if I had been there . . ." She could smell the coffee
now — the *concierge* must be using the large pot, it took so long
to drip through — but somehow the smell didn't mean anything
more. She continued to hear, and to see, and to smell, but the
sensations of it were gone; and fresh coffee had been the one thing
she used to like about waking up in the morning: a cup of hot
black coffee, preferably served in bed. "Liquid lead," her lover
had called it. "Strong enough to rouse a corpse." He had resented
her love of coffee. He had been jealous of it for a while, in the
beginning, offended that she could manifest any desires — any
other desires — in his presence. Perhaps the new woman drank milk
in bed, or fruit juices. . . . Her grandmother's love of coffee. How
could she have missed the resemblance? Her grandmother, clapping her hands as she woke from her nap, pressing down the

silver tail of a turtle-shaped bell, indignant, when she woke earlier, that her coffee wasn't filtering on the table near her head; indignant, when she woke later, that it *had* filtered and surely become lukewarm; clapping her hands, yelling, *"Le café! Mon café!"* Every day the same indignation, summing up the wrongs of the world; the chronic sluggishness of the maids, her family's selfish lack of attention, all conspiring to deprive her of her one small pleasure in life: a hot cup of strong black coffee when she woke from her nap . . . How could she have missed the resemblance? Perhaps her grandmother had not liked herself either. Perhaps resembling her grandmother so much was the reason she had not loved herself (and always felt a little contemptuous of those who did), constantly judging herself, seesawing from over-indulgence to over-severity. Still, her grandmother had not hanged herself. Perhaps she had been satisfied to punish herself by proxy . . . The itinerant colossus of her grandmother, feeding her everlasting wobbling flesh on the lives of those around her. She had outlived generations of squirrels and bluejays and mice, which were killed because they ate the same cheese, and cherries, and nuts she liked to eat and because, each time, her granddaughter cried (The child must learn to control her emotions) and tried to make drawings of them. She had been a coward. She had betrayed the animals she professed to love. She had not disobeyed when her grandmother handed her a dead mouse to cut into little pieces — for the chickens. Everything was always good for the chickens. "A little meat makes the yolk rich and golden," her grandmother would say, and hand her the mouse. Obediently she would seize it by its tail. Sometimes, the outside skin slid off, like a sheath from a tightly rolled umbrella. She would stand, holding the hollow tail between her fingertips . . . When her grandmother finally died, it had been too late to matter. She had outgrown her hatred. Revenge for mice no longer interested her. She had become well intentioned toward people . . . out of cowardice, probably, because she had read Emerson and begun to believe in compensation. She believed that a justly balanced fate would punish anyone who did her harm — to re-establish its balance, which the harm had upset. Revenge would have been meddling. She might have spoiled her beautiful long nails . . . The *concierge* was pouring the coffee. She dropped a lump of sugar in her husband's cup and stirred it

for him. "Life must go on," she said. And then: "Change of life
comes earlier, with some. You can never tell . . ." They drank
standing up. Her husband was rubbing his shoulderblades, back
and forth, against the window frame, slurping as he drank, staring
at the little mound her tongue made under the yellow scarf. The
neighbor asked what time it was. He had to think about getting
to work, he said . . . and tell his wife . . . He wondered how he
should tell her. It would be such a shock. "She was extremely fond
of her," he said, pointing with his chin toward the couch. What a
joke! She wished she could use her throat again, just long enough
to laugh at the neighbor's wife's fondness for her, just long enough
for all of them to hear her laugh . . . Upstairs, her alarm went off.
Her mother must have set it before she left, to make sure that she
got up to go to the Library on time. She would always be up now.
No more sleep. No more forgetting the hurt. She had embalmed
the hurt. It had formed a cud which she ruminated without res-
pite: Her lover was reading a little blue *lettre pneumatique* on the
cagelike balcony outside his hotel room. He was wearing the new
Japanese robe she had bought for him, and when she knocked at
the glass door, he slipped the letter into the sleeve. She would not
have asked about it, if he had not made fun of her hair. (Her
grandmother's hair had been thin with age; islands of pink scalp
glistening through carefully padded strands — the same shiny pink
as the unsheathed tail of a dead mouse.) "Showing off your male
hormones again," he said. "Must you comb it straight back? It
looks balding. You remind me of the great Queen Elizabeth . . ."
That's when she asked, copying his smile, if the writer of the
pneumatique had thicker, curlier hair than she, and he said, yes,
she had, and he might as well tell her: he was in love with the
other woman. "She has none of your intellect," he said. "She admires me." It was the first time that a man wanted to leave her.
Suddenly she understood how much she had made the others suffer,
all those whom she had stopped loving first. She used to think
that she had left them "nicely," that they had parted "the best of
friends." . . . Her lover was assuring her of his unaltered friendship . . . Suddenly she understood the temptation to pry open,
with a knife, the heart which has closed itself against the replaced
lover's love, or tears, or threats . . . Her husband was on the
phone again. He had been telephoning all morning, arranging for
the funeral, ordering flowers. Now he was talking to her lover. She

could tell by his voice, not by what he said. He had been saying the same sentences over and over, describing how he had found her: the empty apartment, the washline, her tongue . . . "I can't understand it," he kept saying. "I don't understand . . ." That was exactly how she had felt about the new woman. How could her lover prefer the new woman? "We have nothing in common," he had said. "I've been monstrously happy for two weeks." . . . He affected a new vocabulary, laced with silly, exaggerating adjectives. He spoke with contempt of the new woman. To flatter me, she thought. To shield her from me, behind my vanity. She cried and they made love, in desperate, unconvinced silence, across the other woman's teasing image. Afterwards they sat on the tiny balcony, apart like bookends. Her lover played with the tassels of the Japanese robe, and because he felt doubly unfaithful now, he tried to fasten his loyalty to the solid presence of objects: "I've never worn my robe with her," he said. "Only with you, or when I'm alone." . . . She wished that he had reserved his touching exclusivity for his body rather than his robe . . . and that she had not told him so. "But . . . you didn't buy me my body," he said . . . How could she stop the hurt? The clothesline had been too short to stop it. Perhaps the justly balanced fate was punishing her for the harm she had done to her body. She had given up her chance to outgrow the hurt, gradually, by living away from it, as she had outgrown her hatred for her grandmother. Growth had been her only chance of change, and she had strangled it with a short piece of clothesline. She had dropped half a story, eloping from life as though she could not wait to join the black, flabby ghost of her grandmother. It had changed nothing. At least not for her. Even her tongue was back inside her mouth. Her hands had been folded around a bunch of Parma violets her lover had brought. They were getting ready for the funeral. The apartment was filled with black-dressed vegetarians. Her mother and daughter were not there, and she was glad. No one knew what a baby saw. Her daughter should remember no mother. She should be free to invent one for herself, beautiful with absence and fantasy, an unequaled mother, composed of the assorted memories of two fathers: her husband and her heartbroken lover . . . Because now that she was dead, he loved her again. She wished that she had her body back to feel his love. The neighbor's wife had come in, looking like an astrakhan muff, with her new permanent.

J. C. OATES

The Fine White Mist of Winter

(FROM THE LITERARY REVIEW)

SOME TIME AGO in Eden County the sheriff's best deputy, Rafe Murray, entered what he declared to the sheriff, Walpole, and to his own wife and man-grown sons, and to every person he encountered for a month, white or black, to be his second period — his new period, he would say queerly, sucking at his upper lip with a series of short, damp, deliberate noises. He was thirty-eight when he had the trouble with Bethl'em Aire, he would say, thirty-eight and with three man-grown sons behind him: but he only had his eyes open on that day, he was just born on that day, he meant to keep it fresh in his mind. When the long winter ended and the roads were thick and shapeless with mud, shot with sunlight, the Negro Bethl'em and his memory both went out of Eden County, and — to everyone's relief, especially his wife's — out of Murray's mind too, but up until then, in those thick, gray, mist-choked days he did keep whatever it was fresh in his mind; so that the fine driving snow of that year seemed to play back again and again Murray's great experience.

He and the Negro Bethl'em, whom he had arrested out in a field, had been caught in a snowstorm driving in to the sheriff's office. Murray had declared, muttering, he had never seen such snow; and every time he exploded into a brief, harsh, almost painful series of curses the snowstorm outside grew thicker. Murray was a big proud man, with eyes that jutted a little out of his head, as if with rage, and these he turned to the swirling world beyond his windshield while the Negro sat silent and shivering beside him, his own eyes narrowed, discreet, while Murray swore at the snow. Never had a man been so tricked by the weather, never so confused by his own country, as Murray thought himself to be; and it seemed to him too, though he pushed the idea right away, that he was lost and would never find his way back again.

Back in the sheriff's office they would be waiting for him, the windows warm and steamy, the men sitting around the stove with their legs outstretched smoking, surely talking of him — of this queer bad luck that had come to Murray, the best deputy, the only man beside Walpole himself good enough to bring in Bethl'em Aire. Murray grimaced to himself at the picture: he saw the men, and he saw their picture of him in turn — Murray with his proud big shoulders, his big hands, but no common farmer either, no common country farmer, Murray with his felt hat stuck tight on his head, the filthy band fitting right on his forehead as if it had grown there, his black felt hat like a symbol of something, or like a pot overturned upon his face. So his face would emerge beneath the hat broad and tanned, stung by the December wind, but raw-looking too, and his eyes blinking and squinting as if there were a glare. He would have his overcoat as great as any horse blanket, stiff and looking like wood, or iron, from a distance, always braced as if in a wind, or just emerging out of one, he would have his leather glove as fine and gleaming as new leather could be, his big boots dully gleaming with grease or melted snow; and these he would kick against the stove, ceremoniously, grunting, first the left foot and then the right, with his chin lowered so upon his chest, or down to where the big coat seemed to swell out from his body: no sheriff's deputy carried himself like Murray, no country son of them had his look, or his voice, could be trusted to bring in such a one as Bethl'em Aire . . . But Murray, sitting in the cold car, felt the vision slip away. He was looking at the snow, the crazy whirling of flakes. Not that these seemed infinite, or even numerous — they looked instead just like a constant shuffling and reshuffling of the same flakes, the same specks which gleamed back at him like little eyes so white in the glare of the headlights. On either side they fell away into a mass of gray, like cloud. Murray grinned and swore, spitting, at the storm. Now and then he saw stiff, shocked trees alongside the road, bare things as naked in the cold as if someone had peeled

all their bark off with a jackknife, peeled it off and tossed it up to
be sucked away by the wind. It was then that Murray noticed the
Negro Bethl'em staring at the trees too. "This won't last long,"
Murray said. "It's just a freak storm, and a freak cold too, and
you know it as well as me."

It was good to hear his voice again. He went on. "When I lived
up north farther there were storms there! That's where they really
were — snow up past the first floor windows of houses, there —
and my father would have to dig his way out, to see about the
stock. People ust to die, there, in storms like that! People who
were alone . . ." He wondered why he had taken that turn. His
voice had just gone that way by itself. He waited for the prisoner
to say something; but they only sat for a minute or two in silence,
listening to the wind. Then he laughed, harshly and humorlessly,
and found himself going on: "They wouldn't find them till maybe
a month afterwards," he said, "old people who lived all alone, old
men, frozen to death in their homes. There was one in a schoolhouse caught, one old man, he'd sleep there to save wood at home.
He got caught in the schoolhouse when a storm come on and he
couldn't get home, and burned all he could — books and desks and
all — That old man, I remember him, I remember him coming
around, asking to shoe horses in the summer — " Murray wondered
at himself, at the odd sound of his voice. He went on, immediately, "That was then. A man caught so all alone in the winter,
that would happen to him — then or now — up there or right
here, anywhere — a man is got to stick with others, doing how they
do, their laws, obeying their laws, living with them — not off by
himself — with his own laws — The ones that think diffrent are
the ones get kilt — or we bring them in to get — "

He quit; he drove on a while, silent, impressed with his own
words, and also with the peculiar closeness of that old man's
death. Then he shook his mind clear of the thought and decided they ought to stop. "We'll wait this goddam wind out," he
said. The wind kept on. Before him the road reared out in
broken, bare stretches, as if it had been torn out of the drifts of
snow on either side. "Wait it out," Murray muttered. He had
not glanced at his prisoner for some time; he did not do so now.
He knew, and the prisoner knew, that he was talking to himself.
But then he went on to say, "You know where we are now?"

The question hung in the air between them. Murray looked around in surprise, as if the Negro had spoken to him. The Negro Bethl'em, however, just sat there, as big a man as Murray, his puffed black face turned right to him, and his eyes, too, small and close together like Murray supposed a pig's eyes would be, these were staring right at Murray's face, or maybe at those queer words Murray had just heard himself say. Bethl'em, a well-known country Negro, well-known up and down the road, who worked for hire in the summertime, hay mowing and such, had come to Murray to look, now, not like himself any more, but like someone else, or a statue of someone else, all hard and cold and ageless, as if he had been staring at Murray or someone like him, so, with those pig's eyes, for centuries. Then he began to cough — not bothering to turn his head aside, coughing in a wracking, terrific, almost spiteful way.

"Ya, you wouldn't know, would you," Murray said. He felt his cold cheeks tighten. "Cough your goddam heart out, your black tonsils out then. Go on." Sitting near the edge of the seat, his knees apart and rubbing against the steering wheel, Murray stared at the storm, his face distorted with the effort of seeing. "There — something over there — " he said. The prisoner had stopped coughing. Murray pressed the car forward slowly. A ridge of land to his left seemed to fly right up out of the ground, a giant swelling of white like the side of a mountain. "There's a garage somewhere here — I'm damned if there ain't — I know it, I seen it enough times — " He spit out his words, as he almost expected the garage to appear as soon as he spoke, as if his words had made it appear. "It must be here somewhere," he said, a little quieter. "Out here somewhere — " Next to Murray the Negro began coughing again. Murray stared at him for a moment; then he looked away. "Are you all right?" he said.

Bethl'em did not answer. "Most likely getting sick," Murray went on, harshly, even angrily, as if he were talking to the snow. "Running all that ways without a coat, like a goddam fool nigger . . . Well, you cough all you like. I'm getting out here." He stopped the car, or allowed it to stop, or allowed the wind to stop it. "I'm going out to see what's here. I think there's a building here." He switched off the ignition but left the lights on. He could barely open the door, and when the first gust of wind hit his face he grunted with surprise, and looked back to Bethl'em. He saw the Negro sitting there, watching him.

Murray carried the picture of the man with him as he made his way, bent awkwardly against the wind, against the terrific onslaught of snow, around the front of the car and off the frozen road. Now the snow seemed to mock Murray, Murray with all his pride, all his strength, stumbling first in one direction and then stopping, slyly, perhaps, and turning in another, now walking as if he had really caught sight of something. When he found himself looking at two shapes, oblong and upright with long narrow drifts extending out behind them like angels' wings, he could only gape at them in confusion. Then he saw behind them the dim flicker of light, a light which grew stronger just as he stared at it, shielding his big face with his hands. Pulsing clouds of snow, like handfuls of fine hard sand, were flung against his face.

While helping Bethl'em out and to the building, Murray had to hold him once from falling — the ground underfoot was ice — and stood with his feet far apart, bracing both of them; the prisoner, with his wrists tied behind him, could not help himself. Murray put his arms right around the man's shoulders and in this way, panting, with both their heads bowed, the line of snow slashing at their foreheads as if they were no different from the gasoline pumps, they made their way through to the little wasteland of shelter before the garage. Murray slammed at the door with his foot. He bent to look through the glass of the door, to a blurred picture of two men, at the back of the garage, and a stove, and a lamp of some sort; he saw, muttering with impatience, that one of the men was advancing slowly and hesitantly toward the door.

When the door opened Murray pushed Bethl'em inside and then stepped in himself to a warm surge of air, and to the vision — how startling only Murray himself could have said, and yet it could not have been really a surprise to Murray, who knew this country so well — of the man in overalls, a Negro, a man with a black and red plaid shirt queerly clean, and, at the back, still another Negro, who sat up straight staring at them with the look of a rabbit or chipmunk or any small animal who believes himself not really seen, but disguised by the foliage around him, and whose belief gives him an air of absurdity. Murray, who was still a little shaken at this time, turned to close the door; and for an instant he stared at the frosted glass, and the sense of his isolation among these men welled up and subsided within him, leaving him a little weak. Then he turned back. "We only come to sit out this storm," he said.

The first Negro was staring at him and, past him, to Bethl'em, with a look of muffled recognition. "You c'n come in here," the Negro said slowly. "By the stove an' get warm . . . I was . . . I was scairt for a minute who was out there."

It was warmer at the back of the garage. The other Negro, a younger man, watched them. He was sitting in a swivel chair before a large office desk, an old-fashioned, ridiculous piece of furniture with scratches and initials on its surface. The older Negro went to the side of the desk and picked up a screwdriver, idly. He looked back at Murray over his shoulder.

"We thank you for this," Murray said, nodding brusquely. He had begun to feel oddly warm. Now, as if performing before these men — whom he believed he recognized, vaguely — but at the same time not really before them at all, but for his own satisfaction, his own delight, Murray began ceremoniously to unbutton his coat. One of his fine leather gloves he had taken off and this stuck, now, in his pocket, as if it were an ornament, and so with one glove on and one off he began to unbutton the big plastic buttons of the coat, frowning, his face distorted with concentration. The Negroes watched him. When he pushed the last button through the buttonhole he sighed and straightened his shoulders and made a gesture — even Murray could not have said how he did it — so that the older Negro started, and went to take Murray's coat. Murray watched him take it gingerly in his arms and hang it on a peg, brushing snow off it, yet gingerly too, as if he knew he was being so closely watched. With his right hand Murray took hold of the red wool scarf his mother had knitted for him the first winter he was a deputy, and now he began to unwind it, again ceremoniously, while the others watched. This too he handed to the Negro, who hung it by the coat. Murray touched his hat, but only touched it; for some reason he thought it might look better on, though it was wet. Then he turned ceremoniously to Bethl'em and, while the others stared, began to brush some of the snow off him. "Stand by the stove," he said. Bethl'em turned blindly — the stove was an old one, made of iron, a large, squat, ancient stove

that gave forth a low roaring murmur and glowed, in spots, a
hard-looking yellow. Murray patted Bethl'em's shoulders and un-
tied his wrists, and he saw now that the cord had cut into the
man's flesh, that it had made raw red lines in his skin. "Look at
that," Murray said in disgust. He held the cord at arm's length.
"Never even told me it was too tight."

He faced the two Negroes boldly, as if they were somehow involved in this. They were watching him, looking at his uniform.
They had been sitting at the desk, on either side of an opened
drawer with a piece of stiff cardboard over it, playing cards —
some of the cards were back against the inside of the desk, blown
there when the door was opened. The fingerworn, soiled surfaces,
the drunken glazed faces of the kings and queens and jacks seemed
to be gazing idly at Murray. "Expect we could offer them some
coffee," the young Negro said. "It's a purely cold night out."

Murray's mouth watered. But no one moved; and he caught his
confusion quick enough to keep it from showing. The older
Negro, who stood picking at the desk half-heartedly with the screwdriver, as if he thought he should look busy, said, "If there's
trouble with the car we ain't any help. We ain't up to these new
cars. We just give out gas, now."

"No trouble with the car," Murray said.

"That's luck for you," the other Negro said. He and the older
man — Murray supposed they were brothers — laughed shortly.
The young man leaned back in the swivel chair. He took a pack
of cigarettes out of his pocket. "Ain't much luck for your friend
you got there, though." Again he and his brother laughed. "Say,
ain't goin' to tie us up with that, are you?"

Murray saw he was still holding the cord. He shrugged his
shoulders and tossed it to the floor. The brothers were grinning
identically. At the stove Bethl'em stood with his arms out as if to
embrace the heat; his eyes were averted. "That had us purely
scairt for a minute," the young Negro said. He was lighting a
cigarette. Still moving slowly he got to his feet. "You, boy. I
expect you'd like a cigarette too." He was grinning at Murray,
showing his teeth; but when he extended the pack it was to
Bethl'em. Murray saw, cautiously, out of the corner of his eye,
the prisoner's fingers take a cigarette. "What's he done to get
himself arrested so?" the young man said. "He hurt some white
folks somewheres?"

His chest seemed swollen when he sat down again, leaning back precariously in the swivel chair; and now his brother had begun to smile too, looking up from the scratches he was making on the desk. Murray felt, alarmed, that they did not only look alike but seemed now to be sharing the same expression, a sly, knowing, inviting look. The young man smoked his cigarette. "Maybe you can't talk none," he said. Murray blinked at his words. "We got to let you in here, or anything you want, but you never need to talk to us. But I expect we already know what he done, anyhow. That Bethl'em Aire, there, there was talking all up an' down here about him . . . He never left off fightin' too early. Ain't that right?"

Murray glanced at the prisoner, who stood with his eyes lowered as if he were listening to something forbidden. His face, though, looked as if it had thawed, and he held the burning cigarette in his hand like a weapon. "What they goin' to do to him?" the older Negro said suddenly.

Murray stiffened. "A matter of the law," he said.

"What they goin' to do?"

Murray stared. The brothers met his stare equally, easily, like burlesques of himself, or like negatives of himself mocking him.

"Seems that takin' a man in to somethin' like he's goin' to get, there, an' not even know for sure what it is — that ain't the way to do," the young man said seriously. "You, Bethl'em. You think that's the way to do? Takin' a man in, an' him sure to be kilt for it — "

"Wait," Murray said. His voice sounded quite young. But what most surprised him is that he felt whatever concern he did, whatever alarm, not for himself but for Bethl'em.

The word, however, came as a pleasant surprise to the young Negro, evidently, who now lounged in the chair with the cigarette in his teeth. "That Sheriff Walpole knows me fine, an' he might of come through here an' tole me somethin'," he said. "Yes. He might of tole me somethin' about Bethl'em. An' I surely wouldn't want to trade no place with that boy there."

Murray glanced from the prisoner's strong back to the brothers. The brothers had drawn closer together; the older man, standing, leaned in against the desk, the younger sat up slowly in the creaking chair. He shook some ashes deliberately onto the concrete floor. "It ain't easy to consider a man that's alive right now," he

said grandly, as if beginning a speech, "an' is goin' to be dead in
a time. Why, that there blood goin' through him right now, only
think — only think — how it'll get all cold an' hard like grease
in the cold — How a man c'n go from alive to dead in such a
time! Not just black but white too or any color. Ain't that so?
A thing no more'n that-there screwdriver, ust to puttin' in screws
an' pickin' around here an' scratchin' the ice off the window, why,
set up against any man's forehead an' pushed in only a bit — any
man at all, why — "

Murray felt his face burn, and he felt something, at first quite
small, like a pinprick, touch coldly at his heart. When he looked
around to the prisoner he saw the man was staring at something
invisible on the top of the stove. Murray could no longer stand
still, but began to shift his weight from one foot to the other
grimacing as if in impatience with the storm. But when he spoke
it was not of the storm. His words seemed to explode from him.
"But I helped him," he said suddenly. "I did. I found him half
a mile out in a field trying to run up a hill that was all drifted,
and it was sundown, dark in a hour . . . and this storm coming
. . . He would have died there."

Now the young man laughed. "One place, here or there, another
place; there ain't much diff'rence." He and his brother laughed
quietly. "You, Bethl'em. You see much diff'rence?"

Bethl'em did not look around. "He would have got lost in the
storm anyway," Murray said. "Lost and frozen, all alone, what
good is it for a man all alone? By himself, thinking by himself . . .
He did that just to get away from me. That's what I can't get
ust to," he said, strangely, "them always running away. Goddam
fools, don't know what's for their own good, what's all thought up
to help them! They don't understand anything but how hungry
they are, they live by their stomach, you can't talk to them for
five minutes explaining any law — about deer or bass or anything
— without their eyes going all around to something else, something
over your shoulder — a bird in a tree, or the tree itself, or the
sky — "

"Hey, what's that?" the young man said. "What's that you're
sayin'?"

Murray was breathing hard. He felt more words crowding and
jumbling inside him.

"Somethin' about a bird in a tree," the older brother said.

"An' the sky too. Bethl'em, you hear that? You s'pose you're goin' to see much of a sky? Huh? Where you're goin'?"

When Bethl'em turned they all must have thought he was crying. Two almost even trickles of water had run down his face. But it was only from the snow in his hair, and he licked his lips and spat and glared at them. He held the cigarette without smoking it. "I got nothin' to say," he muttered.

"Got nothin'? Why, you better have!" the young man said gaily. "What you think they're bringin' you in for? Why, to talk, Bethl'em, to talk — got to answer questions polite. You know that sheriff? Don't you s'pose he's got things to ask you? He'll hit right on that trouble with that-there man, at the saloon, you know, an' how you done somethin' with your knife you oughtn't of; an' you ain't goin' to like it, no, but you got to answer polite for him." The young man began gathering up the playing cards, which had been blown back into the desk. He picked them up one by one, nodding, clicking his tongue as if in agreement with something. "Yes," he said. "You got to answer polite. An' you know what, Bethl'em? You know what?"

The young man's expression was blank, serious, and knowing, all at once, and he sat nodding at the dirty cards, picking them up and inspecting them, putting them into a pile. "You know what?" He looked right past Murray to the prisoner. "There ain't goin' to be a person at that trial, later, only maybe the wife of the guy you cut, an' his kids or somethin', not a person, sheriff or judge or nobody, that ain't goin' to be glad for what you done. They'll all be pleased fine with it." He nodded again, turning back to the cards. Murray could see the glazed faces of the cards, sometimes a king or queen, whose eyes, like those of the Negroes, were turned toward him. "Ain't that right, mister deppity? You tell him. Ain't that right?"

Murray turned away; he walked blindly toward the front of the garage. "Ain't that right!" the young man cried; there was joy in his voice. "Ain't it! An' nobody here ain't explained the diff'rence between lettin' a man die a good way, a clean way, by himself out in the snow, in his own land, an' bringin' him in so they c'n make a fuss out of it — a show out of it — " His words tumbled about themselves. "Yes," he said loudly, "that ain't been tole to me yet.

Or to Bethl'em either. He ain't got much time to be tole it in.
If you're goin' to take a man in to be kilt you better explain to
him why. You — "

Murray calmed his wild eyes. He stared out the window; his
hand was on his pistol. Most of all he was conscious of Bethl'em's
eyes on him, on his back; and he could feel his heart cringing inside him, in shame, a shame that was all mixed up, that had no
direction in which to go. The best deputy, Murray thought, the
best one of them, as good almost as Walpole himself . . . And he
saw a picture of himself, suddenly: tall and proud with his hat
stuck so tightly on his head, his broad face sick and pale, like un-
cooked dough, just a mockery of the old Murray, the one everyone
along the road knew, Murray with his hard chin and his sunburned,
windblown good looks . . . Outside the snowstorm had thinned
a little, the wind had nearly stopped; there was a glaring moon
somewhere that lit up everything with a delicate whiteness, a
crystalline whiteness; it was so clean, so white, it would be painful
to the touch, burning to the breath . . . "A man let loose in all
this cold wouldn't last," the young man said loudly, "he'd walk
off by himself further an' further, all alone, an' never need for any
white folks to do it to him. Any man is got a right . . ."

Murray stared out at the great banks of white, toppled and
slanted in the dark; he felt, beyond his surface paralysis, something
else, something peculiar — a sense, maybe, of familiarity. Such
scenes as this he had seen every night, just about, in the winters
of his childhood farther north, when he would crouch at his bedroom window in the dark and stare out at the night, at the snow
falling on the fine whirling mist which held no strangeness, he
felt, except what people thought strange in it, the chaos of something not yet formed . . . Outside the garage the earth seemed
to roll out of sight, out of mind, too gigantic for Murray's mind
to hold. And Murray felt again the isolation not only of himself
but of the prisoner and the other Negroes as well; he felt their
separate freedoms; and he felt too the time coming on him when
he would have to do something — by himself — not with the
sheriff behind him, or laws anywhere, but only by himself —

When Murray turned back his heart was pounding. Bethl'em
had straightened, he stood, now, taller than any of them, he was
sucking in his breath slowly, moving his eyes slowly about Murray's face and behind his head as if it were all the same thing,

doing something with his hands — rubbing his wrists — he was grinding out the cigarette on the floor. The brothers had not moved but grinned toward Murray, their smiles fixed and expectant, and the younger one went on, quietly, proddingly, "Now you, Bethl'em, you maybe got your only chance now. We're behind you. We ain't goin' to stand by to see such things happen — we ain't now, that's true — An' that-there deppity what's-his-name, that I seen ridin' around in the back seat of Walpole's old car enough times, he knows what's good for him, he ain't goin' to interfere — he ain't — " The young man's arms came loose. "You go on, now, Bethl'em!" he said. "You go on! You are a man, an' you got your right to — "

Murray waited. Both he and the prisoner were breathing strongly, almost at the same time, their big chests taut and falling, stiff, rigid, waiting, their eyes tied up together as if they were counting the steps between each other. But Bethl'em's look was so unflinching, so intense, so knowing of what was right, what was just, that Murray thought he could not bear it any longer — that look pierced him like a sliver of glass — and he looked away. Now the young Negro's chanting voice, even his words, which ought to have been so terrible to Murray, seemed only familiar — only right — exactly what he had expected, almost what he should have said himself — "You are a man," he said, "an' there's no law here — not here, not tonight — Where is there any law? Where is it? Or any one of us better'n another? All of us caught here in a storm, a blizzard, who's to say if there's anything left but us? Any laws? Any ol' sheriff? You surely got a right to your own life. You got a right. You got a right to — "

Neither Murray nor the prisoner had moved. They seemed locked by their eyes, as if in an embrace, with the air swelling about them, about their ears, so that Murray knew in a minute it would explode in to him, crashing and deafening his brain. . . . Then he saw something he did not, at first, believe. Then he saw it again, the young Negro behind Bethl'em's shoulder, winking at Murray himself — There he stood, nodding brightly, grinning incredibly, with one eye shut tight and wrinkled. Murray gaped, he sucked at the air, at its tremendous pressure. "You — you — " he stammered. His fingers were so tight on the revolver handle that he could not move them. "You — what are you — What — "

Just as Bethl'em was about to move the young Negro and his

brother began laughing. Even their teeth seemed to laugh, and
Murray felt, just as he knew Bethl'em felt, their laughter tear
through him. "Look at that Bethl'em, now!" the young man cried.
His delight so shook him that he jerked, his arms loose, his shoulders rocking. "Just look! Here he thinks he's goin' somewhere!
He ain't never goin' to get along with no white men — ain't one
time goin' to learn — "

Bethl'em's shoulders relaxed just a little. His face stayed tight,
like a mask, or a statue, staring right at Murray's shamed face.
"Now, you, Bethl'em, now," the young man said, dancing around,
"don't you get mad at *me*. I ain't done a thing. It ain't a fault of
mine, you come to believe so much!"

Murray went to the prisoner and took his arm. He could not
look at the man's face, so he looked at his collar, and at the wet
hair that grew so long down his neck. Murray stood, so, for a
minute. Then he said, "We're leaving now. The storm let up."
Murray could hear nothing but the prisoner's slow, even breath,
and the almost noiseless laughter of the brothers. "You, Bethl'em,"
he said. "You go on out to the car. You get in and wait." He
waited a moment. "Go on," he said.

Bethl'em went to the door. Murray did not watch him, nor did
he look at the brothers. At first he did not know what to do; he did
not know where to look; he could not, for a minute or so, even
think past the terrible shame he had seen, he felt weak and sickened
before it . . . Then he turned, briskly, he stiffened his shoulders,
he took his red scarf very carefully off the peg and began winding
it around his neck. It took him some time to dress. The young
Negro kept on, a little louder now: "That Bethl'em's a big man,
a good big man, I known him too long a time already. A big man
up an' down this road! Hey!"

Murray finished buttoning his coat. He did not hurry. He
watched himself, and then he watched himself putting on his gloves.
When he was dressed he knew there was something left wrong,
unfinished, but he could not think what; his mind still buzzed and
crowded so. "An' you tell that sheriff, too," the young man was
saying. "Will you? You tell him." The laughter had suddenly
drained out of his face. "Mister deppity — wait — Wait a minute — "

Murray was staring at him. Then he saw the cord on the floor;

then he bent, slowly, and picked it up and put it in his pocket.
He went to the door. The young man hurried along behind him.
He took hold of Murray's arm. "You, mister," he said. "You tell
the sheriff how I did here. You tell him that. An' how you caught
on to the game right away, an' played it too. You tell him. He'll
like that. He will. I know that sheriff, he comes out here sometimes . . . he buys gas here sometimes . . ." Murray stared at
the man. "That black boy out there don't demand no more consideration than any other one. He is got to have it done to him
too. Is he any different?" The young man spoke quickly and a
little shrilly. "Why, there ain't a one of us ain't had it done to
him," he said, proudly, "an' ain't a white man here don't know
it — That's how it is. An' him too, him too, he is got to have it
done to him too — "

He smiled shakily as Murray opened the door and the cold air
fell upon them. Murray stepped out. "Wait, wait," the young
Negro said, pulling at his arm. "Mister, you wait. You tell the
sheriff, huh? Huh? Will you? You tell him how I did — he'll
laugh — you say it was me, here, this garage — He knows me
good — Why, look here, mister," he said, and he pulled one of
his trouser legs up, so fast Murray hadn't time to look away, all
the way up to the knee so that Murray had to look at the queer
mottled scars, "they sic'd the dogs on me, once, had them chase
me for fun down by the crick; I wasn't fifteen then; they chased
me a long ways, I kept runnin' with them right on my legs an'
somebody tole the sheriff an' he come to see me himself an' ast
about it, an' looked sorry, but there couldn't be nothin' done. . . .
Why, I never needed to knife no man first, did I? But I had it
done, it's how it is, I never even thought much on it. So that black
boy you got ain't no different . . . You tell the sheriff. He'll remember which one I am, he'll remember me . . ."

Murray let the door close behind him. Crossing to the car — he
saw with a shock he had never turned the lights off — he believed
he could sense the young man leaning against the glass, his arms
up and embracing the window. Murray did not look back. The
wind pulled at his hat, and he pressed it down tighter. He went
around and got in the car, grunting, his body as heavy as if he
were dragging himself out of water. The air inside the car was
frozen and painful. It turned his breath to steam before him.

Murray sat, quietly, resting, his hands on the steering wheel, looking out at the white world — as Bethl'em himself looked, without speaking — and Murray felt only now the heat of that shame begin to cool, a strange, sinister, diffuse shame, it reached out to all of them, touched them all. He saw that the fine white mist of the storm, all its queer, brutal power, its primeval power, had settled and there was, now, just the same sculptured whiteness of forms, familiar forms, looking just like the same familiar world to which he would return. But he sat behind the wheel, tapping his stiffened fingers on it, thinking, knowing that his behavior did not puzzle Bethl'em but did not even touch upon him. He thought that sometime, before very long, surely in a minute or two, he would again continue on his way.

R. C. PHELAN

Birds, Clouds, Frogs

(FROM REDBOOK)

A HOT BREEZE flapped at each window like a curtain, and yet a housefly cruised easily inside the bus. There were four passengers besides Zachary Calhoun — two country girls traveling together in identical hats, a soldier, and an old woman with bundles. The driver sat squarely in his seat, and beyond him the road flowed smoothly down the windshield. There was a sign that said: "Your driver is Orlando O. Sisler. Courteous — Competent — Careful."

Zachary closed the paperback collection of great short stories. The big spaces of West Texas would not open out around them before dark. He was on his first paid vacation and had forty-three dollars in his pocket. As a graduate of the University of Texas with a B.A. degree in English, he had not been offered the kind of salary that newly graduated engineers, business administration majors or geologists expected and received. For more than a year he had been the junior half of a two-man, one-secretary public-relations firm in a town just barely big enough to *have* public-relations firms. He listened to complaints, drove people to the airport and wrote speeches to be delivered before unimportant groups and letters of condolence for clients too busy to write their own. Now he was on his way to spend two weeks on his great-uncle's ranch south of San Angelo, in the driest, emptiest part of Texas. It was a land that Zachary loved but could find no way to make a living in. On his brief visits to the ranch he was a perennial tenderfoot, but his great-uncle and his various cousins liked him and he was welcome there.

Zachary wondered what the other O in the driver's name could stand for, that he should prefer Orlando to it.

"Hey, *stop that!*" the soldier roared suddenly, in a surprisingly big voice for a little man with glasses. The driver put his thumb on the horn button and kept it there. Zachary saw that the soldier had shouted at two tiny figures far ahead in the road — or, rather, at one of them. A woman lay on the pavement and a man stood over her, kicking her. Near them, standing on the shoulder of the road, was a pickup truck.

As the bus slowed the soldier got up and stood by the door, ready to leap out and save the woman in the road. Zachary, seeing that this was the alert, responsible thing to do and being the only other male passenger, got up and stood just behind him. But the driver's honking, probably, had done what it was meant to do. By the time they stopped, the man was leaning against the back of the pickup truck with his elbows resting on the tailgate. His overalls were dirty and he was drunk.

The soldier walked up to him. With a hand in each hip pocket of his suntans and his elbows pointing back, he tilted his head to one side, looked up at the man in overalls and said, "Boy, just what do you *mean?*"

"That's my wife," the man answered.

Zachary and the driver knelt beside her. She had fresh bruises, but small ones, on her temple and upper arm. Her hair was unwashed and long uncombed, and her dress was very green and rather dirty. Lying on her back, she looked up at them sadly but not perceptively. She groaned, turned on her left side, made herself as comfortable as she could on the warm concrete, sighed, and closed her eyes as if to sleep.

Orlando Sisler touched one of her bruises lightly. "I believe she's drunker than he is," he said to Zachary.

"I think so," said Zachary.

It was only then that he heard the children crying in the pickup truck. He opened the door on the driver's side and there they were, three of them like a nestful of birds, their faces turned up, their mouths open, their tears round, fresh and bright. Zachary took out his handkerchief and then decided there was more work than one handkerchief could do and put it back unused. The oldest and youngest were boys, in coveralls. The middle one was a girl.

"Mister," said the oldest, who seemed to be about ten, "are they going to put us in jay-ul?" Their faces still turned up, they stopped sobbing and waited for the answer.

Zachary leaned in across the seat and looked at them sternly, to give himself added authority. "No, they are not going to put you in jail," he said. "Everything is going to be all right."

All three of them sniffed. They were beautiful children, yellow-haired, barefooted, with perfect complexions under a lot of fresh dirt. Tools and wire and a coil of rope lay on the floor of the truck, and the seat was covered by an old quilt folded to size.

"Is that your daddy out there?" Zachary asked.

"Yes."

"And is that your mama?"

"Yes."

"Did you go to town?"

"Yes, and we had strawberry cones — dime ones," said the girl, smiling. The older boy wiped the younger children's faces and then his own with a corner of the quilt. "Stop crying, Ollie," he told his brother. "They're not going to put us in jail." The boy stopped crying.

"Daniel, let's get out," said the girl briskly.

"You'd better stay here," said Zachary, but Daniel had the other door open. Hooking one arm around his little brother's chest, he slid the boy quickly from the seat to the floorboards, the running board and at last the ground, with Ollie grunting as he went. Then all three of them ran straight to the bus and entered it through its open door.

The children's mother was gone from the highway. "I carried her and put her in the bus," said Orlando Sisler. "She never woke up." He had joined the soldier, and both were staring at the children's father. Zachary walked over.

"Aw, we had a few, but we ain't drunk," the father said. The soldier still had his hands in his hip pockets, but he now was wearing sunglasses, with the case attached to his belt. He was one of those neat, shipshape soldiers with carefully fitted uniforms. In his big, loud voice he now asked the father sternly, "You git your wife down in the road and kick her *ever'* time you had a few?"

"She needed it," the husband answered.

"My schedule is gonna be shot to little bitty pieces," said Orlando Sisler to Zachary. "I'll have to make out a report of this."

Since the bus had stopped no car had passed by. The wind was hot and the sky was clear, except for three buzzards wheeling against a string of white clouds along the south horizon. On the low, dry hills were pastures with cedar and blackjack oak, but there were no houses in sight.

Now a big truck came down the grade eastbound, backfiring gently, and stopped. Its driver lifted his cap by its visor and scratched his head, exchanging a look with the bus driver that was like a lodge handshake.

"Man just got drunk and was kickin' his wife down the road a ways," said Orlando Sisler comfortably. "I reckon he ought to be locked up awhile. You mind phonin' for the sheriff when you get to the junction?"

"Just be glad to," said the truck driver, and pulled away.

"Is the soldier getting off at the next town by any chance?" said Zachary.

"I believe he is," said Orlando. "Why?"

"Well, if he would stay with *him* till the deputy sheriff gets here, we could take her and the children on home; I suppose they live just a few miles down the road. Then the deputy could take the soldier on into town."

"That don't sound like any deputy sheriff I ever heard of," said Orlando, "giving a man a ride. But we'll try it."

The soldier agreed almost eagerly, Zachary thought, to the arrangement. But then, he looked like a man who relished being in charge. Orlando explained matters to the children's father. "We're gonna take your wife and kids on home. This soldier's gonna stay here with you awhile. They gonna lock you up till you get sobered up good."

"I'd stay here all day if I just had a smoke," said the farmer. "I meant to get some in town and be derned if I didn't forget." Orlando gave the farmer his cigarettes. "Got a match, old buddy?" he said to the soldier, offering a cigarette.

The mother was asleep in the seat just behind the driver's. Zachary had expected to find the children playing tag in the aisle, but the three of them were sitting quietly together in a pair of seats, gazing out the window at some sunflowers and a clump of scrub oak. Ollie was standing up on the cushions.

"Daniel," said Zachary, "will you tell the bus driver when we get to your house?"

"Are we going to ride in the bus?" asked Daniel.

"Yes, if you'll tell us when we get to your house."

The children looked at each other and giggled. "We never was in a bus before," said the girl. "Just trucks."

"Edna," Daniel told her, "you get up in that seat and you can look out *that* window. I'll stay here and hold onto Ollie and we'll look out *this* window."

The old woman passenger came along the aisle, steadying herself on the backs of the seats, just as if the bus were moving. "I made this for my grandbabies," she said to the children, "but you'd better have it," and she held out three huge pieces of chocolate fudge on a fresh paper napkin.

Daniel handed the candy around, taking the third piece himself and leaving the napkin in the old woman's outstretched hand. "Thank ye kindly," he said.

"You're entirely welcome," she answered, and turned to Zachary. "Poor little heathen," she said, shaking her head, and then changed the subject. "I shut all the windows, with that awful old drunkard outside, and then I couldn't figure out how to shut the door."

"I'll open them," said Zachary.

"Thank goodness!" one of the country girls said to the other, rolling her eyes to the ceiling, as Zachary began to struggle with windows. They had remained primly in their seats through everything.

Orlando Sisler counted his passengers, took his seat and closed the door. "Wait," Daniel called. "I got to git the groceries." He left the bus, climbed into the back of his father's truck and tugged at a cardboard carton. His father turned and watched him with interest.

"Lord," said Zachary, and he too got out of the bus. But by the time he reached the truck, the soldier had lifted the carton and set it on Daniel's shoulder.

The boy staggered with it toward the bus. "I got it, I got it," he grunted, refusing Zachary's help.

"You kids behave yourself, now, Son," the father called to Daniel, who didn't answer. The father then addressed himself to Zachary. "That oldest 'un's a good little old kid," he said, and exhaled smoke from one of Orlando's cigarettes.

Once more Zachary boarded the bus. As it moved away Edna looked down from her window at the two men beside the truck.

"Goodbye, Daddy and mister," she crooned, smiling at them affectionately.

Zachary sat beside the children's mother. She was asleep until Edna came from across the aisle and touched her arm. "Mama," she said, smiling, "I looked out the window and saw lots of houses and trees and things."

The mother turned her head and looked at Edna. "You sweet, darlin' thing," she said sadly. "Run off now and play nice with Ollie."

Edna returned to her window and the mother went back to sleep. Zachary opened his book and began reading.

It was six o'clock and the sun was low, visible through the windshield of the bus. Daniel came forward and stood by the driver for a while, watching the road. He pointed. "Right there," he said, indicating not a house but a dirt track that led off around a hill.

Orlando Sisler brought the bus to a stop. "All right, lady," he said, turning in his seat. "You're home now."

The woman woke up wearily, rose, and without a word to anyone let herself carefully down the steps to the ground. Orlando set the box of groceries on the shoulder of the road. The children filed out: Ollie, Edna, and then Daniel, who silently held up to the bus driver on his open palm a nickel and three pennies. Orlando looked down at him and shook his head.

"Can you kids carry all that stuff?" he asked, and then added to Zachary, "The house is prob'ly a mile back in the brush."

"We'll hide some under the culvert and come back for it," said Daniel.

Zachary rose and got off the bus. "I'll carry the groceries for them," he told Orlando. "Maybe I'll get to San Angelo tomorrow sometime."

The driver was back in his seat now, with a foot on the accelerator and a hand ready to close the door. "You *might* catch a ride on in tonight," he said. "Anyways, I hope so." He and Zachary exchanged looks of good-humored commiseration — really a complete, miniature friendship of about a second's duration; then the driver closed the door and that particular friendship was over.

"Goodbye," crooned Edna, waving, as the bus pulled away.

The children's mother had not waited; she was about to disappear around the hill now at a dogged, painful gait that suggested she was not so much drunk any longer as hung-over and thinking of sleep. Zachary lifted the carton of groceries to his shoulder and set out with Daniel beside him and the younger children in front. They moved at Ollie's speed, which was slow; they would not overtake the mother.

The road ran gently downhill and entered a stand of scrub oak and cedar. It was nearly sunset. A crow called out a warning as they passed, and the dry wind brought an old skunk smell, faint and antiseptic and, to Zachary, pleasant. His shoulder began to ache. He saw that the printing on the box had rubbed off on his white shirt. His cousins would drive sixty miles to meet the bus in San Angelo, he reflected, and he would not be on it. He might not get to a telephone before tomorrow morning. His toothbrush was in his suitcase on the bus, and the paperback collection of great short stories, for which he had paid fifty cents that morning, was riding west unclaimed on the seat just behind Orlando Sisler. The first day of his two weeks' vacation was gone already and he had not reached the comforting emptiness of the West. Instead he was walking toward a tenant farmhouse that he had never seen, where, at the inexperienced age of twenty-three, he might have to feed and bathe three children. He shifted the groceries and smiled. It was all amazingly irregular and agreeable.

Orlando Sisler had made a good guess; the house was at least a mile from the highway. It was unpainted and sagging, taking some shelter of its own from a big live oak. It had no television antenna and no wires or storage tank to indicate electric lights or running water. Behind the house was a small, weathered barn with a lean-to, and beyond that was a field in which the sunflowers grew taller than the corn. In the front yard were broken farm implements, a few worn-out tires, and a tree stump on which there rested an old dishpan planted with petunias. On the porch sat a little old woman rocking in a wicker chair.

"Grandma, we rode the bus," Edna called.

The old woman sat, rocking only a little, until they reached the porch.

Zachary set the carton down, smiled at her and said, "Here's your groceries."

She had an intricately wrinkled face, sharp blue eyes, and little teeth curved like bird claws. Her ankles seemed to narrow down to the very bones. She wore a black wool dress, hot though it was, and over it a blue cotton apron with a pocket.

"Thank ye kindly," she said. "I was worried when Ruby walked in here drunk a little while ago without the children. She never said a word, just went to bed. Did the truck break down?"

"They both got drunk," said Zachary. "I don't expect he'll be back until tomorrow sometime. I think the truck is all right, though."

The old woman lifted the sparse remains of her eyebrows and pursed her lips as if she were very slightly vexed. "Well," she said, "just sit down and I'll have supper in a little bit. Daniel, draw me a bucket of water, honey; I've been thirsty for an hour. Ollie and Edna, go look for eggs. I fed the chickens." She rose and picked a dead leaf from a geranium in a lard can at the edge of the porch. "I can't lift the bucket out of the well," she explained to Zachary. "I'm eighty-one years old and weigh eighty-seven pounds."

"My, you don't look it," he said.

She smiled. "Wasn't it a fine day?" she asked. "I set on the porch all day, and nobody come to see me but a redbird."

Zachary was hungry; he did not take the trouble to protest that he really ought to be going now. He merely followed the old woman to the kitchen, carrying the carton of groceries. Then he sat on the porch floor, leaned against a post and looked at the trees, the rocky ground and the empty sky. It was dusk. A breeze came and flapped about his legs and shoulders. He heard the sound of a well bucket, the complaint of a hen, the clank of stove lids from the kitchen. Daniel entered the kitchen by the back door and held a conversation with his grandmother. Zachary could hear their two light voices, the old one and the young, but he could not distinguish their words; he didn't try. Then the boy came to the porch and joined Zachary in looking at the trees and sky, waiting for supper. Daniel did not speak. Sitting cross-legged, he scratched one knee through a hole in his coveralls. His blue eyes, paler now than the sky, were fixed on something that Zachary could not see; Daniel was thinking.

They ate in the kitchen at a round table with a kerosene lamp in the center: pork chops, sliced tomatoes, black-eyed peas, hot corn bread and glasses of buttermilk. The children ate busily.

"Grandma," said Ollie, "the little baby squirrel died and we won't get to play together." Ollie stared unhappily at his plate and began to sob. The others looked at him gravely and let him cry.

For dessert there were stewed apricots spread on more corn bread, and coffee for Zachary and the grandmother. Her name, she told Zachary, was Mrs. Sarah Shell; the children's father was her son.

"Do they get drunk every Saturday?" Zachary asked.

"No," said Mrs. Shell, "just when they have the money."

"They didn't get very drunk at all today," said Daniel. "Sometimes they go to sleep in the truck and we don't get back till way late."

"I'll say this for Son, and Ruby too — they buy the groceries the first thing when they get to town," said the grandmother. "If anything's left, they drink it up."

The children left the table, but Zachary and old Mrs. Shell sat on, finishing their coffee. He offered the old woman a cigarette. She looked at it thoughtfully before she refused.

"Have you lived here long?" he asked.

"No. We move to a different place every year. The furniture and the chickens and the six of us all can make it in one truckload. Son's not much of a farmer, though his daddy was. I don't reckon he'll ever have anything." She did not appear to be either sorrowful or worried.

"That was a good supper," he said.

The old woman tried to look severe but managed only to look pleased. In spite of herself, she smiled. "I always say, if you're going to have corn bread, have it *hot*," she said.

"Look, ma'am," said Zachary, "I wish you'd take this. Don't tell your son and daughter-in-law. Just keep it in case you and the kids need it sometime." He put a ten-dollar bill on the table.

The old woman smiled, and her old face somehow looked as fresh and innocent as Edna's. She might have been a little girl with a secret. "Bless your heart, we don't need it," she said. "Daniel and me have got *twenty-three dollars* hid out down by the creek. If me and the kids ever need it, why, it's there. Just as long as Son and Ruby don't wreck the truck and hurt the children, why, we haven't got a worry on God's green earth. Daniel is eleven. It won't be long

before he's big enough to take care of me and the babies, and Son
and Ruby can go their way. They've run off before, stayed two
months, but me and Daniel made out till they got back. I'll leave
these dishes till tomorrow; it's too hot to build up the fire."

On their way to the front porch they passed through a bedroom.
A strip of lamplight fell into it from the kitchen. Ollie lay flung
out on the bed, face up, asleep in his coveralls. "Don't forget to
undress him, Daniel," said old Mrs. Shell when they reached the
porch. Edna was not there. Zachary wondered if she had gone
into the other bedroom to sleep with her mother.

They simply sat — Daniel and Zachary on the porch floor, the
old woman in her creaking wicker rocker — and looked at the magnificent night. After a while Daniel said apologetically, "We had
a radio but the batteries ran down," and he took a harmonica from
his pocket. He played two gentle, sad tunes that Zachary did not
know, and then he stopped.

Zachary felt himself set free, gently, upon the earth. He had not
known that people could be so tenuously attached to a place, so
meagerly equipped with possessions. He thought of his own debts
and duties and possessions. They lay a hundred miles to the east,
weights that he had set down and did not have to pick up again.
His stomach was comfortably filled with pork chops and corn bread
and, just above it, his heart with love for the old woman and the
children. He wanted to join them, take charge of them, protect
them against the caprices of Son and Ruby. But he knew that he
could not join them, any more than he could join a flock of birds.
He was afraid of a freedom based on the possession of twenty-three
dollars and the innocent feeling that the world was made to be
lived in. It was an extension of the choice he had made when he
decided to study English instead of geology, but he could not follow
it that far. He would go on to the ranch, and then back to his job,
debts, books, clothes, promises, phonograph, and camera. Even
his collection of short stories would be returned to him, he knew;
Orlando Sisler would put it with his luggage.

"I have to go," he said.

"Good night," they told him. "Thank ye kindly."

He walked up the dirt track, looking at the sky. The night was
dark and perfect. Winter was somewhere faraway and so was rain;
it was a night, he thought sadly, that was safe even for him to

wander in. He would walk the road and then the highway, enjoying it, and in the morning someone would give him a lift.

From the dark trees on the left came Edna's voice, small, unemotional and clear. "Goodbye," she called, "goodbye."

What was she doing out there? he wondered. Perhaps she chose to sleep there. Zachary answered, but only to himself, "Goodbye, Edna."

MORDECAI RICHLER

Some Grist for Mervyn's Mill

(FROM THE KENYON REVIEW)

MERVYN KAPLANSKY stepped out of the rain on a dreary Saturday afternoon in August to inquire about our back bedroom.

"It's $12.00 a week," my father said, "payable in advance."

Mervyn set $48.00 down on the table. Astonished, my father retreated a step. "What's the rush-rush? Look around first. Maybe you won't like it here."

"You believe in electricity?"

There were no lights on in the house. "We're not the kind to skimp," my father said. "But we're orthodox here. Today is *shabus*."

"No, no, no. Between people."

"What are you? A wise guy."

"I do. And as soon as I came in here I felt the right vibrations. Hi, kid." Mervyn grinned breezily at me, but the hand he mussed my hair with was shaking. "I'm going to love it here."

My father watched, disconcerted but too intimidated to protest, as Mervyn sat down on the bed, bouncing a little to try the mattress. "Go get your mother right away," he said to me.

Fortunately, she had just entered the room. I didn't want to miss anything.

"Meet your new roomer," Mervyn said, jumping up.

"Hold your horses." My father hooked his thumbs in his suspenders. "What do you do for a living?"

"I'm a writer."

"With what firm?"

"No, no, no. For myself. I'm a creative artist."

My father could see at once that my mother was enraptured and so, reconciled to yet another defeat, he said, "Haven't you any . . . things?"

"When Oscar Wilde entered the United States and they asked him if he had anything to declare, he said, 'Only my genius.' "

My father made a sour face.

"My things are at the station," Mervyn said, swallowing hard. "May I bring them over?"

"Bring."

Mervyn returned an hour or so later with his trunk, several suitcases, and an assortment of oddities that included a piece of driftwood, a wine bottle that had been made into a lamp base, a collection of pebbles, a twelve-inch-high replica of Rodin's "The Thinker," a bullfight poster, a Karsh portrait of G.B.S., innumerable notebooks, a ball-point pen with a built-in flashlight, and a framed check of $14.85 from the *Family Herald & Weekly Star.*

"Feel free to borrow any of our books," my mother said.

"Well, thanks. But I try not to read too much now that I'm a wordsmith myself. I'm afraid of being influenced, you see."

Mervyn was a short, fat boy, with curly black hair, warm wet eyes, and an engaging smile. I could see his underwear through the triangles of tension that ran from button to button down his shirt. The last button had probably burst off. It was gone. Mervyn, I figured, must have been at least twenty-three years old, but he looked much younger.

"Where did you say you were from?" my father asked.

"I didn't."

Thumbs hooked in his suspenders, rocking on his heels, my father waited.

"Toronto," Mervyn said bitterly. "Toronto the Good. My father's a big-time insurance agent and my brothers are in ladies' wear. They're in the rat race. All of them."

"You'll find that in this house," my mother said, "we are not materialists."

Mervyn slept in — or, as he put it, stocked the unconscious — until noon every day. He typed through the afternoon and then, depleted, slept some more, and usually typed again deep into the

night. He was the first writer I had ever met and I worshiped
him. So did my mother. "Have you ever noticed his hands," she
said, and I thought she was going to lecture me about his chewed-
up fingernails, but what she said was, "They're artist's hands. Your
grandfather had hands like that." If a neighbor dropped in for
tea my mother would whisper, "We'll have to speak quietly," and,
indicating the tap-tap of the typewriter from the back bedroom,
she'd add, "In there, Mervyn is creating." My mother prepared
special dishes for Mervyn. Soup, she felt, was especially nourish-
ing. Fish was the best brain food. She discouraged chocolates and
nuts because of Mervyn's complexion, but she brought him coffee
at all hours, and if a day passed with no sound coming from the
back room my mother would be extremely upset. Eventually,
she'd knock softly on Mervyn's door. "Anything I can get you?"
she'd ask.

"It's no use. It just isn't coming today. I go through periods
like that, you know."

Mervyn was writing a novel, his first, and it was about the
struggles of our people in a hostile society. The novel's title was,
to begin with, a secret between Mervyn and my mother. Occasionally, he read excerpts to her. She made only one correction. "I
wouldn't say 'whore,'" she said. "It isn't nice, is it? Say 'lady of
easy virtue.'" The two of them began to go in for literary discus-
sions. "Shakespeare," my mother would say, "Shakespeare knew
everything." And Mervyn, nodding, would reply, "But he stole
all his plots. He was a plagiarist." My mother told Mervyn about
her father, the rabbi, and the books he had written in Yiddish.
"At his funeral," she told him, "they had to have six motorcycle
policemen to control the crowds." More than once my father
came home from work to find the two of them still seated at the
kitchen table, and his supper wasn't ready or he had to eat a cold
plate. Flushing, stammering apologies, Mervyn would flee to his
room. He was, I think, the only man who was ever afraid of my
father, and this my father found very heady stuff. He spoke
gruffly, even profanely in Mervyn's presence, and called him Moitle
behind his back. But, when you come down to it, all my father
had against Mervyn was the fact that my mother no longer baked
potato *kugel*. (Starch was bad for Mervyn.) My father began to
spend more of his time playing cards at Tansky's Cigar & Soda,

and when Mervyn fell behind with the rent he threatened to take action.

"But you can't trouble him now," my mother said, "when he's in the middle of his novel. He works so hard. He's a genius maybe."

"He's peanuts, or what's he doing here?"

I used to fetch Mervyn cigarettes and headache tablets from the drugstore round the corner. On some days when it wasn't coming the two of us used to play casino and Mervyn, at his breezy best, used to wisecrack a lot. "What would you say," he said, "if I told you I aim to out-Émile Zola?" Once he let me read one of his stories, "Was the Champ a Chump?" that had been printed in magazines in Australia and South Africa. I told him that I wanted to be a writer too. "Kid," he said, "a word from the wise. Never become a wordsmith. Digging ditches would be easier."

From the day of his arrival Mervyn had always worked hard, but what with his money running low he was now so determined to get his novel done that he seldom went out any more. Not even for a stroll. My mother felt this was bad for his digestion. So she arranged a date with Molly Rosen. Molly, who lived only three doors down the street, was the best looker on St. Urbain, and my mother noticed that for weeks now Mervyn always happened to be standing by the window when it was time for Molly to pass on the way home from work. "Now you go out," my mother said, "and enjoy. You're still a youngster. The novel can wait for a day."

"But what does Molly want with me?"

"She's crazy to meet you. For weeks now she's been asking questions."

Mervyn complained that he lacked a clean shirt, he pleaded a headache, but my mother said, "Don't be afraid, she won't eat you." All at once Mervyn's tone changed. He tilted his head cockily. "Don't wait up for me," he said.

Mervyn came home early. "What happened?" I asked.

"I got bored."

"With *Molly?*"

"Molly's an insect. Sex is highly overestimated, you know. It also saps an artist's creative energies."

But when my mother came home from her Talmud Torah meeting and discovered that Mervyn had come home so early she felt that she had been personally affronted. Mrs. Rosen was summoned to tea.

"It's a Saturday night," she said, "she puts on her best dress, and that cheapskate where does he take her? To sit on the mountain. Do you know that she turned down three other boys, including Ready-to-Wear's *only* son, because you made such a *gedille?*"

"With dumbbells like Ready-to-Wear she can have dates any night of the week. Mervyn's a creative artist."

"On a Saturday night to take a beautiful young thing to sit on the mountain. From these benches you can get piles."

"Don't be disgusting."

"She's got on her dancing shoes and you know what's for him a date? To watch the people go by. He likes to make up stories about them he says. You mean it breaks his heart to part with a dollar."

"To bring up your daughter to be a gold digger. For shame."

"All right. I wasn't going to blab, but if that's how you feel — modern men and women, he told her, experiment *before* marriage. And right there on the bench he tried dirty filthy things with her. He — "

"Don't draw me no pictures. If I know your Molly he didn't have to try so hard."

"How dare you! She went out with him it was a favor for the marble cake recipe. The dirty piker he asked her to marry him he hasn't even got a job. She laughed in his face."

Mervyn denied that he had tried any funny stuff with Molly — he had too much respect for womankind, he said — but after my father heard that he had come home so early he no longer teased Mervyn when he stood by the window to watch Molly pass. He even resisted making wisecracks when Molly's kid brother returned Mervyn's thick letters unopened. Once, he tried to console Mervyn. "With a towel over the face," he said gruffly, "one's the same as another."

Mervyn's cheeks reddened. He coughed. And my father turned away, disgusted.

"Make no mistake," Mervyn said with a sudden jaunty smile. "You're talking to a boy who's been around. We pen-pushers are notorious lechers."

Mervyn soon fell behind with the rent again and my father began to complain.

"You can't trouble him now," my mother said. "He's in agony. It isn't coming today."

"Yeah, sure. The trouble is there's something coming to me."

"Yesterday he read me a chapter from his book. It's so beautiful you could die." My mother told him that Shalinsky, the editor of *Jewish Thought,* had looked at the book. "He says Mervyn is a very deep writer."

"Shalinsky's for the birds. If Mervyn's such a big writer let him make me out a check for the rent. That's my kind of reading, you know."

"Give him one week more. Something will come through for him, I'm sure."

My father waited another week, counting off the days. "E-Day minus three today," he'd say. "Anything come through for the genius?" Nothing, not one lousy dime, came through for Mervyn. In fact he had secretly borrowed from my mother for the postage to send his novel to a publisher in New York. "E-Day minus one today," my father said. And then, irritated because he had yet to be asked what the E stood for, he added, *"E for Eviction."*

On Friday my mother prepared an enormous potato *kugel.* But when my father came home, elated, the first thing he said was, "Where's Mervyn?"

"Can't you wait until after supper, even?"

Mervyn stepped softly into the kitchen. "You want me?" he asked.

My father slapped a magazine down on the table. *Liberty.* He opened it at a short story titled "A Doll for the Deacon." "Mel Kane, Jr.," he said, "isn't that your literary handle?"

"His *nom-de-plume,*" my mother said.

"Then the story is yours." My father clapped Mervyn on the back. "Why didn't you tell me you were a writer? I thought you were a . . . well, a fruitcup. You know what I mean. A long-hair."

"Let me see that," my mother said.

Absently, my father handed her the magazine. "You mean to say," he said, "you made all that up out of your own head?"

Mervyn nodded. He grinned. But he could see that my mother was displeased.

"It's a top-notch story," my father said. Smiling, he turned to

my mother. "All the time I thought he was a sponger. A poet.
He's a writer. Can you beat that?" He laughed, delighted. "Excuse me," he said, and he went to wash his hands.

"Here's your story, Mervyn," my mother said. "I'd rather not
read it."

Mervyn lowered his head.

"But you don't understand, Maw. Mervyn has to do that sort
of stuff. For the money. He's got to eat too, you know."

My mother reflected briefly. "A little tip, then," she said to
Mervyn. "Better he doesn't know why . . . Well, you understand."

"Sure I do."

At supper my father said, "Hey, what's your novel called, Mr.
Kane?"

"*The Dirty Jews.*"

"Are you *crazy?*"

"It's an ironic title," my mother said.

"Wow! It sure is."

"I want to throw the lie right back in their ugly faces," Mervyn
said.

"Yeah. Yeah, sure." My father invited Mervyn to Tansky's to
meet the boys. "In one night there," he said, "you can pick up
enough material for a book."

"I don't think Mervyn is interested."

Mervyn, I could see, looked dejected. But he didn't dare antagonize my mother. Remembering something he had once told me,
I said, "To a creative writer every experience is welcome."

"Yes, that's true," my mother said. "I hadn't thought of it
like that."

So my father, Mervyn, and I set off together. My father showed
Liberty to all of Tansky's regulars. While Mervyn lit one cigarette
off another, coughed, smiled foolishly, and coughed again, my father
introduced him as the up-and-coming writer.

"If he's such a big writer what's he doing on St. Urbain Street?"

My father explained that Mervyn had just finished his first
novel. "When that comes out," he said, "this boy will be batting
in the major leagues."

The regulars looked Mervyn up and down. His suit was shiny.

"You must understand," Mervyn said, "that, at the best of
times, it's difficult for an artist to earn a living. Society is naturally
hostile to us."

"So what's so special? I'm a plumber. Society isn't hostile to me, but I've got the same problem. Listen here, it's hard for anybody to earn a living."

"You don't get it," Mervyn said, retreating a step. *"I'm* in rebellion against society."

Tansky moved away, disgusted. "Gorki, there was a writer. This boy . . ."

Molly's father thrust himself into the group surrounding Mervyn. "You wrote a novel," he asked, "it's true?"

"It's with a big publisher in New York right now," my father said.

"You should remember," Takifman said menacingly, "only to write good things about the Jews."

Shapiro winked at Mervyn. The regulars smiled: some shyly, others hopeful, believing. Mervyn looked back at them solemnly. "It is my profound hope," he said, "that in the years to come our people will have every reason to be proud of me."

Segol stood Mervyn for a Pepsi and a sandwich. "Six months from now," he said, "I'll be saying I knew you when."

Mervyn whirled around on his counter stool. "I'm going to out-Émile Zola," he said. He shook with laughter.

"Do you think there's going to be another war?" Perlman asked.

"Oh, lay off," my father said. "Give the man air. No wisdom outside of office hours, eh, Mervyn?"

Mervyn slapped his knees and laughed some more. Molly's father pulled him aside. "You wrote this story," he said, holding up *Liberty,* "and don't lie because I'll find you out."

"Yeah," Mervyn said, "I'm the Grub-streeter who knocked that one off. But it's my novel that I really care about."

"You know who I am? I'm Molly's father. Rosen. Put it there, Mervyn. There's nothing to worry. You leave everything to me."

My mother was still awake when we got home. Alone at the kitchen table.

"You were certainly gone a long time," she said to Mervyn.

"Nobody forced him to stay."

"He's too polite," my mother said, slipping her tooled leather bookmark between the pages of *Wuthering Heights.* "He wouldn't tell you when he was bored by such common types."

"Hey," my father said, remembering. "Hey, Mervyn. Can you beat that Takifman for a character?"

Mervyn started to smile, but my mother sighed and he looked away. "It's time I hit the hay," he said.

"Well." My father pulled down his suspenders. "If anyone wants to use the library let him speak now or forever hold his peace."

"Please, Sam. You only say things like that to disgust me. I know that."

My father went into Mervyn's room. He smiled a little. Mervyn waited, puzzled. My father rubbed his forehead. He pulled his ear. "Well, I'm not a fool. You should know that. Life does things to you, but . . ."

"It certainly does, Mr. Hersh."

"You won't end up a zero like me. So I'm glad for you. Well, good night."

But my father did not go to bed immediately. Instead, he got out his collection of pipes, neglected all these years, and sat down at the kitchen table to clean and restore them. And, starting the next morning, he began to search out and clip items in the newspapers, human interest stories with a twist, that might be exploited by Mervyn. When he came home from work — early, he had not stopped off at Tansky's — my father did not demand his supper right off but, instead, went directly to Mervyn's room. I could hear the two men talking in low voices. Finally, my mother had to disturb them. Molly was on the phone.

"Mr. Kaplansky. Mervyn. Would you like to take me out on Friday night? I'm free."

Mervyn didn't answer.

"We could watch the people go by. Anything you say. Mervyn?"

"Did your father put you up to this?"

"What's the diff? You wanted to go out with me. Well, on Friday I'm free."

"I'm sorry. I can't do it."

"Don't you like me any more?"

"I sure do. And the attraction is more than merely sexual. But if we go out together it will have to be because you so desire it."

"Mervyn, if you don't take me out on Friday he won't let me out to the dance Saturday night with Solly. Please, Mervyn."

"Sorry. But I must answer in the negative."

Mervyn told my mother about the telephone conversation and immediately she said, "You did right." But a few days later, she became tremendously concerned about Mervyn. He no longer slept in each morning. Indeed, he was the first one up in the house, to wait by the window for the postman. After he had passed, however, Mervyn did not settle down to work. He'd wander sluggishly about the house or go out for a walk. Usually, Mervyn ended up at Tansky's. My father would be waiting there.

"You know," Sugarman said, "many amazing things have happened to me in my life. It would make *some* book."

The men wanted to know Mervyn's opinion of Sholem Asch, the red menace, and ungrateful children. They teased him about my father. "To hear him tell it you're a guaranteed genius."

"Well," Mervyn said, winking, blowing on his fingernails and rubbing them against his jacket lapel, "who knows?"

But Molly's father said, "I read in the *Gazette* this morning where Hemingway was paid $100,000 to make a movie from *one* story. A complete book must be worth at least five short stories. Wouldn't you say?" And Mervyn, coughing, clearing his throat, didn't answer, but walked off quickly. His shirt collar, too highly starched, cut into the back of his hairless, reddening neck. When I caught up with him he told me, "No wonder so many artists have been driven to suicide. Nobody understands us. We're not in the rat race."

Molly came by at 7.30 on Friday night.

"Is there something I can do for you?" my mother asked.

"I'm here to see Mr. Kaplansky. I believe he rents a room here."

"Better to rent out a room than give fourteen ounces to the pound."

"If you are referring to my father's establishment then I'm sorry he can't give credit to everybody."

"We pay cash everywhere. Knock wood."

"I'm sure. Now may I see Mr. Kaplansky, *if you don't mind?*"

"He's still dining. But I'll inquire."

Molly didn't wait. She pushed past my mother into the kitchen. Her eyes were a little puffy. It looked to me like she had been crying. "Hi," she said. Molly wore her soft black hair in an upsweep. Her mouth was painted very red.

"Siddown," my father said. "Make yourself homely." Nobody laughed. "It's a joke," he said.

"Are you ready, Mervyn?"

Mervyn fiddled with his fork. "I've got work to do tonight," he said.

"I'll put up a pot of coffee for you right away."

Smiling thinly Molly pulled back her coat, took a deep breath, and sat down. She had to perch on the edge of the chair either because of her skirt or that it hurt her to sit. "About the novel," she said, smiling at Mervyn, "congrats."

"But it hasn't even been accepted by a publisher yet."

"It's good, isn't it?"

"Of course it's good," my mother said.

"Then what's there to worry? Come on," Molly said, rising. "Let's skedaddle."

We all went to the window to watch them go down the street together.

"Look at her how she's grabbing his arm," my mother said. "Isn't it disgusting?"

"You lost by a T.K.O.," my father said.

"*Thanks,*" my mother said, and she left the room.

My father blew on his fingers. "Whew," he said. We continued to watch by the window. "I'll bet you she sharpens them on a grindstone every morning to get them so pointy, and he's such a shortie he wouldn't even have to bend over to . . ." My father sat down, lit his pipe, and opened *Liberty* at Mervyn's story. "You know, Mervyn's not that *special* a guy. Maybe it's not as hard as it seems to write stories."

"Digging ditches would be easier," I said.

My father took me to Tansky's for a Coke. Drumming his fingers on the counter, he answered questions about Mervyn. "Well, it has to do with this thing . . . the Muse. On some days, with the Muse, he works better. But on other days . . ." My father addressed the regulars with a daring touch of condescension; I had never seen him so assured before. "Well, that depends. But he says Hollywood is very corrupt."

Mervyn came home shortly after midnight.

"I want to give you a word of advice," my mother said. "That girl comes from very common people. You can do better, you know."

My father cracked his knuckles. He didn't look at Mervyn.

"You've got your future career to think of. You must choose a mate who won't be an embarrassment in the better circles."

"Or still better stay a bachelor," my father said.

"Nothing more dreadful can happen to a person," my mother said, "than to marry somebody who doesn't share his interests."

"Play the field a little," my father said, drawing on his pipe.

My mother looked into my father's face and laughed. My father's voice fell to a whisper. "You get married too young," he said, "and you live to regret it."

My mother laughed again. Her eyes were wet.

"I'm not the kind to stand by idly," Mervyn said, "while you insult Miss Rosen's good name."

My father, my mother, looked at Mervyn, as if surprised by his presence. Mervyn retreated, startled. *"I mean that,"* he said.

"Just who do you think you're talking to?" my mother said. She looked sharply at my father.

"Hey, there," my father said.

"I hope," my mother said, "success isn't giving you a swelled head."

"Success won't change me. I'm stedfast. But you are intruding into my personal affairs. Good night."

My father seemed both dismayed and a little pleased that some-one had spoken up to my mother.

"And just what's ailing you?" my mother asked.

"Me? Nothing."

"If you could only see yourself. At your age. A pipe."

"According to the *Digest* it's safer than cigarettes."

"You know absolutely nothing about people. Mervyn would never be rude to me. It's only his artistic temperament coming out."

My father waited until my mother had gone to bed and then he slipped into Mervyn's room. "Hi." He sat down on the edge of Mervyn's bed. "Tell me to mind my own business if you want me to, but . . . well, have you had bad news from New York? The publisher?"

"I'm still waiting to hear from New York."

"Sure," my father said, jumping up. "Sorry. Good night." But he paused briefly at the door. "I've gone out on a limb for you. Please don't let me down."

Molly's father phoned the next morning. "You had a good time, Mervyn?"

"Yeah. Yeah, sure."

"Atta boy. That girl she's crazy about you. Like they say she's walking on air."

Molly, they said, had told the other girls in the office at Susy's Smart-Wear that she would probably soon be leaving for, as she put it, tropical climes. Gitel Shalinsky saw her shopping for beach-wear on Park Avenue — in November, this — and the rumor was that Mervyn had already accepted a Hollywood offer for his book, a guaranteed best-seller. A couple of days later a package came for Mervyn. It was his novel. There was a printed form enclosed with it. The publishers felt the book was not for them.

"Tough luck," my father said.

"It's nothing," Mervyn said breezily. "Some of the best word-smiths going have had their novels turned down six-seven times before a publisher takes it. Besides, this outfit wasn't for me in the first place. It's a homosexual company. They only print the pretty-pretty prose boys." Mervyn laughed; he slapped his knees. "I'll send the book to another publisher today."

My mother made Mervyn his favorite dishes for dinner. "You have real talent," she said to him, "and everything will come to you." Afterward, Molly came by. Mervyn came home very late this time, but my mother waited up for him all the same.

"I'm invited to eat at the Rosens' on Saturday night. Isn't that nice?"

"But I ordered something special from the butcher for us here."

"I'm sorry. I didn't know."

"So now you know. Please yourself, Mervyn. Oh, it's all right. I changed your bed. But you could have told me, you know."

Mervyn locked his hands together to quiet them. "Tell you what, for Christ's sake? There's nothing to tell."

"It's all right, *boyele*," my mother said. "Accidents happen."

Once more my father slipped into Mervyn's room. "It's okay," he said; "don't worry about Saturday night. Play around. Work the kinks out. But don't put anything in writing. You might live to regret it."

"I happen to think Molly is a remarkable girl."

"Me too. I'm not as old as you think."

"No, no, no. You don't understand."

My father showed Mervyn some clippings he had saved for him. One news story told of two brothers who had discovered each other by accident after twenty-five years, another was all about a funny day at court. He also gave Mervyn an announcement for the annual Y.M.H.A. *Beacon* short story contest. "I've got an idea for you," he said. "Listen, Mervyn, in the movies . . . well, when Humphrey Bogart, for instance, lights up a Chesterfield or asks for a Coke you think he doesn't get a nice little envelope from the companies concerned? Sure he does. Well, your problem seems to be money. So why couldn't you do the same thing in books? Like if your hero has to fly somewhere, for instance, why use an unnamed airline? Couldn't he go TWA because it's the safest, the best, and maybe he picks up a cutie-pie on board? Or if your central character is . . . well, a lush, couldn't he always insist on Seagram's because it's the greatest? Get the idea? I could write, say, TWA, Pepsi, Seagram's, and Adam's Hats and find out just how much a book plug is worth to them, and you . . . well, what do you think?"

"I could never do that in a book of mine, that's what I think. It would reflect on my integrity. People would begin to talk, see."

But people had already begun to talk. Molly's kid brother told me Mervyn had made a hit at dinner. His father, he said, had told Mervyn he felt, along with the moderns, that in-laws should not live with a young couple, not always, but the climate in Montreal was a real killer for his wife, and if it so happened that he ever had a son-in-law in, let's say, California . . . well, it would be nice to visit . . . and Mervyn agreed that families should be close-knit. Not all the talk was favorable, however. The boys on the street were hostile to Mervyn. An outsider, a Torontonian, they felt, was threatening to carry off our Molly.

"There they go," the boys would say as Molly and Mervyn walked hand-in-hand past the poolroom, "Beauty and the Beast."

"All these years they've been looking, and looking, and looking, and there he is, the missing link."

Mervyn was openly taunted on the street. "Hey, big writer. Lard-ass. How many periods in a bottle of ink?"

"Shakespeare, come here. How did you get to look like that, or were you paid for the accident?"

But Mervyn assured me that he wasn't troubled by the boys.

"The masses," he said, "have always been hostile to the artist. They've driven plenty of our number to self-slaughter, you know. But I can see through them."

His novel was turned down again.

"It doesn't matter," Mervyn said. "There are better publishers."

"But wouldn't they be experts there?" my father asked. "I mean maybe . . ."

"Look at this, will you? This time they sent me a personal letter! You know who this is from? It's from one of the greatest editors in all of America."

"Maybe so," my father said uneasily, "but he doesn't want your book."

"He admires my energy and enthusiasm, doesn't he?"

Once more Mervyn mailed off his novel, but this time he did not resume his watch by the window. Mervyn was no longer the same. I don't mean that his face had broken out worse than ever — it had, it's true, only that was probably because he was eating too many starchy foods again — but suddenly he seemed indifferent to his novel's fate. I gave birth, he said, sent my baby out into the world, and now he's on his own. Another factor was that Mervyn had become, as he put it, pregnant once more (he looks it too, one of Tansky's regulars told me): that is to say, he was at work on a new book. My mother interpreted this as a very good sign and she did her utmost to encourage Mervyn. Though she continued to change his sheets just about every other night, she never once complained about it. Why, she even pretended this was normal procedure in our house. But Mervyn seemed perpetually irritated and he avoided the type of literary discussion that had formerly given my mother such deep pleasure. Every night now he went out with Molly and there were times when he did not return until 4.00 or 5.00 in the morning. And now, curiously enough, it was my father who waited up for Mervyn, or stole out of bed to join him in the kitchen. He would make coffee and take down his prized bottle of apricot brandy. More than once I was wakened by his laughter. My father told Mervyn stories of his father's house, his boyhood, and the hard times that came after. He told Mervyn how his mother-in-law had been bedridden in our house for seven years, and with pride implicit in his every word — a pride that would have amazed and maybe even flattered my mother — he told Mervyn how my mother had tended to the old lady better than any nurse with umpteen diplomas. "To see her now," I heard my father say, "is like night to day. Before the time of the old lady's stroke she was no sourpuss. Well, that's life." He told Mervyn about the first time he had seen my mother, and how she had

written him letters with poems by Shelley, Keats, and Byron in
them, when all the time he had lived only two streets away and
all she had to do was pick up the phone if she wanted to talk to
him. But another time I heard my father say, "When I was a
young man, you know, there were days on end when I never went
to bed. I was so excited. I used to go out and walk the streets
better than snooze. I thought if I slept maybe I'd miss something.
Now isn't that crazy?" Mervyn muttered a reply. Usually, he
seemed weary and self-absorbed. But my father was irrepressible.
Listening to him, his tender tone with Mervyn and the surprise of
his laughter, I felt that I had reason to be envious. My father had
never talked like that to me or my brother Harvey. But I was so
astonished to discover this side of my father, it was all so unexpected, that I soon forgot my jealousy.

One night I heard Mervyn tell my father, "Maybe the novel I
sent out is no good. Maybe it's just something I had to work out
of my system."

"Are you crazy it's no good? I told everyone you were a big
writer."

"It's the apricot brandy talking," Mervyn said breezily. "I was
only kidding you."

But Mervyn had his problems. I heard from Molly's kid brother
that Mr. Rosen had told him he was ready to retire. "Not that
I want to be a burden to anybody," he had said. Molly had
begun to take all the movie magazines available at Tansky's. "So
that when I meet the stars face to face," she had told Gitel, "I
shouldn't put my foot in it, and embarrass Merv."

Mervyn began to pick at his food, and it was not uncommon
for him to leap up from the table and rush to the bathroom, holding his hand to his mouth. I discovered for the first time that my
mother had bought a rubber sheet for Mervyn's bed. If Mervyn
had to pass Tansky's, he no longer stopped to shoot the breeze.
Instead, he would hurry past, his head lowered. Once, Segal stopped
him. "What'sa matter," he said, "you too good for us now?"

Tansky's regulars began to work on my father.

"All of a sudden, your genius there, he's such a B.T.O.," Sugarman said, "that he has no time for us here."

"Let's face it," my father said. "You're zeros. We all are. But
my friend Mervyn . . ."

"Don't tell me, Sam. He's full of beans. Baked beans."

My father stopped going to Tansky's altogether. He took to playing solitaire at home.

"What are you doing here?" my mother asked.

"Can't I stay home one night? It's my house too, you know."

"I want the truth, Sam."

"Aw, those guys. You think these cockroaches know what an artist's struggle is?" He hesitated, watching my mother closely. "By them it must be that Mervyn isn't good enough. He's no writer."

"You know," my mother said, "he owes us seven weeks' rent."

"The first day Mervyn came here," my father said, his eyes half-shut as he held a match to his pipe, "he said there was a kind of electricity between us. Well, I'm not going to let him down over a few bucks."

But something was bothering Mervyn. For that night and the next he did not go out with Molly. He went to the window to watch her pass again and then retreated to his room to do the crossword puzzles.

"Feel like casino?" I asked.

"I love that girl," Mervyn said. "I adore her."

"I thought everything was okay, but, I thought you were making time."

"No, no, no. I want to marry her. I told Molly that I'd settle down and get a job if she'd have me."

"Are you crazy? A job? With your talent?"

"That's what she said."

"Aw, let's play casino. It'll take your mind off things."

"She doesn't understand. Nobody does. For me to take a job is not like some ordinary guy taking a job. I'm always studying my own reactions. I want to know how a shipper feels from the inside."

"You mean you'd take a job *as a shipper?*"

"But it's not like I'd really be a shipper. It would look like that from the outside, but I'd really be studying my co-workers all the time. I'm an artist, you know."

"Stop worrying, Mervyn. Tomorrow there'll be a letter begging you for your book."

But the next day nothing came. A week passed. Ten days.

"That's a very good sign," Mervyn said. "It means they are considering my book very carefully."

It got so we all waited around for the postman. Mervyn was aware that my father did not go to Tansky's any more and that my mother's friends had begun to tease her. Except for his endless phone calls to Molly he hardly ever came out of his room. The phone calls were futile. Molly wouldn't speak to him.

One evening my father returned from work, his face flushed. "Son-of-a-bitch," he said, "that Rosen he's a cockroach. You know what he's saying? He wouldn't have in his family a faker or a swindler. He said you were not a writer, Mervyn, but garbage." My father started to laugh. "But I trapped him for a liar. For you know what he said? That you were going to take a job as a shipper. Boy, did I ever tell him."

"What did you say?" my mother asked.

"I told him good. Don't you worry. When I lose my temper, you know . . ."

"Maybe it wouldn't be such a bad idea for Mervyn to take a job. Better than go into debt he could — "

"You shouldn't have bragged about me to your friends so much," Mervyn said to my mother. "I didn't ask it."

"*I'm* a braggart? You take that back. You owe me an apology. After all, *you're* the one who said you were such a big writer."

"My talent is unquestioned. I have stacks of letters from important people and — "

"I'm waiting for an apology. Sam?"

"I have to be fair. I've seen some of the letters, so that's true. But that's not to say Emily Post would approve of Mervyn calling you a — "

"My husband was right the first time. When he said you were a sponger, Mervyn."

"Don't worry," Mervyn said, turning on my father. "You'll get your rent back no matter what. Good night."

I can't swear to it. I may have imagined it. But when I got up to go to the toilet late that night it seemed to me that I heard Mervyn sobbing in his room. Anyway, the next morning the postman rang the bell and Mervyn came back with a package and a letter.

"Not again," my father said.

"No. This happens to be a letter from the most important publisher in the United States. They are going to pay me $2500 for my book in advance against royalties."

"Hey. Lemme see that."

"Don't you trust me?"

"Of course we do." My mother hugged Mervyn. "All the time I knew you had it in you."

"This calls for a celebration," my father said, going to get the apricot brandy.

My mother went to phone Mrs. Fisher. "Oh, Ida, I just called to say I'll be able to bake for the bazaar after all. No, nothing new here. Oh, I almost forgot. Remember Mervyn you were saying he was nothing but a little twerp? Well, he just got a fantastic offer for his book from a publisher in New York. No, I'm only allowed to say it runs into four figures in advance. Excited? That one. I'm not even sure he'll accept."

My father grabbed the phone to call Tansky's.

"One minute. Hold it. Couldn't we keep quiet about this and have a private sort of celebration?"

My father got through to the store. "Hello, Sugarman? Everybody come over here. Drinks on the house. Why, of Korsakov. No, wise guy. She certainly isn't. At her age? It's Mervyn. He's considering a $5000 offer just to sign a contract for his book."

The phone rang an instant after my father had hung up.

"Well, hello, Mrs. Rosen," my mother said. "Well, thank you. I'll give him the message. No, no, why should I have anything against you we've been neighbors for years. No. Certainly not. It wasn't *me* you called a piker. Your Molly didn't laugh in my face."

Unnoticed, Mervyn sat down on the sofa. He held his head in his hands.

"There's the doorbell," my father said.

"I think I'll lie down for a minute. Excuse me."

By the time Mervyn came out of his room again many of Tansky's regulars had arrived. "If it had been up to me," my father said, "none of you would be here. But Mervyn's not the type to hold grudges."

Molly's father elbowed his way through the group surrounding Mervyn. "I want you to know," he said, "that I'm proud of you today. There's nobody I'd rather have for a son-in-law."

"You're sort of hurrying things. Aren't you?"

"What? Didn't you propose to her a hundred times she wouldn't have you? And now I'm standing here to tell you all right and you're beginning with the shaking in the pants. This I don't like."

Everybody turned to stare. There was some good-natured laughter.

"You wrote her such letters they still bring a blush to my face — "

"But they came back unopened."

Molly's father shrugged and Mervyn's face turned gray as a pencil eraser.

"But you listen here," Rosen said. "For Molly, if you don't mind, it isn't necessary for me to go begging."

"Here she is," somebody said.

The regulars moved in closer.

"Hi." Molly smelled richly of Lily of the Valley. You could see the outlines of her bra underneath her sweater (both were in Midnight Black, from Susy's Smart-Wear). Her tartan skirt was held together by an enormous gold-plated safety pin. "Hi, doll." She rushed up to Mervyn and kissed him. "Maw just told me." Molly turned to the others, her smile radiant. "Mr. Kaplansky has asked for my hand in matrimony. We are engaged."

"Congratulations!" Rosen clapped Mervyn on the back. "The very best to you both."

There were whoops of approval all around.

"When it comes to choosing a bedroom set you can't go wrong with my son-in-law Lou."

"I hope," Takifman said sternly, "yours will be a kosher home."

"Some of the biggest crooks in town only eat kosher and I don't mind saying that straight to your face, Takifman."

"He's right, you know. And these days the most important thing with young couples is that they should be sexually compatible."

Mervyn, surrounded by the men, looked over their heads for Molly. He spotted her trapped in another circle in the far corner of the room. Molly was eating a banana. She smiled at Mervyn; she winked.

"Don't they make a lovely couple?"

"Twenty years ago they said the same thing about me. Does that answer your question?"

Mervyn was drinking heavily. He looked sick.

"Hey," my father said, his glass spilling over, "tell me, Segal, what goes in hard and stiff and comes out soft and wet?"

"Oh, for Christ's sake," I said. "Chewing gum. It's as old as the hills."

"You watch out," my father said. "You're asking for it."

"You know," Miller said. "I could do with something to eat."

My mother moved silently and tight-lipped among the guests, collecting glasses just as soon as they were put down.

"I'll tell you what," Rosen said in a booming voice, "let's all go over to my place for a decent feed and some schnapps."

Our living room emptied more quickly than it had filled.

"Where's your mother?" my father asked, puzzled.

I told him she was in the kitchen and we went to get her. "Come on," my father said, "let's go to the Rosens'."

"And who, may I ask, will clean up the mess you and your friends made here?"

"It won't run away."

"You have no pride."

"Oh, please. Don't start. Not today."

"Drunkard."

"Ray Milland, that's me. Hey, what's that coming out of the wall? A bat."

"That poor innocent boy is being railroaded into a marriage he doesn't want and you just stand there."

"Couldn't you enjoy yourself *just once?*"

"You didn't see his face how scared he was? I thought he'd faint."

"Who ever got married he didn't need a little push? Why, I remember when I was a young man — "

"You go, Sam. Do me a favor. Go to Rosens'."

My father sent me out of the room.

"I'm not," he began, "well, I'm not always happy with you. Not day in and day out. I'm telling you straight."

"When I needed you to speak up for me you couldn't. Today courage comes in bottles. Do me a favor, Sam. Go."

"I wasn't going to go and leave you alone. I was going to stay. But if that's how you feel . . ."

My father returned to the living room to get his jacket. I jumped up.

"Where are *you* going?" he asked.

"To the party."

"You stay here with your mother you have no consideration."

"God damn it."

"You heard me." But my father paused for a moment at the door. Thumbs hooked in his suspenders, rocking to and fro on his heels, he raised his head so high his chin jutted out incongruously. "I wasn't always your father. I was a young man once."

"So?"

"Did you know," he said, one eye half-shut, "that LIVE spelled backward is EVIL?"

I woke at 3.00 in the morning when I heard a chair crash in the living room, somebody fell, and this was followed by the sound of sobbing. It was Mervyn. Dizzy, wretched, and bewildered. He sat on the floor with a glass in his hand. When he saw me coming he raised his glass. "The wordsmith's bottled enemy," he said, grinning.

"When you getting married?"

He laughed. I laughed too.

"I'm not getting married."

"Wha'?"

"Sh."

"But I thought you were crazy about Molly?"

"I was. I am no longer." Mervyn rose; he tottered over to the window. "Have you ever looked up at the stars," he said, "and felt how small and unimportant we are?"

It hadn't occurred to me before.

"Nothing really matters. In terms of eternity our lives are shorter than a cigarette puff. Hey," he said. "Hey!" He took out his pen with the built-in flashlight and wrote something in his notebook. "For a writer," he said, "everything is grist to the mill. Nothing is humiliating."

"But what about Molly?"

"She's an insect. I told you the first time. All she wanted were my kudos. My fame . . . If you're really going to become a wordsmith remember one thing. The world is full of ridicule while you struggle. But once you've made it the glamour girls will come crawling."

He had begun to cry again. "Want me to sit with you for a while?" I said.

"No. Go to bed. Leave me alone."

The next morning, at breakfast, my parents weren't talking.

My mother's eyes were red and swollen and my father was in a forbidding mood. A telegram come for Mervyn.

"It's from New York," he said. "They want me right away. There's an offer for my book from Hollywood and they need me."

"You don't say?"

Mervyn thrust the telegram at my father. "Here," he said. "You read it."

"Take it easy. All I said was . . ." But my father read the telegram all the same. "Son-of-a-bitch," he said. "Hollywood."

We helped Mervyn pack.

"Shall I get Molly?" my father asked.

"No. I'll only be gone for a few days. I want to surprise her."

We all went to the window to wave. Just before he got into the taxi Mervyn looked up at us; he looked for a long while, but he didn't wave, and of course we never saw him again. A few days later a bill came for the telegram. It had been sent from our house. "I'm not surprised," my mother said.

My mother blamed the Rosens for Mervyn's flight, while they held us responsible for what they called their daughter's disgrace. My father put his pipes aside again and naturally he took a terrible ribbing at Tansky's. About a month later, $5.00 bills began to arrive from Toronto. They came sporadically, until Mervyn had paid up all his back rent. But he never answered any of my father's letters.

WILLIAM SAROYAN

What a World, Said the Bicycle Rider

(FROM THE SATURDAY EVENING POST)

GOING AROUND the world on a bicycle is no longer enough — the daredevil has got to go around the moon on a Pogo stick with one arm tied behind him if he wants to get his picture in the paper. Maybe that's why I wasn't impressed when Amshavir Shamavoor came to my door in Paris, removed a trouser clip from his right ankle, stepped back, his eyes on fire with excitement, and didn't speak, waiting for me (I presume) to get the full picture, which in fact I did get and didn't like.

This has got to be another nut from Fresno, I thought. And while I was trying to think who it might be, he began to speak at last.

"Dan, we went to Emerson together. Amsho? Shamavoor? A block and a half back of your house on San Benito? The little green house by the railroad tracks? In front of the brewery? Hell, Dan, here I am, on my way around the world on a bicycle, and here you are a world-famous picture painter on this high-tone street in the one and only city of Paris, hobnobbing with lords and dukes and high muckamucks. What a world. Amsho?"

I was afraid I might actually know him, might have known him, one of perhaps three hundred Fresno boys I had known thirty years ago, because if I *did* know him I would have to make something of it, and this just wasn't the time for it. But no matter how hard I tried to fix him somewhere in the past, I was relieved that I couldn't. He came from Fresno all right, there was no question about that, but to me he was a total stranger. I couldn't even vaguely remember him — name, face, height, weight, voice, excitement, eyes or manners, which were the traditional high manners of the kids of immigrants in Fresno — comedy, confidence, amazement, health and a determination to be superior in any competitive activity of America. He was of my mob all right, but I didn't know him, and I was glad I didn't, because my wife had just left me.

At four in the afternoon of that magnificent August day she had announced in a kind of nervous frenzy that she had at last found true love and was going straight to him. Would I call a taxi, please? No, I would not call a taxi, but I would like to know what the hell she was talking about. Love, that's what she was talking about — in the person of Al Poufnique, a black-bearded American poet from Greenwich Village we had met at a sidewalk table at the Deux Magots a couple of weeks ago. Well, if I didn't know how to be civilized and call a taxi, she would go out into the street and hail one.

Our two boys and two girls were all over the house, about the big surprise they were going to spring on their mother, on the occasion of the twelfth anniversary of her marriage to their father — me. They had let me in on the surprise while she had been out shopping. So now she was back and she had packed an entirely ridiculous-looking little checkered suitcase, and I wanted to know one thing — what about the kids? I meant of course what about their big surprise for *her?* I knew they had bought peaches and raspberries and had made a great bowlful of something to be eaten with thick cream, because we had all had that dessert the one time we had gone to Maxim's for dinner. That's what I meant, but she said she couldn't decide just now what to do about the kids. She might just throw them all over, the way that woman did who married D. H. Lawrence. Why not? Love and love alone is the thing and don't ever forget it, Dan — in a tone of Eastern philosophic earnestness, or would that be more nearly Western, that love-and-love-alone bazaz, maybe out of old what's-his-name's popular hymn of 1910, "Ah! Sweet Mystery of Life," old Victor Herbert? And then, sure enough, she swung the great door open and flung herself out into the hall, leaving me standing there with my mouth open, thinking, Al Poufnique, Al Poufnique, who the hell is Al Poufnique?

Nelly, eleven years old, the oldest, a lot like her mother, came running to let me see her in the new dress she had put on especially for the occasion: "Mamma go shopping again?"

"Well, yes, I think you could put it that way."

"Just so she's back by six for the champagne part of the party before dinner. And yummy, wait till you see what we're having."

Then Pat, ten, then Della, nine, and finally Rufe, eight, came to the door that was still wide open, and each of them said something about the big surprise for their mother, but I didn't remember (or even really hear) any of it, because all of a sudden I remembered who Al Poufnique was.

Well, it just wouldn't do, that's all. Had three weeks in Paris driven the poor woman mad, just because she was thirty-seven and the mother of four kids, or what?

The kids were all right. I didn't have to worry about the kids. They were always fun. I wouldn't have had four, I wouldn't have had my wife have four if I hadn't always liked kids, always liked the idea of them, the whole incredible reality of them forever underfoot and smelling up the house with their fresh clean smells of intensity, struggle and truth. But now what was I supposed to do? Tell them the truth, or a decent variation of it, ask them to sit tight, and go chasing after her in a taxi to the Deux Magots? I had no idea where else to go looking for her, and it wasn't very likely that she would go there with a small suitcase, so where should I go?

"Back to the living room, everybody."

I shut the door and we all went back to the living room, but after a minute or two Nelly ran off to study the situation in the kitchen. Three days ago the cook had quit because it was too hot to be in Paris and she wanted to visit her mother in Montpellier anyway. And so all of us had got acquainted with the kitchen and how the great gas stove worked. After a moment the others ran off to be with Nelly in the kitchen, because that was where the surprise was getting worked out, and I began to think about the whole situation. I picked up the telephone book to see if Al Poufnique was in it — Poudroux, Pouey, Pougatch, but no Poufnique. Who could I call?

I was sitting on the delicate antique straight-backed chair that belonged to the fragile desk with the telephone on it, with the open book in front of me, trying to think, when all of a sudden I realized that I had fallen into a kind of trance of stupor or disbelief or something, and furthermore that I had been sitting there that way for a long time. The faraway voices of the kids in the kitchen and up and down the long hall had somewhere along the line faded away, and now I had the distinct feeling that this silence was not accidental, that it had something to do with the whole family, with the intended surprise, with their mother, with me. And then without looking up and noticing them standing together in the doorway at the end of the long room, I knew they were there and that they had been there for some time; so now how was I to meet this situation? How was I to look up and find them there, and how was I to come out of it and be alive, and say something sensible? Before I could reach a decision Pat was across the desk from me.

"What's the matter, Pop?"

I got up very quickly and saw the other three still in a group at the end of the room. "Why, nothing. Nothing at all. Why?"

Nelly, coming forward with Rufe and Della beside her: "But you've been sitting there that way for hours, Papa — it's almost half past six. Where's Mamma, for the surprise?"

There wasn't anything else to say, so I said, "A surprise is a surprise; she doesn't know there's a surprise going on, so it's almost half past six, so what?"

"Yeah, so what?" Rufe said, because in that whole household he was the one whose faith in me never faltered.

"I suggest we wait until seven. If your mother isn't home by then, I suggest we postpone the surprise until tomorrow, and we all go out to dinner and then to the circus."

This seemed to make sense to the kids, so we began to wait. The place became quiet again, as each of them picked up a book or a magazine and began to turn the pages, listening all the while for the sound of somebody working a key in the front door. Pages turned one by one, but nobody was really reading anything or really looking at pictures. Everybody was waiting, that's all, and then suddenly everybody was standing, almost as if at attention, or as if in expectation of something possibly wonderful, but also possibly terrible. I myself was standing, a little scared too, because the doorbell had been given a ring of at least fifteen seconds. Now, who could that be? Al Poufnique, to tell me, "I love Susan. I want her to be my wife." Would he be alone, or would she be with him, or what?

"Probably somebody wanting to sell something. You kids stay right here."

I went down the long hall, kind of slowly too, I must say, because I was scared. If it were actually Al Poufnique I was afraid I might not even let him say hello; I might just push him down the stairs and out of the building, and of course that wouldn't be any good at all for the kids. They would grow up believing America should push any nation that got in its way straight down the stairs and out of the building too.

I opened the door, and there stood Amshavir Shamavoor of Fresno. As he talked, I knew the kids were just a little way up the hall, out of sight, watching me, listening to him and waiting.

I heard him out, knowing he in turn was waiting for me to roar with glad laughter at the sight of him, to be a Fresno kid again, to have him meet the wife and kiddies, as he would have put it if he had put it in words at all. But I couldn't laugh; I couldn't ask him in at a time like this and try to be interested in his bike ride around the world. In the first place, I didn't know him. In the second place, I wanted to get out of there with the kids as quickly as possible, because after dinner and the circus they'd be tired and they'd go to bed, and if Susan weren't home by that time, I'd think of something intelligent to do. There is always something intelligent to do, but the trick is to find out what it is. Sometimes the most intelligent thing is not to do anything, certainly nothing loaded with the imbecility of emotionality. And I was so annoyed with Susan that it amounted to the worst kind of emotionality. How could she even think of any other man in the whole world? How unhappy had she been all these years? How pitifully little did our kids mean to her? If she came back in the middle of the night, had I better tell her to keep moving — from Al Poufnique to Hal Fopkin, to Sal Mineo, to the elevator boy next door? I didn't know what to do, but I knew I wasn't going to entertain the forty-four-year-old lad from Fresno who was on his way around the world on a bicycle.

"Amsho." I said at last. "I'm sure you haven't got any time to lose. You've got to jump on your bike and race east to Damascus, and I know the ride is going to make you awfully famous. Thanks for dropping by, it's always good to see a face from the old home-town, and good luck, all the luck in the world, always."

In shutting the door it was actually necessary to have it reach him and move him back into the hall, and during this business he was speechless. After the door was shut I knew he stood there for some time, not believing what had happened. The kids tiptoed up, and I herded them away and up the long hall to the living room again where everybody began to speak at once, calling me names, mainly.

Nelly: "I don't believe I have ever in all my life seen anybody behave with such absolutely lousy manners, Papa."

Pat: "The poor guy was from your hometown. He expected you to bring him in and sit him down for dinner."

Della: " 'Amsho, I'm sure you haven't got any time to lose.' Oh, Papa, how *could* you? Maybe all he wanted was a glass of water or something."

Rufe: "Where's Damascus?"

"Damascus is not far from where his father was born. Not far from Assyria, but of course it's not called Assyria anymore. He's an Assyrian, a first-generation American. I know that from his name, but I never saw him before."

Pat: "He sounded like you were old pals."

Nelly (at the window): "He's standing out there looking at his bike."

"Well, do you want me to go bring him back, or what? It's up to you, but I thought you wouldn't want me to use up the surprise dinner and everything on somebody I can't even remember. I'll run down and get him if you want me to."

Nobody said I ought to go get him. They all stood at the big window looking down at him in the street, but I didn't have the heart to join them. Of course I had been rude, but so had he. I had actually thought of asking him how in the world he had found out where I was living, but it seemed to me that knowing how that had happened wouldn't have done me any good and would only have prolonged his standing in the doorway.

Nelly: "He's just waiting or thinking or something. He isn't getting on his bike or anything. He's just standing there."

Rufe: "Maybe he's crying."

Well, if he wasn't, I almost was. Nobody, under any circumstances, should ever be as rude as I had just been, to anybody, let alone to a perfectly decent bicycle rider from my own hometown.

Della: "He's putting on his trouser clip."

Nelly: "Well, aren't you going to come and watch him get on his bike and ride away?"

"No, I think I'd rather not do that."

Pat: "Seems like a nice guy."

"One of the nicest guys in the world, ordinarily."

Pat: "What do you mean, ordinarily. He's still who he always is, isn't he?"

"Yes, he is, but just now I'm not who I always am."

Rufe: "He's riding to Damascus."

They all watched him ride away, and then they turned and looked at me as if I were the most brutal and insensitive human being that ever lived.

"I'm sorry, I'm sorry, I've told you I'm sorry, what more can I say? He came at the wrong time, that's all. Now, let's go grab a taxi to the Drugstore and have hamburgers and milk shakes, and then let's grab another taxi to the circus. Let's just get the hell out of here, shall we?"

Pat: "Language, Pop!"

The Drugstore was jammed, of course, as I knew it would be, but I also knew it was their favorite place, and the hamburgers and milk shakes were almost as good as the ones they had loved in New York. We waited five or six minutes, and then there was a whole table to ourselves, a table for six, actually. When everybody was comfortable, a man with a tray who had been wandering around looking for a place at a table began to attract their attention. I wasn't watching; I was studying the latest issue of *Allo Paris* to choose between the two circuses that seemed to be open the year around. The kids weren't biting into their hamburgers or sipping their milk shakes anymore; they were just watching, so I looked away from the little magazine to see what it could possibly be.

It was Al Poufnique. Himself. Beard and all.

All right, so where was Susan?

She was nowhere about, although apparently all of the other Americans in Paris were.

He came and took the sixth place, the kids moving some of their stuff out of the way to make room for his tray, and he began to eat his hamburger and drink his glass of milk. The kids fell silent, studying his head and face.

"How are you getting along with your poetry?"

He put down his hamburger, put on his glasses, smiled and said, "Oh, hello. I'm afraid I'm a long way from writing the kind of poetry I *want* to write."

"What kind is that?"

"The best, the way you paint."

The kids watched and listened and finished their hamburgers and milk shakes.

"Thanks, but maybe you're too critical of your stuff."

"That's what my wife says, but let's face it, if poetry isn't the best, it's as good as nothing."

"How *is* your wife?"

"Just fine. A little excited about becoming a mother for the first time."

"*Where* is she?"

"Home, if you can call two little rooms home, and I guess you can." He giggled, and I knew they were almost broke, and pretty worried.

I brought out my wallet and fished out two 100 new-franc notes, each of them worth a little better than twenty dollars, and I placed them beside his plate.

"If that's a loan, thanks a lot. I couldn't accept anything unless it was a loan."

"A loan, and good luck."

"Imagine running into you here. I almost never come here. I just saw some publicity people in the neighborhood about a job, and I have to go back in half an hour. That's how it happened I came in here."

"I'm glad you did. I know you and your wife are going to be crazy about the kid, because I remember how crazy my wife and I were about our first one. That's Nelly here." Nelly nodded. And then I named the other three, and they nodded, and the poet returned each nod earnestly, a man who respected kids, and would be a pretty good father, most likely.

"Biggest event of our lives so far," he said.

In the street the kids wanted to know what that was all about. Who in the world was he, and why had I given him so much money, especially since I had just a little while ago been so rude to a man from my own hometown? I tried to explain, but they weren't especially satisfied.

Well, if Susan hadn't gone to Al Poufnique — and she certainly hadn't — who had she gone to, or where had she gone? What was going on? Had they better go home instead of to the circus, or what?

"Home, or circus?"

"Circus, circus," Rufe said, but the other three, the older ones, the ones who had long ago begun to suspect a thing or two about grownups, were silent. Something was going on that didn't permit them to get excited about going to a place to watch clowns and wild animals and acrobats.

"Home," Nelly said, "and the sooner the better."

"Why?"

"I don't know, Papa, but I think home is where we had better get to as quickly as possible."

A cab slowed down. "OK, let's grab this cab."

The door opened and Susan stepped out. (Where was the small checkered suitcase?)

The kids busted out with laughter, exclamations, gladness, anger and questions, but all Susan did was stand there and look at their father — me. She began to smile, but I couldn't figure out the smile at all. Talk about the smile of Mona Lisa. This one made that smile look like the smile of a simple farm girl.

"Where do you think you're going?"

"I had an idea you'd all be here at the Drugstore if I hurried, so I did."

"What happened?"

"Tell you all about it later."

Nelly: "All about *what*?"

Susan: "Twelve crazy, impossible, miserable years together — and for *what*?"

"Four kids?"

Nelly: "Oh, fine. Talk about us as if we were cattle or something."

"What about this — this whoever the hell it was? Turned you down, did he?"

"On the contrary, I turned him down. I just left him."

"Where?"

"His place."

"What did you do that for?"

"Why should I throw over everything for something ridiculous in a ridiculous movie, or something? I'm too old. It's too hot. What are we going back into the Drugstore for?"

"I just want to pick up a pack of cigarettes."

As luck would have it, as I had hoped, Al Poufnique was just
ahead of me at the cigarette counter. Susan saw him, but he didn't
see her. She looked at me, but I didn't let her know what I was
thinking; I just acted as if Al were somebody I didn't know. She
seemed terrified that the poet might turn and see her. She flung
her arms around the four kids almost as if she were some kind of
animal protecting her family before a storm or something, and she
moved them in the opposite direction, moving away without a
word. Well, what do you know? The things a woman will do to
give a man a surprise, or to hang onto something, or to try to make
it better or different.

In the street she said, "All right, so I didn't see him, I didn't see
anybody, I visited Myra Haley for a couple of hours, but I *could*
have gone to him, I could have gone to anybody I might care to
choose, but I'm too old, and it's too hot. Let's not get into a stuffy
taxi; let's walk home very slowly, because when we get there I want
us to have the surprise, after all. Happy anniversary, and I'm glad
I scared you."

"I thought you'd gone mad, that's all."

Nelly: "I don't understand you two."

Pat: "Pop, what's going on?"

Della: "Mamma, I don't think I've ever seen you more crazy-
beautiful or something. You're different all of a sudden."

We were walking toward the Arc de Triomphe when the kids
suddenly stopped, and Nelly said, "Oh, look!"

I looked, and there, racing around the Arc, came Amshavir
Shamavoor on his bike, moving with the wild circling traffic like
a small colorful bird among a flock of geese.

Pat: "Look at him go, will you."

Della: "I'll never forget your terrible rudeness, Papa."

Rufe: "Goodbye, Amsho, goodbye."

The bicycle rider straightened out when he reached the Champs,
his head down, his legs moving steadily and powerfully. As he drew
nearer I thought I had better shout out to him, stop him, and ask
him to please forgive me, please come with us now to our house
and have dinner with us, but he was going too beautifully, everything was too right for me to spoil it with a little corrective
courtesy. And then he was gone, on his way down the broad road
toward Concorde. The kids and their mother turned and watched

him go, but again I couldn't join them. I still couldn't even remember him. Not until he had disappeared among the automobile traffic did they turn away and begin to walk again.

"Who was that?"

"Some kid from Fresno who doesn't know he's forty-four years old."

"What about him?"

"He's riding around the world on a bicycle."

"So what?"

"Precisely. He's an Assyrian. *They* won't be getting in rockets to the moon or anything like that for some time, most likely, if ever."

Nelly: "I don't think I've seen anything more beautiful."

Della: "Than Mamma, the way she is now?"

Nelly: "Than that nut on the bicycle."

Pat: "What's he want to ride around the world for?"

Rufe: "Will he get there, Papa? Will he get to Damascus?"

"Rufe, maybe I'd better tell you this now, right now, because I might forget later on. You don't *have* to get there, to Damascus, or anywhere else. All you've got to do is *want* to get there. And *try*. That's enough to carry you all the way through. Can you remember that?"

"Sure, Papa. I'll remember it."

We all moved along, on our way to our surprising house in one of the most surprising cities in the world, and to the little daily surprises of our thirteenth year together, in the same boat, so to say, or on the same bicycle, racing through heavy traffic toward another place, and then another, and all the way around, and finally back where we started.

BABETTE SASSOON

The Betrayal

(FROM NEW WORLD WRITING)

I THINK about Hayle all the time and sometimes, for he has truly left a gap in my life, I even wonder what could have happened to him. But mostly I reminisce about Hayle as though he were long dead, as though with his sudden disappearance he had cut himself off not only from us, from Amelia my wife and from me, but from the future too, for I cannot conceive that his existence without us, without Amelia particularly, is not as empty as ours without him, as mine most certainly is. And I think of his eternal laughter which rings in my ears like an echo now, of that loud laughter which reverberated through all his failures, of his uncontrollable good humor which would not be squelched even in the throttling bad luck which he seems never to have been able to evade, of the ill-timed merriment which, appearing at the most uncalled-for occasions, lent to Hayle's enthusiasm, though its gibe was directed against himself, a vast and discomforting impertinence. In the old days I used to be startled at these bursts of hilarious indifference to his own fate, but now I see Hayle as a man who, knowing perhaps from the very beginning that his life would be a hopeless failure, had decided to indulge himself with the comfort of unjustified laughter. And yet even this explanation does not quite make sense, since in the end he did achieve something exquisite and beautiful and perfect, a piece of work so lovely and serene and pleasant in every way that it should have launched him finally into a successful career since it proved at the very least that he was capable of producing acceptable work and yet I cannot help feeling that he saw it in a quite different light. Sometimes I think he was infuriated with us for having forced him into that which made it obvious he really could paint, which removed from then on all excuse for his wasting such a valuable talent on empty experimentation, that he was angry with us for having opened the way for him toward real satisfying accomplishment since perhaps he had become too used to failure to want anything else, perhaps even he did not feel like working any more. And yet Hayle was certainly a worker, I never knew anyone to work as hard as Hayle, and so at times I think the explanation is something which I have always suspected and that is that the artist himself is the last person in the world to know when he has created something good and perhaps he thought that what he had done was really so awful that he did not want to wait for our comments, fearful and humiliated to have failed again in our eyes, since we after all were his very dearest friends.

I think of all that now over and again as I sit in my study all morning long, doing nothing much, while in the background of my musings always I hear Amelia. Sometimes she is in the kitchen giving orders for lunch, and I imagine that all the shining pots which hang in a row against the wall will for a minute clasp against their copper handles the reflection of Amelia who, in her blue dress with little white lovebirds, is talking to the bandannaed cook. Or I hear her in the drawing room where I suppose she is meandering about, feather duster in hand, something like the heroines in opening acts of those long plays whose titles I never can remember, enjoying the sunlight through the blowing curtains which, as I invariably catch a chill in the draft of open windows, are aired only in the mornings. Sometimes I see her in the garden, her silhouette against the formal rows of boxwoods or amongst the flowers growing in geometric patterns. But never do I see her weeding, nor breathless from spading with a hot face and brown hands does she stoop heavily down to plant the rows of flower beds. No, as cool and as desirable as a little river nymph Amelia wanders, as though without a care, while in her arms quite effortlessly to the click click of the sharpened shears are gathered in a gay pell-mell the irises, the tall snapdragons, the sweet peas, and all sorts of wonderfully colored flowers which, try as I may, I will never know the names of; from my study I follow her longingly, imagining the scent of her arms until she disappears from my view leaving nothing to make up for her absence but the empty and cut-down garden.

Then it is I miss Hayle most, for truly he has left a void in my life; as for Amelia I hear her steps, as staccato and as destructive as little hammers, spanning the rooms of the house not only in the long mornings but all afternoon, till I wonder what on earth can she be up to, and how is her time, surely endless now that there is only me to take care of, so precious that she has none left to sit with me and by my side quietly mull over the past, that we might at least be comforted in each other's company by the flickering warmth of a late evening fire. And I suspect all these household duties which have newly sprung up in her life and which keep her so busy and so far from me, and I wonder why it is that the maid these days has become so lax that Amelia must watch continually so that even when the rugs are being shaken out there she is, standing a little apart so that none of the dust will get into her eyes, but there just the same, and why it is that the vacuum makes such a ceaseless hubbub while the rooms, already clean, hardly used as they are, are cleaned again and again and Amelia, as though at work herself, paces from a distance the perambulating maid, as if hypnotized by the droning noise? Why has the furniture become so polished that our hands seem to spring back at us from the shiny surfaces of tables and bureaus? Why since no one ever comes to visit us in our country house are the vases changed so often that the garbage bins are continually full of bright freshly cut flowers? And why has my Amelia who ever since we were married had developed a loathing for the kitchen now taken to spending long hours there with the cook commandeering fantastic banquets which the two of us can hardly begin to eat, so that the food, so heavily spiced the odor of it will linger for days only to mingle with the scents of future menus, sits in abundant heaps between us while I, longing for something simple, peck at hot curries and rich French sauces which I know will keep me awake all night and Amelia, across from me, fidgety with her new restlessness, nibbles half-heartedly and without appetite? Sitting apart at the laden table we barely converse any more, while in the old days when Hayle sat at her left there was hardly a quiet moment; not that Amelia and I were ever very talkative, but that something about Hayle's voice made it seem as though anyone in the room with him, no

matter how quiet, had somehow joined in. For the rhythm of his
speech was so varied that it seemed more like a conversation than
a monologue in which he was constantly asking Amelia questions
which he promptly answered himself, telling jokes which he said
were really mine, and talking so ceaselessly that his words seemed
to fill the room while we, putting in a few phrases here and there,
listening mostly, laughing, assenting, even disagreeing sometimes
with no more than head shakes, felt as breathless as though we had
contributed to the conversation not so much with our attention as
with our voices. And yet all the noise of the old days was not as
noisy as our silence which thrums around me filled with strident
echoes; and not only is the dining room haunted with dead words,
but all the rooms; the house itself is filled with an emptiness so
deep as to seem garrulous in its insistence, the garden down whose
paths we very seldom stroll any more seems blatant in its isolation
and sometimes it even seems to me that the mild slopes of the peaceful rolling hills in whose gentle valley the house as in a loving palm
is protected have become too desolate to give our home back its
tranquil atmosphere; the house which in the old days held us so
soothingly in its arms that even the fervor of Hayle's presence could
not ruffle us, now that we do very little and have in a sense retired
into ourselves, seems to loom about us huge like a phantom, laying a net of shadows around us until I who have always been so
happy in my own home, the home where as a child I was already
content in the knowledge that here I would spend the rest of my
life, sense, going from one tidy room to another, by day the per-
sistent dull irritation of nothingness and by night the strangeness
of the void into which Hayle has already gone and into which all
will follow, Amelia, me, the wilting garden, the crumbling house,
the eroded hills. And I know that Amelia feels it too for in the
dark the anxious shades creep between our sheets, keeping us far
apart, till finally she gets up in the middle of the night when she
thinks I am asleep and I hear her soft steps tiptoeing down the
corridor, fading on the staircase and lost downstairs in the carpet.
Then I wish, for Amelia's sake, since it is she who is really full of
sorrow and in whose sorrow my existence seems to have ended,
that she had either never met Hayle or that he had never left her.

Poor Amelia, poor innocent little Amelia, what could she possibly have done to lose us a friendship which even I, less interesting

certainly, less entertaining, and less deserving of Hayle, was able to
keep throughout all the years I had known him, from the time we
were first quite by chance assigned to be roommates in the university where, having no one, his parents having died years before,
and with nothing but a legacy left to him by an aunt, the last of
his relatives, a tiny pitiful legacy all of which was tied up in fees,
for she had made the money payable only for his education, he was
always deriding himself as a poor penniless orphan quite dependent
on his old roommate, to the time fifteen years later when I per-
suaded him to live on my estate, in the little studio which I had
built expressly for him and which stands empty now, with its blank
and curtainless windows, its door hinges rusting, its roof beginning
to sag, awaiting still his occupancy, just like my Amelia, and myself
too. I often think of that old dead aunt of Hayle's with gratitude
and think it was thanks to her that I got through college at all, for
it was Hayle who, never stooping to do any homework himself,
helped me by the hour with mine, so that finally with none other
than his assistance I passed, and almost made the honors list, while
poor Hayle, laughing away as usual, had the dubious distinction of
being expelled on the last day, having given fantastic and incom-
prehensible answers to the simplest questions on all his examina-
tions and having behaved in so extraordinary a manner at his orals
that no one recovered from the sight of Hayle dressed up in a white
sheet with a crown of boxwood on his head in time to ask him a
single question. Five professors shuffling their papers looked up
through their spectacles in utter disbelief, Hayle's voice reaching
them through a miasma of whiskey fumes. "O suppliants," he
chanted, quavering theatrically, "at the ancient Delphic oracle, well
known to me by your pensive and lamentable misery, ask and ye
shall receive the answers for I, the prophet of Apollo, shall put
wisdom into your hearts; do but ask and the fumes of my sacred
intoxication shall rise unto almighty Apollo and through me the
godhead shall send you riddles, conundrums, enigmas, puzzles,
dilemmas, answers aplenty. O divine Apollo, hear your suppliants."
How I laughed to hear Hayle re-enact all this expressly for me later
on and how he laughed when after four years of what he called in-
terminable penance he after all received no diploma. "Poor Aunt
Lizzy, I have nothing with which to assuage your angry shade, I have
no scroll to use as a passport into the trembling pride and love of

your long-dead bosom. But wait, Aunt Lizzy, O fortunate Aunt
Lizzy, I do have a token with which to allay your displeasure, a
living sacrifice to offer at your altar, this young man, this prepared
young man, this young man filled with teaching, this devoted
young man; I, Aunt Lizzy, it is I who have trained him to be your
disciple, he has the scroll, he has the learning, and it is I who have
infused him with it, and now I offer him up to you as my four
years' handiwork, so you see, dear Aunt Lizzy, that you have not
wasted your money." And he took up his pen, a sort of quill left
over from the time that Hayle was going to be a poet, and pretended to plunge it through my head. "A new mode of sacrifice,
the ink is ejected through the cranium to pour in a blue flood
through all the vessels of the brain where turning into an azure
glacier it immobilizes all future functions of the brain and assures
that what is there will remain inviolate through life." And he
intoned in the most comical accents, "Now I sacrifice you to the
shade of my Aunt Lizzy, as a victim to her will. You will never
learn another thing." I canot imagine why Hayle bothered so
with me. But perhaps in a way I acted as a ballast to him who,
having pathetically cut himself off from all 'ordinary,' as he called
it, life had at least the companionship of one ordinary person, a
kind of assurance for poor Hayle who would otherwise have been
without any assistance except for the unwanted aid of the idiot aunt
as he called her. Exacerbated by his forced incarceration in college,
in the world itself for all I know, he was also without friends, for
no one really took him seriously. But of course I felt differently
about Hayle; I was sorry for him; but much as I admired him I
really wondered at times if there was not a lot of bluff to Hayle
and I wondered this for no reason at all except that I could not
understand why he refused to turn his talents to some kind of use.
Even the fact that he was so entertaining he refused to make use
of, spending half his time in gloomy perusal of books which weren't
even on the reading list, talking to me constantly about the characters in them, so that he said wherever he went multitudes traveled
in his head, all sorts of villains and heroines cloyed to his elbow,
endless nonsense, but with real people, besides myself of course,
Hayle would have no recourse. And it was exasperating, this
apathy really so close to contempt that he regarded the world with.
Had he been conceited, had he set himself up above the rest, that

would at least have been something, but he refused to be better, he refused to be worse, he refused to compare himself or to justify himself for anything; he was quite simply filled with the utmost indifference toward us, toward himself, and toward all mankind. Except of course when he was discoursing wildly about his favorite mysteries. Then everyone listened and at those times he loved to have people gathered around him and to have everyone laugh at him, and he too would laugh; it was the only thing which linked him with the rest of the world, this laughter of his turned against himself, and I can hear him ranting now the day he had decided to become an archaeologist.

"Imagine, just imagine that most beautiful and fantastic moment when out of the earth — can't you see the earth, black and secret, which has been sucking up the sun's energy for centuries, millenniums, who knows, and which the dusty-cheeked farmers, intent only on their produce, have been cursing for barrenness — can't you see it, that dry empty patch, and suddenly deep within there will be discovered a little mound, round and polished and sprouting its smoothed age — and I, one day, after months and years of work and all sorts of research will bring out of the sterile land, with the cloggy field still clinging like a jealous veil all about it, a dazzling, incredible, perfect Aphrodite. And then with her white breast how she will flaunt our silly wasted lives that up to this moment have not looked upon her nor know the meaning of love, though our barren steps plodded mechanically, trudged daily over her splendid wings. I feel it, oh I really feel it, the fantastic miracle of it." And he looked around him at his classmates and from the corners of their snickering mouths picked up their derision and gathered it into a great peal of roaring merriment until we all laughed together. "And not only that, not only that, but a whole city stretched out before me with the blue sea down below the promontory just as it was time immemorial when the palaces glimmered whitely and the temples breathed the adoration of a myriad worshipers and in the graveyard curled around the beehive tombs of the ancient kings and intertwined in their fingers the strings and weights of their riches awaiting life again, the sharp air treading itself through the old stones. I just see that moment before the vases and jewels and all sorts of innumerable gorgeous objects are dusted and catalogued and placed in the metropolis under glass to slowly perish in the Sunday crowd, how unbelievable that moment of discovery when it is something glorious after all, something almost heroic to be the descendant of all this, and worth perhaps even the eternal hack work of the days and weeks of dead existence with dead people."

As if Hayle were in the least bit involved with hack work or with people for that matter; not that he was totally unconcerned with people but that he always had amazing ideas about them, ideas which were not in the least bit true; he saw them as images, as relics, as statues, as characters out of books, as anything but what they really were and there was no difference to him between living people and the imaginary ones of literature. He would not even admit the obvious fact that no character in a book, no matter how great the masterpiece, is as real as an ordinary human being, for characters in books I know have been too stepped up, too illuminated, too vivified to be true, though of course it does seem to me that they would be so much easier to cope with than people in life, and even today there are times when I think that if Amelia were only a character in a book I could deal with her so much easier, words would trip off my tongue with so much more grace, gestures of comfort and affection would be second nature to me, and Amelia's moods now that I find myself in this obscure rut with her would be clearer to me were she but a character in a book. And yet I would not for anything miss the lovely sight of Amelia nor exchange the vision of her golden hair as she combs it out like so much wheat in front of the mirror, her eyes so focused in its effulgence that never once does she notice me several feet away watching her, for a literary description, no, not even for Hayle's. But Hayle, of course, never saw anything for what it was. I think that was his downfall, his inventing everything; there was no reality, and therefore no truth in his vision, and often I used to say to him, "Hayle, why is it you don't know anyone? Not as they are, not really in a down-to-earth manner. You go on long discourses and you make up the wildest theories, but your psychology is incorrect, it's all invented, you know."

And he would answer, "You see, my idea is motivating them, no, not my idea, but my ferreting out the idea which motivates them. So if there is no idea there at all, which I begin to think is quite possible, it's better just to make one up, it does no harm, and it amuses me."

"Then you're simply using people."

"Why would I do that? I'm not using anyone in particular. I'm just peopling the world."

"No. You're using people grossly to illustrate your ideas. Your idea comes first. The illustration next."

"But you," he said eagerly, "I see just as you are. Generous. Kind. Firmly planted in the earth, and I envisage that when the roots go way down, they will bring forth a fine plant, a sturdy flag to champion the trunk of good sense."

"You see, there you go again, Hayle."

"No! I mean it. I see that good sense which will save you from feeling too much, and from working too hard, and which will find you the right wife, and make you a happy home, with the right amount of love, and which will always keep you within the bounds of success."

"But do you see me now as I am?"

"Oh . . . now . . . but yes, yes, I see you as the best of friends. And then you know there is something about your patience, the way you listen to me, the way you look at me when I talk, the way you wait for me to laugh before you start laughing, something about your concern for me, and I do feel it, you know, this concern of yours which is so much deeper than mine, so that you care more what happens to me than I do myself, and the thought of this one straw of caring in the wind even if it is not one's own straw almost makes life worthwhile. You see how it is, your concern balances my indifference."

"But truly don't you care about your future?"

"Oh, I'm curious. And you? Do you care so much about yours?"

"Of course I do. But then I am all set, you know. Once I get out of here all I shall have to do is nestle into my lovely house that I know so well, gather the roof over me, so to speak, and all the year I shall watch through the French doors the seasons changing in the garden, my seasons revolving in my land. There are no surprises in store for me unless it be she who is fated to share all this with me."

"Ah yes, a woman."

"A lovely girl!"

"Oh yes, I can see her now, she'll be ever so coy, slim and twisting with transparent eyes and not a thought in her head and lovely arms to drape sweetly about your neck and pert ankles which she'll show off to great advantage and which will never grow thick, and all day long she'll wander in your famous garden like a kind of female Narcissus — Narcissa — looking at herself in pools and watching her reflection in fountains, falling deeper and deeper in love with herself till all she will vouchsafe you will be the very remotest corner of a smile just glancing off the edge of a mirror. But your Narcissa will have you so in thrall you'll think yourself the luckiest man in the world, proud possessor of a pretty wife."

"Well, I don't know that I would mind suffering for such a pretty Narcissa as all that."

"Perhaps you won't suffer, though. After all, suffering takes practice and you aren't likely to be practicing pain and sorrow, etc., eh?"

"Nobody would be likely to do that, now would they?"

"I think that one should not be able to avoid it."

"But Hayle, even you would not have to suffer if you would only settle down. Because I know you suffer, you look sort of miserably lost all the time, and then you keep changing your mind about what you're going to do, you won't settle for anything, and the world has only so much to offer. You're always dissatisfied. I don't believe you're going to be an archaeologist either."

"Oh yes I am. I'm going to roll in the sacred furrows of Greece."

"Seriously, what are you going to do?"

"Paint."

"What?"

"Since I can't go digging in Greece, having learned none of the essentials of spade work as you would so correctly put it, and since after all I have decided that it might be more exciting to discover something completely new, I shall paint."

"But you can't draw."

"Oh, I'll learn. Simple mechanics, just like grammar. The main thing is that I shall be constantly on the point of discovery. The opaque, dense form of matter will suddenly as it were become transparent and I shall see within the suggestion of different patterns, new forms evolving within each other. I, Hayle, shall be present at the very act of creation, when life, tired of its protective husk and worldly expression, exposes to me its true varied and faceted core. Imagine, to be offered daily the inventiveness of a novel existence. For, that we should look every day upon the world only physically and not demand to know the meaning of it, the shapes below the surface, the possibilities behind the closed lips and vague eyes, the energies under the passive expression, that we should look without seeing, without even wanting to see, each with a separate and unique method, is utterly bestial and inhuman. And only if I could see this way, if I could really see, could I consider my fate as anything but an indifferent matter."

Poor Hayle, I felt even then he had made a terrible decision, if it really was a decision, that he was hurling himself quite untrained and unprepared into the unknown, that he would never care what other people, critics even, who knew more than he, said about his painting, and so would never get anywhere, that he would just be pursuing painting, and it might just as well have been anything else, to satisfy some personal craving, some bottomless greedy and unnecessary yearning of his own and that if he was unable to make a success even of college, he would certainly never get anywhere in the volatile and unstable world of art, and I was immediately against this idea of his to be an artist, knowing all along that it was just these notions of Hayle's that made him so attractive and different and enjoyable and, yes, even inspiring to me.

And yet in the end it was I who benefited most by his decision. For now, what has poor Hayle got to show for it? Nothing but those terrible sketches in which no human being is recognizable, those paintings which did nothing more than emphasize his apparent lack of skill, for it turned out just as I had feared, that he would not stick to the simplest rules of drawing, so with what a shock did it come to us, that lovely painting of Hayle's, that masterpiece which proved so amazingly that after all he did have talent. And why, I have been wondering ever since, why had he never once employed it before, why had he agonized so over his monstrous grotesqueries, when all along he truly was a great artist, and why am I so certain that this masterpiece of his which I have, not he, was his very last? But it is at any rate entirely fitting that it is we, and not he, who own his last painting since it is Amelia who inspired him to it, Amelia who from the very beginning loved Hayle in her sisterly fashion and covered him with the tenderness of a devoted companion, Amelia who added the weight of her womanly friendship to our old alliance; how happy I was to present this charming wife of mine to Hayle, and yet I cannot help at

moments conjecturing that it is something Amelia has done or perhaps not done which has so disintegrated the old peaceful existence
of we three, for why should Hayle have so trusted me in the old
days — many times he said to me, "I trust you, you know I trust
you. You know nothing about anything, and you understand
nothing, but I trust you. Oh, I think I trust you because you need
me, and I need your need in me, and I feel about you that eternal
status quo, that nothing with you will ever change, and need to
need will always remain constant, permanent, trusty" — why should
Hayle have felt this way about me in the old days, and not now,
and especially not about Amelia, for it is Amelia I feel certain he
has left more than me or why else should she be so particularly
wretched, it is Amelia he has left just as it was she who kept him
with us all those years for I, after all, had nothing to offer Hayle
but Amelia, Amelia whose gracefulness and prettiness and sweet
ways in some measure could soothe the daily irritations of his utter
lack of success, for Amelia is like a balm, like a solacing emollient
against life; if ever in this lovely retreat of mine anything evil
should reach me to irritate me, to annoy me, to hurt me even, I
shall be protected by my Amelia whom only to look at is to be
soothed and to realize that there is nothing so sharp and so poison-
ous that she cannot remove its pain, for there is that about her
which tranquillizes, there is the gentleness of her eyes that lullabyes
and pacifies, those eyes which are pale and surface-colored and not
at all the way Hayle described them, purple and mysterious and
turned in upon themselves with secrets, but like a thin stream of
the most transparent water running smoothly over the iris, and yet
when I first heard Hayle speak of her eyes in this extraordinary
fashion I could not help but feel a stab of excitement, a catch at
the heart, something almost pleasantly jolting like the first difficult
breath on a very cold day, harsh in its suddenness but bracing
nonetheless, and I felt also a new pride that I, I who had always
merely listened admiringly to Hayle at long last was able to surprise
him, to show myself capable of having done something all on my
own without his help, to present him to a wife he never expected
me to have. "Why she is not Narcissa at all," he said delightedly,
and my dear little Amelia, who was still so shy in those days when
we had only been married a month, looked down at her toes and
only when Hayle had become quite solemn, quite grave, did she

dare glance curiously at him. Because of course I had already told her all about him and she longed to meet him and strangely enough what had interested her about him, that is before she had met him, was the paltry fact that he was as poor as she had been. When first she came into my beautiful house, her eyes widening in amazement because, poor thing, she had never seen such a garden before, had never seen a library, had never seen so much furniture, she said, when I laughed at her, "Why, your friend Hayle would feel the same as I do, I'm sure, such a big house for two little people, what ever will we do in all this space? Oh, but it's grand, grandly lovely, and I do love you for having it."

"And now it is yours," I said.

"All of it?"

"All of it," I said. "And I am yours too to do with what you will."

"Oh," she laughed, "I won't do much to you, you know, but to the house I may make a few changes." For in my presence she had never been shy, though I was older than she, and had from our very first meeting acted toward me in the most natural and delightful manner. I never could resist Amelia. It was really, I think, love at first sight with us. "No," Hayle pronounced, "she is not Narcissa. She hides, but not as Narcissa. She has secrets after all, deeper than the pretty little mirrors of selfdom," and he would talk about Amelia, so coy, so nymphlike, as though she were some sort of august goddess, talk about her pretty ways not as if they were pretty ways at all but solemn symbols of something or other and, though I did not believe him, still I would feel something of an emotion which on my own I could never have conjured up; so if he misinterpreted Amelia was it not after all to my advantage, since it kept us all so satisfied, we happy three, for strangely enough from Hayle's errors I have unaccountably and unwittingly reaped great advantages, even from the greatest mistake of all, his choosing to become an artist: what of that dreadful miscalculation has poor Hayle to show, while I, I have the lovely portrait he did of Amelia.

It hangs even now in my study, a constant reminder of my wife's charm, her graceful ways. She looks out over my room in her characteristic mock-serious way, as if teasing me on the heaviness of the ponderous volumes, the encyclopedias, the history sets, the leathered Dickens and George Eliot, while in her eyes there darts that little

mischievous glance I love so much, as though she had perhaps
cunningly hidden the tiniest meadow flower between the heavy
pages of a Thucydides I would not dream of actually opening, and
is now lightly, prettily, warning me of how the scent of her wild
weed pressed in my book will one day invade the entire room, till
all the volumes, the gilt bindings, the fine paper, will topple down
in the dizzying perfume, leaving the polished shelves quite bare;
while at the same time she is smiling at me for comprehending
nothing of these tomes which are after all no more than the traditional decorations of country homes but which I love nevertheless for their comforting antiquity; whenever I go into my study
now I stand as if lost in wonder at all these books and stare at
them as if I had never seen them before and only slowly, so slowly,
do I let my eye travel across the shelves, pretending all along that
I am doing no more than reading the titles, ruminating, planning
research, anything to keep up the delicious suspense as my eye ap-
proaches that spot over the mantelpiece where, every time feigning
surprise to amuse myself, I am truly surprised to discover Amelia,
for the portrait is so strikingly real, so very much like her and she
is there before me on the canvas exactly as she is in real life except
of course that here above the mantelpiece I really have her, she is
truly mine and does not elude me and, along with everything else
I feel for Hayle, I feel deep gratitude for this painting, for it is
exactly as if Hayle had given me Amelia, had given her to me to
cherish and to gaze at forever. And how pitiful it is that Hayle
should have done this too for me since he must have had to rally
himself, to make a great effort, to put all his concentration together
to render Amelia up in this lifelike manner, poor Hayle who never
thought of anyone sensibly, he must have summoned all his energies
to understand her so well, as well as I do even, and who knows if
perhaps it was too much of an effort so that he never wanted to see
her again, never wanted to be asked to repeat the effort, never
wanted to see even me, afraid perhaps that I would expect him
from then on to buckle down, so to speak, to really work now that
he had finally shown his ability. Perhaps also the sight of Amelia
seen truly as herself for what she really is was too much for him,
for the magician who was never satisfied with letting people be,
but had always to see them through the distortion of his own
imagination, for even Amelia he used to say extraordinary and

quite incorrect things about, speaking of her as though she were
a myth and not a woman at all, so that sometimes she would look
at him quite bewildered and not understand a word he was addressing to her, though he always insisted that she was only pretending for some secret reason of her own, "secret" and "mysterious"
still being Hayle's favorite words; poor Hayle, he had hardly
changed from college days, he had in fact changed so little that
although we were the same age I could not help thinking of him as
much younger than myself, as though he were still in college and
only I had grown up so that he and Amelia, who is much younger
than I, seemed to be the same age and I would feel myself almost
an older brother as I watched them meandering down the garden
paths or welcomed them in with huge bouquets of weeds from the
fields which Hayle immediately pronounced to be in actuality
scarce and rare flowers which should be seeded in the garden, as if
I could really allow the formal beds of flowers which had remained
in the same patterns throughout all the generations of my family
to be disturbed by Hayle's weeds, and Amelia would always cry out,
"Oh yes, yes, right away, let's ask the gardener to plant some in the
rose garden."

"But they're just common buttercups, you know, they wouldn't
do at all in the rose garden."

"No," said Hayle, "I suppose it really wouldn't do, all your ancestors would be turning over in their graves."

"Yes," echoed Amelia, dear Amelia, she was always echoing
Hayle, "wouldn't they just turn over in their graves. Oh, it would
be so amusing."

"Amusing!" cried Hayle. "My dear girl, it would be horrifying,
for one thing they wouldn't just turn over once and go back to
sleep quietly, quite the contrary, they would heave and snort and
come shrieking right out of their graves and spill all over the land
till hills and garden and house would be filled with death and
nothing in the land would ever move again and all the living would
be invaded by death and you, sweet girl, without even knowing it
would become the widow of a living man."

"How silly you are, Hayle, how could I become a widow without
knowing it?"

"Why, your husband would only have the appearance of being
alive, but in reality he would be dead, stone cold dead."

"Then I would feel the cold."

"The cold would have a semblance of warmth, see, you touch his hand and the fingers seem to clasp you but it is only an illusion, you feel his cheek and you think you see the blood coursing below the skin but that too is just an illusion, and when he speaks you think you hear words, but that also is an illusion because really he is as dead as his ancestors."

"Hayle," I begged, "do stop. You'll frighten Amelia." But it was I who was frightened, as I always was when Hayle was in his spooky vein.

And Amelia said to me, "I can just look right through you, I see nothing at all. You're as dead as a doornail."

"You shouldn't sound so jovial about it," said Hayle.

"Why, I can't possibly be expected to mourn, can I?"

"No, cruel one, savage and unsatisfied crone, you cannot be expected to mope over one death." And I could sense Amelia beginning to pout.

"I don't think he means crone the way you think he does, Amelia, do you, Hayle? You don't mean it quite that way, do you?"

"I don't really know what I mean, old man, I don't suppose I have anything much at all in mind; I believe I was thinking of the moon goddess in her three phases or some such thing I have been reading about, young and white and full of seed in the pale crescent, and then round and red, the goddess of love and fruition, and lastly the old moon, the crone, black, powerful."

"Hayle, really, what nonsense, what has all this to do with Amelia, or with any of us; just some discarded myth or other you've picked up."

"But the myths haven't changed, they are after all not just inventions, and the moon goddess may be in eclipse for the moment but there just the same. Dear Amelia, forgive me for calling you an old crone, you are also Persephone in the springtime."

"And the middle thing, is she that too?"

"The whole works," he said, bursting out laughing so that we all joined him. "The white goddess herself." And looking at Amelia with great bunches of field flowers in her arms and her golden hair coming out of its pins and curling moistly around her white forehead and her cheeks pink from sun and with pleasure too at the turn the conversation had taken and her blue eyes pale in the brilliant sunlight, I could not help thinking of her as something too pretty to be true; I could hardly believe in my luck, and I would like to have folded her up in my arms and tasted the moist hair upon her cheek, and even now when I sit in my study I feel that same pleasure to look up at her, perhaps even more here in my study for I know that here at least she will be stationary under my gaze and I am quite willing to look up forever, even to reverence her a little, for am I not like a worshipful suppliant down below, she way above the fireplace smiling down at me from her frame till I am quite ready to agree that compared to her I understand nothing, know nothing, am perhaps nothing; and then, how I wish to hear all her thoughts, but the vagueness of her look coupled with the impatience of her pose seems to tell me that I would not comprehend, for Hayle has captured also that little jerk of her head with which she will terminate the conversation, though it has barely begun, or will at least slip out of her part of it, and with a maddening, intriguing, goddess-like movement, turn away from me in her chair.

For Amelia is always turning away from me. I often think it is just that which so attracts me to her, that elusiveness which I find especially charming in her. For she is so simple and so ingenuous, that her evasiveness never fails to surprise, to give to her simplicity almost an air of complicity, and it is such a delightful thought to think of my naïve Amelia putting on airs, pretending to be sophisticated, a woman of the world even; she does it very well too, sure as she is that my mind and heart are following her, that my eyes are watching her, that when she cuts off her talk to me after a few impatient minutes my imagination continues the conversation long into the morning, that when she disappears into the fields and is lost around the curves of the garden so that I see no more than the spray into which she seems to have melted my fancy continues to see her before me, that my arms still dream of holding her long after she has gone to sleep, her back turned to me, and now I have become so accustomed to these delightfully feminine love games that without them my life would be quite dull. And then she is much more alluring this way than if she presented herself to me outright, if she said, Look, I love you, here I am, take me in your arms, kiss me, fondle me; I doubt if I should want to touch a woman who would so brazenly present herself, and is it not after all the preliminary, the dreamed-of caress, the long-sought kiss, the imagined embrace which is the most intense? When Amelia first met Hayle I saw through the lowering of eyes, the blushes, the confusion and shyness, that she did not grace him with the same attention as she did me, she did, not turn away from him, she treated him differently, she did not give him the intimacy of her delightful aloofness as she did to me; it was only her shyness which might have made it appear to be so and I suppose she had every reason to be shy of Hayle, as I had spoken of him so much that she was quite nervous at meeting him. Oh, how I looked forward to that meeting between the two people I loved most in the world. We had been married but a month when I asked Hayle down, Amelia begging me to put off what she had herself so looked forward to, seized by apprehension as she was, terrified of meeting people. Poor little Amelia, she was only seventeen when I plucked her right out of her home where she had known no one but her five brothers and her four sisters; whenever I went to see her, and I had plenty of opportunity to do so as in those days her family lived as tenants on our land, she was always ironing, washing, doing innumerable household chores, her sleeves rolled up to the elbow, her cheeks gleaming red in the laundry steam; now if her family could see her, but they have moved away, they would hardly recognize her, so ladylike is my Amelia, but oh, how I yearned for her from the very beginning, how enticed I was by her air of utter indifference to my visits, how charming I found her sitting by me quite ingenuously at her mother's request with soap suds still ringing her fingers and asking me why I was disturbing her from her work. I knew right then that I had to have her for my own, and was she not after all something like a gift from my ancestors who had generations back leased land to her ancestors, was she not like a wild flower on my property to be gathered up ever so tenderly and made to grow in my garden, cultivated and beautified; and how well she took to all the smoothing and pruning, how she shot up beyond me really, so that Hayle was always saying, You would never know it, you'd think she was the one who had been educated, and not you. And as far as Hayle went certainly Amelia must have been very much more interesting to talk to than I, who am not artistic, and although I have on occasion when I was young visited museums it always seems to me that it is Amelia and not I who has seen them, little Amelia who has really never done anything in her life at all or been anywhere, almost one could say that she has never left my property, and yet that too she is able to suggest, that she has been places, secret places as Hayle used to say, made mysterious forays into the underworld, and soarings into other universes, so charmed did she have him that he could not believe that poor Amelia had never even seen the ocean: "Why, she would be bored stiff, old man, to live in this green retreat if at night she did not ride a golden panoply over the five oceans down to grottoes purple and coral." And she would smile at him as if this really was so, my little scrubber of the old days, who had so grown up in Hayle's imagination and fanciful tuition. Oh, but he had an easy lovely time of it, she responded so well, so much better than I had in college to Hayle's tutoring, she developed so prettily and listened so sweetly with head cocked on one side when he spoke to her about painters and writers and told her all sorts of amazing tales which I was quite sure he was inventing on the spot to amuse her while she sat in the evening by the fire and the light glimmered wildly through her hair and her eyes took on an added brightness, and looking at her as, lips slightly opened, she stared intently at Hayle I was grateful to him for the prettiness of the moment and the comfort of happiness. And really we were so content the three of us, we in our house and Hayle in the little studio in the back I had built expressly for him, that I was reminded of some sort of Arcadia, and I was inexpressibly moved that I, who on my own could never have achieved this unique existence, had managed it through Hayle and Amelia, and watching them always deep in conversation, or rather Hayle talking and Amelia listening, I could have hugged them both just for being themselves and for making my life so worthwhile, and for those two I think I would have done anything. I somehow never could help thinking of them as illusively alike, Amelia's real youth, and Hayle's appearance of youth, Hayle's vivid imagination and Amelia's being the material on which his fancy grew, Amelia's loveliness and Hayle's longing for loveliness, Hayle's artistry and Amelia's artistic nature — real and imaginary, true and illusionary, they seemed in my mind to be linked together like twins that shadowed and mirrored each other, and for Amelia it must have come quite naturally, quite emphatically, to comfort Hayle in all his failures, and for Hayle Amelia must have been a very apt pupil, for I imagine it was of art he discoursed on those long walks of theirs.

For Amelia is almost as artistic as Hayle. She has artistic ideas. She designed the curtains in the pantry, painting them herself with a stencil, all sorts of sweet buttercups trellised with bluebells, and she does wonderful flower arrangements. Hayle, at her insistence, even tried to teach her drawing, but nothing much came of it as she did everything so small that he joked he could not see it, though she has a pretty sense of color. He always said, "What on earth does perspective matter, just carry on in your own way, my dear Amelia, and as far as I am concerned you are the Muse herself, so stay on Mount Olympus and don't grovel in swamps of charcoal and oil like the rest of us mortals with our puny little-teeny mimicking mirroring shallowness." But I, I loved to watch my dear little Amelia tinting in her tiny sketches because she sat so gracefully with the brush in her lily fingers, and when she showed us what she had done, I for one could never look at it objectively. Of course I suppose I understand nothing about art. "Nothing," said Hayle. "Nothing, nothing, nothing, a visual moron." I know this must irritate Amelia since she herself has developed such good taste over the years. Even I can be witness to that just by looking around the house and seeing how nicely decorated it is. For instance, we have a lovely print which hangs in our drawing room called "The Lacemaker," which always gives me a special feeling of sweet studiousness, of concentration and usefulness. I would think of that girl with her strange hair-do, oblivious of herself and her surroundings, bending all her soul toward the threads and I, dreaming, would imagine how the lace would come out the intricate pattern of herself. But Amelia, as serious as the girl in the picture, would show me how foolish I was, for I had no concern, she said, for the picture itself and she pointed out how prettily the red threads blend in with the white, and how well the background suits the golden blouse, and how the blue-green pillow sparks up the general effect till I was amazed to have missed all this artistry, and begged her to explain more as if she were Hayle himself, but she with a contemptuous shrug turned away from me while still I stood, staring into the frame and seeing nothing but the flat expanse of my own ignorance. For Amelia is quiet and does not advertise all that she has learned over the years.

She is not like Hayle, who seemed to be always talking, in a constant struggle to keep conversations going, ideas proliferating, as though the mere contact with another person necessitated a furious exchange of words; and nervously he would work up the stray vague ends of phrases, stuffing up the pauses and full stops with his own ideas until he so fired himself with verbal enthusiasm that the very conversation he had tried to inaugurate would finish up a soliloquy; then only if our admiring silence became too obvious would he pause, as if suddenly aware that he was drowning us in the torrent of his words, and every time he would say, "But I talk too much. I am inventing a lot of rubbish. Come, you must force me to be quiet, for it is to you that I want to listen." And he would turn, always to Amelia, and quickly, nervously, words would pour out of him again, this time a string of questions as though he were interviewing her, questions about anything, politics, the theater, how she felt about the weather, gardens, anything, trying as it were to draw her out, but even as she was attempting to answer, flustered and stammering, he would interrupt her with an understanding nod as though he knew that she could not express herself so quickly and in the atmosphere of his inquisition and as if he had already grasped the hints and signals of her peripheral answers; after which he would deluge her with more talk, more ideas, more merriment of his own and she, sighing with relief, would break into laughter with him.

But there were rare times when Hayle gave us a momentary glimpse of another mood. I remember one evening when I was just coming in from the veranda with a load of firewood, for it was a cold evening and we had gathered around the fireplace, I in my stuffed chair and Hayle and Amelia on the floor, their faces red in the reflection of the firelight, when over the rattling panes of the French doors I could just hear Hayle making an extraordinary confession to my wife.

"Amelia," he said, "we three have been practically living together for almost four years, and your husband from long association I know very well, but you, Amelia, are a mystery to me, and I think it irresponsible of me not to know you better." At which I saw her lower her head but what she answered I never heard and when I came into the room they were both laughing.

"I have just told Amelia a joke she doesn't understand."

"Try me," I said.

"No. If Amelia doesn't understand me, how could you? Don't you remember how I had to help you in college? No, decidedly your spouse is cleverer than you, not cleverer but deeper. Except it was arch cleverness on your part to have caught her. How ever did you do it? How ever did you lure a woman, a wild, untamed figure of mystery, into your safe, obscure retreat?"

"I fooled her. She never got to know me."

"Aha. And did you get to know her? Or did you just offer her the security of your portly years? No, you must have offered her something else or she would surely not have accepted you. What did you place on the altar of mystery, eh? And did you, did you see into the mystery? Did you become intimate with it? Did you, who remained unknown to her as you said, did you ever get to know her?"

"Why really, Hayle, I don't know, I don't know, Amelia, did I?"

"Really," she answered, "let's not be silly. A joke's a joke. And," she added sweetly, "everybody knows me now."

"Yes, so long, so long . . . but now what has that to do with it?" Hayle said to me, "Your Amelia is not easy to tame. She must be very moody, no, and changeable, with many possibilities, how should we two know the meaning of all those existences, how should you, even you, her husband, guess at it all? I wonder, Amelia, would you allow for such a conquest?"

"You're in fine form," she said. "I love to listen to your talk." And although all this speech about Amelia really was quite untrue, quite foolish, it was really wonderful to hear him voicing it with all his eloquence.

"I hate it," he said all of a sudden, so maliciously that we both started. "All these words just fill out the droning minutes."

"Why Hayle, whatever is the matter?" I asked.

"I really don't know. I'm just depressed, I suppose. Please excuse me, I'm having a bad time with a painting; it isn't worth thinking about." But he did think about it, frowning furiously until Amelia became so distressed at his unaccustomed brusqueness that she started to leave the room, and suddenly her movement brought him back to us, as if on top of all his aggravations that she too should add her displeasure were the utter last straw; he hurriedly stood up beside her, smiling apologetically at her and down at me, the smile spreading over his face till he burst out into that loud laughter against himself in which we always joined.

And yet I could not help feeling sorry for Hayle. Fifteen years had passed since he had left college and still he was getting nowhere; there was something about Hayle despite all his talk and enthusiasm which struck one as being negative and immaterial, as if he did no more than float above the world in a state of flux; it gave the impression of lack of seriousness; and yet notwithstanding his vagueness, his lack of purpose, he did at least stick by that decision of college days, disastrous as it was; he was plugging away at his painting, producing one failure after another with dogged determination; late at night we would see the light on in his studio and I would think of him desperately dabbing away at some horrible canvas, trying his best perhaps to retrieve some sense out of an unrecognizable mass of blobs and lines, and then it seemed to me that my life was a veritable heaven compared to Hayle's, for it must have been an unbearable disappointment to him that after fifteen years of painting he still had made so little money that, happy as I was to have him living near me, he could not have done otherwise. But sometimes I did wish just the same that I might have felt a little more like a patron of the arts and not just a patron of Hayle, but to have encouraged him in what he was doing would have been out of the question, harmful as it was to him never to achieve success, and exhausting as it must have been for him to be always courting something he could not achieve; for he was always rushing off into the city with great piles of canvases and returning defeated two days later, or careening off to try to get a commission out of someone he had met or attending what he called invaluable parties from which he would sometimes return triumphantly with a portrait commission; then off to the city he would go with all his gear, but somehow things always went wrong, the portrait would not be purchased, or, if it was, Hayle said they would not hang it, or they asked of Hayle so many changes that he had refused, and we would be called in to see the canvas in question, and really every time it did seem to me that it was quite impossible, unflattering, ungraceful, not pretty, though Amelia never ventured to say anything; sometimes even he would pose someone in his studio, then Amelia would be so pleased, acting like his housekeeper, bringing in tea at four o'clock and clearing up and putting all sorts of little feminine touches in the studio so that she could be present in the background while he painted, and I was glad to see her there because I knew it eased Hayle and when the painting would not be accepted I thought at least Amelia is on his side, at least she is there to smile away the hurt; and Amelia would say yes, we must not criticize, we must try to praise because it would be too much for us to join in against him too, and for all I knew perhaps Hayle really would get sick from disappointment; certainly he was thin, always rushing to the city and hurrying back empty-handed, much too thin, Amelia would say, too pale and too thin, and needed taking care of. But I felt that as a true friend I should speak to Hayle, for it was just the same extraordinary that after all the experience he must have had Hayle's portraits hardly resembled living people and I used to say to him, "Hayle, you don't look at people. You invent their features to match some idea of your own. It simply won't work."

"What you're saying holds no interest for me, don't you see, I'm not concerned with my model, not in the sense of skin and features and resemblance, though I am trying for a resemblance, if you want to use that word, but a resemblance which I for one can only achieve by becoming it myself, for it must come out of me and not be reflected at me, only if I could achieve this would I discover through paint and form that the physical world which is static and dogmatic and an obstacle is only the crust that has jelled over a world full of vibrancy and mutability. That is the real inspirational moment, to discover that the dull is only a casual camouflage to be divined, that the body is only a veil, and that all which seems opaque and heavy is only a misleading decoy."

"You used to say that in college," I reminded him.

"Oh then, then I had hopes of really being an adventurer."

"Hayle, why not complete one portrait the way your sitter wants it and get your commission? After all, if you're going to start out on a project why not complete it? A little success would do you a world of good."

"Oh . . . that kind of success . . ."

"You don't realize it, but it's worrying you."

"Certainly. I have financial troubles. And I am grateful, you know what I mean, for all you've done. Perhaps one day I'll be able to pay you back . . ."

"No, no, Hayle, you must not talk like that, but you know you said you were full of hope in the old days. With a little success you'll get it back."

"Oh . . . well . . . you know . . . no, you don't know . . . you couldn't possibly imagine, for fifteen years I've been working hard, really working hard, do you know what that means, to concentrate on one thing for fifteen years, and to find that you can't do that one thing . . . for I can't do it . . . mechanically I'm good, even very good, and if I just weakened and gave the public what it wants I would be praised, that is sure, for technically and mechanically there is no doubt that I am a good painter, and yet give in that way I never will do, I would sooner throw up the whole business or go into an office or just do nothing, just retreat and do nothing at all; but what I really want to accomplish I can't because if you knew, if you could only know how deeply there is something wrong with me, with my soul and my heart, because I can't be moved. I can't fall in love with the lovely earth. With it all laid out before me, the earth, the seasons, the beasts, everything, the human form, the sea, everything moving full of lightness and dark with suggestion, I still can't tremble because I am not a part of it, it has no meaning for me. Perhaps when one is not a part of it it is too general, too vast; and when it enters my eye it dwindles and becomes insignificant, for I look at all this radiance quite unmoved, imagining the end, the death, quite calmly, almost with relief, and I cannot for one instant fall in love with it. I'm like a man who, confronted with an immense glittering diamond, is appalled in contemplation of its one blind spot. And that blind spot he has either invented or it is the reflection of himself, because he has not a soul grand enough to be lost in the overwhelming brightness but must moor himself continually upon a fancied blemish. He hates himself for it but he does not dare let go, because the light is too much, too unrelenting, and there is not one facet on which he can lay himself to rest, and through which the light could reach him with some kind of significance, a light for himself alone, since he would be a part of it, and yet the universal light at the same time. Can't you see how I resemble him? I cannot lose myself in what I paint, not just each individual subject, but in the whole thing, the significance of the search really, since I cannot fall in love with the divine creation of the world, for my soul is drowning in myself and in egocentric artistry. It is not honest, it is not even painting, it is just a grotesque mechanical parody, and I who, so full of conceit, wanted to discover what energy shaped the world, what lay behind the veils of earth, of foliage, of bone, have been strung up in that same veil."

"You might have found out that the veil was all there was, that there is nothing behind it."

"Well now, you know, I never conceived of it that way . . . now wouldn't that be a good joke on us all." And suddenly he burst into such hilarious laughter that I had to join him.

And so, talking, joking, and practically living together, five years passed for us like one. Often we would spend the evening in Hayle's little studio, although it was only one room with a cupboard-like kitchen, but going there was like going out into the world, for it was so different from our neat and warm house, what with all the clutter of sketches and the smell of oil paint and charcoal smudges which Hayle had somehow even managed to get on the walls and the atmosphere of feverish work; it was like entering a world of delirium and it made a nice change from our house, and then Amelia liked it, she would get all rosy with pleasure when we went over there, her hair blowing in the inevitable draft, for Hayle insisted on open windows — "Air out the blasted work room," he would say, opening them wide and laughing at my protestations — and she went over more and more often, taking him tea in the afternoons and sometimes later on a dish of something, fruit, or even wine — "He will be working late and need something" — and I could imagine her, a pretty maid serving him buttered toast, holding his cup for him while he finished the day's work, or clearing the table of old sketches and paint rags to set her tray down; once she even became incorporated into a background arranging flowers into a blue vase. But it turned out to be one of those unfortunate commissions which never came through, and Hayle was so exasperated that he started to mess it all up with black paint.

"Ah," he said, "I have just noticed the background. What have we here? Why, it's too ravishing, is it not? To think of that great frog squatting in the foreground and taking up all the room while the beautiful Amelia skulks like a slave arranging flowers in the background. Well, since the ingrate does not fancy herself through my eyes I offer her up to you, Amelia, as a sacrifice, if you will be

so kind as to deface her hideous features." And he handed her a
brush.

"But I really would love it, Hayle, and I do wish you hadn't
spoiled it. I liked it, even if it didn't look like her. You know
we haven't anything much on our walls, and nothing by you."

"Would you really like to have something?"

"Of course, even if it isn't of me."

"But Amelia, my God, do you mean that you would pose for
me?"

I cannot imagine how such a little portrait, which to me was
almost like a miniature, could have taken six whole weeks to paint,
and yet I am most grateful, for now as I sit in my study, or as I
listen to Amelia walking alone through the rooms, or in the garden
watch the birds who are busy with their endless routine, I realize
how fast that time, the happiest of my life, went by. Now that it is
all over I look at myself, and sometimes even at Amelia, and wonder at our existence, so quiet and drab it has become, as though our
home which had floated on air with joy has now fallen to accusing
us of its old age and, folding its wings, holds us close in its damp
embrace. For the house, along with us, is lost in creaking memory;
never again will we three attain the vision of those six weeks which
were the apex of our long friendship, the apogee of the very best in
us all. Ah, then, how glorious we were. Amelia herself was never
more beautiful; her loveliness was like the flag of our happiness;
she was younger, her step was quicker, her arms were whiter and
slimmer, and her face was radiant as it must have been when she
was a very young girl, even before I knew her, and in love for
the first time. Even her hair, which I had always admired for its
blondness, was transformed by the alchemy of our days into a
stream of gold; when at night it fell heavily down her back so
brightly did it ripple in my eyes that I longed to lose myself in its
spray, for it was the golden river to paradise; in the daytime I imagined her posing before Hayle, her grace mirrored in the canvas,
and I waited with impatience to see this painted reflection, for I
had always suspected that Amelia was more beautiful than I was
myself able to realize. In her visage when she emerged from the
sittings I had already a hint of what I had been missing, for she,
who had never had much confidence in her looks, became through
Hayle's attentions radiant with self-knowledge.

As for Hayle, there was a complete change in him, and I felt that even he had finally arrived at some sort of peace with himself, for he dropped his joking manner, and even that hilarity which was forever bursting out of him at the most inappropriate moments was quelled; for the first time since I had known him, he became serious, even tranquil, and I guessed that unbelievably and at miraculous last he was happy. Often in the evenings after dinner we three would sit peacefully together, without any talk, just glad of each other's company, and Hayle, so different from his old self, would seem contemplative, at rest after his long day's work, and in his voice there was no longer that sharp witty tone punctuated by laughter, but a softer evenness and for the first time a smile almost, and his painting which had always agitated him, made him restless with himself, had really dissatisfied him, seemed now to calm him; almost I would describe Hayle in those weeks as being in a state of inspiration in which we, as in the sun, basked.

How hard he worked, and in his work how close we became. For at last I knew that Hayle was going to create something great and I was not only happy that my confidence in him was finally to be rewarded but that he too would regain his lost hopes, and I was impatient for that moment when we should all three have the beautiful proof that Hayle was truly an artist. I remember one afternoon as we were having tea I felt so happy, so justified for my existence in this new anticipation that, unable to restrain myself, I took Amelia's hands into mine and right in front of Hayle without even the customary embarrassment I called her darling wife. With her hands in mine I turned to him and said,

"Paint us together, for you see we are inseparable." In the mirror in back of him I could see our reflections sitting close to each other on the sofa, and then oddly it seemed to me that Amelia was smiling at Hayle and that as she smiled she was slowly shaking her head. Instantly he burst out laughing and really she did have a droll expression on her face; but he laughed so raucously that I forgot all about Amelia and only now does the incident seem slightly puzzling, though perhaps only puzzling since it brought on the sole echo of Hayle's nervous laughter in that entire six weeks.

There were only a few days left now, during which he painted feverishly and Amelia posed until she was aches all over and could hardly sleep at night, so that she finally took to walking restlessly about the garden at all hours. I could see her in the moonlight through the bedroom window pulling up flowers which she left to wilt on the ground; once she wound some through her hair and smiled to herself, not knowing that I could see her, but the next moment she ran her fingers impatiently through them so that they fell out in little bruised clumps, and when I would see her coming into the house it would be ages before I would hear her step coming up the stairs and even once in the room she would stand for what seemed an eternity by the window, as if loath to come to the bed, where in her fatigue she would toss and toss before finally going to sleep. And then one morning Hayle burst into the dining room to announce the completion of his greatest masterpiece; he wanted us to see it right away. We were so terribly excited we did not even wait to finish breakfast; Amelia got up so abruptly she spilled her coffee, so anxious was she, for though she had been posing all these weeks, Hayle had never allowed her to view the work in progress and she had no more idea than I what it would be like. Never were three people's hearts more in unison than when we rushed over to the studio to see Hayle's portrait of Amelia.

It was in the middle of the room on an easel, and Hayle was already beside it full of anticipation and, my God, the hideous contrast of his smiling expectant eyes and the painting; I could not believe it, that during these innocent weeks this cruel travesty of my wife had slowly, carefully, been fashioned into the ugly and unrecognizable thing that Hayle so happily presented to us, as if offering up in a sacrifice all the toppled empty blocks of the tricked past.

It was a tiny oval canvas in which the figure was cramped and forced as if through a hand mirror; the head looked straight out with no attempt at grace, the shoulders were squarely forward, and all was unbendingly strict down to a tiny rigid waist. I cannot understand what he meant to convey by this pose, for it is most unlike Amelia who, far from sitting so stiffly serious, is always curled into a sofa, kittenish, presenting her profile at most, her hands in a constant fluttery movement, and while the figure was on the one hand all too tiny, the little oval miniscule head placed on a tremendously long neck, minute wrists and fingers, the absurd waist, the composition was on the other hand so cramped that the body, though ridiculously small, seemed at the same time too large, as if at any moment it might loom menacingly out of its frame and with one fatal blow cover the whole world in darkness. The expression also was immense, horrifying, way out of proportion to the features, and the eyes, whose focus was on nothing, took in the entire scene with their steady gaze, until one felt uneasy staring back into those irises which saw too much and held too many secrets. Indeed the whole painting had a secretive air about it, down to the oval canvas, itself like an eye into whose sight one had an uncomprehending glance. And the hair, that hair like running gold, had become truly grotesque, for he had pictured it hanging thinly all about her, absolutely straight and without a ripple, as though she were enclosed in a veil in whose dark tented confines was hiding her soul. I cannot imagine how he could have conceived such a style. Out of all the horrible paintings that I had seen of Hayle's this one was truly the most horrible. The clasped hands, while assiduously hiding something, were on the point of disclosing their treasure, for the arms were held out from the body in a strange manner as though the figure might at the next moment, declaring all her secrets, her hidden possessions, her heart even, fling herself upon the onlooker in an eternal and uncontrolled embrace. And the promise of that embrace was both shocking and undesirable because it was too immense and too revealing.

Hayle cried out triumphantly, "Well?" We both looked to Amelia. I heard him give out the horrified gasp I felt rising in my own throat. She had turned dead white; I really thought she might collapse. Rushing forward with a chair, I put my arm out to steady her while Hayle held her hands in an agony of suspense. I shall never forget the look she turned on us both, accusing one of us of having left her unprotected against the treachery of the other and, dominating us with her hate, she joined Hayle and me in a common plight, a common guilt. But the next minute she was sitting huddled and pitiful while Hayle was frantically patting her face with water as though she had fainted. He too was trembling and unbelievably pale and he spoke to her in jerks, using the most extraordinary words.

"Darling Amelia, darling, what is it, oh please, my God, what's wrong? What have I done? Give me a chance, both of you, give me a chance." But it was not to me he paid attention nor was bent on justifying himself; it was Amelia that he hovered over, his arms ready to hold her, trying to open a chip in her hurt which he still could not understand, that she might disclose its source to him.

"Amelia, are we not very close, do you not see how close we have become, that this is not my work alone? You must see in it all the effort you too have made, all the concentration we have together exerted, so that in this feat we have become a part of each other, and because of that have accomplished this wonderful thing, this revelation, this portrait of woman which is at one time you and the spirit of all womankind; she who is at the secret core of everything, whose wisdom coupled with man's energy has created all that is best in him; who is waiting to be conquered by man only that she may reveal to him her soul and inspire him out of the four walls of his ignorance. She who is more than dust and more than temporal because, wound and veiled in mystery and half-tones, she has suggested the impossible journeys, the preposterous feats, all the fantastic adventures of the world and, looking man straight and magnificently in the eye, she challenges him to fall in love with the great radiant creation of God's world of which he and she are a part. And when at last he accepts that challenege, she will be for-ever in his mind, and never, never, will she desert him again, for she is the muse and the muse will not deceive her true disciple."

Finally by dint of hearing his voice, and it was growing more and more positive, clear, assured, for he, poor deluded Hayle, was actually growing inspired with his own words, nonsense as they were, Amelia looked as if she were beginning to listen and he, heartened by this, brought the picture down from the easel and held it close between them.

"See, Amelia, how I have shown everywhere the mystery which engulfs the muse, she who answers more than is ever asked, and understands more than one ever dreams of knowing, for she beck-ons the artist further and further into her maze while he, poor fool, is frightened, not knowing that at the intricate toiling end there shall be complete union and understanding. Don't think that I have held back in my feelings or that I ever shall again, for now my entire life is changed, and it is you who have shown me how empty my egoistic, inhuman ideas were, for I recognized and saw nothing but myself with whom I was disgusted and out of love. I was not a man, but because of you I am."

During this speech he had become quite steady again, speaking with great calm, but suddenly he faltered, for Amelia seemed at last to be understanding his words, but instead of reassurance they produced in her the utmost horror. If she looked at him now it was only because she could not escape his nearness while he, seeing her as if for the first time, crouching there pitiful in front of him, tried to fathom her misery as though she were posing for him all over again. He said, "You cannot mean that I have misunderstood you or your intentions toward me or your feelings toward me, for if I have, I have misunderstood all the meaning of my happiness, and all that is profound and sacred in existence, and all of the work I shall do in the future, all of my painting apogeed in your likeness." But she did not answer. "Amelia, you never say much, and I have always admired you for it. I have admired that you speak only in hints and suggestions and found more in your gestures than in most people's speeches but, Amelia, this once you must speak out plainly to me, you must tell me where I have failed, what I have done. You must tell me. You cannot be so cruel as to leave me forever cut off in this failure. You must tell, whatever the cost to me."

We both turned to Amelia. Poor thing, she sat there wringing her hands, and so great was her discomfort that she even looked to me as if for assistance, and still she sat there. But he was determined to hear. Her cheeks turned an ugly brick red and even her neck was suffused and, glancing at me once again with a look full of constraint, she let out in a high, uncertain, sobbing voice, "You don't love me."

If Amelia's words momentarily shocked me, they did not affect me half as much as they did Hayle. For I knew what she meant. I was not misled. No, she did not fool me, is there not after all the love one owes a husband and cannot there be love at the same time, a different sort of love, of course, but love just the same, for an old family friend? There was nothing extraordinary in what she had said. But Hayle on the other hand behaved like a man completely stunned. At first he only stared at her utterly incredulously and then slowly a look of almost contempt passed over his face and with his contempt mingled a sort of shame. He looked first at Amelia and then suddenly at me and turned as red as Amelia had a moment ago; I thought for one horrible moment he was going to break down himself, but he only shouted, "What?" at Amelia as though he had not heard properly, but when her silence made it quite certain he had not heard wrong he stared at her as if he would obliterate her from the earth; grasping her suddenly by the shoulders, he held her tightly as if she were no more than a puppet to be scrutinized at will or an object to be examined, and then all at once, before I could move to her assistance, he had shoved her away from him so brusquely and so roughly that she almost lost her balance. Then he took the painting up and examined it too in the same harsh, disgusted way; even then I pitied him because I knew him in great distress. By now, having recovered from my surprise, I had just gone up to Amelia, when he wheeled on us both, brandishing the painting high above us as though it were a sort of sword out of our reach and said, "You are right," and the hard, precise tone with which he with difficulty controlled himself was more alarming than the sincerity of his previous emotion: "You are right. What is more this painting is not of you. It is not of anyone. It is an invention, a figment of the imagination. A mistake. That is all. But do not worry, you two, I will make it good. You will not be able to claim," he said, looking coldly at me, "that you have wasted your time, or your money either, nor you," he said cruelly, looking straight at Amelia, "that you have not received a fit reward for your affections." I went up to him, because I did not want Hayle to feel his debt to us so heavily, and said, "Hayle, no hard feelings, on my part. Perhaps we just don't understand art."

"On the contrary," he said, "you have brought me to my senses. I shall dedicate my first success to you, to you both, my patrons." And suddenly he shook hands with me, but he did not look at me. Amelia stood up and he shot his hand out to her too, and there was something odd and strange in this formality, it was even odder that, emphasizing each word, he should have repeated my own words to her, "No hard feelings, on my part." Abruptly he turned away. We had just started to leave when he said, "Don't you think that it's a good joke on the three of us, the way we have all betrayed each other?" And right in the face of all this failure, as if it were nothing more than a source of amusement to him, Hayle burst out into a long, frenzied, gasping fit of laughter.

And yet during the next week we too began to smile, realizing we had all taken the episode too seriously, and even Amelia, who had been so shaken that she had stayed in bed a whole day, began to revive and was her pretty self again. As for me I looked at her with a new wonder that she, my own dear wife, had made so deep an impression upon Hayle who had never really noticed anyone before. But him we did not see. At tea we were just the two of us and our silence marked his absence. In the evenings we sat alone by the fire, the anxious thought of him between us, and at the dining-room table the noise of our eating sounded terribly amplified without his conversation. And yet we expected him constantly. There was a cup ready for him, a place set at the table, on Amelia's left. The house itself was in a hush awaiting his return. The third day, unable to contain ourselves any longer, we went to his studio, thinking he was naturally embarrassed on account of the portrait, but when we knocked there was no answer, although I was sure he was inside. In the evening long after our lights were out we could still see his on, and Amelia said he must be working, and I thought tomorrow we must get in, for I felt very badly to be thus excluded from Hayle's activities. Amelia became agitated. One morning she called to him, begging him to come out, to join her for a walk, to just come out a second and see her, and he answered that she was to leave him alone as he was busy. Then she reported to me that he sounded strange, that he was perhaps ill, that she was sure he was ill, that I was to do something about it, as if I could have, that she wondered if he was eating, what he was doing, that she was nervous; and really she did become nervous; in that one week she became restless, pale, older even, and sometimes I think that week was like a taste of what was to come, for I do not think that Amelia was ever quite her old self again; it was then too that she began that eternal pacing of hers, from bedroom to corridor to staircase and back again till, perambulating with her in my mind, I feel quite worn out; often I hear her steps on the gravel outside and see how she walks to the farthest confines of the garden before she starts back again. One afternoon toward the end of the week she went over with a little bunch of flowers she had picked herself and when Hayle would not let her in she left it on his windowsill, where I suppose it must have withered. I was sad to see her this way, so anxious, so unsuccessful, almost as if she had been spurned, when all she was trying to do in her kindness was to reach him, to bring him back to us where he belonged. Perhaps too she was trying to restore the old times, the old relationships.

But finally the week ended. We found the little note tacked on the studio door: "Please accept what you will find inside for yourself as it is yourself and belongs to you and not to me."

We entered wondering what we should find. We found the room utterly bare. The table, the two old familiar chairs, the bed which was a sofa, all ranged against the wall neat as phantoms; the walls too which here and there had been stained with paint were now washed clean, so that there were only faint anonymous marks. Even a garden which has been cut down here and there will show the skeleton of its old walks and arbors, but this room had been picked so clean that only the nakedness was a living presence. The brushes which used to stand in pots and look like clusters of dried flowers and pods full of colored seeds had vanished, and the comfortable smell of turpentine had been overpowered with a sterile angry soap. The curtains were drawn so that the morning light filtered in like twilight. He must have gone during the night, I thought helplessly. We stood there, listening to the silence which we, without Hayle's assistance, were unable to break, our eyes growing accustomed to the darkness.

And then, as if I had always expected it, here in this room, at this moment, I saw it, hanging in the corner, coming as if to meet me from the desert of the room, the likeness of Amelia, so real as to be startling, in all her feminine prettiness, her coyness, her flirtatious playfulness. It was the best painting he had ever done, and she had not even posed for it.

And now when I sit day after day in my study with nothing much to do I gaze upon his lovely portrait of Amelia till I am filled with admiration for Hayle who created it and for Amelia who inspired it and even for myself to whom it is after all half dedicated, and I wonder what has happened to him, how he is getting along now that he is utterly alone; but sometimes I feel as if it were not quite fair that I, with my house, and my leisure, I who have Amelia too, should have exacted from Hayle his very soul in this final prize, and then I long that Hayle might return, Hayle with his conversation always whipping around us, daring us on and up to follow him, until we skimmed on the bark of his imagination heights which we could never have reached on our own, while he with his jokes, his enthusiasm, his praise, his hard work, and even his failures full of laughter guided us far above and out of ourselves.

IRWIN SHAW

Noises in the City

(FROM PLAYBOY)

WEATHERBY WAS SURPRISED to see the lights of the restaurant still lit when he turned off Sixth Avenue and started up the street toward the small apartment house in the middle of the block in which he lived. The restaurant was called The Santa Margherita and was more or less Italian, with French overtones. Its main business was at lunchtime and by 10:30 at night it was usually closed. It was convenient and on nights when they were lazy or when Weatherby had work to do at home, he and his wife sometimes had dinner there. It wasn't expensive and Giovanni, the bartender, was a friend and from time to time Weatherby stopped in for a drink on his way home from the office, because the liquor was good and the atmosphere quiet and there was no television.

He nearly passed it, then stopped and decided he could use a whiskey. His wife had told him she was going to a movie and wouldn't be home before 11:30 and he was tired and didn't relish the thought of going into the empty apartment and drinking by himself.

There was only one customer in the restaurant, sitting at the small bar near the entrance. The waiters had already gone home and Giovanni was changing glasses for the man at the bar and pouring him a bourbon. Weatherby sat at the end of the bar, but there were still only two stools between him and the other customer. Giovanni came over to Weatherby and said Good evening, Mr. Weatherby and put out a glass and poured him a big whiskey, without measuring, and opened a soda bottle and allowed Weatherby to fill the glass himself.

Giovanni was a large, non-Italian-looking man, with an unsmil-
ing, square, severe face and a gray, Prussian-cut head of hair.
"How's Mrs. Weatherby tonight?" he asked.

"Fine," Weatherby said. "At least she was fine when I talked to
her this afternoon. I've just come from the office."

"You work too hard, Mr. Weatherby," Giovanni said.

"That's right." Weatherby took a good long swallow of the
whiskey. There is nothing like Scotch, he thought gratefully, and
touched the glass with the palm of his hand and rubbed it pleasur-
ably. "You're open late tonight," he said.

"That's all right," Giovanni said. "I'm in no hurry. Drink as
much as you want." Although he was talking to Weatherby,
Weatherby somehow had the feeling that the words were addressed
to the other man at the bar, who was sitting with his elbows on the
mahogany, holding his glass in his two hands in front of his
face and peering with a small smile into it, like a clairvoyant who
sees something undefined and cloudy, but still agreeable, in the
crystal ball. The man was slender and graying, with a polite, educated face. His clothes were narrow and modish, in dark gray, and
he wore a gay striped bow tie and a buttondown oxford white shirt.
Weatherby noted a wedding ring on his left hand. He didn't look
like the sort of man who sat around alone in bars drinking late at
night. The light in the bar was subdued and Weatherby had the
impression that in a brighter light he would recognize the man and
that he would turn out to be someone he had met briefly once or
twice long ago. But New York was like that. After you lived in
New York long enough, a great many of the faces seemed tantaliz-
ingly familiar to you.

"I suppose," Giovanni said, standing in front of Weatherby,
"after it happens, we'll be losing you."

"Oh," Weatherby said, "we'll be dropping in here to eat again and
again."

"You know what I mean," Giovanni said. "You plan on moving
to the country?"

"Eventually," Weatherby said, "I imagine so. If we find a nice
place, not too far out."

"Kids need fresh air," Giovanni said. "It isn't fair to them,
growing up in the city."

"No," Weatherby said. Dorothy, his wife, was seven months

pregnant. They had been married five years and this was their first
child and it gave him an absurd primitive pleasure to talk about
the country air that his child would breathe as he grew up. "And
then, of course, the schools." What joy there was in platitudes
about children, once you knew you could have them.

"Mr. Weatherby . . ." It was the other man at the bar. "May
I say good evening to you, sir?"

Weatherby turned toward the man, a little reluctantly. He was
in no mood for random conversation with strangers. Also, he had
had a fleeting impression that Giovanni regretted the man's advance toward him.

"You don't remember me," the man said, smiling nervously. "I
met you eight or ten years ago. In my . . . ah . . . in my shop."
He made a slight sibilant sound that might have been the beginning of an embarrassed laugh. "In fact, I think you came there
two or three times . . . There was some question of our perhaps
doing some work together, if I remember correctly. Then, when I
heard Giovanni call you by name, I couldn't help overhearing. I'm
. . . ah . . . Sidney Gosden." He let his voice drop as he spoke
his name, as people who are celebrated sometimes do when they
don't wish to sound immodest. Weatherby glanced across the bar
at Giovanni for help, but Giovanni was polishing a glass with a
towel, his eyes lowered, consciously keeping aloof from the conversation.

"Oh . . . uh . . . yes," Weatherby said vaguely.

"I had . . . have . . . the shop on Third Avenue," Gosden said.
"Antiques, interior decoration." Again the soft, hissing, self-dep-
recating half laugh. "It was when I was supposed to do over that
row of houses off Beekman Place and you had spoken to a friend
of mine . . ."

"Of course," Weatherby said heartily. He still didn't remember
the man's name, really, but he remembered the incident. It was
when he was just starting in, when he still thought he could make
a go of it by himself as an architect, and he had heard that four old
buildings on the East Side were going to be thrown together and
cut up into small studio apartments. Somebody in one of the big
firms, which had turned the job down, had suggested it might be
worth looking into and had given him Gosden's name. His memory
of his conversation with Gosden was shadowy, fifteen or twenty

minutes of rather distracted talk in a dark shop with unlit brass lamps and Early American tables piled one on top of another, a sense of time being wasted, a sense of going up one more dead-end street. "Whatever happened?" he asked.

"Nothing," Gosden said. "You know how those things are. In the end, they merely pulled the whole block down and put up one of those monstrous apartment houses nineteen stories high. It was too bad. I was terribly impressed with your ideas. I do remember, to this day." He sounded like a woman at a cocktail party, talking swiftly to a man in a corner to hold him there, saying anything that came to mind, to try to keep him from escaping to the bar and leaving her there stranded, with no one to talk to for the rest of the evening, for the rest of her life. "I meant to follow your career," Gosden went on hurriedly. "I was sure you were meant for splendid achievements, but a person is kept so frantically busy in this city — with nothing important, of course — the best intentions . . ." He waved his hand helplessly and let the complicated sentence lapse. "I'm sure I pass buildings you've put up every day, monuments to your talent, without knowing . . ."

"Not really," Weatherby said. "I went in with a big firm." He told the man the name of the firm and Gosden nodded gravely, to show his respect for their works. "I do bits and pieces for them."

"Everything in due time," Gosden said gaily. "So you're one of those young men who are putting us poor New Yorkers into our cold bright glass cages."

"I'm not so young," Weatherby said, thinking, grimly, *That's the truth.* And, at the most, Gosden could only have been ten years older than he. He drained his drink. Gosden's manner, gushy, importunate, with its hint of effeminacy, made him uncomfortable. "Well," he said, taking out his wallet, "I think I'd better . . ."

"Oh, no, please . . ." Gosden said. There was a surprising note of anguish in his voice. "Giovanni will just lock up the bottles and put me out if you go. Another round, please, Giovanni. Please. And please serve yourself, too. Late at night like this . . ."

"I really must . . ." Weatherby began. Then he saw Giovanni looking at him in a strange, imperative way, as though there were an urgent message he wanted to deliver. Giovanni quickly poured a second Scotch for Weatherby, a bourbon for Gosden and a neat slug of bourbon for himself.

"There . . ." Gosden said, beaming. "*That's* better. And don't think, Mr. Weatherby, that I go around town just offering rounds of drinks to *everybody*. In fact, I'm parsimonious, unpleasantly parsimonious, my wife used to say, it was the one thing she constantly held against me." He held up his glass ceremoniously. His long narrow hand was shaking minutely, Weatherby noticed, and he wondered if Gosden was a drunkard. "To the cold beautiful lonesome glass buildings," Gosden said, "of the city of New York."

They all drank. Giovanni knocked his tot down in one gulp and washed the glass and dried it without changing his expression.

"I do love this place," Gosden said, looking around him fondly at the dim lamps and the gluey paintings of the Ligurian coast that dotted the walls. "It has especial memories for me. I proposed marriage here on a winter night. To my wife," he added hastily, as if afraid that Weatherby would suspect he had proposed marriage to somebody else's wife here. "We never came here often enough after that." He shook his head a little sadly. "I don't know why. Perhaps because we lived on the other side of town." He sipped at his drink and squinted at a painting of sea and mountains at the other end of the bar. "I always intended to take my wife to Nervi. To see the Temple," he said obscurely. "*The Golden Bough.* As the French would say, *Hélas,* we did not make the voyage. Foolishly, I thought there would always be time, some other year. And, of course, being parsimonious, the expense always seemed out of proportion . . ." He shrugged and once more took up his clairvoyant position, holding the glass up with his two hands and peering into it. "Tell me, Mr. Weatherby," he said in a flat, ordinary tone of voice, "have you ever killed a man?"

"What?" Weatherby asked, not believing that he had heard correctly.

"Have you ever killed a man?" Gosden for the third time made his little hissing near-laugh. "Actually, it's a question that one might well ask quite frequently, on many different occasions. After all, there must be quite a few people loose in the city who at one time or another have killed a man — policemen on their rounds, rash automobilists, prizefighters, doctors and nurses, with the best will in the world, children with air rifles, bank robbers, thugs, soldiers of the great war . . ."

Weatherby looked doubtfully at Giovanni. Giovanni didn't say anything, but there was something in his face that showed Weatherby the barman wanted him to humor the other man.

"Well," Weatherby said, "I was in the war . . ."

"In the infantry, with a bayonet, perhaps," Gosden said, in the new, curious, flat, noneffeminate voice.

"I was in the artillery," Weatherby said. "In a battery of 105s. I suppose you could say that . . ."

"A dashing captain," Gosden said, smiling, "peering through binoculars, calling down the fire of the great guns on the enemy headquarters."

"It wasn't exactly like that," Weatherby said. "I was nineteen years old and I was a private and I was one of the loaders. Most of the time I spent digging."

"Still," Gosden persisted, "you could say that you contributed, that by your efforts men had been killed."

"Well," Weatherby said, "we fired off a lot of rounds. Somewhere along the line we probably hit something."

"I used to be a passionate hunter," Gosden said. "When I was a boy. I was brought up in the South. Alabama, to be exact, although I'm proud to say one would never know it from my accent. I once shot a lynx." He sipped thoughtfully at his drink. "It finally became distasteful to me to take the lives of animals. Although I had no feeling about birds. There is something inimical, *prehuman* about birds, don't you think, Mr. Weatherby?"

"I haven't really given it much thought," Weatherby said, sure now the man was drunk and wondering how soon, with decency, he could get out of there and whether he could go without buying Gosden a round.

"There must be a moment of the utmost exaltation when you take a human life," Gosden said, "followed by a wave of the most abject, ineradicable shame. For example, during the war, among your soldier friends, the question must have arisen . . ."

"I'm afraid," Weatherby said, "that in most cases they didn't feel as much as you would like them to have felt."

"How about you?" Gosden said. "Even in your humble position as loader, as you put it, as a cog in the machinery — how did you feel, how do you feel now?"

Weatherby hesitated, on the verge of being angry with the man.

"Now," he said, "I regret it. While it was happening, I merely wanted to survive."

"Have you given any thought to the institution of capital punishment, Mr. Weatherby?" Gosden spoke without looking in Weatherby's direction, but staring at his own dim reflection above the bottles in the mirror above the bar. "Are you pro or con the taking of life by the State? Have you ever made an effort to have it abolished?"

"I signed a petition once, in college, I think."

"When we are young," Gosden said, speaking to his wavery reflection in the mirror, "we are more conscious of the value of life. I, myself, once walked in a procession protesting the hanging of several young colored boys. I was not in the South, then. I had already moved up North. Still, I walked in the procession. In France, under the guillotine, the theory is that death is instantaneous, although an instant is a variable quantity, as it were. And there is some speculation that the severed head as it rolls into the basket is still capable of feeling and thinking some moments after the act is completed."

"Now, Mr. Gosden," Giovanni said soothingly, "I don't think it helps to talk like this, does it, now?"

"I'm sorry, Giovanni," Gosden said, smiling brightly. "I should be ashamed of myself. In a charming bar like this, with a man of sensibility and talent like Mr. Weatherby. Please forgive me. And now, if you'll pardon me, there's a telephone call I have to make." He got off his stool and walked jauntily, his shoulders thrown back in his narrow dark suit, toward the other end of the deserted restaurant and went through the little door that led to the washrooms and the telephone booth.

"My Lord," Weatherby said. "What's *that* all about?"

"Don't you know who he is?" Giovanni said, in a low voice, keeping his eyes on the rear of the restaurant.

"Only what he just told me," Weatherby said. "Why? Are people supposed to know who he is?"

"His name was in all the papers, two, three years ago," Giovanni said. "His wife was raped and murdered. Somewhere on the East Side. He came home for dinner and found the body."

"Good God," said Weatherby softly, with pity.

"They picked up the guy who did it the next day," Giovanni

said. "It was a carpenter or a plumber or something like that. A foreigner from Europe, with a wife and three kids in Queens somewhere. No criminal sheet, no complaints on him previous. He had a job to do in the building and he rang the wrong doorbell and there she was in her bathrobe or something."

"What did they do to him?" Weatherby asked.

"Murder in the first degree," Giovanni said. "They're electrocuting him up the river tonight. That's what *he's* calling about now. To find out if it's over or not. Usually, they do it around 11–11:30, I think."

Weatherby looked at his watch. It was nearly 11:15. "Oh, the poor man," he said. If he had been forced to say whether he meant Gosden or the doomed murderer, it would have been almost impossible for him to give a clear answer. "Gosden, Gosden . . ." he said. "I must have been out of town when it happened."

"It made a big splash," Giovanni said. "For a coupla days."

"Does he come in here and talk like this often?" Weatherby asked.

"This is the first time I heard him say a word about it," Giovanni said. "Usually, he comes in here, once, twice a month, has one drink at the bar, polite and quiet, and eats by himself in back, early, reading a book. You'd never think anything ever happened to him. Tonight's special, I guess. He came in around eight o'clock and he didn't eat anything, just sat up there at the bar, drinking slow all night."

"That's why you're still open," Weatherby said.

"That's why I'm still open. You can't turn a man out on a night like this."

"No," Weatherby said. Once more he looked at the door to the telephone booth. He would have liked to leave. He didn't want to hear what the man would have to say when he came out of the telephone booth. He wanted to leave quickly and be sure to be in his apartment when his wife came home. But he knew he couldn't run out now, no matter how tempting the idea was.

"This is the first time I heard he asked his wife to marry him here," Giovanni said. "I suppose that's why . . ." He left the thought unfinished.

"What was she like?" Weatherby asked. "The wife?"

"A nice, pretty little quiet type of woman," Giovanni said. "You wouldn't notice her much."

The door at the rear of the restaurant opened and Gosden came striding lightly toward the bar. Weatherby watched him, but he didn't see the man look either left or right at any particular table that might have held special memories for him. As he sprang up on his stool and smiled his quick, apologetic smile, there was no hint on his face of what he had heard over the telephone. "Well," Gosden said briskly, "here we are again."

"Let me offer a round," Weatherby said, raising his finger for Giovanni.

"That is kind, Mr. Weatherby," said Gosden. "Very kind indeed."

They watched Giovanni pour the drinks.

"While I was waiting for the connection," Gosden said, "I remembered an amusing story. About how some people are lucky and some people are unlucky. It's a fishing story. It's quite clean. I never seem to be able to remember risqué stories, no matter how funny they are. I don't know why. My wife used to say that I was a prude and perhaps she was right. I do hope I get the story right. Let me see — " He hesitated and squinted at his reflection in the mirror. "It's about two brothers who decide to go fishing for a week in a lake in the mountains . . . Perhaps you've heard it, Mr. Weatherby?"

"No," Weatherby said.

"Please don't be polite just for my sake," Gosden said. "I would hate to think that I was boring you."

"No," Weatherby said, "I really haven't heard it."

"It's quite an old story, I'm sure, I must have heard it years ago when I still went to parties and nightclubs and places like that. Well, the two brothers go to the lake and they rent a boat and they go out on the water and no sooner do they put down their lines than one brother has a bite and pulls up the hugest fish. He puts down his line again and once again immediately he pulls up another huge fish. And again and again all day long. And all day long the other brother sits in the boat and never gets the tiniest nibble on his hook. And the next day it is the same. And the day after that, and the day after that. The brother who is catching nothing gets gloomier and gloomier and angrier and angrier with the brother who is catching all the fish. Finally, the brother who is catching all the fish, wanting to keep peace in the family, as it were, tells the other brother that he will stay on shore the next day and let the one who hasn't caught anything have the lake for himself that day. So the next day, bright and early, the unlucky brother goes out by himself with his rod and his line and his most succulent bait and puts his line overboard and waits. For a long time, nothing happens. Then there is a splash nearby and a huge fish, the hugest fish of all, jumps out of the water and says, 'Say, Bud, isn't your brother coming out today?' " Gosden looked anxiously over at Weatherby to see what his reaction was. Weatherby made himself pretend to chuckle.

"I do hope I got it right," Gosden said. "It seems to me to have a somewhat deeper meaning than most such anecdotes. About luck and destiny and things like that, if you know what I mean."

"Yes, it does," Weatherby said.

"People usually prefer off-color stories, I notice," Gosden said, "but as I said, I don't seem to be able to remember them." He drank delicately from his glass. "I suppose Giovanni told you something about me while I was telephoning," he said. Once more his voice had taken on its other tone, flat, almost dead, not effeminate.

Weatherby glanced at Giovanni and Giovanni nodded, almost imperceptibly. "Yes," Weatherby said. "A little."

"My wife was a virgin when I married her," Gosden said. "But we had the most passionate and complete relationship right from the beginning. She was one of those rare women who are made simply for marriage, for wifehood, and nothing else. No one could suspect the glory of her beauty or the depths of her feeling merely from looking at her or talking to her. On the surface, she seemed the shiest and least assertive of women, didn't she, Giovanni?"

"Yes, Mr. Gosden," Giovanni said.

"In all the world there were only two men who could have known. Myself and . . ." He stopped. His face twitched. "At 11:08," he said, "they pulled the switch. The man is dead. I was constantly telling her to leave the chain on the door, but she was thoughtless and she trusted all the world. The city is full of wild beasts, it is ridiculous to say that we are civilized. She screamed. Various people in the building heard her scream, but in the city one pays little attention to the noises that emanate from a neighbor's apartment. Later on, a lady downstairs said that she thought perhaps my wife and I were having an argument, although we never fought in all the years we were married, and another neighbor thought it was a program on a television set, and she was thinking of complaining to the management of the building because she had a headache that morning and was trying to sleep." Gosden tucked his feet under the barstool rung in an almost girlish position and held his glass up again before his eyes with his two hands. "It is good of you to listen to me like this, Mr. Weatherby," he said. "People have been avoiding me in the last three years, old customers hurry past my shop without looking in, old friends are out when I call. I depend upon strangers for trade and conversation these days. At Christmas, I sent a hundred-dollar bill anonymously, in a plain envelope, through the mails to the woman in Queens. It was on impulse, I didn't reason it out, the holiday season perhaps . . . I contemplated asking for an invitation to the . . . the ceremony at Ossining tonight, I thought quite seriously about it, I suppose it could have been arranged. Then, finally, I thought it wouldn't really do any good, would it. And I came here, instead, to drink with Giovanni." He smiled across the bar at Giovanni. "Italians," he said, "are likely to have gentle and understanding souls. And now, I really must go home. I sleep poorly and on principle I'm opposed to drugs." He got out his wallet and put down some bills.

"Wait a few minutes," Giovanni said, "until I lock up and I'll walk you home and open your door for you."

"Ah," Gosden said, "that would be kind of you, Giovanni. It is the most difficult moment. Opening the door. I am terribly alone. After that, I'm sure I'll be absolutely all right."

Weatherby got off the stool and said to Giovanni, "Put it on the bill, please." He was released now. "Good night," he said to Giovanni. "Good night, Mr. Gosden." He wanted to say more, to proffer some word of consolation or hope, but he knew nothing he could say would be of any help.

"Good night," Gosden said, in his bright, breathy voice now. "It's been a pleasure renewing our acquaintanceship, even so briefly. And please present my respects to your wife."

Weatherby went out of the door onto the street, leaving Giovanni locking the liquor bottles away and Gosden silently and slowly drinking, perched neat and straight-backed on the barstool.

The street was dark and Weatherby hurried up it toward his doorway, making himself keep from running. He used the stairway, because the elevator was too slow. He opened the metal door of his apartment and saw that there was a light on in the bedroom.

"Is that you, darling?" He heard his wife's drowsy voice from the bedroom.

"I'll be right in," Weatherby said. "I'm locking up." He pushed the extra bolt that most of the time they neglected to use and carefully walked, without haste, as on any night, across the carpet of the darkened living room.

Dorothy was in bed, with the lamp beside her lit and a magazine that she had been reading fallen to the floor beside her. She smiled up at him sleepily. "You have a lazy wife," she said, as he began to undress.

"I thought you were going to the movies," he said.

"I went. But I kept falling asleep," she said. "So I came home."

"Do you want anything? A glass of milk. Some crackers?"

"Sleep," she said. She rolled over on her back, the covers up to her throat, her hair loose on the pillow. He put on his pajamas, turned off the light, and got into bed beside her and she lifted her head to put it on his shoulder.

"Whiskey," she said drowsily. "Why do people have such a prejudice against it? Smells delicious. Did you work hard, darling?"

"Not too bad," he said, with the freshness of her hair against his face.

"Yum," she said, and went to sleep.

He lay awake for a while, holding her gently, listening to the muffled sounds from the street below. God deliver us from accident, he thought, and make us understand the true nature of the noises arising from the city around us.

PETER TAYLOR

At the Drugstore

(FROM THE SEWANEE REVIEW)

MATT DONELSON was back home on a visit. He rose early, before any of the others were awake, and set out on foot for the drugstore, where he was going to buy a bottle of shaving lotion. He had left a pretty wife sleeping in the family guest room, two little sons snoozing away in the next room down the hall — both the wife and the sons being exhausted from the long train ride of the day before — and a mother and a father snatching early-morning, old-folksy naps in their adjoining rooms at the head of the stairs. At this early hour the house seemed more like its old self than it usually did on his visits home. Though he knew it was a house that would be politely referred to nowadays as "an older house," for a moment is seemed to him again "the new house" that the family had moved into when he was aged six. His room had been the one his father now occupied. He was the baby of the family; his mother had wanted him nearby. His two big brothers had shared the room where his own two boys were sleeping this morning. And his sister, for whose coming-out year the house had been bought, had claimed the guest room for hers during the brief two years she remained at home. She and the brothers had long since, of course, had houses and families of their own. When Matt came back to see his parents he seldom caught more than a glimpse of any of them, and to their children he was a stranger.

Downstairs, just before he left the house, Matt had a brief exchange with the colored cook who was a recent comer and whose name he did not even know.

"I suppose it feels good to you to be back home," she had said. "There's nothing like it," Matt had replied. "Absolutely nothing."

On his way to the drugstore Matt realized that this was an expedition he had not given any real forethought to. For several days before he left New York he had been intending to buy the bottle of shaving lotion, but he had kept forgetting it or putting it off — refusing somehow to let his mind focus on it. And he had risen this morning and left the house — hatless and on foot — without really thinking of *what* drugstore he was going to. It was with a certain wonderment even that he found himself hiking along a familiar thoroughfare in this sprawling inland city where he had grown up. It was a street that led through what he as a boy had thought of as a newish part of town but a part which he knew must now of course be regarded as "an older section." Once, along the way, he stumbled over an uneven piece of pavement which the roots of one of the maple trees had dislodged. Next he found himself looking up at the trees, trying to determine whether or not they had grown much since the days when he first remembered them. It seemed to him that they had not. The trees had not leafed out yet this year and even the patterns of the smallest branches against the dull March sky seemed tiresomely familiar. Somehow he felt both bored and disquieted by his observations. And when finally he stood opposite the drugstore and realized that this was his destination, the very sight of the commonplace store front was dismaying to him. How had he got here? It all seemed unreal. It was as though he had climbed out of his warm bed, without thought or care for his wife, his sons, or his aged parents, and walked off down here in his sleep — to a drugstore that he had not thought of in a dozen years.

But it was no dream, not, that is, unless all visits back home be dreams of a kind. He was wide awake, no doubt about that. He was fully and quite properly dressed, except that he wore no hat — he never wore a hat when he was back home — and he was bent on a very specific and practical piece of business . . . But what was the business? Ah, of course, the shaving lotion! He pushed open the heavy glass door and entered the drugstore rather breezily, just as though it were any other drugstore in the world. Fluorescent lights, giving everything an indigo tint, gleamed overhead and behind the counters and even inside some of the glass cases, as they would have done in any other modernized, up-to-date drugstore. But it was still so early in the day that there wasn't another customer in the place. In the artificial light and in the silence, there was the timeless quality of a bank vault. Or, more precisely, the atmosphere was that of a small, out-of-the-way museum where the curator doesn't really expect or welcome visitors.

To call attention to his presence Matt began dragging his leather heels on the tile floor. But at once he checked himself. The black and white tile under foot had suddenly caught his eye! How well he remembered the maddening pattern of it! And he was struck by the thought that this tile was the only feature of the once-familiar drugstore that remained unchanged. Even more striking to him, however, was the coincidence that last night in the railroad station he had had very nearly the same experience. The old Union Depot had, sometime very recently, undergone complete alteration, and when Matt had walked into the lobby just after midnight, he had believed for one moment that he was in the wrong city. During that terrible moment he had looked over the heads of the two sleepy boys at his wife and had given such a hollow laugh that Janie took a quick step toward him, saying, "What is it, dear? What is it, Matt?" Then the expanse of two-toned beige tiling, on which he had long ago played hopscotch, had seemed to come right up at him, and he felt such relief that he had sighed audibly.

Now in the drugstore, with his eyes fixed on the hypnotic black and white diamonds and octagons, he gave another such sigh. He felt relieved all over again not to have gotten Janie and the boys off the train in a strange city in the middle of the night. It really was not something he could possibly have done, of course, but that didn't diminish the relief he felt — last night or this morning. And while he continued to wait in the front part of the drugstore for someone to take notice of him, his mind dwelt further on his confusion last night . . . "What is it?" Janie had asked still again, placing a gloved hand on his sleeve. He had tried to turn his sigh into a yawn, but that had not deceived Janie for one second.

"It's nothing," he had said, watching now for the porter to bring in their luggage. "I was only thinking how I used to play a kind of hopscotch on this floor whenever we came here to meet people."

Janie had looked at him with narrowed eyes, not at all convinced;

on their visits home — especially just before they arrived — she always developed her own peculiarly mistaken ideas about what thoughts he was having. "Surely," she said now, "surely you can't have expected anyone to meet us at this hour, Matt. Especially after you insisted so that they not." . . . He wasn't even annoyed by her misreading of his thoughts. In fact, he had had to smile. And he even seized the hand that was resting on his sleeve and whispered, "My little worry-wart!" It was so *like* the notions she always took about his homecomings. She was ever fearful that in these occasions there would be some misunderstanding or quarrel between him and his father, or between him and one of his brothers, or even his gray-haired brother-in-law. Moreover, he knew that in her heart she was firmly convinced that there was some old quarrel between him and his family that had sent him to live away from home in the first place — some quarrel that he would not tell her about. In the early years of their marriage she had not let it bother her very much. But ever since the first baby came she had devoted considerable time to "winning him back to his family." She never put it into so many words — they were *his* words — but he knew what her thoughts were. (She had taken to writing regularly to his mother and even began remembering his father's birthdays.) It had originally seemed to him a good joke on her that she thought there were hidden wounds to be healed, but the joke had gone too far and she had at last become too serious about the matter for him to do more than smile and call her a worry-wart. Yet it really was laughable, almost incredible, to think how little she understood him with respect to his relations with his family. His was simply not a quarreling kind of family! They didn't have the passionate natures for it! — and particularly with respect to how he was affected by the prospect of a short visit with just his two parents.

His confusion last night, however, had been a rather extraordinary thing. And he had to acknowledge that it was due partly to the fact that none of the family was there to meet him. Always in the past at least one of them had been here. They thought it silly of him to insist upon coming home on the train instead of flying (they didn't understand what he meant by the transition's being too abrupt — and the difference in the fares was *so* trivial), but still one of them had always trekked down to the dingy old railroad station to welcome him — him and his family. Usually it was his father or one of his two brothers who came, because they considered it strictly a man's job to meet a train that arrived so late at night. They usually seemed amused to find themselves in the depot again. They hadn't been there since the last time Matt came home! (Who else rode the trains nowadays but Matt?) And Matt was merely amused at their amusement. Why should he take offense at their condescension when he would only be home for a few days? . . . With whoever came to meet the train — father or brother — Matt and Janie and the boys would walk the length of the great depot lobby, between the rows of straight-back benches on one of which a pathetic family would be huddled together and on another a disreputable-looking old bum would be stretched out, asleep with his head on his bundle and with his hat over his eyes. And when the party came directly under the vast dome that rose above the lobby, Matt's father or brother would tell the boys to look up and see the bats whoozing around up there or see the absurd pigeon that had got himself trapped in the dome and was flapping about from one side to the other.

It had been a very different scene last night, however. The dimly lit lobby of old had been transformed. A false ceiling had been installed no more than ten or twelve feet above the floor. And a new, circular wall, with display windows for advertisers and with bright posters declaring how many people still rode the trains, altered the very shape of the room, hiding the rough stone columns around which children had used to play hide and seek. As for the wooden benches, they were replaced by plastic, bucket-bottomed chairs on which huddling together would have been difficult and stretching out alone quite impossible. And the lighting, though indirect, was brilliant; there were no dark corners anywhere.

In view of these changes Matt felt his moment of consternation and confusion upon entering the lobby a very natural response. He did not have to lay it, even in part, to his weariness from the long train ride. Yet when the porter had finally appeared with their luggage and he and his little family had passed out of the lobby and into the large vestibule at the main entrance of the depot, something even more absurd, if no more confusing, happened. In a huge wall mirror which had always occupied its place there in the vestibule, Matt saw his own reflection; he mistook that reflection for some other male member of his own family. "Oh," he said under his breath. But his "oh" was not so soft that Janie didn't hear it. She perceived at once the mistake he had made. This time he might almost have shown annoyance with her. Her smile said, "You see, you *were* expecting to be met," but the smile was also full of love and was so overly sympathetic — be it sympathy ever so uncalled for — that he could only gently push her and the boys through the doorway and follow them silently to the waiting taxi.

In the drugstore none of the clerks had come to work yet. Only the druggist himself was there, and as soon as he appeared, Matt apprised him of the business he had come on. "What kind will it be — what brand?" the old fellow asked. Matt gaped across the counter. He couldn't believe his eyes at first. It was the same old Mr. Conway who had been the druggist there twenty-odd years before. It was the same old Mr. Conway, and yet of course he didn't recognize Matt.

"I don't know, sir," Matt said respectfully. "Any kind."

The old druggist looked up suspiciously and with obvious irritation. "*Any* kind?"

Matt began to smile, but then he realized his mistake. One large vein stood out on the druggist's forehead precisely as it had used to do whenever he was vexed . . . (Incredible, incredible that he should remember Mr. Conway's vein!) . . . The broad, flat nose twitched like a rabbit's . . . (To think that he should remember. How annoying it was.) . . . One more thing. The small, close set eyes seemed to draw closer together as the druggist bent across the counter peering up at him. Then the total personality of the man came back to him, and somehow it was all too much to be borne at this hour of the morning. He shifted his gaze away from Mr. Conway. But in the mirror behind Mr. Conway he saw another familiar face (oh, *too* familiar) and was struck by the guilty expression in the round eyes that ogled back at him there.

"*Any* kind?" Mr. Conway was saying again. For a moment the voice seemed to be coming from away at the back of the store. But that was absurd. Mr. Conway was right here before him. There was something back there, however, tugging at Matt's attention.

"Yes, *any* kind," he repeated. They were like two birds or two insects answering each other. Finally Matt broke the rhythm of it.

In the most impersonal, hard, out-of-town voice he could muster, he said, "Any kind, my friend. And I'm afraid I'm in a hell of a hurry."

He even managed to sound a little breathless. Unfortunately, though, it wasn't a very manly breathlessness. It was a boy's breathlessness. It was as if this very morning he had run all the way from home with his school books under one arm and his yellow slicker under the other and was now afraid that the streetcar — the good old Country Day Special — would pass before he could get waited on. How terrible it had been being a boy, and the world so full of Mr. Conways.

Mr. Conway turned away toward the shelves on the wall behind him, to the left of the mirror and toward the rear of the drugstore. (Still, still there was something back there trying to claim Matt's attention. But he couldn't, or wouldn't, look.) He tried to watch Mr. Conway as he examined the various bottles. He was of course searching out the most expensive brand. The old guy's rudeness was insufferable and at the same time fascinating. As soon as his back was turned, Matt felt himself seriously tempted to snatch up some article off the counter and slip it into the pocket of his topcoat. As a boy he had never for a moment been tempted to do such a thing, though he had seen other boys do it. They had taken the most trivial and useless articles — ladies' lipsticks, manicure scissors, get-well cards, though they would not have stooped to stealing candy or chewing gum. Not Country Day boys! But something distracted Matt from his temptation, and distracted him also from watching Mr. Conway's evil, grasping fingers. (The fingers moved with awful deliberation and seemed bent on strangling every bottle they picked up.) What distracted Matt, of course, was that same familiar face in the mirror, his view of it now unobstructed by the figure of his malefactor.

Yet somehow or other it wasn't the same face in the mirror this time. The eyes weren't the guilty eyes of a schoolboy. The face wasn't really familiar at all — not *here*. The person in the mirror now eyed him curiously, even incredulously, and momentarily he resented the intrusion of this third, unfamiliar person on the scene, a person who, so to speak, ought still to have been asleep beside his wife back there in the family's guest room. But he accepted the intrusion philosophically. In effect said to himself, "Look, look,

look! Have your fill and let me get back to my important business
with Mr. Conway." But the face had a will of its own. It had an
impersonal, hard, out-of-town look, like the faces one gets used to
seeing everywhere except in the mirror. It was one thing consciously
to put those qualities into your voice; it seemed quite another to
find them translated and expressed in your face without your even
knowing about it.

But the impression lasted only for a moment. The eyes in the
mirror grew warm and sympathetic. They were the same fine old
eyes. It was the same fine nose too, just the littlest bit beefier than
the boy's nose had been. The blond hair was as thick as ever
through the temples. (If it lay flatter on top, you could not say for
certain that it was really thinner even up there.) And the ruddy
complexion was the same as of old, or was except for the "slight
purplish cast" that his mother was always imagining when he came
home, and had got his wife to imagining, and now had him half
believing in.

By the time Mr. Conway had set the bottle on the counter before him, Matt Donelson had recovered himself — had been recovered, that is, by the grown-up self. The thought of his mother
and wife had reminded him of the real circumstances of this day
in his life. At seven forty-five A.M. on a Saturday morning he was
in the drugstore where he used to hang out as a boy. It was the
man to whom the strange cook had spoken so politely and respectfully that looked at Mr. Conway now — the mature Matt Donelson,
aged thirty-five, a man with a family of his own but still a faithful
and attentive son, a man whose career was such a going thing that
he could easily spare an occasional four or five days for visits back
home.

Poor old Mr. Conway. His hand trembled as he set the bottle
down. Matt seemed to feel something inside himself tremble.
Pitiable little old fellow, he thought. What kind of a career had
he had? Probably the most that could be said for him was that he
had held his own and kept up with the times. Instead of the white
linen jacket that had once upon a time made him look like a butler,
he now wore a sleazy, wash-and-wear tunic (with short sleeves and
a tight collar) that suggested he was an elderly surgeon fresh from
the operating room. Besides the addition of fluorescent lights, his
drugstore had been refurbished throughout. The soda fountain was

no more, and of course the tables and the booths were gone. There was now a large toy department, a hardware counter, shelves containing men's socks and jockey shorts, a serve-yourself freezer with half-gallon packages of ice cream, cartons of milk, even loaves of bread. Instead of the old lending library, innumerable paperbacks were offered for sale on two revolving stands. Mr. Conway — bless him, dear old fellow — had always had an eye for what brought in the money. No doubt he had a goodly sum stashed away. No doubt he was highly respected by the other storekeepers along this street. Within his lights, he was probably a considerable success. Perhaps his kind was, as everybody always said, the backbone of the community, even the backbone of the country. Matt was on the verge of making himself known to the old man and of reminding him of the days when Country Day boys waited for the streetcar in his store. He was on the verge; then he pulled back.

What was it now? Out of the corner of his eye he had caught a glimpse of the giant mortar and pestle that squatted on a shelf above the entrance to the pharmacist's prescription room. It had squatted up there in the old days; it seemed to be the only piece of the old decor that had been allowed to remain. The bowl was about the size and shape of a large wastebasket, and the boys, who had somehow always hated the sight of it, used to toss candy-bar wrappers and other trash up into it . . . Was that what had made him pull back? Was it only this that had been calling for his attention back there all along? Or was it the electric light burning with such fierce brightness in the prescription room beyond the doorway? (How keenly he had felt the fascination of that intense light when he was fourteen.) But presently he answered his own question very positively. It could not be any of that. Surely not. No, it was the bottle of shaving lotion itself that had made him recoil and refuse to introduce himself to Mr. Conway. For, almost without realizing it, he had observed that Mr. Conway had actually set before him — albeit with trembling hand — the most expensive brand that such a drugstore as this would be likely to stock. Matt recognized the label, and despite the bottle's being tightly sealed and neatly cartoned he imagined he could detect the elegant scent.

"Didn't you have something cheaper?" he said.

Mr. Conway grinned, showing — yes — the same old dentures, row upon regular row. And when he spoke there was the familiar clamp and clatter. "I thought you didn't mind what brand," he said. His hand rested solidly on the carton now.

Without seeing himself in the mirror, Matt knew his face was coloring. His lips parted to speak, but at that instant he heard the sound of footsteps in the front part of the store. Someone else had come in.

"You want something cheaper, then," Mr. Conway said, in a loud voice.

"This will do," said Matt.

He quickly drew out a bill and handed it to the druggist. Just as quickly the old man drew change from the cash register and counted it into Matt's open palm. Before Matt's fingers had closed on the change, he glanced over his shoulder to see who it was that had come in. From the first sound of the footsteps he had felt an unnatural curiosity to know who this other person was. He had imagined that it might be someone he knew. But his shock upon glancing back now was greater than any he had received from the face in the mirror.

A rosy-cheeked young man had come up directly behind him — a man ten years or so younger than himself. And the face of this young man, who was at the moment removing from his head a checked cap which matched the checked raglan coat he wore, was indisputably the face of old Mr. Conway as it had been forty years ago — long before even Matt had ever set eyes on him. A black fright seized Matt Donelson. Either this *was* a dream from which he could not wake himself or he was in worse trouble than any of those friends of his and Janie's back in New York — the ones they laughed at so for feeding the revenues of the analysts.

He looked back at Mr. Conway to make out if he saw the apparition too. But Mr. Conway's eyes were on the big clock above the entrance to the store. Matt looked up at the clock; and now he had to concede that there was, after all, another fixture that had been here in the old days. But *had* the clock been there when he came in five minutes ago? Perhaps before his eyes this modern drugstore was going to turn back into the place it had once been. Worst of all, the clock hands said that it was ten minutes to eight! — the time when the Country Day Special was scheduled to pass this corner. *Would* have been the time, that is, on a week day. *Had* been the time, that is, in the era of streetcars. Nowadays, he re-

minded himself, the boys rode to school on buses . . . He put his
two hands to his head and massaged it gently. He felt a swimming
sensation.

"It's ten minutes to eight," Mr. Conway said flatly. Matt sensed
at once that the old man wasn't addressing him. He felt better, and
removed his hands from his head.

From behind him came the equally flat response: "I know."

And now Matt had no choice but to turn around and determine
finally whether or not the young man were real. When he confronted him it was really as if he himself were the ghost, because
the young man with the rosy cheeks and the shock of dark brown
hair did not seem to see *him*. The young fellow was real enough
all right but he seemed lost in a dream of his own.

Despite his being the youthful image of old Mr. Conway, with
the same squashed nose and small, close-set eyes, he was a pleasant-
looking young man. And judging from the dreamy expression on
his face, from his snappy clothes, and from the easy way he was
now slipping out of his coat, he was a person fairly pleased with the
world and not totally displeased with himself. Matt was a trifle
offended by the way he seemed to be blind to *his* presence, regarding him as a mere customer and therefore not worthy of his direct
gaze. (A family trait, no doubt, since this was certainly Mr. Conway's own flesh and blood.) But still, even before he heard him
speak again, Matt was more attracted to the young man than put
off by him.

Matt had already turned away and was moving toward the front
of the store when he heard the young Conway addressing the old
man: "We've morning sickness at our house again this morning."
The voice was very masculine, very gentle, expressing keen pleasure
in the tidings he brought. "It's a pretty sure thing now," he said.

Matt could not resist taking another glance over his shoulder. He
saw that old Mr. Conway was already off to his prescription room,
padding down the aisle behind the counter. He responded to his
son's good news without bothering even to look at him. But he was
clacking away as he went along, his plate making more noise than
his footsteps, and speaking so loud that Matt heard him quite distinctly: "Well, that doesn't alter its being ten to eight when you
turned up. And there have already been four prescriptions called
in which I haven't got started on good."

The old Scrooge, the old bastard! . . . Tyrannizing over this
easy-going young fellow! . . . Making no concession even at such
an important moment! . . . Matt felt it behooved him almost to
go back and shake the young man's hand. But he didn't, of course.
He had almost reached the front door now. He halted by the long
magazine rack just to the left of the door. (Yes, there had always
been such a rack there. Yet the rack was something else he hadn't
noticed at first.) From the rear of the store he could hear the young
Conway whistling. He let his eye rove over the display of magazines. Somehow he could not bring himself to leave. He tried to
identify the jazzy tune young Conway was whistling, but it was
something too recent for him. He continued to study the magazines.
There was the same old selection. Only *Collier's* was missing. He
remembered how the Country Day boys had been forbidden to
touch a magazine they were not going to buy.

Presently the whistling was interrupted by the old druggist's
voice.

"Is the music necessary?"

The reply was cheerful enough: "Not if you say so."

There was a moment's silence. Then, lowering his voice so
slightly that it was only the more insulting to Matt, Mr. Conway
asked, "Is that the same customer up there, still hanging around?"

"Yep. The same."

"Better keep an eye on him. He let on to be in 'one hell of a
hurry' when he came in."

"All right," said the young man, and Matt thought he heard an
indulgent snicker. Boldly Matt turned around and looked the
length of the store at the two men. The older man stepped back
into the prescription room. Matt could not be certain but he believed the younger man, who was now in shirtsleeves, winked at
him.

He turned back toward the magazines and gazed unseeing
through the broad window above the rack. He was reflecting on
the young man's undisturbed good spirits, on his indulgence toward
his crotchety father. Mr. Conway was lucky indeed to have a son
with such an understanding and forgiving nature. And suddenly
it was as though the young Conway had communicated to Matt an
understanding of the old man's ill humor and impatience this
morning: It was due to Matt's interruption while he was trying to

get those prescriptions filled. Matt could not restrain a malicious little smile. It was *so* like old times. They had always delighted in interrupting Mr. Conway when he was at work back there in the prescription room. Poor guy seemed to have had a lifetime of having his most important work interfered with. Whenever there was a piece of roughhouse up in the front part of the drugstore and Mr. Conway had to be called from his "laboratory" to deal with it, the boys became almost hysterical in their glee. They were apt to be good as gold if he stood idly here by the front window with his hands behind his back. But somehow they could not bear his being at work in the prescription room crushing a mysterious powder with his pestle or turning up the blue flame of his Bunsen burner under a vial. It was wonderful the things they used to do in order to distract the druggist.

At the soda fountain, in those days, there was a youngish black-haired woman who was believed by some of the boys to be Mr. Conway's wife. Sometimes four or five of the boys would line up on the stools at the soda fountain and place orders for cokes. Then when the glasses were set before them they would pretend to have no money. At first the dark-haired woman would merely threaten to call "Dr. Conway." The boys, winking at each other, begged her not to, and even pretended to try to borrow the money from some of the other boys who were looking on. Finally the woman would throw back her head and call out at the top of her voice: "Oh, Dr. Conway! Dr. Conway!"

But the boys continued to search their pockets until the very moment the druggist appeared. (Apparently he worked with his plates out, because he always came through the door of the prescription room with his hand to his mouth as though he were just shoving them in.) Only at that moment did each of the boys make the miraculous discovery that he had the needed money after all. With one accord they all bent forward and plunked their money down on the marble counter. And when they had done this they would be overcome by such a fit of giggling that they couldn't drink their cokes. Sometimes they would have to go off to school without tasting the drinks they had ordered and paid for.

At another counter in the drugstore, where cigarettes and toilet articles and candy bars were sold in those days, there was usually a somewhat older woman, a woman who was generally believed to

be Mr. Conway's mother. Sometimes Mr. Conway himself presided
at that counter; that was when the boys actually swiped the useless
articles they found on display. But when his "mother" was in
charge they always made a point of fumbling . . . As a matter of
fact, there was a school of thought which maintained that this
older woman was the druggist's wife and the younger woman
was his daughter. Since in the boys' eyes Mr. Conway was of an
indeterminate age, all of them conceded that the truth might lie
either way; and the women themselves would not tolerate questions
about their identity. It remained always a mystery . . . At any
rate, in an emergency, "mother" Conway would place her two hands
on the glass case before her, fix the suspect with her feline eyes,
and call out in a coarse, plangent voice: "Do—oc—to-or!"

And the thief stood looking at her blankly until at last the druggist came in sight. The trick as this point, for the boy, was to stoop
down and pretend to find the missing article on the floor where
he had unknowingly knocked it. Then, handing it to the druggist
himself, his next move was to begin making profuse apologies
which could not be heard above the gleeful convulsions of the other
boys and which continued until some boy at the front door shouted,
"Special! Special!" After that, came the chaos of a general exodus.
Amid the grabbing up of books and football gear and sheepskin
coats, and against the clamor that accompanied the rush for the
door, Mr. Conway was helpless. He stood watching them go, his
nose twitching, the vein standing out on his forehead, his false
teeth no doubt clacking, and holding in his hand a dented lipstick
case or a pocket comb with possibly half its fine teeth broken.

Matt felt that he had seen each of these pranks played at least
a dozen times. But Mr. Conway seldom took any action against
the pranksters; these Country Day boys were the children of his
best customers; their parents had the biggest charge accounts on
his books; and Mr. Conway had always had a good head for business. Matt had seen even worse tricks than these played on the
old man, though he himself had always been a little too timid, a
little too well brought up, to have any part in them. He had
generally looked on with amusement, but also with a certain disapproval. He had never so much as snatched up a magazine and
stuck it under his jacket, or even broken the rule against glancing
through a magazine one was not intending to buy. Suddenly now

he realized he was at this very moment holding a copy of a news magazine in his hand. He pushed it back into the rack. Then he eased it out again. He held it in his two hands a moment, gazing blankly at the newsworthy face on the front cover. And before he could stop himself he stole a glance over his shoulder . . . From beside the cash register the young Conway was watching him . . . Slowly Matt turned around and, with the magazine he didn't want in one hand and with his other hand delving into his pocket for change, he walked back toward the young man. He had got sufficiently hold of himself to make it a thoroughly casual performance.

The young Conway accepted the payment for the magazine with a positively friendly kind of smile. In fact, when Matt turned away he was again not sure that the young man had not winked at him. Despite his unfortunate resemblance to his father, the young man was obviously a sensitive, reasonable, affable sort. Matt felt drawn to him, wished they could have some conversation, longed to congratulate him on his wife's morning sickness. Matt felt also that there was some other purchase he had been intending to make which had escaped his mind this morning; surely there was *some* reason why he should not leave the drugstore yet.

This time he stopped before one of the revolving stands that held the paperback books. He began turning the thing slowly. What else was it he had recently been intending to buy in a drugstore? He imagined that it had almost come to him the first moment he had looked back and seen the young Conway removing his checked cap from his head. Perhaps if he went back and made conversation with him now, the thing would come to the surface of his mind. Maybe the young Conway would enjoy hearing about the pranks that the schoolboys used to play on his father. No, that would not do. Especially not if one of those women who used to clerk in the store had been his mother; because, somehow, the worse the prank had been, the more it had always involved one or both of those women. It did seem to Matt in retrospect, however, that probably neither of the women was the real Mrs. Conway. Very likely they were both merely hired clerks, and the real Mrs. Conway — and her mother-in-law too, and the daughter if there were one — kept at home and looked after the young Conway, who would have been a mere infant at that time. Yes, there was a

gentleness about the rosy-cheeked young Conway, as seen today,
that suggested a careful upbringing by women who didn't go out
to work . . . Yet one could not be sure, because those two women
clerks, even if they were not in the mother-wife-daughter category,
could not possibly have been more respectful of Mr. Conway than
they were, or seemed more dependent upon him for protection.
They believed absolutely in the old man's authority, and their confidence in him was resented by the boys. What strange power had
he over those two women? This question, in the boys' mind, was
lumped in with all the other questions they had about Mr. Conway.
And all their pranks, if not intended to satisfy their curiosity, were
at least intended to show that they knew there was something to be
curious about . . . There was the time, for instance, when Ted
Harrison threw the stink bomb. The stench of the sulfur made
Matt shake his head even now. The memory of it was that vivid.
The two women didn't understand what had happened. The odor
hadn't yet reached their nostrils when some of the boys began ex-
claiming in girlish voices: "Oh, that *awful* Mr. Conway! That
dreadful Mr. Conway!" The two women stared at each other across
the store for a time, then each of them began to spread her nostrils
and sniff the malodorous air. The boys all set their faces toward
the back of the store, focusing their eyes on the lighted doorway
beneath the huge mortar and pestle. Presently, in a dramatic stage
whisper, Ted Harrison asked: *"What* can Mr. Conway have *done?"*

Matt himself, standing near the soda fountain that day, had fixed
his attention on the face of the younger woman. He was watching
her when she inhaled the first whiff of the stink bomb. Suddenly
her nostrils quivered, her swarthy skin took on a curious glow, her
dark eyebrows contracted. He could tell that her eyes had met those
of the older woman, who was behind him at the other counter.
Then simultaneously the two women fled their posts, running behind the counters toward the rear of the store. What indeed *had*
their Dr. Conway done? They met at the entrance to the prescription room and disappeared through the doorway. There came the
sounds of the three excited voices back there, and then presently
Mr. Conway emerged, pushing in his dentures. The two women
followed close behind him, but he soon sent them scurrying back
to their places.

As Mr. Conway aproached from the rear, the boys drew away

from him toward the front of the store. They really were afraid of him. With downcast eyes they pretended to be looking and smelling all about to find where the stench came from. But suddenly Ted Harrison made a dash for it; he rushed right past Mr. Conway. "It's somewhere back here, I think," he shouted. He rounded the big glass case where hot water bottles and syringes and enema bags were displayed. And then, to the consternation of all, Ted Harrison passed beneath the mortar and pestle and through the bright doorway. He was out of sight for only one second, certainly not long enough to have done any damage or to have had more than a glimpse of the sacrosanct prescription room, but when he reappeared a cheer went up from the other boys. In fact, Ted was already outside again by the time Mr. Conway roared back at him to "get the hell out of there." And when the old druggist slipped in between the counters to try to head him off, Ted was already among his companions again in the front part of the store. Somebody shouted, "Special!" The front door was flung open. The crowd surged out onto the sidewalk, and without slowing their pace moved on into the street, and then, heedless of angry horns and shrieking tires, clambered aboard the waiting streetcar, some of them still chanting, "Special, Special!" until the streetcar doors were safely closed behind them.

There was probably never a worse incident than that one — except one, except one. There was that morning when some boy wrote with soap on the mirror behind the soda fountain. Another boy, probably an accomplice, had fallen or been pushed out of his chair at the little round table where he had gone to drink his morning coke. As he fell, his knee struck the tile floor — or so he pretended — and presently he lay on the floor moaning and groaning, and writhing in his pain. Of course the two clerks, those same two helpless, artless females, came hurrying to his succor. But he would not let them come near enough to examine the injured knee. "It's killing me!" he wailed, and he began thrashing about as though he were going into a fit. What else were the two honest women to do but cry out for their lord and master? And what else could Mr. Conway do but come forward?

He came warily, though, this time, shoving at his dentures and keeping an eye out for anyone who might make a rush for the prescription room. But his wariness and his precaution were needless and to no point on this occasion. Even before he appeared, a hush had come over the dozen or so boys who were present. Further, silently they had begun to gather up their possessions and to creep toward the front entrance. There was no cry of "Special" this time, and nothing false or pretended about the urgency they felt to be out of the place. Literally they had seen the handwriting on the wall. Clearly the consensus was that this time someone had gone too far. Matt, like a good number of the others, probably had not really seen which of them had done the writing. His whole attention had been directed toward the boy who squirmed on the black and white tile in the center of the store, and as Matt moved with the group toward the entrance, his eyes avoided another contact with the soapy writing on the mirror. But he had no need to see it again. It was written before his mind's eye forever. Twenty years later he could still see it just as distinctly as he could smell the sulfur of the stink bomb: the crude, hurriedly written letters spelling out the simple sentence, "Mr. Conway sleeps with his mother."

And at the door, as he passed out with the others, Matt had looked back to see that the boy on the floor had got to his feet and, with only the slightest pretense at a limp, was running on tiptoes to join his schoolmates.

Nobody waited to see how the writing on the mirror would affect Mr. Conway or the two women. But during the following two weeks Mr. Conway stationed himself at the entrance each morning and would not let the Country Day boys come inside the drugstore. It was in the dead of winter, and the boys had to wait outside in the cold, stamping their feet and beating their hands together until the Special arrived. When at last Mr. Conway did relent, there was a period of a month or more when the boys came into the drugstore every morning and behaved like the real little gentlemen that Country Day boys were sempiternally and without exception supposed to be. And during that period it was only with the greatest difficulty that Matt had been able to look directly into the eyes of either of the two women clerks. Whenever he wished to make a purchase he couldn't find his voice. If he did finally find his voice it would be either too soft or too loud. Or in the midst of whatever he tried to say his voice would break and change its pitch from high to low, or the other way round. The most painful part, though, was that before he could speak he would stand before the one or the other of the two women for several seconds, scratching his head and looking down at his feet.

That memory of the head-scratching! It was to mean Matt's release and salvation after standing there so long hypnotized by the revolving book stand. He came out of his trance, and he realized that he was actually at this moment scratching his head. And that was it. It was something to soothe his troublesome scalp that he had been meaning to buy in a drugstore. With great self-assurance he strode back to the counter where the young Conway was still on watch.

But when he stood face to face with the amiable sentinel there — so smiling, so fresh-complexioned, so luxuriantly thatched (and with the luxuriant thatch so lovingly groomed) — he understood that it was not really he that he wanted to see again. It was the older man. And once again, some twenty feet from where he now stood, it was the giant mortar and pestle with the bright doorway underneath that caught his eye. It was a red flag waved before him — maddening. Ted Harrison had actually got inside the prescription room. But Matt Donelson had never even taken part in any of the pranks. He heard himself saying to the young Conway, "There's a matter I'd like to speak with the pharmacist about. I'd like to get some advice. I'd like him to recommend something."

The young man stopped smiling, and tried to look very serious and professional. "Maybe I can help you," he said. "As a matter of fact, I am a pharmacist myself. And my father is tied up with some prescriptions just now."

Matt continued to look at him for a moment or so without saying more.

The gentleness and sensitivity that showed perpetually in the young man's eyes was momentarily translated into a look of professional consideration for the feelings of a customer. But Matt would have none of that. The young Conway was obviously a mere slave — no man at all really. Else how could he consent to live under the domination of that brute of an old man? Moreover, Matt could tell that the young man thought he had guessed the nature of his ailment. He thought it was hemorrhoids that Matt was so hesitant to mention. "It's my scalp," Matt said abruptly. "I have a more or less chronic scalp complaint. No dandruff, but itching and an occasional breaking out."

"Ah, yes, I see," the young pharmacist began. And lifting his eyebrows he actually looked directly at Matt's head.

Matt looked back at *his* head. "If you don't mind," he said, "I'd like to speak with the senior pharmacist." He relished that last phrase, and he was pleased to observe that finally he had managed to offend the junior pharmacist.

Now the young Conway looked at Matt for a moment without speaking. Presently the inane smile returned to his lips. "Just one moment, please," he said to Matt. He turned and walked away, back to the prescription room. Matt could barely restrain himself from following. The young man stood in the doorway, leaning one shoulder against the jamb while he spoke with his father. Then he came back with a message.

"My father," he said quietly, "suggests that you probably ought to see a doctor."

Matt understood at once that there was more than one interpretation that could be made of that message. "I believe I'd like to speak to the pharmacist myself," he said, and was already striding alongside the counter and toward the doorway to the prescription room. But the young Conway was moving at the same speed behind the counter. They converged at the entrance to Mr. Conway's prescription room. And simultaneously the figure of the old druggist was framed in the doorway. Matt went up on his toes and peered over Mr. Conway's shoulder! He saw it all, the white cabinets and the bottles and the long work shelf, all so like a hundred other pharmacists' shops he had had passing glimpses of. Everything about it looked so innocent and familiar and really quite meaningless. There was no satisfaction in it for him at all — not even in the glass of water which he identified as the receptacle for Mr. Conway's teeth. But what kind of satisfaction should he have got? he asked himself. What had he expected? Something inside him which a moment before had seemed to be swelling to the bursting point suddenly collapsed.

"You told my father you were in a hurry," he heard the young pharmacist say. "I think you'd better get going now." Looking at the young man, Matt observed that he definitely had a nervous tic in one eye. And all the blood had gone out of his cheeks now. He was in a white rage. Why, he even had his right fist tightened and was ready to fight Matt if necessary to protect the old druggist. The incredible thing was that only a moment before, Matt himself would have been willing to fight. Why? What had possessed him? Already the whole incident seemed unreal. Surely he had been momentarily insane; there was no other way to explain it. He backed away from the two men, turned his back to them, and quickly left the drugstore.

On his way back to his parents' house he kept shaking his head as if to rid himself of all thought of his absurd behavior in the drugstore. But at the same time he kept reminding himself of how near he had come to getting into a scrap with the young druggist, and perhaps the old druggist too. How unlike him it would have been, what an anomaly, how incongruous with everything else in a life that was going so well. He would never have been able to explain it to anyone. But even without the incident's ending in a real brawl, his behavior was nonetheless appalling. The only difference was that nobody ever need know about it. Finally he would be able to put it out of his own mind.

Back at the house, he found everyone up and stirring. The odors of the coffee and bacon greeted him in the front hall. From the living room he heard the voices of his two little boys commingled with those of his parents. "There he is now," he heard his mother say. He stepped to the cloak closet and hung up his topcoat, and while still at the closet he slipped the bottle of shaving lotion into the pocket of his jacket. He hesitated a moment, undecided about what to do with the magazine he had bought. It was a magazine he never read himself and one his father "thoroughly detested." Suddenly he stuffed it into the pocket of his father's heaviest winter coat. He knew it wouldn't be discovered there until his mother packed away the winter clothes the first week in May, and it pleased him to think of the mystery it would make and how they would talk about it for days . . . As he left the closet, his father hailed him from the living room doorway with: "Where have you been?"

"Just out," Matt said, and then out of long practice was able to soften such smart-aleckness toward his father with: "Just out for a walk."

"I might have gone with you if you had given me a knock," said his father. The two boys appeared now on either side of their grandfather.

"So would I," said the older boy. He was ten and was beginning to want to dress like a man. He had put on a tie this morning and kept running a finger around the inside of his collar.

"Me too," said the little brother, who was eight and affected nothing.

Matt eyed the three of them. He observed that the old man was wearing the silk smoking jacket he and Janie had sent him at Christmas. "You were both slugabeds," he said to the boys. He went past them and into the living room to kiss his mother on the forehead. "That's a good-looking smoking jacket *he's* wearing," he said to her. His father shruggged, feigning indifference.

"He saves it for special occasions," his mother said. "It's very becoming to him."

"I'm going to run up and shave," Matt said.

On the stairs he met Janie. She had done her long, dull-gold hair in the way his mother liked it, *not* with the dramatic part in the center the way she and he liked it best but parted on the side and brushed softly across her brow and low over her ears to an upsweep ratted effect on the back of her head. She looked old-fashioned, like some girl in a 1917 poster.

"Early bird," she said, as he came up toward her.

As they passed, he gave her hand a quick squeeze. "I must shave," he said, rubbing a hand upward over his cheek. "They wouldn't like it this way."

"Oh, must you?"

"I don't look civilized," he said. "I'll hurry."

"No, don't hurry. You're sure to cut yourself if you hurry."

"Worry-wart, I never cut myself," he said.

From the top of the stairs he heard her addressing his parents a good morning . . . It was wonderful being home. It was wonderful having his wife be so attentive to his parents, and his parents so admiring of Janie. It was fine having his parents enjoy the boys, and the boys and Janie enjoy his parents, and fine enjoying them himself the way a grown man ought to do.

He felt that everything was under control and that it was going to be a good visit. Once while he was shaving, in the bathroom, he saw his hand tremble slightly just before he was going to bring the razor up to his bristly throat. But he steadied the hand, and a little smile came upon his lips as he did so. He had already shaved around his mouth, and in the mirror above the lavatory he observed there was a certain cynicism in the smile. It was strange.

When he came down to breakfast, the others had already taken their places around the big dining table. They were all sipping at some kind of juice, but at his plate there was an orange and a fruit knife — as of old. His mother was watching his face, and he smiled at her appreciatively. There was also a box of cigars at his place. He picked up the box, examining it and reading the brand name, holding it gingerly in one hand as though trying to guess its weight. "I haven't had any of these in a long time," he said to his father, who pretended not to be listening. "I can't afford them." He took the box over to the sideboard, aware that his father was watching him, and put it down there. "You'll have to join me in one after breakfast," he said to his father.

"Not for me," the old man said. "Not any more."

Matt stood with his back to the room, looking down at the cigar box on the dark sideboard. Somehow his father's words held him there; he could not turn away. And suddenly a great wave of despair swept over him. It caught him completely off guard. He felt his heartbeat quicken beneath his shirt, and he realized that his shirt was soaked with what must be his own sweat. He placed his two hands on the sideboard as if bracing himself against another wave, which came on now with more fury than the first and which was not of despair but of some other emotion less easily or less willingly identified. It was like regret for lost opportunities, or nearly like that — but already it had passed and already still another wave was imminent. And then it came, the inevitable feeling that Janie had been right last night, and always, about what was happening inside him at these homecomings. His first impulse was to hurl the whole weight of his great good sense and reason against the flood of feeling, but the deeper wisdom of a longtime swimmer in these waters prevailed. He yielded a little to the feeling and let himself be carried out a certain distance, striving only to keep his head clear; and meanwhile he kept telling himself, warning himself, in big, easy strokes . . .

"What are you doing over there?" his father was saying now. Matt rummaged in his pocket for the small silver knife he always carried (mainly for the purpose of paring his nails). He opened the knife and began slitting the paper that sealed the cigar box. He did a very precise job of it, careful not to dig into the surface of the soft wood because he knew one of the boys would want the box. Presently he turned to the table with the lid of the box open and exhibited its fragrant, orderly contents. Everyone strained to see. The smaller boy stood up beside his chair and peered across the table. Apparently everyone took satisfaction from the symmetry of the cigars and the orderly way they were lined up inside the box.

Matt stepped toward his father and said, "Take one for after breakfast."

"I told you I've given up all that," his father said calmly, looking Matt in the eye. His father always sat very erect in his chair, especially at breakfast. And at that hour the old man's bald pate had a smoother, rosier look than it would have later in the day. His face stayed always the same, but by noon the top of his head would have a tired look.

"We'll see," Matt said, winking at his mother, and flipping the box lid closed. He had never felt more self-possessed.

But when he turned again and replaced the cigar box on the sideboard, he again found that something barred his rejoining the family group. This time there was no nonsense about waves sweeping over him or about keeping his eye on the shore. There was a different kind of nonsense: It seemed to him now that he had gone to that drugstore on purpose this morning, that he had planned the whole adventure before he ever left New York. It had been intended to satisfy some passing and unnamed need of his, but the adventure had cut too deep into his memory and into what was far more than mere memory. Inadvertently he had penetrated beyond all the good sense and reasonableness that made life seem worthwhile — or even tolerable. And through the breach, beyond, behind or beneath all this, he was now confronted by a thing that had a face and a will of its own. It was there threatening not only him and his father but the others too. Its threat was always present really, in him and in every man. It was in women too, no doubt, but they were so constituted that they never lost sight of it, were always on their guard, were dealing with it every moment of their lives.

Above the sideboard hung a dark still life done in oils. It was protected, in the fashion of an earlier day, by a rather thick pane of glass. Behind this glass a dead fish lay upon a maroon platter, and beside the platter were stretched two dead pheasants in full

plumage, their necks drooping over the edge of what seemed to be
the same sideboard that the picture hung above. They were not
very colorful pheasants, all dull browns and reds; and the leaden-
eyed fish, with its lusterless scales and its long tapering tail, bore
more resemblance to a dead rodent than to any game fish. He had
been at once fascinated and repelled by the picture as a child, then
when he was older he had come to despise its triteness, and later he
had learned to find it amusing. It had been painted by one of his
great-grandmothers, and like the mahogany sideboard was counted
among the family treasures. Suddenly now the limp tail of the dead
fish stiffened and moved! Or perhaps it was the neck of one of the
lifeless pheasants! . . . It was neither of course. The movement
had been the reflection of his own face as he lifted it. He was not
amused by the illusion. Momentarily the dim reflection of his face
in the glass, superimposed upon the dark, unreal fish and pheasants,
appeared to him as the very face of that Thing he had uncovered.
The dark face loomed large in the glass and it was a monstrous
obtrusion on the relatively bright scene that was reflected all around
it — the innocent scene at the breakfast table behind Matt. In the
glass he could see his mother nodding her head as she spoke. She
was saying that one of his brothers was going to stop by the house
to see them on his way to work this morning. And he heard Janie
asking whether that brother's oldest child was going to graduate
from high school this year. . . . How dearly he loved them all!
And how bitterly the Thing showing its face in the glass hated
them!

"Only out for a walk, eh?" his father was saying, just as though
Matt's back were not turned to the room. The tone was playfully
sententious. It was their old accustomed tone with each other. Matt
massaged his face, as if to transform his features before presenting
his face to the family. He reached into the cigar box and took out
one cigar for himself, then headed toward the empty chair beside
his mother.

"Yes, only out for a walk," he replied cheerfully. "And why not?"

"I don't know. You had a guilty look when you came in."

Matt was standing behind his chair at the table. Already he was
able to laugh inwardly about the business of the boogy man in the
glass. What nonsense! Perhaps it was a sign of age, letting a visit
home upset him so. The truth was, it wasn't just waking up in his

father's house and the visit to that drugstore. He had come to the
age where waking up anywhere but in his own apartment or in any
city but New York could throw him out of kilter. And he reflected
that ever since he could remember, his father had disliked sleeping
anywhere but in his own bed. It was very wise of the old man,
very wise.

As he was getting into his chair he heard the older boy say to his
grandfather, "Yes, he looked guilty all right. I noticed it."

"Yes, he sure did," added the younger boy.

"You two little parrots," Matt said fondly. And to his father he
said, "*They're* just *like* you."

Janie burst out laughing. He could feel her relief. And his
mother said, "You men."

Matt smiled at his father, waiting a moment before taking up
his napkin from the table. He was aware that his smile was the
same smile he had given his trembling hand upstairs.

"Just out for a walk, eh?" his father said again, childlike in the
pleasure he took from the attention his remark had drawn the first
time, and even more childlike in his effort to repeat or extend the
pleasure. But Matt knew he wouldn't pursue the subject further.
He felt that in a sense his father understood him better even than
Janie did. And the old man had his own way of communicating it.
Yes, it seemed to Matt that he and the man sitting at the head of
the table had long, long since reached an understanding and come
to terms with one another. Surely no one could say that either he
or his father had not made those adjustments and concessions that a
happy and successful life requires. They played at being father and
son still, played at quarreling still, but they had long ago absolved
each other of any guilt. They were free of all that. As two men,
they respected each other and enjoyed each other's company. All
the rest was nonsense!

Presently the conversation around the table became general.
Everyone chattered while they waited for the cook to come and
remove the fruit-juice glasses. The two boys were behaving extremely well with their grandparents, and Janie had never seemed
easier or more at home in the house of her in-laws. Everything was
going splendidly. Matt unfolded his napkin and stretched it across
his lap. He experienced an exhilarating sense of well-being. He
took up his fruit knife and began to peel his orange. He worked

with a steady hand, displaying consummate skill, and was conscious that everyone else was looking on admiringly while he performed the rite. As he peeled away at the orange, making the coarse rind come out in long curls like apple peels, it was as though he could already taste the fruit in his mouth. Yet when finally he had put down his knife he observed with satisfaction that there was nowhere a break on the thin, inner pellicle of the orange. His satisfaction was so complete, in fact, that he could not resist lifting up the piece of fruit — unscathed and whole — between the fingertips of his own hands for a general inspection. Then for a moment he sat looking over the orange and into the faces of his loved ones, and he did not wonder at their grateful smiles.

NICCOLÒ TUCCI

The Desert in the Oasis

(FROM THE NEW YORKER)

WHEN THE DESERT is born in the oasis, it is time to take leave, because silence is back and love is finished. When the lies that were used to keep solitude out of the bedrooms have been stuck into window frames and soaked with dampness, it is time to go home — because this is the end. But when the time comes to go home, there is no home, there is no time, there is nothing but a great desert everywhere.

The lovers know this very well, but neither dares be the first to say it. They wait, believing this is not happening to both at the same moment. They send out feelers. ("Do you love me?" "More than ever before.") And it is true. The heart of their love is still intact. And when disease creeps in, the heart will pump more strenuously to bring fresh blood and heat to organs that don't live any more, and be the last one to give up. The throbbing at the collar which enlivens the shirts of the dying is a symptom of this. Dying loves become feverish. They flare higher, people who watch them think they have just only begun, and this is what the lovers themselves want the whole world to believe, but they know very well it is not so, and they throw everything into it, still refusing to share this supreme secret with their partner; thus the first patches of desert become visible. Chairs and tables and beds, books and clothing, all go, one after the other, to feed that awful fire, and every time it ebbs, under mountains of smoke, there is less furniture, less clothing, and less friendliness; life becomes more and more impossible, until even the roof is gone. It rains inside the house. The neighbors know it. Beggars have more to give than these two millionaires, but they go on, they destroy one another and themselves, and even now the supreme secret is not told, until the whole oasis turns to cinders and stone. They have behaved like governments.

On a Saturday morning he set out for the oasis — Jacques's apartment, where they were in the habit of meeting. Jacques was such a good friend, he was always away, mostly in Paris, and before coming to New York he called, and when he came he often stayed at a hotel, so as not to desecrate someone else's oasis. Now all these precautions would be useless; to tell Jacques was almost like the official announcement of her death. He would write to Jacques tomorrow. Today he was going to the apartment only to remove his belongings and to burn all her letters, without touching the telephone. It would not take more than ten minutes to do this. He did not have to watch the letters burn. The fireplace was huge, the letters on thin paper. He would pour all the liquor he still had on the heap and let the orgy have itself; her written self and his lost self could burn together without witnesses. The apartment had, in recent weeks, become a tomb and a place of self-torture, where he spent a few hours or a few minutes every day, to hear the telephone not ring and to remember everything about her, and to imagine her elsewhere, in somebody else's arms.

But the moment he entered the door he heard the telephone. He had heard it from the end of the hall, and even from inside the elevator, without thinking for a moment that it might come from that place.

"Who is that?" he asked, angrily, into the mouthpiece.

"Darling . . . darling . . . How are you?"

"Very well, thank you."

"Are you angry?"

"Angry? How could I be?"

"Oh, thank God. Tell me you are not! But are you well?"

"Yes, very well. Why, what happened?"

"I thought you had been murdered. I thought something awful had happened. Oh, thank God you are safe! Thank God, thank God a thousand times! Thank God . . ." She began to cry.

"*Chérie*, what is it? Tell me."

"May I come?"

"Yes, of course you may come. What a silly question. Come at once."

It was exactly as in the old days; they had to do away in the first

seconds of their meeting with the void of their arms, the blindness
of their eyes, and they sniffed at each other for that good perfume
of cleanliness and health in which they each recognized a discreet touch of the other's identity, almost a guarantee of faithful-
ness: *You are all here and nowhere else.*

But these very good signs did not yield the expected results.
There was impatience in him, and she noticed it. She said, "*Chéri*,
please, let us talk. I had such a terrible night. Give me a sip of
whatever that is. I see you, too, needed a drink today, my poor
chéri . . . it was all my fault."

"Tell me what happened."

"Let me look at you first." She looked at him severely, drawing
two or three steps away from him and then studying him with her
head sidewise, as if he were a fur coat in a shop. "Do you realize
that if you were to die I would never be able to do *anything* for the
rest of my life?"

"That's very kind of you — or is it kind of me to stay alive?
Anyway, here I am, so come, lie down, put your head in my lap and
talk. What happened?"

"Yesterday afternoon he came to me and said, 'I don't want to
know anything about the distant past. I know enough. But you
told me, weeks ago, in the course of your many confessions, that
there was nothing now, and I want you to swear it.' I did . . .
Why do you look at me like that?"

"No, go ahead."

"I did, and he said, 'Thank you for your truthfulness. But now
he must be punished, because he slandered you. If he had told the
truth, it would be different.' 'What do you mean?' I asked, and he
said, 'You will learn it early enough — if not from me, from the
newspapers.' . . . I did not think he would do anything silly, because I knew he had several appointments that were urgent. But
then he didn't show up at the office, and his secretary called several
times. That was what frightened me. I thought what if he really
was out looking for you with a gun. I began calling you. I called
here forty-nine times in succession. Then my maid, who had seen
and heard everything, and who in the past had never dared speak a
word about you, said, 'Madame, I cannot bear to see you in such
a state. What about calling that other number? I shall call it for
you.' I would have wanted to say no, or to put her in her place,

but I confess that I no longer cared who was involved or disturbed at that point. I let her call and listened in from the extension. And this anguish of women, which had started with the voice of his secretary, working me up to a state of vague fear, then my maid worked up by *my* voice as I answered his secretary, and finally your wife alerted by the voice of my maid, who stood there like an arbiter, working on both of us who were so close to each other through this stranger — oh, I can't tell you what I suffered, and how tempted I was to break through this thin veil of absurd secrecy, plead with her to help me, and offer her my help . . . If I did not, it was through sheer self-control, and also partly out of superstition. Breaking that veil, it seemed to me, might mean the two of us mourning together over your corpse. So now you understand why at a certain point I told my maid to stop calling. The temptation was too great. Later on in the evening, my maid pleaded with me to let her try once more. I forbade her to touch the telephone."

"Well, that was very silly. If you had let her, you would have spared yourself a frightful night."

"Easily said. When a number has been so consistently inhuman with you, it should be changed. It has become the very essence of bad luck. I tried this number; I called here again. At least it still conveyed my question to this room, as a good number. And I called exactly one hundred and seventeen times, letting a few moments pass to allow my husband to call me or to allow you to get here. And this morning I finally got you here, thank God. Yes . . . this is you . . . safe, in good health . . . Thank God! Thank God! Thank God . . ."

Her trembling hands touched the contours of his face. Her wrists and then her thumbs came very near his lips several times. He could have kissed them by just turning his face one inch to the right or the left, but he preferred to wait, trusting time and in-difference for results, and, to keep his rising hopes from upsetting this cold calculation, he counted by fours until he reached seventy-two, but still there was no change in her face or in her movements. The same tenseness in her hands — they seemed, if anything, more stiff, barely touching his skin and repeating that gesture of worship. The same fixity in her eyes, the lips parted, and voiceless, still set in the groove of the same words: "Safe, in good health. Thank God! Thank God! Thank God!" — all of this, so much like himself in the last months, so much like her in previous years, and so true, so beautiful, and all brought about by the stupidity of that man, the same stupidity that had given him everything. What spontaneity, what guarantee was that? Could he thank *her*? Then why not him?

Oh, how he wished he could break loose from his inner counting self and let his worship melt with hers. The meeting of two worships would have melted the world. But no, he thought. When I was calling her two hundred times a night and she was nowhere to be found and then I told her the next day, where was her understanding then? And had that fool not tried his silly blackmail yesterday, where would she be today? Not in my arms, not worshipping my face like the image of Christ, but in some restaurant, or shopping, or just home, still refusing to see me. Oh, no. This time I shall be a spectator.

She went on worshipping his face and did not even ask to be admitted to the mysteries behind it. This infinite respect, which could pass for indifference, reminded him of home. It was irksome and wonderful. It made him grateful and suspicious. He understood the meaning of her old accusation: *There is no room for me in your love of me.* So, gently, imitating her voice, he said, "There is no room for me here," and she sprang to her feet.

"I am sorry, *chéri.* You were uncomfortable."

"Not at all. Come back here, you fool. I meant it differently. Or have you forgotten?"

"Oh . . . Oh . . . Oh-h-h, how stupid of me. But it is so long since I spoke those silly words."

"They were not silly at all."

"Yes, they were. I should have been contented with whatever I got."

"Which happened to be everything."

"But as you rightly said, speaking of other people's possessive generosity: 'Anything is better than Everything.'"

He laughed.

She pulled him by the hair and said, "I like you when you laugh. I don't like your tragic moods. They somewhat don't seem serious, but your laughter *is* serious — too much so for my own good. If I spent two more days with you in a cheerful mood, I would find myself in exactly the same spot where I was eight years ago, when it all began."

"And why not?"

"Are you insane?"

"What's wrong with that?" he said. But his cheerfulness was gone. He was now in the same pit of despair from which he had just rescued her. Now she could feel excused and watch him suffer. This was going to destroy all his good resolutions, and he saw that the only way out was to destroy every bit of desirability still lingering about her person. All of it must be burned in one great fire, not a speck must be left on which to build a future capital of love. In my wife's interest, he thought, but he knew this was a lie, because he already wanted much more than the destruction of the past; he wanted the whole future. He had been much too decent in the past, always yielding to sound arguments such as "You cannot do this to your wife, I cannot do it to my husband." But he now realized that he must bring about a new situation with entirely new reasons for her to trust him and to lie in his lap. The old reasons were out.

He sprang up from the couch and asked her, with an air of professional interest, "Tell me now, clearly and coldly — what do you intend to do when your husband comes home?"

This was an excellent move. It surprised her, and she seemed disappointed. To conceal it, she kissed him.

"This is what you are going to do to him?" he said mockingly. "I don't think he deserves it."

"No, but *you* do. Because you are my greatest friend. I had never expected you to be so understanding. I was quite resigned to a long scene, with tragic explanations that men are not made of wood, etc. You are the only clean person I know, and he is a mean, dishonest, sneaky, miserable little idiot. Now listen to me and tell me what you think." (As if the week before, in the same posture, in the same tone of voice, she had not said, "My husband is the only clean man I know . . .") "In my opinion, his saying this was pure blackmail. Don't you think so?"

He did. Pure blackmail of the type he himself could have tried. But he said nothing.

"Why don't you answer me? Or don't you agree?"

"Yes, I agree. I excuse him. He and I are alike."

"Nonsense. You were never so mean."

"Would you have said so a week ago?"

"Of course I would. Your scenes were never in bad taste. And besides, you had a right to make scenes and even to be mean, because I loved you."

"Love-*dddd?*"

"I still do. I always will. But what right does he have?"

"Besides, he has nothing to go on. Unless you told him something."

"I never told him anything about us."

"Not even weeks and weeks ago, when you decided to be frank with him?"

"Yes, I was frank with him, and I regret it. He certainly did not deserve it. Few men do. You are one of them."

She kissed him again, but a bit hurriedly. He noticed this, and managed to keep up the pretense of detachment.

"Try to remember exactly what you told him about us."

"I said we were very great friends. I admitted that I could have fallen in love with you, had it not been for the salutary memory of a frightening experience which took place years and years ago and which cured me forever of any such temptations."

"I see. Something of which not even I had been informed."

"Oh, it would not have been worth the effort. Ancient history, anyway."

"I see."

"Don't tell me this upsets you now, or I won't really know where to go for advice. *Chéri,* this happened long before I met my husband. Don't slip into your tragic mood again, please."

"No, no, I am not. I was just concentrating on your husband. Don't forget that this man still loves you and he is about to lose you. He is very unhappy."

"Come, don't try to defend him now. He is incapable of loving and of suffering. With him it is only hurt pride."

"This may well be the case, but hurt pride hurts. Come, let me ask you another question. Did he cry when you said, 'This is all ancient history'?"

"How do you know I said this? And how do you know he cried?"

"Intuition."

"You are a genius."

"No, I just observe things."

He began to count again. The temptation to take her in his arms was strong, but so was the memory of his recent errors of judgment, and he watched her shoulders and her neck for any signs of breaking down. She was struggling with her tears, and she must lose that struggle first. Her face was almost ugly from the effort.

"Tell me," she asked, in a faint and discouraged voice. "Why is it that I always hurt the people I love?"

The kindest thing he found to say was "You only hurt the people you don't love."

"Oh, but I do love him . . . in a way. Or I would never have married him."

"You are a bit confused, but so is everybody else."

"Am I not worse than the others?"

"N-n-n-no . . ."

"You must despise me very much."

"Not at all."

"The way you say that. Yes, you do. I am only good for pleasure." And she looked deep into his eyes from a great distance, and yet reading his thoughts as if she were inside him. A great pity for her, and with it the whole love of the world, upset and drowned his shameful calculations. He moved closer, with the courage of honesty. All he wanted to do was to pat her on the back and perhaps touch her cheek very lightly and paternally. She took his hand and kissed it, sitting down on the couch.

"Put your other hand here, behind my neck. Protect me against myself."

He did, and the telephone rang close to his hand, on the edge of the table behind her.

"Don't answer it," she said. "Who could that be?"

"My wife, perhaps. But I don't have to answer it."

"Your wife knows you come here?"

"I told her recently, in an impulse of . . . frankness, when it was no longer dangerous. I told her I came here sometimes alone, to work. I wanted to be able to tell some sort of truth, after so many lies."

The telephone kept ringing.

"But I don't think she ever would call. This might be Jacques, from Paris. Let me try. If it is from out of town, I shall answer it." He picked up the telephone.

The operator said, "Greenwich, Connecticut, calling Mr. Jacques d'Untel."

"He is not here."

"Operator," said a shaky voice. "Let me talk to the person who is answering the telephone." It was her husband.

Their faces touched again, only to share reception of that voice.

"I'm so glad I found you," the voice said. "I called Jacques because I know you are great friends. But I was really looking for you. I tried your home first, and your wife didn't know where or when I could reach you. I hope I didn't do anything wrong?"

"Of course not."

"That's very kind of you. I'm sorry to disturb you. May I speak?"

"Why, of course you may speak. I am all alone here."

"Oh, I see. And may I ask you a favor, even though I don't, ah, know you very well? If you . . . speak to my wife, would you . . . *not* tell her I called you?"

"Why, certainly I won't tell her. If I call her. I had no intention of doing so."

"You have not spoken to her yet?"

"No . . . not for the last . . . three days."

"So I may count on this? I have your promise?"

"Yes, you do."

"Thank you. And may I . . . see you for a moment?"

"Do you want to come here? Jacques is due back any moment. But we can go into another room."

"Oh. No . . . I'd rather . . . see you somewhere else. And don't tell him anything, either, if I may ask you again. I would prefer to have this remain something between you and me alone."

"Of course. I am sorry I mentioned it at all."

"No, you were very kind to invite me there. But I would rather meet you . . . let's say at the men's bar in the Waldorf? Or the Biltmore?"

"Wherever you say."

"I'm out of town. I don't know anything about trains. I came here yesterday. Let me find out. Would you . . . mind very much waiting for me to call you back in, let's say . . . five or . . . ten minutes?"

"Not at all. I can wait. Wouldn't you rather we met tomorrow?"

"No, no, it must be tonight, if you don't mind. I will call in a few minutes."

"Very well."

As he put down the receiver, she withdrew to the very end of the couch, as if to establish a clear space between them. "Poor boy . . . What horror. How I hate myself. And it was all my fault. You should never have let me come in here, never have put your arms around me . . . Do you think he heard me breathing? Was I careful enough?"

"I don't know, and I don't care. The problem is, what shall I tell him?"

"Deny everything!"

"Even if he heard you breathe?"

"Even if he had seen me here, you should!"

"How can I?"

"One always can. Just think of *him* for a moment, and not only of yourself. I can just see you with your best Dostoevski-like attitude, itching to tell. But I won't let you. You have no right to completely destroy another man for the egotistic pleasure of unburdening your conscience. Do you realize that, after what I have sworn to him, and after all the suffering I have already inflicted on him, he would lose the last bit of faith in humanity he may still have? You yourself were reproaching me only a minute ago, and now you want to do worse than I did."

"But look, I mean —"

"Look, nothing. Rather, do *not* look for an easy way out. Have the courage to stay what you are, and don't pamper yourself with undeserved forgiveness."

"But what if he has evidence?"

"There is no evidence that a denial cannot shake in the mind of a person in love. He will try to make you speak, because he wants to suffer now, that being the only thing he still can do in connection with me. It is his way of asserting his rights. But even if he should beg you on his knees to let him suffer, you will not give him the poison. Understand?"

"If you insist, all right."

"Insist? I *order* you to do as I tell you. And if you don't show real strength on this occasion, I shall hate you to the last breath of my life, and nothing in the world will make me forgive you."

"All right, all right. I still contend that he would suffer less if — "

"Whose husband is he — yours or mine?"

When the telephone rang again, she crouched, with her knees pressing on her eyes and both hands held tightly over her nose and mouth. The one ear that emerged from under a thick cloud of hair, to be close to the phone, was red with shame; she was a little girl, not a grown woman. And the two men were little boys; they spoke at such a high pitch of sincerity that they did not just make an appointment but they *pledged* one another to meet at seven-thirty, at the Ritz-Carlton bar on Forty-sixth and Madison and nowhere else, at seven-thirty sharp — as if that were high strategy in the noblest endeavor ever engaged in by two heroes.

"And remember — not a word to my wife."

"Count on me. Not a word."

"Seven-thirty."

"Seven-thirty, at the Ritz."

"Right. The Ritz."

When he hung up, her eyes emerged from behind those pale knees. "Why do you always have to exaggerate?" she asked. "Can't you be natural? This is exactly what I mean when I say that you cannot be trusted. If that is to be the tone of your meeting, it will take you exactly five minutes to spill everything! You can't be truthful when you tell a lie!"

"You said be natural . . ."

"Men are so stupid — all of them. A woman is always alone."

He apologized and wanted to console her, but she petrified him with a terrible look so charged with virtue that he apologized again and felt like a criminal.

And this time the door closed like the back cover of a book on his last hope to become truthful to himself, to save his work, and to get rid of her. As the noise of her steps receded in the corridor he turned and saw that it was not even noontime. Could he go back to his family now, for a walk with the children? They would enjoy it so. What a surprise to see him suddenly in a state of vacation, all theirs to play with or to work with, and his wife, grateful for this personal Saturday, would only accept it after trying to transform her peaceful working day and the children's playday into that ghastly jail of every moment, every movement, every noise, "to protect Father in his work." That was what made him decide not to go home. He had a clear image of her ready to receive him at the door with a huge bath towel in her arms, as she received the children from his hands after he gave them their evening bath. He could already hear her voice: "But are you sure you want to spend the day with us? Won't the children upset you? And if you suddenly should feel inclined to exchange a few words with other scholars, would it not be quite unrewarding to find only me here, busy as I am, ignorant as I am, utterly inadequate to give you what you need?"

As for spending the day where he was, that seemed the worst of all. There were books he could read, in fact — some of the same books he had at home, and at the library, reserved for him day after day. But what usually happened was that instead of availing himself of this excess of comfort — three sets of the same books waiting for him in his three whereabouts — he had three places in which to be ashamed that he wasted his talent like a fool. Why did she have to leave, now that she needed his last lie? He also needed hers, and for a better purpose than to prevent her husband from losing his last faith in humanity. She could have stayed and calmed him down, not by giving in to him — oh, no; on the contrary, by hooking their relationship on to some higher, if impossible, flagpole, like a tent that is lifted again on a new pole after the old one has been cut down. This alone could have lifted their passion from the flat goal of a bed and the blindest of senses. They could have made a deal; he could have said to her, "I'll protect you tonight by protecting your husband from despair, and you protect me now by protecting my wife from despair. If she understands that I am still unhappy, and torn by doubts, she, too, may lose all her faith in humanity. While if she sees me smiling and contented, this will be good for her, no matter what may have produced this state in me. She will never be curious. So now sit here in this corner and read while I sit there and read in that corner; then we can eat something together, and then perhaps go out and laugh — yes, laugh. This is my greatest need today. We may go to the movies, for example, even without holding hands, and rehearse my next lie, prepare for it as for a test in school, so that tonight I may remember: yes, today we were friends, excellent friends and nothing else. And extend this good truth to have it cover the whole past.

That is the way to serve your lies — a seven-layer cake of lies and truth, with a frosting of truth, and 'Happy Birthday' across it, written in more truth."

He called her up and told her. She was furious. "Is this all you could think of as an excuse not to do as I told you?"

"Not at all. I just meant it as a plan to bridge over these hours between now and seven-thirty."

"Oh, I see, you need company. But do you think that other people have nothing else to do than to keep you company?"

"I never said that. I only thought that it would make things easier. We don't have to meet here at all. I would much prefer that we go to the movies together."

"And if I had just made another engagement for the afternoon?"

"With whom?"

"What right have you to know?"

"Only an hour ago I had every right on earth."

"That was an hour ago."

"And two hours ago you were the most desperate woman in the world. Had you not found me here, where would you be now?"

"I am sorry, *chéri*. But I am apt to lose my temper these days."

"So am I, and forgive me."

"To tell you the truth, I feel exhausted and I wanted to stay home. Do you still love me a little bit?"

"Immensely so."

"Thank you. And what are you going to do?"

"Going to the library for the rest of the day."

"To work?"

"Yes, to work."

"You say that as if it were a curse. Your work is still the only thing that counts. I hope you can work. And don't hate me too much. And call me before *he* gets home tonight. And don't ruin him, please. Don't make him lose his last bit of faith in humanity."

"No, I won't."

He loved the library. It was to him a tiny concentration of insanity in that great island of insanity that is New York. In the library, at least, everyone was insane for his own private reasons, and these reasons were public in expression, in that no one was ashamed of exhibiting his manias or his elaborate idea of what constitutes a hat, a coat, a necktie, or a shirt, not to mention a pencil or a comfortable sitting posture, while outside everyone was insane in the same conformist and expressionless way.

There he sat, in a state of irritated somnolence, hoping that he might doze for a few minutes without being aroused by the usual attendant in charge of public dignity. It was five-thirty. He still had two full hours before meeting her husband at the Ritz. Faith in humanity, he thought. She is so self-effacing that she becomes identified with the whole world. What if her husband lost his faith in her alone? He could still have humanity as an object for his faith . . .

He made an effort and concentrated on the thoughts in his book, which had nothing to do with her and with her modesty or conceit, her lies, her truth, her husband, or her lover. He kept reading and reading, and all he could retain and whisper to himself was "Faith in humanity." Then came the struggle between headache and book, head and hands; the head was resting on the well-balanced scaffolding of hands and elbows, but the whole structure kept crumbling. My hands have no faith in humanity, he thought. This book is called "Faith in Humanity" . . . When he realized this, he protested in a very loud voice, "Faith in humanity, my foot!"

Several people said, "Sh-h-h," looking up from their reading. Somebody giggled. Others became more interested in him than in their books, and were now reading him from under the green lampshades on the library tables. He exhibited all the hate of which he was capable, to dismiss their tactless interest in one so empty and tired as he was. The little old woman who occupied the seat across from his had such a kind, sympathetic expression in her eyes that he almost apologized to her for his outburst. He tried to concentrate on the clock. She leaned over the table, concealing all her neatly written filing cards and her book, to whisper to him, "You seem rather upset. Could you tell me precisely what has shaken your faith in — "

"Sh-h-h!"

"Let's go out into the hall," she said, and he got up and followed her with pleasure, because that was at least a waste of time. Sitting there as he had been for the last two hours, he had wasted no time, but what a waste of hope, of love, of nervous energy, even perhaps of his precious virility, which could not find itself much strengthened by that agony of self-hate and contempt for the woman he loved.

"If you have no faith in humanity," the old woman continued

when they were outside the reading room, "then you simply cannot find enough energy to live — let alone read or study. Could you tell me what happened to — "

"Oh, nothing. Nothing at all. I have great faith in humanity."

"I am sure of that," she said, shaking her head and smiling up at him. "But still, something must have made you say that. I, too, have faith in humanity, and I have faith in you. May I ask what you are? A scholar, of course, but in what field? I see you at times with books of history, at times with poetry, at times with novels. What are you?"

"Do you really want to know? A liar," he said, and ran downstairs to the telephone booths and dialed her number. But it was busy. He tried a dozen times, then gave up, in great anguish, because it was past seven-thirty.

"Yes, gentlemen?" asked the waiter.

"Make mine Drambuie, double," said that poor devil slumped in his chair in the Ritz-Carlton bar with arms outstretched on the low table in front of him, as if ready for a manicure. "How about you?"

"Er . . ." He looked up at the waiter for help, unable to stand the sight of those suffering eyes in that pale, unshaven face before him.

"Same?" asked the waiter.

"No . . . er . . . What do I want?" And he kept thinking of the various drinks: arsenic, prussic acid, strychnine . . .

"Martini?" suggested the victim.

"No, not a Martini."

"Champagne *rosé*? You like champagne *rosé* . . ." (He is informed. And this is only the beginning.)

"No, no champagne *rosé* . . ."

"Cordon Rouge? Moët et Chandon? A highball?"

"No . . . a small cognac," he said to the waiter, and the well-informed husband added, "*Fine champagne* Rémy Martin. I am sorry to put you to all this trouble."

"No, no, it is for me to be sorry. I am late . . ."

"Never mind. Aaah. This has been one hell of a day."

"Trains crowded?"

"No. This was counter rush hour. I was coming in from the suburbs at six."

"Oh yes, of course . . ."

"I often wonder how can there be people who do this twice a day all their lives, on overcrowded trains. They come in every morning and go back every night — millions of them. How can they stand it? Not for me. I'd rather die than live like that. Waiter! Waiter? He can't hear me."

"Shall I — "

"Never mind, he will come. I shouldn't have too many all at once anyway. Well, I imagine you know all about yesterday."

"Yesterday?"

"Yes. All the foolish things I did."

"What foolish things?"

"Come on, don't play that game. I'm not a baby. Besides, you do know, because I told you so myself this morning, when I called you."

"You mean when you called me from out of town?"

"When else? I called you only once, didn't I?"

"No, you called twice, but you didn't mention any foolish things that you had done. All you said the first time was that you were out of town and didn't know about trains."

"Is that all I said? Are you sure?"

"Absolutely sure. I could swear to it. You may ask — " He stopped too late, and felt his ears grow purple while his victim watched him.

"I *may* ask who?"

"No one. I was thinking that Jacques had come back, but that was later."

"And you told him the whole story? After I had asked you to keep it to yourself?"

"No, no, no, I told him nothing. I just said someone had called. You remember you were trying to get him and not me?"

"But then I got you, and I asked you *specifically* if you were alone in the room."

"And I was."

"So you said. But do I know that you were?"

"I beg your pardon."

"Well, I have your word for it, but so I also thought I had for your keeping this a secret. And the first thing you do is go and tell your friend Jacques."

"Jacques knows nothing at all. *This* I can swear. In fact, I said to him, 'Someone just called you,' and at that moment I remembered that they had called me, so I said, 'Never mind, it was for me.' He was surprised, because this was a strange coincidence — that someone calling *him* to ask *him* about *me* should find me in his apartment. And I said to him, 'I not only can't speak, because this is a confidential matter, but even if I wanted to there is nothing I could tell you, because I don't know what this man wants from me.' Is that satisfactory?"

While waiting for his lie to go down into his victim, thick as it was, he put a hand to his neck to conceal the vibrations that his jugular vein was transmitting to his collar.

"So your friend Jacques knows nothing at all?"

"Shall I call him in your presence? You will hear him insist that I tell him what happened between us."

"*Between us?* Then he knows about *me.*"

"I tell you he does not. Shall I call him?"

"No, I believe you."

"Thank you so much. It's about time."

Fear of falling, after not having fallen, finds its natural outlet in righteous indignation. The two feelings cannot be told apart. And the victim gave in because he just could not afford to be particular. There was so much he still wanted to know.

"I am sorry," he said. "And my wife has not told you about yesterday?"

"You asked me not to speak to her."

"Only about my call. But I thought you'd spoken to her anyway, or that she had called you."

"No, she has not. I was not home all day."

"She . . . calls you at home?"

Now the fear was preventive, but the indignation just as righteous. "What *do* you mean? Of course she does, *when* she does, and she has *not* for a long time."

"Oh . . . I see. That surprises me a bit, if I may say so."

"Why?"

"Because . . . May I be frank?"

"What else? We did not meet here to be . . . less than frank."

"Right. I apologize. The reason it surprises me is that until quite recently — until yesterday morning, let's say — she seemed utterly unable to decide whether she should sneeze or not unless she had consulted with you first. How can she have lost confidence in you between one day and the next?"

This hurt immensely. It struck at the heart of his pain, and at the same time it felt soothing, for here was the one person in the world who still believed in his lost privilege.

"And how come you did not call her today? Or have you quarreled?"

"What a word to use. Lovers quarrel. Friends have disagreements. We had many in the course of our long friendship. But we never *quarreled,* as you say. I only called her much less frequently these last few months because I knew she had . . . difficulties, and I also felt that if she wanted my advice she knew where to reach me. Especially as I have always been most violently opposed to her ideas of independence — I mean her breaking up the family."

"I am glad to hear that from you directly. I had always suspected you were behind all this."

"Me? No, no, no, no. I could not have been more explicit in my advice against it. And I still believe that you should give it a new try."

"You really do? I'm afraid it's too late. Frankly, I don't know whether I would want it now. So you did not speak to her today?"

"I tried several times, but the line was always busy."

"I know. I tried her, too, and, in a way, I was pleased I could not reach her. Again I was suspecting you, but it must have been that fellow from Paris. You know him?"

"Yes, of course I do — Jacques."

"Jacques? But you said Jacques was in town. We were going to call him."

"*Of course!* How *stupid* of me! He arrived *this morning* from Paris. In fact, that is why I had gone to his apartment — to see him and to help him with some papers."

"Then it was *not* Jacques."

"Of course not. It must have been either Etienne or Robert."

"You are giving me all these names as if I knew. I don't know any of them. I only know that the person she mentioned was neither of these two."

"Impossible."

"She even said he was a friend of yours. Wait a moment. Perhaps it will come back to me."

"But I don't *want* to know! That is all utterly unimportant, and besides, it is her business. It seems to me that what the two of us are doing here is highly uncivilized . . ."

Here righteous indignation worked too well; the victim stared at him, then sat back with his eyes closed, and seemed about to faint.

"Are you ill?"

"No. You frightened me. For a moment I thought she was here. You spoke in her voice, the words were hers, and you even looked like her. My God! How can you do that?"

"I'm sorry, I was not aware of it. It is true, I am often told I have a gift for imitating voices, and, as I happened to be thinking of her reaction to all this, perhaps — "

"Never mind. You were right. I could not agree more. And I hope I have your word that this remains between us."

"But I gave it to you. Must I repeat it all the time?"

"No, no, I'm sorry, but you don't know what she's like when she flies into a temper."

"Don't I."

"Oh, you do? Why? Was she ever like that with you?"

"No, of course not, but I saw her — frequently, too. These tempers were never directed against me, I want you to understand, always against herself."

"Against *herself?*"

"Against herself."

"Not against *me?*"

"No. Only against herself."

"How strange. I never knew she had a conscience."

"Oh, she has, she most definitely has. And a very sensitive one."

"How many things you know about my wife that I don't know."

"Why, that is only natural. An outsider at times — "

"An outsider? Who is the outsider here? You have been inside her bones."

"Yes, but a stranger very often, like a confessor, who . . . It is an entirely different kind of relationship. Body and soul cannot always be relinquished together. One must be held back. Only in rare cases of great love, and a great love is rarer than a great violinist, a great painter . . ."

"I know, I know. These are her words, or perhaps they are yours. But, to be quite sincere, she held back her body from me, too. She was incapable of giving. . . . Am I being indiscreet? It seems to me there is no point in talking if we don't talk of everything. It hurts much less, you know. Tell me — why against herself? What was she doing to cause this feeling of regret, of repentance, that she had to show to you and not to me? You can speak freely, you know."

"Nothing that I could see."

"Yes, but . . . where did this take place? I am not trying to cross-question you, I am just trying to get an image of the person I have been living with for twelve years."

"Well, anywhere. At the public library, in a restaurant, over the telephone."

"Did she . . . just come and tell you? Did she cry?"

"I really don't remember. She was usually depressed. She felt . . . she had been very unfair to you."

"Oh, yes? To me? In what specific way?"

"In a number of ways. By sudden tempers. By ridiculing everything you did. By . . . not being appreciative enough, or helpful . . . or . . . I don't know what."

"She did not like the way she was behaving toward me? Is that what she said?"

"Yes."

"What a strange creature! And she never told me. . . . She certainly had reason to be ashamed of herself. . . . At times I did not know: Was this a stranger in my house? Was this my wife? Why did she have to antagonize me in everything I did, make me feel worthless, ignorant, and stupid . . . after having done everything for me, broken off with her friends, overcome the resistance of her family, extolled me as a God, imposed me upon them, made me feel that together she and I could conquer the whole world. And then, less than three months after we were married, she became a different person. This was years before you met her. When you came along, there was a marked improvement. At least she became interested in things again, and even with the children she became a real mother, which she had never been before. And she loved books and music, and she sang, and she went to museums and concerts. This lasted . . . quite a number of years, I should say. For which I am still grateful to you, even if yesterday — Waiter? Waiter? Two more here."

"Yesterday what?"

"Oh, never mind. I am ashamed of what I did."

"What did you do? Come, it is your turn to be frank now. I have done my bit."

"Yes, you have, I must say. I owe you a full confession. But before I begin, here come our drinks — let's give ourselves a little energy, for I at least will need it all tonight. And I don't care how long I keep you here. As for your wife, she can wait . . . Sorry, I was only joking. Am I detaining you?"

"Not at all."

"Don't you really want to call your wife and tell her you are detained by some important conference? This time it happens to be true. You should jump to take advantage of the occasion . . . I am joking again. But if you want to call, go ahead."

"No, I don't have to call."

"I must say you have trained her better than I did mine. Years ago, when *I* had to tell these lies, I got hell from her every time, even on those rare instances when I was being truthful. Well, let's drink, then. Here's to you."

They drank.

"I really do not hate you at all, even if I said so yesterday. Because I know that you have had a remarkable influence on her, through the contact with your mind, your ideas, your whole world, which has a value of its own. I am the first to admit it. I am not like those fellows who despise everything intellectual or artistic. Art has its place in the world, so has philosophy, so has poetry . . . Where would we be without them? Can you answer me that? . . . You won't answer my question. I know why. You think I'm drunk. Well, I'm not. I am only just beginning to see clearly. What made me black out yesterday was that I felt I had to know. That I had to or I would die. That I couldn't go on groping in the dark. Women don't understand that they can drive you insane . . ."

The listener was beginning to gulp down too much liquor for his own good. The temptation to confess was becoming too strong. And it would have been silly, after weathering such storms, to sink the ship a few minutes from the port of arrival. "Look, my friend," he said, and the victim wiped his first tear, smiled, and said, "I'm *looking*. Speak."

"I know very well what drove you insane with jealousy, because I am a few years older than you, and in my stormy life I have had some of the same experiences. As you know, she has confidence in me. Well, some time ago she told me exactly what had happened, and she regretted it so much that it was painful to watch her suffer. She destroyed your illusions of the past by confessing to things that had happened long ago and that were of no importance to her any more. But they still were to you. She . . ."

He could not go on, because the victim seemed amused — so much so that he began to laugh. "So you, too, now know all of her most intimate secrets."

"I'm sorry I mentioned this. I am very, very sorry indeed. And you can trust me to forget what I was told. But you must not let yourself be destroyed by her confession of old things. Those don't count. If she married you, she must have loved you, and — "

"Did she tell you all that? And you believed it? . . . See what a damn liar she is! She was trying to fool you, too. Now, she can do that to *you*, because you are up in the clouds with your art and stuff, but not to *me*. Oh, no. I won't buy it. What a bitch! Forgive me for using that word, but at times I could strangle her. To take advantage of a poor, innocent fellow like you — that's what I can't forgive. And did she say I was upset? Did she describe the pathetic scene as she alone can describe scenes? Did she? I want to know that. Just that. Come on. She did, didn't she? She said I cried bitterly?"

"What's wrong with that? Men do cry."

"I don't have to be told by you that she loved me at one time. She was mad about me. Trouble with her is she is not a grown person at all. She is sexually immature, and mentally even more so. She is full of complexes, she has no sense of reality, no sense of money, and she hasn't got a logical bone in her whole body, if you want to know the truth. I'm positive she is hiding something from me, and I decided I'd find out, no matter what it cost. And it has already damaged me a good deal in my work. Yesterday I fouled up four important appointments in my office trying to get her to confess about you. It would have cost me less in money, time, and energy had I come straight to you, instead of going the whole damned long roundabout way to discover in the end that you are even more of a fool than I am! Now tell me, frankly, man to man — are you in love with her?"

"No."

"And were you ever in the past?"

Over him weighed his pledge to her, like a huge gravestone, and inside him this torment, which perhaps could become a liberating force if concentrated only in one direction: upward, against the gravestone. "No, I don't think so. Let me explain. I have for her an affection such as I have almost never had for anyone before. I would do anything to see her happy and steady . . . I know she needs someone to guide her, someone she can obey and trust. And, of course, she needs affection — all women do. She is, in many ways, a child. And yet, in other ways, she is two thousand years old."

"A hell of a problem, in other words."

"All women are a hell of a problem. They adapt themselves instantly to the emotional climate of the times, because they are adaptable by nature. That is what makes them frigid in our age. Love in our world is out of fashion. Look at these women executives; they are harder than men — they have to be. But they are also living schools for homosexuals. They are effeminate instead of being feminine. Any adolescent coming near them is instinctively repelled and made to seek refuge in his own immature self, by the lack of affection and the weakness they exude. But they exude that which they were given. It is a vicious circle: violent men are weak, they breed weak women, who in turn become violent and destroy the upcoming generation. This, then, gives up even the initial violence, which has lost every function — "

"We have gone far afield."

"No, we have not. Now, for example, take your case. Had you, who are strong, aggressive, and intelligent, lived in an age when love was still in fashion, you would never have made such a mess of your marriage. To turn detective at the very last moment — and to what purpose? You would have recognized your rival from the very first day. You would have fought him openly in a tournament. You would have won, because you are more aggressive and also more athletic. This would have given you, together with the joys of triumph, the necessary ambition to achieve success in love, instead of only in your various industrial endeavors — " The exam had been brilliant. He could easily graduate *cum laude*. But the teacher was asleep.

"Aaah. I was not asleep at all, I heard everything you said. In fact, I could repeat the whole damn essay if I only applied myself. But I don't go in for essays much. I'm after facts. Did you ever sleep with her?"

"Of course not."

"Really, really, really? Cross your heart and may you die?"

"Cross my heart and may I die."

"Not even once?"

"Absolutely never!"

"Then . . . there was nothing."

"No, nothing."

There was a great sigh and then another. The prosecution was resting. In a tone of real glory came these words: "Well, that's too bad. You missed your chance. Perhaps with you it might have worked. You have so much in common with her, but so much. It's not only that you imitate her voice without knowing it; you are so alike in many, many ways that I would feel much better if I knew she was going to start a new life with someone who had a good influence on her, as you have. And then, I trust you instinctively. God knows what she is going to do, and who will influence her now. And then, she's in love with you."

"What nonsense. In the first place — "

"Yet me finish. As far as she is capable of real feelings, she is. And you are in love with her."

"But I told you I was not."

"Yes, you are. Anyone who can gulp down that kind of a sob story from a woman is either madly in love with her or he is a drooling Mongoloid idiot. You are far from being an idiot, so you must be in love. Very simple."

"I admit that there is a certain logic in your reasoning, but then I told you that I trust her immensely. I adore her, in fact. But between that and being in love there is quite a way. And besides, I am happily married, and I worship my wife . . . I would never think of leaving her and the children . . . Oh, no."

"These things happen, you know."

"Well, it has not happened here, this I do know," he said, and smiled to himself, lost in sweet thoughts of her and waiting for another crushing proof of his love.

"You know nothing at all. But it shows — "

"*What* shows? If there is *absolutely* nothing — " But he wouldn't say. Instead, he went on shaking his head and fumbling with his empty glass.

"Come, let's have another drink. Then before I let you go I must ask you just one more indiscreet question. It may shock you. You may decide to tell me a lie. But I am going to ask it all the same, whether you like it or not. Waiter? Waiter?"

"No, thank you, none for me."

"Well, I'll have one. Waiter! . . . One more double Drambuie for me." When the drink arrived, he said, "And now tell me — who is her lover? You must know, and I swear to you that I'll never let her know that I know. But I must know."

"She has no lover."

"Are you sure? And how about that Frenchman?"

"What Frenchman?"

"The one whose name I can't remember. But you know him. You even went with him, and with her, to Southampton for a long weekend almost a year ago. Or don't you know about that? You seem surprised. Are you surprised? You look awfully pale to me."

"Pale? Nonsense. I've had too many cognacs, that's all. But I remember that weekend very well. Only there were three French-men present, and also several other people. And the three were those whose names I mentioned before: Etienne, Robert, and Jacques."

"I see. And still, I am sure of one thing: the name she gave me was another one. And I just hate to be left in doubt."

"Sorry, but that is all I remember."

"On your honor."

"On my honor."

And to himself he said, with a mixture of infinite compassion and contempt, "It *is* hurt pride; she's right."

It seemed as if a whole crowd of people were rising from those two seats, one after the other, by twos: victim and executioner, teacher and pupil, investigator and suspect, prosecutor and crimi-nal, outgoing husband and outgoing lover. These two were the last ones to get up and leave. As they neared the bar, where now a new constellation of drinkers were nursing their glasses, these two self-conscious fools became suddenly friends.

"I'll stop here for a quick one before facing the storm," said the outgoing husband, as he motioned to the bartender. "Won't you join me, this time?"

"No," said the outgoing lover. "I had more than I could take."

"Well, I'm so glad we spoke. I hope we will stay friends. Let's have lunch one of these days, when things calm down."

"Yes, let's. I'll call you soon."

The outgoing lover was now faced with a problem of exit. He had holes in his socks and did not want to exhibit them on his way out. His shoes were old and quite loose on his feet. So he backed up until he reached the door, as one does in the presence of kings.

JESSAMYN WEST

The Picnickers

(FROM THE KENYON REVIEW)

IN THEIR BEDROOM under the roof, where Jess and Eliza slept, the July morning was already warm at 5.30. Though he hadn't roused her when he got up, Eliza knew before she opened her eyes that her husband was no longer beside her. She awakened slowly, listening . . . "What do I expect to hear?" she asked herself sleepily. The answer brought her awake with a start: gunfire. She had been listening, even in her sleep, for gunfire. Why, on a farm in southern Indiana . . . Then she remembered, all at once, not piece by piece. The whole of the day before crowded her mind. Yesterday there *had* been gunfire . . . and she and Jess had listened with their very veins . . . not out of any fear for themselves but because their eldest was off with the Home Guard, every one of his Quaker principles thrown to the wind, trying to save Vernon from Morgan, the raider.

As her memory of Josh and their fear for him came to her, Eliza threw back the already too warm sheet and hurried across the rag carpet to the windows. She felt thirsty for the reassurance of the known landscape, parched for it. The air outside the window was cooler than that inside the room and she leaned as far out as she dared, grateful for the freshness. Rolling summer fields, wheat yellow, corn green. Cows, already milked, standing switch-tail in the sycamore shade. Summer haze in the hollows mingling with morning mist off the Muscatatuck. Crows flapping by, early to work. An old hen, deceived by early warmth, letting off a premature midmorning cackle. A few Juneberries, escaped the children

by some miracle, hanging drawn and dried like summer raisins on
the Juneberry tree. Nothing changed. Nothing bearing the signs
of disaster. And there had been a disaster yesterday, had there not?

It was odd for Eliza to ask herself such a question. It showed
what the day before had done to her. You do not bear five children,
become a recorded Quaker minister, and survive twenty years as
Jess Birdwell's wife without knowing a disaster when you see it.
Yet she was uncertain as to the proper name for yesterday's hap-
pinings; yesterday, toward the end of the day, "picnic," instead of
"disaster," had seemed as good a name as any. Labe had found his
brother Josh, who, except for a head cracked in a fall over a cliff,
was none the worse for the wear. None the worse physically, anyway. Spiritually was another matter, for Josh was convinced that
by his warlike valor he had single-handed saved Vernon from the
enemy. And for any outward indication Jess believed the same.
Jess had welcomed his prodigal home with a few prayers and many
helpings of food. When she had rebuked Jess for giving Josh his
best horse to ride off to war on, Jess had quoted George Fox to her.
When Penn asked Fox what he should do, now that he had become
a Quaker, with the sword he was accustomed to wear, Fox had replied, "Wear it as long as thee can."

That quotation had been a mistake on Jess's part. "Fox didn't,"
Eliza reminded Jess, "*give* Penn the sword. Nor let him go off to
a real war with it, telling him to lop off heads and arms as long
as he could. That's what thee did, sending Josh off armed, on thy
fast horse."

This conversation had taken place before Josh's return. And it
had reminded both Jess and Eliza that lopping off was a two-way
street. What Josh could do, he could also suffer. And being the
boy he was, to suffer would more likely be his fate. Jess had turned
away, sick at heart, she knew. But she had let him go without a
word of comfort. There was no honest way for a Quaker to let his
son go off to fight, and at the same time be comfortable — and she
wasn't the woman to try to deceive any man, let alone Jess.

But after Josh's safe return Jess had become more and more
comfortable; and, when the children had finally gone to bed, every
one of them was in a war fever of some kind: Mattie, proud of
Gardiner Bent, her Methodist beau, who was a full-time soldier;
Labe, resisting soldiering but banged up from a private fistfight he

had won; Josh, with his cracked skull, evidence of his warlike courage; Little Jess, only eight, but in a swivet to land a blow somewhere on someone himself.

After the children were all asleep, she and Jess had stood on the back porch, breathing the cool and the peace of the evening. She, with two minds about the day's events: rejoicing in Josh's return, but downcast that he had gone at all; and Jess, for all of his talk of how bright the stars were and how well the peaches were ripening, was not, she could tell, completely easy in his mind either. Jess, when happy, never lacked for a subject for conversation, particularly late at night when everyone else was ready for sleep. But last night he had finally found nothing to say. And it was in this silence that he had heard the sounds down by the springhouse, and, investigating, had found the poor Southern boy.

Jess had carried him into the kitchen. The boy had been hurt several days earlier at Dutch Ford and since then had been hiding, living off the country and trying to catch up with Morgan. He had been trying to find something to eat in the springhouse when he had fallen down the steps and reopened his wound. It was this fall and the moans he had tried to stifle which Jess had heard. In the beginning the boy was in too much pain and too hungry to worry about being caught by the enemy. And after Jess had bound up his leg, and she had fed him, he was too worn out and too sleepy to care. They had half led, half carried him to the spare room, and, before Jess could get him undressed, he was already sound asleep.

The arrival of the rebel boy had done wonders for Jess's peace of mind. After he had put him to bed, Jess had become as talkative as ever, his qualms about the day's events washed away in the flood of his happiness at being able to care for one of the enemy. That proved, didn't it, that he was free of hate? Eliza didn't know what it proved. But Jess, cleaning up the kitchen after the bandaging and feeding, had hummed as carefree as if the morning's gunfire had been nothing more than the sounds of an Independence Day celebration. Or real gunfire, but of no consequence, because he *didn't* hate.

He had stuffed the last of the soiled bandages into the cookstove, and had momentarily paused in his humming. "I'll set some buckwheat batter for breakfast," he said. "We'll have a hungry crew on our hands in the morning. How about my bringing up a crock of sausage meat from the springhouse? Buckwheat cakes and sausage gravy? How's that strike thee, Eliza?"

It struck Eliza as something she had no heart for. If Jess was in a picnic mood, she couldn't stop him. But she couldn't pretend to share it, either. She went upstairs to bed leaving all the breakfast preparation to him.

These were the events of the day before. Thinking about them, it took her a half hour instead of ten minutes to dress. It was 6.00 when she came downstairs. When she opened the kitchen door she saw that the picnic mood of the day before was still in full swing. Jess, in one of her checkered aprons, motioned to her with the griddle-cake turner to come in and to be quiet. When she had closed the door behind her, he said, "No use rousing up all the others. Jimmy and Little Jess are keeping me busy as it is."

"Jimmy?" she asked, and Jess, like a schoolmaster with a backward pupil, pointed to the soldier boy.

Little Jess and Jimmy were seated at the end of the table next to the stove. The gravy bowl was already half empty and the sorghum molasses pitcher needed refilling.

"Good morning, boys," Eliza said.

Little Jess, who was in his own home, and besides had a mouthful of buckwheat cake and gravy, didn't reply. The boy, Jimmy, said, "Good morning, ma'am."

He looked worse to Eliza than he had the night before. In morning light she could see that the rising above his left temple was big as a turkey egg, but less solid, discolored and wobbly. She looked away quickly.

"I thought thee'd like to sleep late this morning," she told him.

"I'm out of the habit of sleeping after daylight." He appeared to think this over. "Out of the habit of sleeping, you might say. Anyway, I was hungrier than I was sleepy this morning, ma'am."

"Thee could've had thy breakfast in bed."

The boy looked at Eliza, amazed. "I ain't sick, ma'am." He had lifted his head quickly and the rising on his head trembled.

Eliza, courteously ignoring the ugly rising, motioned to his leg. "I been hit," he said, "but I ain't sick."

"Doesn't thy head hurt?" she couldn't help asking.

"I know that bump don't look nice, ma'am," he said, "but it's a real good sign. I got a shell splinter in there and it's working its

way out. It's just like a splinter in your thumb you can't dig out.
It's got to fester its way out. Don't cause me no pain. It did at
first, but it don't any more. My leg hurts. That's a good sign too,"
he said. "It's beginning to draw. That's a sign of healing."

"Did a doctor tell thee all this . . . about your head and leg?"
Eliza asked.

"Doctor?" He repeated what she had said as if she had spoken in
a foreign language. Then he understood. "I was with Morgan,
ma'am, and we been riding real hard. If you get hit, Morgan don't
get off his horse and fetch you to a doctor." Jimmy laughed, and
in spite of herself Eliza looked again at that soft-shelled, egg-shaped
rising. "No, not Morgan," he said quietly. "No, ma'am, you ain't
with Morgan for your health. That's a dead sure cinch."

Eliza didn't need any argument to convince her of that. If Jimmy
had ever had any health, he had lost it a long time ago. He was
rawboned, though the bones he had were small. Under his tan was
the yellow of fever. His blue eyes were back in his head like an
old man's. His hair, which in health had been black, was as dingy
and matted as an old worn-out buffalo robe. Eliza didn't know
where he got the energy to eat and talk as he was doing. From fever,
probably. But back of the courtesy and the conversation, the "yes,
ma'ams," and the apparent willingness to answer all questions, Eliza
saw a constant wariness. He was practising half-forgotten parlor
tricks. A sudden sound or movement and his sunken blue eyes were
hard as stones. The skin would tighten across his sharp little jaws.
Then he would go back to his eating, spooning sausage gravy onto
buckwheat cakes, like a mannerly fox or stoat.

"How old is thee, Jimmy?" Eliza asked.

"Nineteen." He saw her surprise. "I know I'm kind of runty,"
he admitted. "Two years with Morgan's kind of shook me down in
the saddle. A good thing. You ain't such a good target down
low." Then he laughed again and touched his forehead. "Sat up
too high once, though. I sure did."

"We'll get thee to a doctor this afternoon, Jimmy."

Jimmy, all fox now, put down his fork quickly. "No," he said,
"I don't need any doctor. I'll stay right here if it's all the same
to you."

Jess, who had been keeping the supply of griddle cakes coming,
intervened. "Eliza, I've got a cake here for thee."

"I'm not hungry," she said. "I'll bake while thee eats." She poured herself a cup of black coffee and managed it with one hand, the cake turner with the other.

At the table Jess began, and Jimmy unbelievably continued, to eat. Little Jess, a knife and fork winner himself in lesser company, gave up, pushed back his plate, and settled down to a steady stare at the Johnny Reb . . . a man, Eliza knew, Little Jess had expected to carry some sign of the nether regions upon him: a brimstone smell, or even horns. Maybe he thought that Jimmy's rising was horns beginning to sprout.

"Can thee give a Rebel yell?" Little Jess asked.

For a minute Eliza saw the boy thought Little Jess was making fun of him. Then he said, "Is that what you Yankees call it?"

"What do you Rebels call it?"

"We don't call ourselves Rebels."

Little Jess wasn't interested in the names for things. "Can thee give the yell?" he persisted.

"Sure," Jimmy said.

"Will thee give it now?"

"Now? No, it wouldn't be right, here in the house."

"Couldn't thee give a quiet Rebel yell?"

"You can't give that yell quiet . . . any more than you can shoot a quiet cannon."

This gave Little Jess ideas about an even more interesting subject. "Did thee ever . . ." he began; but Eliza stopped that question before he could finish it.

"Fill up the woodbox, Little Jess," she said. "Now, this minute."

Little Jess, no soldier, still knew a command when he heard it. He left the table promptly. Eliza, when Jimmy had finally pushed back his plate, urged him, if he wouldn't see a doctor, to go back to bed. But he refused to budge, too proud perhaps to show any weakness before his enemies. All his signs were good, he said again, head easy, wound drawing, belly tight as a drum. He tilted his chair against the wall and looked at her and Jess and the room: house, furniture, and civilians — all curious and faintly ridiculous to him after two years on a horse's back. He answered Jess's questions, though plainly puzzled by many, without hesitation. Jess wasn't as simple as Little Jess. Rebel yells didn't interest him, but Rebels did. Where was he from? What was he fighting for? He was from Plum Tree, South Carolina. And as to what he was fighting for, Eliza had heard the same story word for word from Josh a dozen times in the last two months: honor and freedom and self-preservation. The Mason-Dixon line hadn't changed that story a whit.

She cleared the table, washed the dishes, swept the floor around the two men. Jess lifted his feet to make way for the broom, but didn't pause in his talk. By midmorning she had fresh peach pies in the oven. The heat from the cookstove, which she was keeping fired up, would surely drive them out, she thought. Jess gave no sign of feeling it. He was making a day of it, celebrating something, peace or victory or Josh's return or the enemy made welcome. He was waiting for the surprise the children would have when they finally got up and saw who had spent the night with them. He was anticipating the love feast they'd all celebrate at dinner, North and South united around his table. Eliza, stringing green beans for a mess of succotash, listened to the talk and, through the opened window, to the summer sounds: the regular creak of the windmill and the papery ruffle of the big-leafed maples. Over the smell of the baking pies, she caught whiffs from the Prairie Rose now in full bloom, and, over that, all the mingling of scents of fruity ripenings from Jess's orchards. She could see the big cannonball clouds at the horizon and above them the arch of deep summer blue. Stretch her senses in every direction, there was nothing but felicity; nevertheless she could not manage happiness. Children at home and in health; enemy routed; Jess in high fettle. She counted her blessings; and, like women at weddings, had to squeeze back her tears, for at the heart of the tulle and the orange blossoms there is a core of sadness: and the fairer the bride, the higher the wedding cake, the greater the cause for sorrow; for life, which is going to contradict these things, will be, by contrast, the darker.

As if to tell her how silly tears were on such a day, she heard singing. The trees hid arrivals from her sight, but Little Jess brought in the news with his armload of wood.

"Enoch," he announced in great excitement, "is bringing home a prisoner."

Enoch was the Birdwell hired man and hadn't been, insofar as Eliza knew, mixed up with the fighting.

Jimmy, at the word "prisoner," brought his chair down on all four legs. Jess, stopping his talking to listen, said, "Mighty happy prisoner, sounds like."

Eliza, who could see the porch, said, "It's no prisoner. It's Clate Henry."

Eliza often thought Jess could have a hired hand a little less talkative and self-assured than Enoch. But Enoch came in now, meechin as you please, holding Clate Henry up with one hand and quieting him down with the other.

"You folks know Clate Henry, don't you?" Enoch asked. "From over Sand Creek way? He's been in the Guard for the last couple of days."

Clate Henry was a straw-colored, pudgy little man. Eliza didn't know a thing about guard duty, but she'd think twice before she'd give Clate a job of egg-hunting after dark. Clate sat down suddenly and looked surprised.

"What's the matter with him?" Eliza asked Enoch.

"He's a little under the weather at the minute," Enoch, as slick with words as Jess when he wanted to be, answered.

Clate, as if embarrassed by the silence which followed this, lifted his round face, shut his round eyes, and began to sing.

> *"Oh Lily up and Lily down*
> *And lay them on the side wheels."*

He delivered the two lines loudly but plaintively, then stopped suddenly as if he'd received an order.

There followed another silence, which Little Jess finally took care of. "That don't make sense," he said.

Ordinarily, Eliza would have rebuked Little Jess for such discourtesy. Under the circumstances it seemed a mild observation. She herself said, "Enoch, Clate Henry is drunk."

At the sound of his name Clate Henry roused up for an encore.

> *"Oh Lily up and Lily down*
> *And lay them on the side wheels."*

He kept his eyes shut; for a man as small, round, and pale as he was, he had a resounding voice.

"Is that all he knows?" Little Jess asked Enoch.

"No," Enoch said shortly, "it ain't." He turned, as if fearful that the question would refresh Clate's memory, to Clate himself. "Hush up, Clate," he said. "Hush up your noise."

Clate opened his eyes and looked at his friend as if he couldn't believe his ears. Eliza looked at Jess, waiting for him to take charge. Jess didn't say a word, he didn't make a sign. So she herself spoke.

"Enoch," she said, "thee knows I won't have a drunkard in the house."

"Clate ain't a drunkard, ma'am," Enoch protested. "He's a farmer and not used to fighting — or drinking either. If I turn him loose he'll just do himself harm. He was lost for the last two nights as it was."

"Lost? How could he be lost? He's lived around here all of his life."

Clate roused himself to answer Eliza. "The first night," he said, "I was lost because I was scared and running and hiding. Then somebody offered me a jug of corn likker to get me over being scared. From then on I was drunk *and* scared. But I was lost both nights. Where am I now?" he asked, looking around wildly.

Eliza would have nothing to do with such play-acting. "Thee knows where thee is, Clate Henry. This isn't the first time thee's been here. Thee's drunk."

There was no arguing with such a man. He agreed with, then enlarged upon, her accusation. "Drunk," he repeated. "Dead drunk and sick to boot. I ain't real stout, ma'am. Fleshy, but that's not the same. I've never slept out of my own bed a night in my life — let alone on the ground. There was a heavy dew the last two nights. I've got a weak chest. They say summer nights are short. They're long. Longer than any winter night I ever knowed."

Eliza didn't feel melted by his story. Her boy had been out those nights too; one of them spent at the bottom of a cliff with a cracked skull. *He* hadn't taken to corn likker.

"Why did thee join the Guard," she asked, "in the first place?"

"I didn't know my own nature, ma'am," Clate said sadly. "I wasn't prepared for what I'd see and hear. I wasn't prepared for the screeching."

"Screeching?" Eliza asked. "Josh didn't mention any screeching."

"He's deef then. Or calloused. Them Rebs kept up a-screeching like hoot owls fresh from hell. Excuse the bad language, ma'am. But they're bloodthirsty. They're white Comanches."

Without warning Clate Henry cut loose with a couple of terrible screeches. Hoot owls and Comanches would've turned tail at the racket he made. Eliza would never have guessed the pursy little fellow had such sounds in him. She felt as stunned as though he had struck her a blow.

Clate appeared well satisfied. "Bloodcurdling, ain't it?"

But Jimmy wasn't stunned and his blood wasn't curdled. He leaned forward in his chair, his rising livid. "That's no Rebel yell," he said.

"How do you know?" Clate asked.

"He's a Rebel," Little Jess said. "That's how he knows."

Clate stared at Jimmy for a few seconds; then he closed his eyes and began once again to sing.

> "Oh Lily up and Lily down
> And lay them on the side wheels
> And everytime the wheel goes round . . ."

Enoch took his friend by the shoulders and shook him out of harmonizing. "What he needs," he told Eliza, "is a pot of strong coffee, hot and black. Hush up," he told Clate, who was showing signs of continued melody.

Before Eliza could get the pot on the stove, Clate had collapsed, head on his arms and arms on the table. At that minute Labe, still tucking his shirt in his pants, appeared in the doorway, blinking around at everyone sleepily.

"A diller-a-dollar, a ten o'clock scholar," Jess greeted him.

Labe smiled. It was no trick to make Labe smile. He had a mop of curly tow-colored hair, a black eye, and a dingy unwashed look. He was big-framed, man-sized, but his seventeen-year-old face showed that he hadn't met any man-sized troubles yet.

"I thought I heard something," he said.

"If thee's up," Jess said, "thee heard something."

"It was a Rebel yell," Little Jess said.

"No," said Jimmy.

"Who's he?" Labe asked, staring at Jimmy.

"A Rebel," Little Jess said proudly.

"He give that yell?"

"No," said Jimmy.

"Where'd he come from?"

"He come from falling down our springhouse steps."

Labe was much too polite a boy to say, "What was he doing on our springhouse steps?" Instead, taking in head and leg, he said, "Must've been a pretty bad fall."

"He got *them* in the war," Little Jess explained. "He's one of Morgan's men."

"*Was* one of them," Enoch corrected him.

"Am," Jimmy said. "I'll catch up with him. Men are away a month and catch up. I've only been away a week."

"And every time the wheels go round . . ." Clate muttered.

Labe turned his attention to Clate's collapsed figure. "Who's he?"

"Home Guard," Little Jess replied promptly.

"That's Clate Henry from out Sand Creek way," Jess told him. "You've seen him before."

Clate moaned or snored. "What's the matter with him?" Labe asked. "He hurt too?"

Little Jess was happy to give him the answer. "He's soused," he said.

With that word Eliza ended the picnic. Picnic was one thing, but circus was another. She was not going to have a circus in her kitchen. Drunkenness was no subject for fun. Wars, simply because they had moved from your neighborhood to someone else's, were no cause for rejoicing. Under her roof were three men who had been ready to kill: Josh, spared that evil by falling over a cliff, Clate saved by cowardice, and Jimmy maybe not saved at all. If you wanted a picture of war and death, she thought, take Jimmy. His own mother, like as not, wouldn't recognize him. He had shed his humanness. He was shrunk down to bullet size. He carried a thing on his head that looked like the grave. The bones of his head were saved by the thinnest of coverings from being a skull. Yet he was a boy. She tried to find in the back of his sunken eyes the boy he had been, before he rode off with Morgan. She turned on him every bit of motherliness and love she had. She had as well said "son" to a rock. She was an enemy, a part of a household whose people had been out to kill him and who called him "Reb."

"Get out of my kitchen," she said to all of them but Jimmy. Jess turned to her in surprise, but she cut him off before he could say a word. "I need the room for cooking."

It wasn't true. She could cook in a nest of them. Rebelling against ugliness and blindness, she had lied. So far as she knew, none of them was a liar.

"It's not true," she said. "You're not in my way."

But Jess herded them out. She and Jess were as divided as the states, and she let him go without attempting to explain. Jimmy rose with the rest of them, but some weakness in head or leg made him hang onto the chair back. Outside, Eliza could see the others settling down in the side garden where there was a lawn swing and a hammock slung between two cedars. There, on the hottest days, the air in the clumps of cedar needles moved with a mountainy sound and smell. Clate was singing again. The picnic was not much interrupted.

Eliza did not make the mistake of saying "bed" again to Jimmy. "If thee stayed inside, thee might help me later," she told him. "Come on into the dining room. Thee'll be out of my way and handy for table setting later."

She went to him but didn't offer to help him. A pulse was beating in his rising like a misplaced heart.

"This way," she said, and went, without looking behind her, into the dining room which opened out of the kitchen. It was a long narrow room, papered green, and dark now with blinds pulled to keep out the sun and discourage flies.

She turned and Jimmy was on her heels. "Thee can sit there," she said, pointing to a narrow black leather lounge with a built-in hump at one end to support the head. She said "sit," but no one could sit on that narrow leather thing and Jimmy, once seated, lay back against the bulge of the built-in pillow.

"You let me know if there's anything I can do to help you," Jimmy said, as if this readiness excused his stretching out.

"I will," Eliza said.

The voices of the picnickers could be heard. "I hope you didn't think that yipping was the real thing," Jimmy called to her.

"It scared me," Eliza said, "I suppose that's what it's supposed to do."

"No," Jimmy said. "We ain't trying to scare anybody." In the gloom Eliza could see the little fox skull part at the mouth, and yellow teeth, whiter than yellow skin, show in a smile. "We don't need to, once they know Morgan's around."

"Why do you do it, then?" Eliza asked.

"We do it," Jimmy said, "because it's what we feel like doing. We feel better doing it."

He would've talked more about it; Eliza, however, didn't want to hear any more about it. She went back to her work, but Jimmy called after her, "That's why I wouldn't do it. You can't do it except *then*."

"Then" was what Eliza wanted to forget. She went upstairs and wakened Josh and Mattie. Josh came down to breakfast, his shame at blundering over a cliff less, and his pride in being one of the defenders greater. Fear had sent Josh toward the enemy and Clate Henry away from them. But fear was the master of both. Mattie came downstairs, hung uneating over her cakes, her throat too thick with worry about Gardiner Bent to swallow.

"There's a wounded Southern boy in the dining room," Eliza told her children. "He's lost from Morgan. He stumbled in here last night. Maybe you'd like to talk to him."

Neither one wanted to. Josh felt embarrassed at the idea of sitting down and talking to someone he'd spent a couple of months screwing up his courage to take a shot at. He felt funny enough already, falling over a cliff, without finding out that he'd taken all of his trouble and done all of his shaking because of some poor, starved, done-in, bunged-up Johnny. This was the very reason Eliza wanted him to see the boy. It would take some of the false pride out of his sails; make him see how big Goliath really was, this poor boy of bones and festerings. But Josh wouldn't budge. He didn't want to see any Rebs who weren't fire-eaters. And Mattie wouldn't go either.

"If Gard gets home safe," she said, "I'll see him."

"All right," Eliza said. "Outside, both of you. Out with the picnickers."

"Picnickers?" Mattie asked.

"Look," Eliza said, and she pointed to the side garden. There they were, spread around under the cedars amid the phlox and the snowball bushes, the lawn swing creaking, the hammock swaying. "What's thy name for them?"

Josh looked at his mother and left. Mattie put a hand on her mother's arm. "Come on out, Mama," she urged. "Isn't thee glad Josh is home? And that Vernon's saved from Morgan?"

"Morgan's in some other town today."

"But, Mama, thee can't be sad for every town in the county."

"I don't know why not," Eliza said.

There was sorrow in her, though whether enough for every town in the county she wasn't sure. But she didn't want to make any big claims. Mattie made a pitcher of lemonade and took it outside, but Eliza stayed in her kitchen working, halfway between Jimmy and the picnic — able to see one and talk to the other. She took her pies out of the oven and put her light bread in. She scoured the case knives with brick dust and scalded all the milk pans and put them in the sun to sweeten. Blackbirds were at the cherries. White butterflies hovered over the little cabbage heads. The Dominique rooster's colors were faded in the heat. She picked enough Summer Sweetings for a dish of applesauce.

Little Jess came in for more lemonade. When she made it, he said, "Can I take a glass to Jimmy?"

Eliza poured the glass. "If he's asleep, let him sleep. He needs that more than lemonade."

Little Jess tiptoed in and Jimmy must have been awake.

"I brought thee a glass of lemonade."

There was a silence followed by, "Does thee want another?"

"Why do you folks say 'thee'?" Jimmy asked.

"We're Quakers."

"What's Quakers?"

"A church."

"Like Baptists?"

"Is thee a Baptist?"

"Yes."

"We don't believe in being baptized."

"What do you believe in?"

Eliza waited.

"God."

"So do Baptists. You're no different from us."

"We're different," Little Jess said. "We don't believe in fighting."

Jimmy hooted. "Who don't? Your Mama?"

"Father don't."

"He didn't keep his son home from fighting."

"Labe don't believe in it."

"How'd he get that black eye?"

"That was a private fight, not war."

"What was your hired man doing?"

"Saving Vernon from Morgan."

"Same as me. Saving the South from the Yanks. If I say 'thee'

I reckon I'll be a Quaker. Little Jess, will thee bring me some more lemonade?"

Little Jess brought the glass out to Eliza to be refilled. "He said 'thee' to me," he complained.

Eliza was short with him. "He can if he wants to," she said.

After Little Jess went outside with his lemonade, Eliza took a piece of warm peach pie in to Jimmy. The boy was lying back, flat as the hump would let him, one hand picking at the nub of the rag carpet. "I'm too full of lemonade — to eat any more right now," he said.

Eliza shooed a couple of big black flies away from him.

"Those buzzards have smelled me out," he said.

"It's my pie they smell," Eliza said. She apologized to him. "I'm sorry thee had to get in a house that's so mixed up with the war."

"That's what you got to expect in wartime, ma'am."

"Not in a Quaker house," she said.

She decided to give the family their dinner outside. It was hotter out there and succotash, light bread, and peach pie could've been served easier at a table. But if she set the table Jimmy would get up and she didn't want to disturb him. Besides, in serving the meal picnic style there'd be so much running back and forth and waiting on, she'd have an excuse not to sit down with them — and no excuse to make, either, for not doing so. She was disturbed by her reluctance to break bread with her own family — but she had it; and once they were attended to she sat down with Jimmy.

"You got some kind of an old rag I could have?" Jimmy asked. "This here thing's begun to run."

She brought him clean cloths, saved from worn-out pillow shams, and would've brought him a basin and water too, but he wouldn't hear to it. "Don't want to get in the habit of washing again," he said. "I'd just have to break it. I'll be well in no time now, soon as the corruption drains off. That's what's been making me dauncey. It's been poisoning my system."

There was a smell now and Eliza would've liked to shut it away from her kitchen. "Does my clattering out here bother thee, Jimmy? Could thee doze, if I closed the door?"

"No, ma'am," he said. "Leave it open. It sounds good. I ain't heard anybody stirring around in a kitchen for quite a spell."

After a while he called to her, "What's that click-clack I hear?"

Eliza went to the dining room door. "That's the windmill," she said.

"I don't feel any wind moving."

"The windmill catches it when we can't feel it."

As they listened to the windmill, the voices of those on the side lawn came through the opened window — still eager and rejoicing in midafternoon, recalling each incident, real or reported, of Morgan's routing.

"They sound happy," Jimmy said. "All safe at home and happy."

"Yes," Eliza said.

"Like a party."

"That's what it sounds like."

"I could watch your cooking if you want to set outside for a spell."

She felt more at home with Jimmy, with his wounds and dirt and bad smell, than with those high-spirited ones out there.

"No," she said. "I feel like cooking this afternoon."

"What's for supper?" Jimmy asked.

"What strikes thy fancy?"

"Corn bread," Jimmy said, "greens, and custard pie."

"This time of year, I can't manage greens, but the corn bread and custard pie I can."

"I forgot what time of year it was," Jimmy said.

She was glad for the need of cooking, of keeping the stove going, of stirring and peeling, mixing and washing. Sometimes she stood at the back door and looked at the view which for twenty years had sustained her as much as food. Jess was in it. Jess had made it, except for the rise and dip of hills beyond the farm's boundaries. Apple orchard, berry patch, vegetable garden, snowball bushes and syringa, and a graveled path edged with bleeding heart and sweet alyssum. She couldn't joy in what she saw without taking joy in Jess too. Maybe what made Jess such a good nurseryman made him a man not easily separated from the joy of others — even when they were wrong. When she wasn't with Jess, she imagined conversations with him. Now she could hear him in defense of himself quoting more George Fox to her; reminding her of the time when George, no smoker, had put a proffered pipe in his mouth to show "he had unity with all creation." "That's all I'm doing, Eliza," she could hear him say, "out here with the returned warriors showing them I have unity with all creation." In her imagined conversation she was able to have, what wasn't always so easy when she was face to face with Jess, the last word. "What thee's showing them thee has, Jess Birdwell, is unity with all destruction."

She felt better after that, the way Jimmy said he did after he gave the yell. It wasn't said to put Jess in his place; but it did tell her something about hers. Behind her, the kitchen clock struck 5.00. The afternoon was ending. A wind out of the southeast had sprung up, changing the windmill's tune and spattering the pathway with the green-white litter of broken snowball blossoms. Away off westward past Jess's handiwork, where the joining of Sand Creek and the Muscatatuck showed in a thicker mounding of sycamore green, the sky was murky, gray-yellow, like some old fire-opal in need of a cleaning. The wind which was turning the windmill, scattering the petals, banking the clouds was strong enough to feel now. Eliza turned back the collar of her gray dress—but there was no refreshment in warm sultry air.

It must've been around 5.30 when Gardiner Bent trotted into the yard, tied his lathered horse at the upping block, and got a hero's welcome from everyone on the side lawn.

Mattie flew into the house for more lemonade and to ask if Gard could stay for supper.

"Won't he want to go home to his own folks?"

"He's been there already."

"It'll make quite a crowd."

"That Clate Henry won't want anything to eat. He's been sick and now he's asleep."

"He'll wake up the hungriest of all."

"Please, Mama. I'll help."

"I don't need help," Eliza said. "Tell Gard he's welcome. Everyone else is. I don't see why we should draw the line at him."

Mattie turned to go, then stopped. "How's the boy?"

"Don't pretend thee's given him a thought all afternoon."

"I haven't," Mattie said. "I'm not pretending. It was Gard I was thinking about. This boy might take it in his head that he ought to keep on fighting."

"No matter what he takes in his head," Eliza said, "he's too sick to fight. Thee just see to it that Gard stays peaceable and we'll have nothing to worry about."

One outdoor meal a day, Eliza decided, was enough. She was not going to carry fried chicken, mashed potatoes, corn bread, and custard pie outdoors. She'd have a sit-down meal at the table. But instead of moving Jimmy upstairs to the spare room—where he'd be shut away from everything (and refuse to go, anyway, probably) — she'd move him out to Enoch's room. That was only a step away, off the kitchen, a part of the porch roofed over and sided up. It was nothing but a hired man's room. Nothing fancy, but Jimmy wasn't in shape or practice for enjoying anything fancy.

He surprised her by being perfectly willing to move. He sat up, holding the cloths she had given him wadded against his head.

"Who was that rode in a while back?"

"A neighbor boy," Eliza told him.

"He had on a uniform."

"He's a soldier," Eliza admitted.

"He's a Quaker, too?"

"No," Eliza said, "he's a Methodist."

"I reckon it don't make much difference," Jimmy said.

Jimmy followed through the kitchen, across the back porch, and into Enoch's room. He walked as if the floor under his feet were uneven, and as if Enoch's door shifted from left to right. But he was in good spirits. When he saw the custard pies lined up to cool he said, "If some of them turn up missing you'll know where to look for them."

Eliza, after she had settled him unresisting on to Enoch's bed, brought him a half-pie on a plate, and a supply of clean rags.

"Thank you, Mama," he said.

Eliza was at first pleased; then, after she went back to her work in the kitchen, puzzled. Had he spoken jokingly — or in a minute of lightheadedness did he think he was back in Plum Tree with his own mother? But she was too busy frying chicken with one hand and mixing a batch of corn bread with the other to worry about it.

Jimmy asked to be excused from going to the supper table. "I ain't a very pretty sight for eaters. Besides, I spoiled my appetite with pie."

Eliza was glad he felt that way. Apart from his looks and his smell, something might be said he would take exception to.

She got them all down to the supper table before lamplighing time, all hungry after the pick-up dinner, the fighting, and the talk of fighting; and Clate Henry, just as she'd guessed, was the hungriest of them all. Eliza served them like a woman working in a stranger's house. She knew that this day of estrangement would pass; that it signified nothing but the dying down in her of a spirit of perfect sympathy which would rise again and would embrace them all. But she accepted the lull and the separation, fought neither it nor them — and moved back and forth silently with platters and pitchers to be refilled.

She had brought the supper plates from the table and gone to the porch for the pies when she saw Jimmy — who had seen her first — standing on the steps below her, immovable. He had the rations bag he'd arrived with over his shoulder, and one side of his face, for all that he had tied up his head with a bandage torn from one of her pillow shams, was covered with the bloody outpouring from his rising.

"Jimmy," she said, "what's thee doing?"

Jimmy didn't stop to argue. He hurried down the step in his hobbling, stiff-legged gait.

"Jimmy, thee's not fit to travel."

Fit or not, he traveled, his gait uneven, his hands to his head as if afraid it might, in spite of the bandage, split open. He took off down the pathway littered with the false snow, under the green-yellow Summer Sweetings, heading for the main road. He was running, but weaving and stumbling as he ran.

"Jimmy," Eliza called, "Jimmy, let me help thee."

With skirts lifted she was far fleeter footed than he. He barely missed trees, stumbled over hummocks of grass, lost his bandage and kept going.

At last Eliza understood that he was running away from *her* and stopped. "Jimmy," she called. "I'm not following."

It was too late. The boy tripped, fell over, and lay where he had fallen. When Eliza reached him, he struggled to sit up and Eliza, kneeling beside him, supported him. Half of his head seemed to have fallen away. From the brain-deep cavity where his rising had been, blood and pus covered his face. Eliza cradled his head against her shoulder and rocked him a little before it occurred to her that this might be bad for him.

He appeared to be trying to say something. An indistinguishable sound filled his throat and Eliza thought, when no words took shape, that he might be trying to give that yell, the one he believed the others had mismanaged and that made him feel good. She hoped he could do it. But it wasn't a yell he had in mind. He said perfectly clear and quiet, "Be good to Jimmy," and underneath the blood he closed his own eyes.

Eliza sat flat on the ground under the apple trees with the boy in her arms. She felt guilty, as if she had killed him herself. Not by running after him, which might have hurried things — but no more than that. But because when the others came down from the house, as they would in a few minutes, and found her here with the boy dead in her arms, he would say to them what she had been saying all day, "Don't rejoice so much." And they would listen to him as they hadn't to her. He would be her "I told you so." With all her heart she wished him a live boy and no sign. But he was both: a boy and a sign and she couldn't separate them — and shouldn't try. Whatever message he had for those who found him, he had earned the right to say.

Biographical Notes

U. S. ANDERSEN was born in Portland, Oregon. His parents, who had been born in Norway, liked the United States so well that they gave him its initials. A Stanford graduate, he has played professional football, gone around the world on a merchant ship, and served on a destroyer in the Second World War. Mr. Andersen has worked in advertising and in the oil business, and currently teaches a course of his own creation, Psycho-Ontology. Married, with four children, he has published three non-fiction works and three novels, and his short stories have appeared in *Esquire* and *The Saturday Evening Post*.

H. W. BLATTNER was born of Swiss parents in Buenos Aires. As a child she lived in New York, in Havana, Cuba, and in Switzerland. As a result, she speaks, reads, and writes German and Spanish, is competent in French, and speaks the German-Swiss dialect. Married to an American, she and her husband have lived in California since 1941, where she works as a secretary.

JOHN STEWART CARTER was born in Chicago, and still lives next door to the house in which he was brought up. He attended Northwestern and Harvard Universities, and received a Ph.D. from the University of Chicago. Except for a four-year stint as a lieutenant in the Navy, one year's research under a Ford Foundation grant, and a year's leave as Fulbright Professor of American Literature at the University of Teheran, he has spent all his professional life at Chicago Teachers College, where he is a professor of English. Married, with two daughters, his poetry appears frequently in "little" magazines, and he has contributed to *The New Republic*. "The Keyhole Eye" is the first of three stories with the same narrator, of which two stories are complete.

JOHN CHEEVER was born in Quincy, Massachusetts, in 1912, received his only formal education at Thayer Academy, served four years in the army, and has published one novel and three collections of stories. A second novel, *The Wapshot Scandal*, which includes a scene from "A Vision of the World," will be published in January. He lives with his wife and three children in an old farmhouse in the Hudson Valley.

CECIL DAWKINS was born in 1927 in Birmingham, Alabama. She was graduated from the University of Alabama, and received an M.A. in English Literature from Stanford University. In 1952–53, she was awarded a Stanford Writing Fellowship. Miss Dawkins taught for four years at Stephens College in Missouri, and her stories have appeared in *Pacific Spectator*, *The Sewanee Review*, *The Paris Review*, *Southwest Review*, *Charm*, *The Saturday Evening Post*, and *The Georgia Review*. A collection of her stories is being published this year in New York and London. Miss Dawkins lives presently in Riverdale, New York.

GEORGE DICKERSON was born in Topeka, Kansas, in 1933. He graduated from Yale, and did one year of graduate study in English at Columbia University. Presently managing editor of *Cavalier* Magazine, Mr. Dickerson has worked on the editorial staffs of *The New Yorker* and The Macmillan Publishing Company. He has also worked as a producer for a feature film, put out a newspaper on a transatlantic liner, "sweated it out in various factories, construction jobs, and in an insurance company," and taught prep school in Vermont. Never having lived in one place for more than two years, he now considers New York his home. His short stories and selections from two novels have appeared in Voices and in Phoenix. A one-act play may be produced on off-Broadway in the fall of 1963.

MAY DIKEMAN was born in Baldwin, Long Island, majored in painting at the High School of Music and Art, and was graduated from Vassar, where she encountered the strongest direct writing influence in John Malcolm Brinnin. In 1961 she was given the Atlantic First Award for her short story "The Tender Mercies." Other stories have appeared in Harper's, and an early novel, The Pike, was published in 1954. Now finishing a second novel, she lives in New York City with her three children.

STANLEY ELKIN was born in New York City and raised and educated in Chicago. He attended the University of Illinois "for seven hundred years and received at its hands a Bachelor's, Master's and Ph.D. degree in English." He has taught English at Illinois and is now an Assistant Professor at Washington University in St. Louis. His stories have appeared in Epoch, Views, Perspectives, Accent, Chicago Review, and Southwest Review. Two years ago he received a Longview Foundation Award for two of his stories, "Among the Witnesses," and "In the Alley." He and his wife and son have spent the past year in Rome, where Mr. Elkin has completed a novel.

DAVE GODFREY was born in St. Vital, Manitoba, in 1938, and raised in Canada. He attended Harvard, Toronto, Iowa, and Stanford universities, and is at present working toward a Ph.D. at Iowa, where he taught fiction writing this past year. He has worked as potato picker, timekeeper, butt sawyer, boilermaker, ad writer, parts picker, and extra ganger. His stories and other pieces have appeared in The Canadian Forum and The Tamarack Review. Mr. Godfrey plans to teach, with his wife, in Africa for CUSO in 1963–64, "before, or after which he intends to finish a novel."

W. J. J. GORDON was born in Boston and educated at the University of Pennsylvania, the University of California, and Harvard, where he is on the faculty in the Division of Engineering and Physics. He is the author of short stories in The New Yorker and The Atlantic Monthly, and articles in the Philosophical Journal and the Harvard Business Review. His Synetics, an operational theory of creative process, was published in 1961. He holds a considerable number of patents in fields ranging from bio-chemistry to thermodynamics.

JOHN HERMANN was born in Wisconsin and lived there the early part of his life. After three and a half years in the army, he took graduate degrees at the University of Wisconsin and at the University of Iowa. For the last eight years he has been teaching at Long Beach State College in California, where he lives with his wife and daughter. His short stories have recently appeared in Western Humanities Review, Northwest Review, and The Kenyon Review.

KATINKA LOESER was brought up and went to school in Chicago. She attended Mount Holyoke and the University of Chicago, after which she taught school and worked for Chicago newspapers and Poetry Magazine. The latter awarded her the Young Poet's Prize. Following her marriage to Peter DeVries, she moved to New York and became a housewife. She left New York for Westport because of two children and lack of closet space. Now the mother of three children, she writes that "the mice have got all the tulips again . . . the story of my life." Miss Loeser's stories have appeared in The New Yorker, McCall's, Redbook, the Ladies' Home Journal, and her poetry in The New Yorker and Poetry.

ST. CLAIR McKELWAY was born in Charlotte, North Carolina, and educated in public schools in Washington, D.C. After one year of high school, he went to work on the Washington Times as an office boy, became a reporter, and was assistant city editor when he left Washington to go to New York, by way of Philadelphia, in 1925. He worked as a reporter of the old New York World, later the Herald Tribune, then spent five years in the Orient, where for three years he was editor of the Bangkok Daily Mail, returning to the Herald Tribune in 1933, and thence to The New Yorker the same year. During the Second World War he served in the Air Force. He is the author of Gossip: The Life and Times of Walter Winchell, and True Tales from the Annals of Crime and Rascality. Mr. McKelway was for many years one of the editors of *The New Yorker*, as well as a contributor, and is now a member of the writing staff.

URSULE MOLINARO was born in France, educated in London, and now lives in New York with her husband and a cat. She is an editor of *Chelsea*, and her work has appeared in a great number of publications, including *Cosmopolitan*, *San Francisco Review*, *Swank*, *Harlequin*, and *Noonday*. Her first novel, *The Imposture*, will be issued as an original paperback next fall, and will also be translated into French. She is now at work on her second novel.

J. C. OATES was born in Lockport, New York, received her B.A. degree from Syracuse University, and her M.A. from the University of Wisconsin. She and her husband now live in Detroit, where she is on the faculty of the University of Detroit. She was the winner of the 1959 *Mademoiselle* College Fiction Contest, and her stories have appeared also in *Epoch*, *Arizona Quarterly*, and in *Prize Stories, 1963: The O. Henry Awards*. Critical pieces have appeared in *Renascence*, *Texas Studies*, *Bucknell Review*, and *The Dalhousie Review*. A book of her stories, *By the North Gate*, will be published this year.

R. C. PHELAN was born in McGregor, Texas, in 1921. He is a veteran of World War II, a graduate of the University of Texas, and a former Fulbright student in Paris. He has worked as a newspaper reporter in Houston, a magazine writer in New York, and a teacher of English at the University of Arkansas. His stories and articles have been published in *Vogue*, *The Reporter*, *True*, *The Yale Review*, *The Saturday Evening Post*, *Redbook*, and a number of European magazines. At present he lives and writes in the Missouri Ozarks.

MORDECAI RICHLER, born in Montreal in 1931, attended Sir George Williams University, but quit after two years to go to Europe. His stories have appeared in *The Kenyon Review*, *Commentary*, *Encounter*, *Spectator*, and *The New Statesman*. His books include *The Acrobats*, *Son of a Smaller Hero*, *A Choice of Enemies*, *The Apprenticeship of Duddy Kravitz*, and *Stick Out Your Neck*. Mr. Richler has been the recipient of the Canada Council Junior Arts Fellowship and a Guggenheim Fellowship in Creative Writing. Married, with three children, Mr. Richler has made his home for the past seven years in London.

WILLIAM SAROYAN was born in 1908 in Fresno, California. His new book, *Not Dying*, will be brought out this year.

BABETTE SASSOON was born of English parents in Paris, but she has lived most of her life in the United States. At present she lives with her husband in Maine. She is working on a collection of short stories.

IRWIN SHAW was born in New York, in 1913, and was graduated from Brooklyn College in 1934. He has written many plays, short stories, and novels. His last novel was *Two Weeks in Another Town*. He now lives in Europe, dividing his time between a village in the Alps and the city of Paris.

PETER TAYLOR was born in Tennessee, in 1917, and grew up in Tennessee and Missouri. He attended schools in Nashville, Memphis, and St. Louis. He was married in 1943, and now lives with his wife and two children in North Carolina, where he teaches courses in creative writing at The Woman's College of the University of North Carolina. Mr. Taylor has published three volumes of short stories, a novel, and a play. A collection of twenty-four of his stories will be published this fall. He is currently working on a novel and a group of plays.

NICCOLÒ TUCCI was born in 1908. His stories have appeared in a number of magazines, and he has written a book in Italian, as well as a novel, entitled *Before My Time*, four more volumes of which will be forthcoming.

JESSAMYN WEST was born in southern Indiana, brought up in southern California, and is now a resident of northern California. She "always wanted to write but was afraid to try, until illness shut all other doors." Tuberculosis prevented her taking the oral exam for the Doctorate, and sent her instead to a sanatorium. Sent home from the sanatorium to die, she graduated, after ten years, to couches and pens, and from there to gymnasia. She has appeared three times before in *The Best American Short Stories*. Now married to a college classmate, her latest novel was *South of the Angels*, her latest work, *A Quaker Reader*. "The Picnickers" is part of a new group of "friendly persuasion" stories, on which she is working.

THE
YEARBOOK
OF THE
AMERICAN SHORT STORY

January 1 to December 31, 1962

Roll of Honor, 1962

I. *American Authors*

ANDERSEN, U. S.
  Turn Ever So Quickly. Saturday Evening Post, Nov. 3.
ARKIN, FRIEDA
  A Ride In. Massachusetts Review, Summer.
  Madeline. Transatlantic Review, Summer.

BLATTNER, H. W.
  Sound of a Drunken Drummer. Hudson Review, Autumn.
BONOSKY, PHILLIP
  The Flood. Mainstream, May.
BUTLER, FRANK
  The Watchers in the Dark. Hudson Review, Winter.

CARTER, JOHN STEWART
  The Keyhole Eye. Kenyon Review, Autumn.
CHAIKIN, NANCY
  Afternoons in an Office. Colorado Quarterly, Summer.
CHAY, MARIE
  Gringos Are Fools. Arizona Quarterly, Summer.
CHEEVER, JOHN
  A Vision of the World. New Yorker, Sept. 26.
  Reunion. New Yorker, Oct. 27.
  The Embarkment for Cythera. New Yorker, Nov. 3.

DAWKINS, CECIL
  A Simple Case. Southwest Review, Winter.
DE PAOLA, DANIEL
  The Last Rebel. Arizona Quarterly, Spring.
DICKERSON, GEORGE
  Chico. Phoenix, Spring.
DIKEMAN, MAY
  The Sound of Young Laughter. Atlantic, June.
DUKE, OSBORN
  Big Foot Country. Southwest Review, Winter.

ELKIN, STANLEY
  Fifty Dollars. Southwest Review, Winter.
  I Look Out for Ed Wolfe. Esquire, Sept.
EPSTEIN, SEYMOUR
  The Girl with the Golden Hair. Redbook, Jan.

FETLER, ANDREW
  Longface. Atlantic, Dec.
FRANCIS, H. E.
  As Fish, As Birds, As Grass. Minnesota Review, Summer.

GARRETT, GEORGE
  More Geese Than Swans Now Live. Sewanee Review, Spring.

Sweeter than the Flesh of Birds.
Virginia Quarterly Review,
Autumn.
GODFREY, DAVE
Newfoundland Night. Tamarack
Review, Spring.
GORDON, WILLIAM J. J.
The Pures. Atlantic, May.

HALL, JAMES B.
In the Eye of the Storm. San Fran-
cisco Review, Spring.
HERMANN, JOHN
Aunt Mary. Perspective, Spring.
HOOD, HUGH
The Changeling. Canadian Forum,
March.

JACOBS, WILLIS D.
Treason in English I. Arizona Quarterly, Summer.

KIMBER, ROBERT B.
Maine April Morning. Antioch Review, Spring.

LA FARGE, OLIVER
The Mutineers. New Yorker, June
30.
LOESER, KATINKA
Whose Little Girl Are You? New
Yorker, July 7.
Beggarman, Rich Man, or Thief.
McCall's, Sept.

McCLURE, J. G.
The Rise of the Proletariat. North-
west Review, Winter.
McKELWAY, ST. CLAIR
The Fireflies. New Yorker, Feb. 3.
MARSH, WILLARD
Honor Bright.   Southwest Review,
Autumn.
MINOT, STEPHEN
Sausage and Beer. Atlantic, Nov.
MOLINARO, URSULE
The Insufficient Rope. Prism, No. 1.

NABOKOV, VLADIMIR
The Late Mr. Shade. Harper's
Magazine, May.

NEMEROV, HOWARD
The Escapist. Virginia Quarterly
Review, Spring.

OATES, J. C.
The Fine White Mist of Winter.
Literary Review, Spring.
O'HARA, JOHN
The Bucket of Blood. New Yorker,
Aug. 25.
How Can I Tell You? New Yorker,
Dec. 1.
OLIVE, JEANNIE
The Summer of the Windfall.
Prairie Schooner, Spring.

PETER, JOHN
Tom's A-Cold. Tamarack Review,
Spring.
PHELAN, R. C.
A Special Joy. Redbook, April.
POWERS, J. F.
The Most a Man Can Do. Critic,
February–March.

RICHLER, MORDECAI
Some Grist for Mervyn's Mill. Ken-
yon Review, Winter.
ROBIN, RALPH
You Don't Need No Mediator in a
Two-Group. Western Humanities
Review, Summer.

SAROYAN, WILLIAM
In the Land of the Midnight Sun.
Saturday Evening Post, Sept. 22.
What a World, Said the Bicycle
Rider. Saturday Evening Post,
Nov. 3.
SASSOON, BABETTE
The Betrayal. New World Writing,
No. 20.
SASSOON, R. L.
In the year of Love and unto Death,
the fourth—an Elegy on the Muse.
Northwest Review, Winter.
The Restless One. Northwest Review,
Fall.
SHAW, IRWIN
Noises in the City. Playboy, June.
STEGEMAN, JANET ALLAIS
Mr. Murphy's Garden. Georgia Re-
view, Summer.

SWADOS, HARVEY
  Bobby Shafter's Gone to Sea.
  Kenyon Review, Winter.

TAYLOR, PETER
  At the Drugstore. Sewanee Review,
  Autumn.
THURBER, JAMES
  The Danger in the House. Harper's
  Magazine, Sept.
TOBIAS, JOHN
  The Year After the Magician. Vir-
  ginia Quarterly Review, Spring.
TROMPETER, DON
  Bounty Hunters. Kenyon Review,
  Winter.
TUCCI, NICCOLÒ
  The Desert in the Oasis. New
  Yorker, Oct. 6.

TUSHNET, LEONARD
  A Pious Old Man with a Beard.
  Prairie Schooner, Fall.

WEST, JESSAMYN
  The Picnickers. Kenyon Review,
  Spring.
WETZEL, MARY FOSTER
  Fly Away Home. Southwest Review,
  Winter.
WHITE, ELLINGTON
  Iago and the Tired Red Moor.
  Kenyon Review, Winter.
WULLSTEIN, MAUD
  First Victory. University of Kansas
  City Review, Autumn.

YATES, RICHARD
  Out with the Old. Atlantic, March.

II. *Foreign Authors*

ANDRIĆ, IVO
  Neighbors. Atlantic, Dec.

CHEKOV, ANTON
  Two Tales. Quarterly Review of
  Literature, Vol. XII, Nos. 1/2.
CORKE, HILARY
  Someone with Whom to Converse.
  Kenyon Review, Summer.

FORD, FORD MADOX
  Zeppelin Nights. Minnesota Review,
  Summer.

GORDIMER, NADINE
  Through Time and Distance.
  Atlantic, Jan.

JACOBSON, DAN
  A Gift Too Late. New Yorker, June
  9.

LESSING, DORIS

From the Black Notebook. Partisan
  Review, Spring.

NOMA, HIROSHI
  A Red Moon in Her Face. Literary
  Review, Autumn.

O'BRIEN, EDNA
  Come Into the Drawing Room,
  Doris. New Yorker, Oct. 6.

PRINSEP, SARAH
  The House at Two Falls. Trans-
  atlantic Review, Summer.
PRITCHETT, V. S.
  Noisy in the Doghouse. New Yorker,
  Nov. 10.

SILLITOE, ALAN
  To Be Collected. Transatlantic Re-
  view, Summer.
SINCLAIR, ANDREW
  A Head for Monsieur Dimanche.
  Atlantic, Sept.

Distinctive Short Stories in American Magazines, 1962

I. *American Authors*

ANDERSEN, U. S.
  Turn Ever So Quickly. Saturday Evening Post, Nov. 3.

ARKIN, FRIEDA
  A Ride In. Massachusetts Review, Summer.
  Madeline. Transatlantic Review, Summer.

BARTHELME, DONALD
  The Big Broadcast of 1938. New World Writing, No. 20.

BEMELMANS, LUDWIG
  On Board Noah's Ark. Town and Country, May.

BERRIAULT, GINA
  The Diary of KW. San Francisco Review, Sept.

BLATTNER, H. W.
  Sound of a Drunken Drummer. Hudson Review, Autumn.

BODE, ELROY
  An Excursion into Mr. Reade. Southwest Review, Winter.

BOLES, PAUL DARCY
  What a Bit of Moonlight Can Do. Saturday Evening Post, April 21.

BONGARTZ, ROY
  Twelve Chases on Ninety-Ninth Street. New Yorker, April 21.
  They Want You In. New Yorker, June 23.

BONOSKY, PHILLIP
  The Flood. Mainstream, May.

BRENNAN, MAEVE
  The Bohemians. New Yorker, June 9.
  A Young Girl Can Spoil Her Chances. New Yorker, Sept. 8.

BRYAN, C. D. B.
  So Much Unfairness of Things. New Yorker, June 2.

BURNS, REX S.
  The Net Fisherman. Coastlines, Vol. 5, No. 2.

BUTLER, FRANK
  The Watchers in the Dark. Hudson Review, Winter.

BUTLER, WILLIAM
  Who Stopped By a Tree. Critic, February–March.

CARTER, JOHN STEWART
  The Keyhole Eye. Kenyon Review, Autumn.

CASEY, BILL
  Loss. Southwest Review, Spring.

CHAIKIN, NANCY
  Afternoons in an Office. Colorado Quarterly, Summer.

CHAY, MARIE
  Gringos Are Fools. Arizona Quarterly, Summer.

CHEEVER, JOHN
  A Vision of the World. New Yorker, Sept. 26.

GRAU, SHIRLEY ANN
The Empty Night. Atlantic, May.
The Reach of the Fog. Saturday
Evening Post, Oct. 6.
GREENE, GEORGE
A Cat Named Dempsey. Critic, Dec.
GREENLEAF, WARREN
The Marksman. University of Kansas City Review, Spring.

HALL, JAMES B.
In the Eye of the Storm. San Francisco Review, Spring.
HAWKINS, D. G.
Seeing Nellie Home. Canadian Forum, August.
HAZZARD, SHIRLEY
Cliffs of Fall. New Yorker, Sept. 22.
The Party. New Yorker, Dec. 8.
HELWIG, DAVID
Deerslayer. Canadian Forum, Sept.
The Winter of the Daffodils. Canadian Forum, Nov.
HENDERSON, ROBERT
Carolina Moon. New Yorker, Oct. 20.
HERMANN, JOHN
Aunt Mary. Perspective, Spring.
HISE, JESSE, JR.
End of School. Colorado Quarterly, Autumn.
HOOD, HUGH
The Changeling. Canadian Forum, March.
The End of It. Tamarack Review, Summer.
HOWER, EDWARD
Galina. Epoch, Fall.
HUNTINGTON, GALE
Blow the World Away. Saturday Evening Post, Dec. 22–29.
HURST, JAMES
Once There Came a Cobra. Transatlantic Review, Spring.

JACOBS, ELIJAH
Shivaree. Southwest Review, Spring.
JACOBS, WILLIS D.
Treason in English I. Arizona Quarterly, Summer.
JONES, BARTLEY
The Old Middleton Place. Virginia Quarterly Review, Summer.

JURKOWSKI, JOHN
A Walk on the Sweet Side. New Yorker, Aug. 11.

KEARNS, WINIFRED
The Twist. Minnesota Review, Fall.
KEVELSON, ROBERTA
Mourning Into Dancing. Southwest Review, Autumn.
KIMBER, ROBERT B.
Maine April Morning. Antioch Review, Spring.
KING, FRANCI
Kind. Gentlemen's Quarterly, Winter.
KLEIN, NORMA
The Grandmother. Southwest Review, Winter.

LA FARGE, OLIVER
The Mutineers. New Yorker, June 30.
LAMOTT, KENNETH
Colonel Higashi. Massachusetts Review, Autumn.
LARSEN, ERLING
The Season Coming. Antioch Review, Summer.
LAVIN, MARY
The Lucky Pair. New Yorker, Apr. 28.
LAWSON, JACK B.
The Tears of Things. New Mexico Quarterly, Winter.
LEAHY, JACK THOMAS
The People Are Coming. Northwest Review, Spring.
LEOGRANDE, ERNEST
Tomorrow Is Yesterday. Kenyon Review, Summer.
LICHT, FRED S.
Visit the Sick. New Yorker, Apr. 28.
LISH, GORDON
Flower. Chrysalis Review, Spring.
LOESER, KATINKA
The Permanent End. New Yorker, Apr. 7.
Whose Little Girl Are You? New Yorker, July 7.
Beggarman, Rich Man, or Thief. McCall's, Sept.
The Departure of Mr. Katt. Ladies' Home Journal, Oct.

LOVERIDGE, GEORGE
The Toaster. Woman's Day, Sept.

McCARTIN, J. T.
A Romance. Arizona Quarterly, Spring.
The Shawl. Arizona Quarterly, Autumn.

McCLURE, J. G.
The Rise of the Proletariat. Northwest Review, Winter.

McCONNELL, WILLIAM
Our Ballast Is Old Wine. Canadian Forum, July.

McKELWAY, ST. CLAIR
The Fireflies. New Yorker, Feb. 3.

McKINLEY, GEORGIA
The Fragile Heaven. Virginia Quarterly Review, Winter.

MADDOW, BEN
Christmas in Another Skin. Hudson Review, Winter.

MANOOGIAN, KATHRYN
Everyone's Got to Die Sometime. Ararat, Summer.

MARSH, WILLARD
Honor Bright. Southwest Review, Autumn.

MATTHEWS, JACK
The Failure. Epoch, Fall.

MELLON, WILLIAM
A Race of Heaven. Quarterly Review of Literature, Vol. XII, Nos. 1/2.

MILLER, WARREN
Thirty Years on the Estoril. Colorado Quarterly, Spring.

MINOT, STEPHEN
Sausage and Beer. Atlantic, Nov.

MOLINARO, URSULE
The Insufficient Rope. Prism, No. 1.

MONTGOMERY, MARION
The Birthday Party. Shenandoah, Autumn.
Graduation Snapshots. Northwest Review, Spring.

MOORSE, GEORGE
Bright Daylight. San Francisco Review, March.
Hub Caps. Transatlantic Review, Spring.

NABOKOV, VLADIMIR
The Late Mr. Shade. Harper's Magazine, May.

NEMEROV, HOWARD
The Escapist. Virginia Quarterly Review, Spring.

OATES, J. C.
The Fine White Mist of Winter. Literary Review, Spring.

O'CONNOR, WILLIAM VAN
The Picture Window. Prairie Schooner, Spring.

O'HARA, JOHN
Money. New Yorker, March 24.
The Bucket of Blood. New Yorker, Aug. 25.
How Can I Tell You? New Yorker, Dec. 1.

OLIVE, JEANNIE
The Summer of the Windfall. Prairie Schooner, Spring.

PERLONGO, ROBERT
Cousin Karl. Massachusetts Review, Autumn.

PETER, JOHN
Tom's A-Cold. Tamarack Review, Spring.

PHELAN, R. C.
A Special Joy. Redbook, April.

POWERS, J. F.
The Most a Man Can Do. Critic, February–March.

QUENTIN, AMES ROWE
If I Lived Through It. Atlantic, April.

REBSAMEN, FREDERICK
You Better Pay Attention. Antioch Review, Winter.

REYNOLDS, TIM
A Banal Miracle. New World Writing, No. 20.

RICHLER, MORDECAI
Some Grist for Mervyn's Mill. Kenyon Review, Winter.

RINTOUL, WILLIAM T.
Admiration. University of Kansas City Review, Autumn.

ROBERTS, PHYLLIS
Saluda Berkeley, Passerby. Saturday Evening Post, July 14–21.

ROBIN, RALPH
You Don't Need No Mediator in a Two-Group. Western Humanities Review, Summer.

ROTH, PHILIP
Novotny's Pain. New Yorker, Oct. 27.

RUSHWORTH, EMILY C.
The Dance. Georgia Review, Summer.

SALERNO, GEORGE
The Ghost of Fisherman's Ledge. Transatlantic Review, Spring.

SAROYAN, WILLIAM
The End of the War and Robert Burns. Ararat, Summer.
In the Land of the Midnight Sun. Saturday Evening Post, Sept. 22.
What a World, Said the Bicycle Rider. Saturday Evening Post, Nov. 3.

SASSOON, BABETTE
The Betrayal. New World Writing, No. 20.

SASSOON, R. L.
In the year of Love and unto Death, the fourth—an Elegy on the Muse. Northwest Review, Winter.
The Restless One. Northwest Review, Fall.

SCHULZE, GENE
Conversation Piece Unspoken. Transatlantic Review, Summer.

SEGARD, JUDITH
The Wealthy Monkey. Arizona Quarterly, Summer.

SHAW, IRWIN
Noises in the City. Playboy, June.

SHORE, WILMA
The Man in the Subway. Antioch Review, Summer.

SHOWALTER, DAVID W.
Sparrow! Sparrow! Virginia Quarterly Review, Winter.

SIEBEL, JULIA
A Maintenance of Love. Kenyon Review, Autumn.

SOUTHERN, TERRY
The Road Out of Axotle. Esquire, Aug.

SPACKEY, JAMES
Welcome to the Picnic. Esquire, Sept.

STEGEMAN, JANET ALLAIS
Mr. Murphy's Garden. Georgia Review, Summer.

STUART, JESSE
The Finder, Arizona Quarterly, Winter.
Drink to the Man. Arizona Quarterly, Summer.

SWADOS, HARVEY
Bobby Shafter's Gone to Sea. Kenyon Review, Winter.

TAYLOR, PETER
At the Drugstore. Sewanee Review, Autumn.

THURBER, JAMES
The Danger in the House. Harper's Magazine, Sept.

TOBIAS, JOHN
The Year After the Magician. Virginia Quarterly Review, Spring.

TOPKINS, KATHERINE
The Family Way, Prairie Schooner, Fall.
Free and Accepted. Genesis West, Winter.

TROMPETER, DON
Bounty Hunters. Kenyon Review, Winter.

TUCCI, NICCOLÒ
The Desert in the Oasis. New Yorker, Oct. 6.

TUSHNET, LEONARD
A Pious Old Man with a Beard. Prairie Schooner, Fall.

TUTT, RALPH
Grapes. Shenandoah, Autumn.

UNGER, LEONARD
"Deja Vu Etcetera." Minnesota Review, Fall.

VLIET, R. G.
The Journey. Quarterly Review of Literature, Vol. XII, Nos. 1/2.

WEAVER, GORDON A.
When Times Sit In. Perspective, Autumn.

WESELY, DONALD
  The Rooking. University of Kansas City Review, Autumn.
WEST, JESSAMYN
  The Picnickers. Kenyon Review, Spring.
  The Last Laugh. Redbook, July.
WETZEL, MARY FOSTER.
  Fly Away Home. Southwest Review, Winter.
WHITE, ELLINGTON
  Iago and the Tired Red Moor. Kenyon Review, Summer.
WIBBERLY, LEONARD
  The Man Who Lived on Water. Saturday Evening Post, March 31.

WINDHAM, DONALD
  Gentian. New Yorker, Nov. 7.
WOLFE, LINDA
  With Appetite for None. Southwest Review, Winter.
WULLSTEIN, MAUD
  First Victory. University of Kansas City Review, Autumn.

YATES, RICHARD
  Out with the Old. Atlantic, March.

ZIVKOVIĆ, PETER D.
  Behind the Circle. Arizona Quarterly, Spring.

II. *Foreign Authors*

ABBAS, KHWAJA AHMAD
  The Sword of Shiva. Literary Review, Spring.
ANDRIĆ, IVO
  Neighbors. Atlantic, Dec.
ASHTON-WARNER, SYLVIA
  Toll Call. New World Writing, No. 20.

CHEKOV, ANTON
  Two Tales. Quarterly Review of Literature, Vol. XII, Nos. 1/2.
"CLARIN," LEOPOLD ALAS
  A Repatriate. Prairie Schooner, Summer.
CORKE, HILARY
  Someone with Whom To Converse. Kenyon Review, Summer.

DES FORÉTS, LOUIS RENÉ
  The Children's Room. New World Writing, No. 20.

FORD, FORD MADOX
  Zeppelin Nights. Minnesota Review, Summer.
FRAME, JANET
  The Reservoir. New Yorker, Jan. 12.

GILL, RAJ
  Outcast. Transatlantic Review, Spring.
GORDIMER, NADINE

Through Time and Distance. Atlantic, Jan.
  Tenants of the Last Tree House. New Yorker, Dec. 16.

JACOBSON, DAN
  A Gift Too Late. New Yorker, June 9.

KAZAKOV, YURI
  The Outsider. Esquire, Nov.
KHAING, DAW MI MI
  A Sawbwa Dies. Antioch Review, Fall.
KHAN, ISMITH
  A Day in the Country. Colorado Quarterly, Autumn.
KIELY, BENEDICT
  The Shortest Way Home. New Yorker, March 17.
  The House in Jail Square. New Yorker, Dec. 8.

LESSING, DORIS
  From the Black Notebook. Partisan Review, Spring.

MILLARD, OSCAR
  Time Enough for Glory. Atlantic, Oct.
MONTALE, EUGENIO
  A Meeting. Quarterly Review of Literature, Vol. XI, No. 4.
  The Slow Club. Quarterly Review of Literature, Vol. XI, No. 4.

Addresses of American and Canadian Magazines Publishing Short Stories

Antioch Review, 212 Xenia Avenue, Yellow Springs, Ohio
Ararat, 250 Fifth Avenue, New York 1, New York
Arizona Quarterly, University of Arizona, Tucson, Arizona
Atlantic Monthly, 8 Arlington Street, Boston 16, Massachusetts
Audience, 140 Mount Auburn Street, Cambridge 38, Massachusetts
Audit, Box 92, Hayes Hall, University of Buffalo, Buffalo 14, New York
Between Two Worlds, Inter American University, San Germán, Puerto Rico
Canadian Forum, 30 Front Street West, Toronto, Ontario, Canada
Canadian Home Journal, 71 Richmond Street, Toronto, Ontario, Canada
Carleton Miscellany, Carleton College, Northfield, Minnesota
Carolina Quarterly, P.O. Box 1117, Chapel Hill, North Carolina
Catholic World, 180 Varick Street, New York 14, New York
Charm, Glamour, 420 Lexington Avenue, New York 17, New York
Chicago Review, Reynolds Club, University of Chicago, Chicago, Illinois
Chrysalis, 5700 Third Street, San Francisco, California
Coastlines, 2465 North Beachwood Drive, Hollywood 20, California
Colorado Quarterly, University of Colorado, Boulder, Colorado
Commentary, 165 East 56th Street, New York 22, New York
Commonweal, 386 Park Avenue South, New York 16, New York
Contact, 749 Bridgeway, Sausalito, California
Contemporary Fiction, Box 1323, Milwaukee, Wisconsin
Country Beautiful, Elm Grove, Wisconsin
Critic, 210 Madison Street, Chicago, Illinois
Descant, Texas Christian University, Fort Worth, Texas
Ellery Queen's Mystery Magazine, 527 Madison Avenue, New York 22, New York
Epoch, 252 Goldwin Smith Hall, Cornell University, Ithaca, New York
Esquire, 488 Madison Avenue, New York 22, New York
Evergreen Review, 64 University Place, New York 3, New York
Fantasy and Science Fiction, Box 271, Rockville Centre, New York
Four Quarters, LaSalle College, Philadelphia 43, Pennsylvania
Genesis West, 711 Concord Way, Burlingame, California
Gentleman's Quarterly, 488 Madison Avenue, New York 22, New York
Georgia Review, University of Georgia, Athens, Georgia

Good Housekeeping, 57th Street and Eighth Avenue, New York 19, New York
Harper's Bazaar, 572 Madison Avenue, New York 22, New York
Harper's Magazine, 49 East 33rd Street, New York 16, New York
Holiday, 477 Madison Avenue, New York, New York
Hudson Review, 65 East 55th Street, New York 22, New York
Husk, Cornell College, Mount Vernon, Iowa
Inland, P.O. Box 685, Salt Lake City, Utah
Kenyon Review, Kenyon College, Gambier, Ohio
Ladies' Home Journal, 1270 Sixth Avenue, New York, New York
Literary Review, Fairleigh Dickinson University, Teaneck, New Jersey
McCall's, 230 Park Avenue, New York 17, New York
MacLean's, 481 University Avenue, Toronto, Ontario, Canada
Mademoiselle, 575 Madison Avenue, New York 22, New York
Mainstream, 832 Broadway, New York 18, New York
Massachusetts Review, University of Massachusetts, Amherst, Massachusetts
Midstream, 515 Park Avenue, New York, New York
Minnesota Review, Box 4068, University Station, Minneapolis, Minnesota
MSS, 670 Fifth Avenue, Chico, California
New Mexico Quarterly, University of New Mexico, Albuquerque, New Mexico
New World Writing, 521 Fifth Avenue, New York 17, New York
New Yorker, 25 West 43rd Street, New York 36, New York
Northwest Review, Erb Memorial Union, University of Oregon, Eugene, Oregon
Paris Review, 45-39 171 Place, Flushing 58, New York
Partisan Review, 22 East 17th Street, New York 3, New York
Perspective, Washington University Post Office, St. Louis, Missouri
Phoenix, Ida Noyes Hall, 1212 East 59th Street, Chicago 37, Illinois
Prairie Schooner, Andrews Hall, University of Nebraska, Lincoln, Nebraska
Prism, University of British Columbia, Vancouver, British Columbia, Canada
Prism, 250 Park Avenue South, New York 3, New York
Provincetown Quarterly, P.O. Box 473, Provincetown, Massachusetts
Quarterly Review of Literature, Box 287, Bard College, Annandale-on-Hudson, New York
Queens Quarterly, Queens University, Kingston, Ontario, Canada
Redbook, 230 Park Avenue, New York 17, New York
Reflections, Chapel Hill, North Carolina
San Francisco Review, P.O. Box 671, San Francisco 1, California
Saturday Evening Post, 666 Fifth Avenue, New York 19, New York
Seventeen, 488 Madison Avenue, New York 22, New York
Sewanee Review, University of the South, Sewanee, Tennessee
Shenandoah, Box 122, Lexington, Virginia
Show, 140 East 57th Street, New York 22, New York
Southwest Review, Southern Methodist University, Dallas, Texas
Tamarack Review, Box 157, Postal Station K, Toronto, Ontario, Canada
Texas Quarterly, Box 7527, University Station, Austin 12, Texas
Transatlantic Review, 821 Second Avenue, New York 17, New York
University of Kansas City Review, University of Kansas City, Missouri
Virginia Quarterly Review, 1 West Range, Charlottesville, Virginia
Wagner Literary Magazine, Grymes Hills, Staten Island, New York
Weird Tales, 9 Rockefeller Plaza, New York, New York
Western Humanities Review, Building 41, University of Utah, Salt Lake City, Utah
Yale Review, P.O. Box 1729, New Haven, Connecticut
Yankee, Dublin, New Hampshire